ALL HE
NEEDS

ALSO BY C. C. GIBBS

All He Wants

ALL HE NEEDS

NEEDS

C. C. GIBBS

FOREVER

NEW YORK   BOSTON

Forever
Hachette Book Group
237 Park Avenue
New York, NY 10017
www.HachetteBookGroup.com

Printed in the United States of America

RRD-C

First Edition: December 2013
10 9 8 7 6 5 4 3 2 1

Forever is an imprint of Grand Central Publishing.
The Forever name and logo are trademarks of Hachette Book Group, Inc.

The Hachette Speakers Bureau provides a wide range of authors for speaking events. To find out more, go to www.hachettespeakersbureau .com or call (866) 376-6591.

The publisher is not responsible for websites (or their content) that are not owned by the publisher.

Library of Congress Cataloging-in-Publication Data
Gibbs, C. C.
    All he needs / C. C. Gibbs.
        pages cm. — (All or nothing)
        Summary: "Kate Hart and Dominic Knight's volatile love affair continues in the next book from C. C. Gibbs"— Provided by publisher.
        ISBN 978-1-4555-2833-2 (pbk.) — ISBN 978-1-4555-2834-9 (ebook)
        I. Title.
    PS3607.I2254A53 2013
    813'.6—dc23

                                                            2013027725

ALL HE
NEEDS

ONE

Paris, February

Dominic Knight glanced out the car window and half smiled. Even on a gray winter day, even with the clusterfuck going on in his head, Paris made him feel as though life might be worth living. Of all the cities in the world, only this one offered pleasure with an urbane practicality: suave, cultured, rowdy, risqué, money-making, or money-spending. Whatever got you up in the morning or kept you up at night.

There weren't a lot of rules of the road here.

Unfortunately, even the *thought* of pleasure suddenly dredged up a flood of treacherous memories, needle sharp, frozen in time, beautiful, and a fresh, raw sense of deprivation twisted his gut. Uttering an almost imperceptible sigh, Dominic slid down lower in the seat, grim-faced and moody once again. Christ, how the hell long would this misery last?

An amateur when it came to personalizing emotion, he didn't have a clue. Which pretty much characterized his entire relationship with Katherine Hart.

She'd signed on for a two-week IT consulting contract at Knight Enterprises and, in that brief period of time, she had completely fucked up his life. Prior to Katherine, his relationships with women had fallen into a well-established pattern: you meet a woman, you want her, you screw her, you politely say good-bye.

All perfectly normal.

Then you meet someone like Katherine and screw her continuously for a week. That's seven whole days.

Definitely not normal. You leave her. Back to normal. But you can't get her out of your mind. Can't eat. Can't sleep. Booze is suddenly your best friend. That's where it gets crazy. That's where the norm completely goes to hell.

Where the fucking misery quotient powers up big-time. You're thinking too much, he muttered under his breath. Stop thinking about it. *Do* something.

And *what the fuck?* was always a useful game plan.

Tired as hell of debating the issue, he pulled his cell phone from his T-shirt pocket, sat up in the backseat of the black Mercedes, and scrolled through his directory of contacts. He hesitated for a fraction of a second more before he tapped the name, knowing this call might reopen doors better left closed. Then he inhaled a quick breath, dismissed the last pang of doubt, and thumbed the name.

When his contact in London picked up, Dominic said, "Nick here. Got a minute?"

"What the hell do you want?" The accent was wiseass Brooklyn.

"Your wife but she keeps saying no," Dominic answered with a faint smile in his voice.

"That's because your track record with women is crap. Where are you?"

"I'm on my way into Paris from the airport. Just came in from Hong Kong. I need a favor."

"Since I owe you a couple dozen, ask away." Dominic had introduced Justin Parducci to his wife, which was reason enough for Justin to help him. But the business deals Dominic had moved through Justin's investment division at CX Capital had made him a fortune.

"This is for your ears only," Dominic cautioned. "I'm not involved in any way."

"Christ, did you kill someone?"

"If I had, I wouldn't be calling you."

"Speaking of which—how's Max?"

"Steeped in domestic life in Hong Kong at the moment." Justin softly whistled. "Who would've thought?"

"You should talk. I hear another one's on the way. You're keeping Amanda busy."

"She wants four. I have no idea why, but…"

"You're willing to help out," Dominic drolly said.

"I'm more than willing. Thanks by the way for bringing her over at George's wedding reception. At the risk of sounding maudlin, we're over-the-moon happy."

"Good to hear," Dominic said, keeping his voice neutral with effort, the nihilistic state of his own life oppressive.

"It's even better than I thought," Justin cheerfully noted, completely unaware of the nuances of Dominic's tone. "I never thought I'd leave New York, but I'm beginning to think of London as home now that I have a wife and kid and another on the way. How about you? Are you in Paris long or just passing through?"

"I haven't decided."

That Justin noticed—the terse reply was more than Nick's usual reserve. Not that he was about to ask for an explanation from a man like Dominic Knight, whose personal life was hermetically sealed. "So what can I do for you?"

"I need someone who can offer a woman I know a consulting contract; someone in IT who's in charge of their own budget and hiring. Someone who can keep his mouth shut. Know anyone like that?"

"IT's a little out of my bailiwick, lemme think…"

"Ask around if you have to. Give me a call back."

"Wait, wait…I think Bill might be your guy. Tight-lipped, indifferent to the herd mentality, accommodating. He's at CX Capital Singapore, VP of Security now, used to be their head tech guru. He owes me for past favors rendered."

"Perfect," Dominic said. "Her name's Katherine Hart. I'll pay all the expenses: food, lodging, transportation, salary, flowers…she should have fresh flowers in her suite every day. Have your man at CX Capital send the charges to me through you. And Miss Hart is to be paid *well*, not your well, mine," Dominic specified. "After the recent scandals at CX Capital Singapore, I should think they'd be in the market for someone with her skills anyway. As for a plausible story, have your guy—"

"Bill McCormick," Justin interjected. "He's Boy Scout dependable."

"He'd better be. Have McCormick tell Miss Hart that he heard about her from the bankers at Sander Global who were crying in their drinks at the Racket Club. The Singapore bank was sitting on twenty million of mine that had been siphoned from a factory I own in Bucharest. Miss Hart tracked down the twenty mil to one of their accounts and with her explanation and my threats, I got my money back. Have McCormick contact the Accounting Department at MIT with his job offer for her, so everything looks reputable...McCormick can name his price for his cooperation; let me know the amount. But his pitch has to be convincing. I can't stress that enough. If Miss Hart finds out I had anything to do with this, I'll personally cut off your balls."

"Okay, okay, got it. This babe must be special." Since Nick never allowed it to get personal with women, the subject was fair game.

"She's not just a babe. She's smart—one of the best forensic accountants in her field. I want her to make some money."

"Whatever you say," Justin smoothly remarked, figuring the lady also had been smart enough to play hard to get. "Why won't she take money from you?"

"Fuck if I know."

"Losing your touch, Nick?"

"Yeah, along with every other fucking thing."

Holy shit. If that wasn't a bottomless pit of sullen. And over a goddamn woman. "I'll get right on it," Justin said immediately, thinking he had to give Max a call and get the story on this woman. "As soon as the setup's in place, I'll get back to you. Quick question. What if she says no to McCormick?"

"The guy's not an idiot is he? See that he makes her an offer she can't refuse. And keep me posted," Dominic said briskly. "Daily."

Two days later, Kate Hart's phone rang. She was lying in bed, her Boston apartment dark with the curtains drawn, the samurai movie she was watching even darker. When she pulled her cell phone from under the Dunkin' Donuts bag and a pile of cheeseburger wrappers, she had to squint to see the display. Department of Accounting, MIT? Really? Was she up to being polite now that the one-person pity party she'd been indulging in since she left Hong Kong was in full swing?

But curiosity got the best of her. She took a deep breath and picked up.

"Miss Hart? Jim Henderson."

Jeez, the head of the department, no less. "Hi, Professor Henderson." *Were they taking back her diploma?* The way things were going for her, she wouldn't be surprised.

"I have an attractive job offer. Interested? Or are you already gainfully employed? Jenny tells me you've decided on consulting work."

Her advisor, Jenny Fields, stayed in touch. Not that Kate had given her more than the most superficial details of her work for Knight Enterprises. "I don't know if I've decided yet. But so far the fees are intriguing."

"Then you'll like the sound of this offer. I've been contacted by a banker in Singapore who heard about you from some colleagues. He wants to know if you can fly out to Singapore for an interview. Or if not, accept a call from him. They're paying well."

"I'll take a call. Anytime. And thank you, Professor Henderson," she remembered to say, with her thoughts already racing. Because this job offer was way too suspicious. Puppet master that he was, Dominic was probably involved.

But when she spoke to William McCormick he seemed

authentic. He'd heard of her from the bankers at Sander Global in Singapore, who were friends of his. The bank had been pissed about having to write off the twenty million, of course, but impressed with her expertise. And CX Capital Singapore needed someone to run a thorough security check on their major investment accounts. Their IT watchdogs had given them a clean bill of health, but after the scandal two weeks ago when access to their accounts had been shut down for an entire day, they wanted a second opinion, particularly on possible inroads into their monetary funds.

After a few probing questions, Kate was 99 percent sure that William McCormick had never met Dominic. Didn't even know of him, besides what he'd heard from his friends at Sander Global.

He mentioned that both Sander Global bankers had a personal security team now.

If McCormick was looking for gossip, she was the wrong person to ask. Kate explained that a good deal of the conversation with the bankers in Singapore had been in Mandarin and had been meaningless to her. And honestly, since she didn't know what Dominic had said to threaten the men, she couldn't have told him anyway.

William McCormick went on to offer her a hefty fee for the project. He also said he'd have a first class ticket e-mailed to her if she was willing to take on the assignment.

"May I think about it overnight?"

"Certainly."

"I'll call you tomorrow," she politely said.

After she hung up, she lay back on her pillows, weighing,

digesting, and reviewing every word of the conversation, trying to decide if there was any possible way Dominic had a
hand in the offer.

She finally decided—most likely not. And after having
seen how Sander Global operated, if CX Capital was using
similar crap security, they needed her.

Tossing back the covers, she climbed out of bed, where
she'd been wallowing in her own misery for days. Even
though she knew it was incredibly stupid to cry over someone who could have any woman he wanted and probably
had. Maybe this call was gypsy fate telling her it was time
to forget about the shameless, heartless, *unfortunately jaw-
droppingly beautiful* prick.

Straightening her Road Runner sleep shirt, which was
a mess of wrinkles after days in bed, she made her way
through the pile of luggage and fast food containers clutter-
ing her apartment, stopped at one of the windows, pulled
back the drapes, and blinked like she'd just walked out of
a cave. Brilliant sunshine, the outside world was still intact.
The street was empty, melting snow piled up on the curb,
grimy and gray—city snow. Not like the snow at the lake.

She *could* go home. Nana was waiting.

But she'd be better off *doing* something rather than
going home and being depressed in different surroundings.
She *had* been thinking about checking to see if some of her
job offers were still open; *thinking about it* being the key
phrase.

Nibbling on her bottom lip, she reviewed her conversation with William McCormick, parsing and dissecting each
of his replies. Simple, uncomplicated answers, no hesitation

when it came to Dominic's name. If she had to bet, she'd say he really didn't know the selfish fucker.

And she couldn't deny that the idea of working for herself *was* appealing.

So really…she was being offered the consummate work experience.

She refused to let anything dampen her excitement. This was a glorious prospect and what seemed like a fabulous job. Furthermore, with Dominic's fee and the one from McCormick, she'd be financially secure for at least three years—maybe more.

She suddenly smiled, feeling a little bit cheerful, even faintly inspired, for the first time since she'd come home. She adored matching wits with possible hackers, peeling back the layers of potential fraud, and entering the murky waters where the dark market operated.

So why not? There really wasn't a down side.

And it was a game she loved to play.

Oops, wrong words; the thought of playing games generated a hot rush of lustful memories: the feel of Dominic's body pressed against hers, the quiet authority in his soft, deep voice, the exquisite pleasure he so casually delivered. Seriously, that was another reason she had to reenter the work force. She needed a distraction. Masturbation was all fine and good but it wasn't nearly enough.

Turning from the window, she went to call her grandmother.

"Guess what, Nana?"

"It must be good. You sound cheerful."

"It is. I was just offered a great assignment. Lots of money, nice hotel, first class airfare, even my food—it all comes with the deal."

The fact that Katie wasn't on the verge of tears was the best news of all… "Give me the who, what, when, where, and why, sweetie."

"CX Capital, a bank that recently was shut down by hackers. As soon as I want. Singapore. And they need me—"

"For their fix-it-up chappie," Nana finished.

Kate laughed. "You betcha. Dr. Seuss and me to the rescue." She'd loved those books so much as a child, she'd memorized them all before she was four. "I'll stop and see you before I go."

"Lovely. Although I warn you, you might have to endure a coffee party with my bridge club. I've been telling them how you've become a world traveler."

"An opportunity to jerk Jan Vogel's chain is not to be missed, I see."

Nana chuckled. "That goes without saying. When it comes to bragging rights, no one outdoes Jan anyway. I'm years behind her since I'm polite, so I expect you to tell a good story."

Kate had a story to tell that would curl Jan Vogel's toes, but it wasn't for public consumption. "I did see how the rich and famous live. I could describe Dominic Knight's house in Hong Kong, his private plane, and the fleet of Mercedes-Benzes at his beck and call…"

"Sounds exciting," Nana said. "But really, I just like to show you off. You know that. So talk about whatever you want."

"It was another world, Nana. You wouldn't believe the

luxury, the huge number of servants, the beautiful surroundings, the incredible food and expensive wines. And
it's all just taken for granted."

"I'm glad you had a chance to see it," Nana gently noted.
"Most people don't. At least people we know."

Kate sighed, feeling a pang of heartache. "You're right.
It was definitely a not-to-be-missed opportunity."

"Perhaps Singapore will be equally exciting. You never
know."

"It might be," Kate politely replied, even though it
couldn't possibly be without Dominic. "I'll call the banker
and tell him I'm taking the job, then I'll let you know when
I'm coming home."

"Anytime, sweetie. Leon and I will be waiting. Did I tell
you he's gained another twenty pounds? He's like the pony
you always wanted."

Kate chuckled. "The one Gramps didn't want in his
garage."

"One of the few times your grandfather didn't give you
everything you wanted," Nana said drolly.

"Only that once, Nana." Kate's voice trembled and tears
blurred her vision. Her Gramps had been a kind, generous
man with rock-solid convictions who was devoted to her.
Who challenged her to try anything and everything. Her
Santa Claus and badass drill sergeant rolled into one.

"I think he was saving himself from mucking out a
pony's stall. You would've done it once or twice at that age
and then it would have been his job. Your grandfather was
a practical man. Now we better change the subject or we'll
both be crying."

"Right," Kate said briskly. "So let me call McCormick back, then I'll make my reservations for Minnesota."

Kate called Mr. McCormick, accepted his offer, made her flight reservations, and texted Nana with the numbers. Then she ordered a pizza and watched the end of the tragic samurai movie while she waited for the pizza delivery. Yet another reason for returning to work: her eating habits were lamentable. If she continued lying in bed and having food delivered, she'd soon weigh two hundred pounds.

After the movie ended, Kate decided on the spur of the moment to call Meg and tell her she'd stop by Missoula for a day or two on her way to Singapore.

It was time to see if some other man could ignite her libido. After three solid days of misery, she was willing to try anything to put Dominic behind her. And who better than Meg to set her straight—the queen of "sex is for fun, check your heart at the door, last names aren't necessary."

Meg squealed when she heard Kate would be visiting. "Really! Really, you're coming to visit! I can hardly wait!"

"It sounds like you're having fun out there," Kate said. "Missoula's not much out of the way to Singapore, and I'm *not* having any fun here so I thought—"

"Hey, what's with the someone-died voice? Oh, shit, don't tell me—"

"No, no, Nana's fine. But"—Kate sighed—"tell me you can't die of a broken heart."

"Ohmygod! You didn't! Oh Christ," Meg said as though she were telepathic. "You really did. You slept with the billionaire."

"Kinda, sorta"—a grumbling sigh this time—"yeah. Now all I do is cry."

"Listen to me, sweet pea." Meg spoke in her it's-for-your-own-good tone of voice. "I'm going to be brutally frank. First—you're not Cinderella. Second, even if you were, Dominic Knight's definitely not prince material. Third, whatever happened had nothing to do with love, it was sex. And fourth and most important, even if you think your heart is broken, no one *ever, ever* dies of a broken heart. Got it?"

A lengthy pause.

"Trust me. Okay? I know. Remember Johnny Dare? I got over him."

"In less than a day," Kate pointed out sarcastically.

"So you're behind the curve. I'll get you back up to speed. I got to tell you, the men out here are prime examples of heavy-duty testosterone. They hunt, fish, break horses, and—I don't know—probably chop wood in their spare time."

That brought a reluctant chuckle from Kate. "So you're saying if I have a wood stove—they can help me out?"

"They can help you out in even better ways than that. Guaranteed."

"You're right." Kate put a little briskness in her tone, as if she actually believed Meg's guarantee. "Why mope."

"Hey, I'm not pretending Dominic Knight isn't dazzling. I've seen him in enough tabloid magazines, always with a Barbie doll on his arm. But you know he's only shopping, never buying. Hey, speaking of shopping"—the sudden animation in her voice was familiar to Kate, who'd known Meg since they'd been dorm mates freshman year—"you can do a little shopping too. I'll invite all of Luke's gorgeous, studly friends to a party, and you can look them over and take your pick. When are you coming?"

"Probably Friday."

"Perfect. I'll have a complete lineup on hand. You choose your favorite one night stand, have some fun and forget billionaires who have dollar signs where their hearts should be. Seriously, sweetie, one has to be practical about men who own half the world."

"I know. Really, I'm trying."

"Good," Meg said warmly, like a teacher praising a slow student who finally gave the right answer to two and two is four. "Now—any preferences for your rebound sex? Tall, muscular, dark, blond, blue eyes—give me a hint."

"Blond's good." Someone who wouldn't remind her of Dominic, someone who wouldn't trigger even the tiniest memory of a tall, dark, handsome jerk.

"Blond it is. God, I'm so glad you're coming out! We'll have a ball!"

After ten drinks maybe. "I'm looking forward to the party," Kate fibbed. But she knew once she was in Missoula at least she'd be busy. Meg was a full-steam-ahead, egocentric personality who didn't sit still. "And thanks," she politely added. "I feel better now." But she knew it was a lie, even as she said it.

"I'll have a full roster of studs waiting for you," Meg replied gleefully. "All blondes. And, may I say, it's about freaking time."

TWO

At the same time Kate was making plans with Meg, Dominic was seated across the dinner table from a beautiful, blond divorcee whom he'd known for years.

"I can't believe my luck, darling." Victoria Melbury smiled at Dominic over the rim of her wineglass. "What are the odds of bumping into you on the street in Paris?"

Factoring in the population of Paris and his previous plans to fly home from Hong Kong, he smiled and said, "Definitely a long shot." He'd been getting out of his car in front of his apartment on the Île Saint-Louis a few hours ago when Vicky had called out his name. Dominic had met Vicky at a London party three years ago and had fallen into bed with her soon after. It was a pattern he'd repeated several times since.

"I hope you don't mind," she said in a seductive purr. "But I wasn't about to be shy in asking you out when you said you weren't in the city for long."

Dominic smiled again. "Not a problem. I was about to invite you out to dinner anyway," he lied. He'd actually planned on sitting alone in his apartment and drowning his sorrows in whiskey.

"This is such a darling little restaurant." She lifted her perfectly manicured hand in a flighty little wave that encompassed the room before reaching out to lightly brush her fingers across Dominic's hand, which was resting on the table. "I'm so glad you brought me here. I gather the chef is a good friend of yours." The chef had come out to greet them when he heard Nick was in the house.

"Guillaume and I met in Nice a few years ago. I was pleased when he moved to Paris." The restaurant was on a quiet, tree-lined street in Montmartre, on the ground floor of a small house that had been converted into a neobistro thanks to an investment from Dominic.

"He reminds me of that lovely young chef in Monaco. Do you remember that little café by the water?" She giggled prettily. "We were a little risqué that night."

"I remember. We were both pretty loaded." He picked up the bottle on the table, uninterested in reminiscing about their public sexual escapades. "More wine?"

She readily held out her glass and gave him a playful smile. "Are you trying to get me drunk, Nicky dear?"

He shook his head. "It's just a good wine." *He actually was trying to get himself drunk.* He didn't want to be here. He didn't want to see Vicky across the table from him, full of flattery and artifice, showing off her boobs, taking it for granted that they were her best calling card. He had wanted to leave twenty minutes ago...alone.

The way Vicky ate the first course of white asparagus with anchovy dressing almost took away Dominic's appetite. Although, realistically, it wasn't her fault, it was his. Pre-Katherine, watching Vicky delicately place the tip of the asparagus in her mouth and slowly nibble on it until she'd consumed the entire stalk would have been amusing. Now it was unappealing on so many levels.

Daintily wiping her mouth when she finished, she smiled and pointed at Dominic's barely touched asparagus. "Aren't you hungry, darling?"

Not anymore. "I should have ordered the ravioli," he said with a quick glance at his watch. Then he caught the waiter's eye and nodded at their plates.

As their first courses were whisked away and their glasses refilled, Vicky leaned forward to better display her impressive cleavage, beautifully framed by the deep V of her white angora knit dress. "You seem moody." Her voice softened. "All dark and dangerous. I like that," she whispered.

If she mentioned whips he might lose it. "I'm just a little tired. Long day at work." He smiled tightly and wondered if he was being punished for all the iniquities in his past. "Guillaume's blanquette de veau is amazing," he said, determined to change the subject. "You'll enjoy it." And reaching for his wineglass, he drained it, nodded at the waiter for a refill, and drank down the next glass without tasting it.

Two bottles later, he was marginally relaxed *or* mildly anesthetized. The food was superb as usual, the veal spectacular, the wine cellar excellent, the waiter alert to his glances for more wine, the low buzz of conversation tranquilizing. Vicky was persistently flirtatious, doing her best to lure him in.

Unfortunately, he was unaffected by her overtures.

She obviously was planning on staying the night.

He'd previously thought the same; a fuck was a fuck. But each minute that passed, each perfumed remark directed his way, each seductive smile, left him not only indifferent but seriously demoralized by his own apathy. Since when had he become a eunuch? *Don't answer that*, he quickly warned the insinuating little voice in his head.

His unprecedented feelings aside, what he really needed was a way out. But his escape mechanisms were rusty from neglect; he couldn't remember when he'd last turned down a woman. Calling for another bottle, he hoped alcohol would quash his aversion to fucking Vicky.

Sadly, it only made him more averse.

Long before dinner was over, he knew that there was no way he was bringing Vicky back to his apartment. He ordered a rare port to prolong the meal, then another for tasting, at which point Guillaume came out to the table and politely said, "I have two of those bottles left in the cellar. Come, Dominic, you decide which you prefer."

Dominic experienced such a feeling of deliverance, he was momentarily touched by a flash of religiosity. But his voice was calm as he came to his feet. "If you'll excuse me, Vicky, I'll be right back."

Dominic shot a glance at Guillaume as they entered the back hallway. "How the hell did you know I needed rescuing?"

"You don't normally drink so much. Bertrand noticed and told me."

"Bertrand must be the mother I never had," Dominic said with a grin. "I've been trying to think of some way to end this dinner date. Vicky's lovely but I'm not in the mood for more of her tonight." Smiling, Dominic shook his head when he saw Guillaume's quizzical look. "Don't look at me like that—I haven't a clue why either." The men had partied together in Nice and Paris; they both loved women. "I need an escape plan she won't find insulting. Although, if necessary, I'll go with insulting."

"Are you unwell, *mon ami?*" Guillaume looked at Dominic with male understanding. "I know a good doctor; he doesn't mind if I call day or night. He's a friend from Nice."

Dominic smiled. "Thanks for the concern, but I don't need any penicillin. Although maybe I should mention I do. That might put a damper on Vicky's plans."

Guillaume spoke over his shoulder as he started down the basement stairs. "It's not like you to turn it down. If you're not temporarily *hors de combat*"—a Gallic lift of his shoulder that was both query and commiseration—"why not just politely decline?"

"Because Vicky won't accept it, polite or otherwise. She's a taker. So help me out. What the fuck can I say to her that's semipolite but clear?"

Guillaume came through with flying colors. Five minutes after Dominic returned to the table with his bottle of port, Guillaume brought over his newly pregnant wife and asked Dominic if he'd accompany her to the hospital. It wasn't serious, he said, but she'd been instructed to come in the next time her pulse rate accelerated so they could check her on a monitor. She didn't want to bother Guillaume when he was busy.

"I'm sorry, Vicky," Dominic said gently with what he hoped was tangible regret. "I'll have my driver take you home. I'll call you tomorrow."

After some minor resistance, Vicky was placed in his car, his driver quietly instructed to *not*, under any circumstances, take her to Dominic's apartment and Dominic watched the car drive away with a profound sense of relief. It didn't bear close scrutiny.

Nor did he give it any.

When it came to his sex life, he wasn't introspective.

He was however, careful to stay out of sight. Moving into the kitchen with his port, Dominic sat down and poured himself a glass.

Guillaume's wife, Amalie, gave Dominic a kiss on the cheek before she went back upstairs. "I never thought I'd see the day," she said with a twitch of a smile, her pretty face tipped slightly, her dark gaze assessing. "You uninterested?"

"I'm as surprised as you." Dominic glanced up, a touch of amusement in his eyes. "Must be old age."

"Hardly. Is there something you'd like to tell us?" Her female intuition was working overtime because she'd seen Dominic with the blond beauty in Nice two years ago and he hadn't been running away.

"I wasn't going to mention it yet, but I'll buy you a bigger restaurant if you name the baby after me."

She sniffed, gave a little toss of her head. "Keep your deep, dark secrets then. But the lady was angry. She'll make you pay."

"She'd have to find me first."

Amalie lightly tapped his cheek. "Don't forget, I met your little Vicky. She might find you after all."

Dominic groaned.

"You'll have to leave town to escape her," Guillaume said, looking up from the roux he was stirring. "You've done that before."

"I can't. I'm here for a meeting. I'll have to go with plan B."

Which turned out to be a suite at the George V. Upon registering, Dominic asked for privacy. Assured that his presence there was completely confidential, Dominic settled into the presidential suite until the rescheduled meeting with his rare earth investors. In the intervening days, he immersed himself in company business, desperate for a distraction from his own chaffing discontent. Each day he read a dozen proposals for new speculative ventures, discussed the undertakings with the various Knight Enterprises personnel involved, responded to his constant barrage of e-mails, and limited himself to a bottle of single malt a night to avoid calling Katherine and saying something he shouldn't.

The fact that he didn't choose to call any of the other women he knew in Paris or pay a visit to one of the private sex clubs he used to frequent didn't bear reflection. It was too unnerving to contemplate the extraordinary changes in his life. He resorted to masturbation and used a photo for inspiration.

Actually, two photos: the ones he'd taken of Kate sleeping in his bed just before he left Hong Kong. He'd had the cell phone photos enhanced and edited at a commercial lab in Paris, printed into 8 x 10s, and framed in a folding titanium case he could carry with him when he traveled. He didn't question his unusual behavior. But then he rarely questioned any of his actions, particularly when his personal pleasure was involved.

He'd settled into an evening routine that began with

dinner in front of the TV in the suite's living room, followed by half a bottle of any of the single malts on hand in
the liquor cabinet. Or vice versa, depending on his mood.
Although the hotel's famous chef was beginning to question
his skills when many of his dinners went untouched.

Dominic had tried watching porn in an effort to distract
his thoughts from the continuous images of Katherine loop-
ing through his brain. To no avail. His body's total lack of
response gave him pause—but only briefly, because he had
no trouble getting hard when he thought of Katherine.

Inevitably, he'd take the half-drunk bottle to bed, flick
on the TV, mute the sound, direct his gaze to the photos
of Katherine opened like a book on a table at the foot of
the bed, and slowly begin masturbating. He always took
his time, remembering only the pleasure they'd shared, not
the ruinous end—when they'd both reached a point of no
return. But neither his mind nor body could forget the inex-
pressible wonder of their time in Hong Kong.

THREE

While Dominic was staring at the muted TV, enduring another sleepless night, waiting for the sun to come up in Paris, Kate was tossing down a tequila shooter in Meg's kitchen, wondering if there was enough liquor in the world to make her hook up with the really sweet premed rodeo cowboy who kept telling her how beautiful she was. The ear-blasting music from the ad hoc band playing in the living room was only a few decibels quieter in the kitchen and tall, handsome, blond, blue-eyed Ben had his mouth near her ear so she could hear him.

"Let's find a little quiet. That okay with you?"

"Sure." Because she was here for a reason tonight, because she'd silently picked Ben out of Meg's lineup and there was no point in putting off her rebound sex.

Grabbing the tequila bottle, Ben took her hand and led her through the kitchen and down the hall to the bedroom. He knocked, saying with a grin, "Just in case. Or we could go to my place if you like."

She smiled. "Here's good."

"Hey, we lucked out." He shoved the door open.

Or Meg had warned everyone else off, Kate thought, but was too tipsy to give it much thought. Because, bottom line, this was about her leaving the past behind. This was the night she erased Dominic Knight from her memory.

Ben pulled her into the bedroom, shut the door, and walked to the bed, where he placed the bottle on the bedside table, sat down, and drew Kate down on his lap. "You should stay in Missoula for a while," he whispered, kissing her lightly. "You could stay with me. I'll show you how to ride."

"Maybe," she murmured, because it was easier than explaining why she couldn't. And reaching up, she took his face in her hands and kissed him hard, shoving her tongue down his throat, wanting to *feel* something. She felt something all right, but it was his erection swelling against her bottom. Nothing for her. Not a scintilla of emotion. She might as well have been kissing the mirror. Christ, she could see a future devoid of mind-blowing sex stretching before her and she knew where the blame lay—with Dominic's goddamn sexual prowess. She reached for the tequila bottle. "Want some?" She held it out.

"Nah. I'm good." Ben smiled. "Take your time."

Tipping the bottle to her mouth, she smiled back. "You're way nice."

"I'm not in a rush."

Jeez, he was really nice. Although a guy with his looks wasn't hard up for women to fuck. Swallowing, she took another quick shot, then put the bottle back and wrapped her arms around Ben's neck. "There. Sometimes I'm real small town. Sorry about that."

"Not a problem. Everyone in Montana's from a small town." He dipped his head and brushed her lips with his. "I can relate."

In an effort to overcome her body's stunning indifference

to Ben's delicate kiss and huge erection, Kate moved her bottom in a gentle undulation over his rigid dick.

With a low groan, he fell backward, taking her with him, and stretched out on the bed—cowboy boots and all. Shifting her slightly on his lean, muscled frame to accommodate the hard swell of his erection, he cupped the back of her head and pulled her closer for a kiss. "We'll take it easy," he said, his smile only inches away. "Small-town easy."

Maybe that was the problem. Ben was too polite. Dominic often wasn't; he was demanding, occasionally coercive, always in control. Jeez, did that make her some kind of masochist? Did normal sex leave her cold? But then she remembered their days on the *Glory Girl* when Dominic had been all tenderness and affection, when he'd made plans for their future, when he'd not said no to her even once. And suddenly, her eyes filled with tears and she was choked with grief. "I can't do this," she said on a suffocated sob, shoving herself upright. "I'm sorry." Her tears spilled over, and sniffling and sniveling she said in a cracking voice, "I just broke up with someone. I'm a basket case."

"I know. I'm not here to push you."

Her eyes flared wide. "You know!"

"Luke told me. Hey, it's no big deal."

"Oh God," she groaned, the shock at least drying up her tears. "How pathetic is that?"

"Hey, babe." He slid his finger over her bottom lip. "I'd take on any guy to have you. Okay?"

"I don't suppose this has ever happened to you? Only women cry about this shit."

"Everyone's gone through a breakup." He smiled. "I didn't cry, but I know what you mean."

The way he said it, she doubted his world had gone dark. And for a second she debated shutting her eyes and going through with it. She sighed. "I guess I'm too much of a wuss." And rolling off him, she sat on the edge of the bed.

He brushed her arm in a light downward drift of his hand. "We don't have to do anything. We could go see a movie or something."

"I feel really dumb," she whispered.

"I could kick his ass for you."

That brought a small smile to her face; she turned back to him. "I might take you up on that."

"Anytime."

Meg was right. There was no lack of testosterone in Montana. "I'll let you know." She came to her feet. "And thanks. Really." Then she left the bedroom, walked to the bathroom, locked herself in, and quietly cried.

Ben followed her and talked to her through the door. Still polite. A real gentleman.

"Maybe next time," he said. "Call me." And he walked away.

What was wrong with her?

Did only arrogant pricks turn her on?

The day of Dominic's rescheduled meeting finally arrived. Max, along with the other attendees, met in the sumptuous conference room of the Paris office, with Dominic lounging at the head of a long Empire table that had once graced the Château de Malmaison. Coffee, tea, and pastries were available, the cups set before each man Sèvres porcelain contemporary with the table. Small flower arrangements offered scent and color without blocking any sight lines. Dominic's office staff was efficient.

As the investors found their seats Dominic dispensed with a greeting. "This shouldn't take long," he said curtly. "Everyone's familiar with the prospectus?" It wasn't really a question.

Mindful of the last aborted meeting, the fact that Miss Hart was not in attendance was noted by all the industrialists as they settled back in their chairs. Very soon, the attendees also took note of Dominic's poisonous mood. *Related? No, not with Dominic*, they all individually concurred. But he was conspicuously less accommodating, more prickly, quick to reject any quibbles about money. And in the end, he essentially offered them a *take it or leave it* proposition.

With Dominic's track record they all took it, but they grumbled after he got up, brusquely said, "You gentlemen will be much richer after today," and walked out of the room without so much as a thank you. A little courtesy wouldn't have been out of place when they were investing billions.

Max was left to soothe outraged egos.

Sometime later, Max walked into Dominic's office, bit back his comment about the half-empty bottle on Dominic's desk, and forced himself to speak in a measured tone. "You could have been more polite, Nick. It's going to take them a while to cool off."

Dominic drained his drink before looking up, his half-lidded gaze indifferent. "I gave them the full extent of my charm in Hong Kong. I didn't feel like kissing ass again. If

they want to make money, they can buy in. If they don't"—
Dominic shrugged—"I don't give a shit. I'll cover it myself."
He coolly met Max's gaze. "Is there anything else?"

"You're drinking a lot and you're drinking alone," Max
said pointedly. Dominic had never been a solitary drinker.

"So?" He refilled his glass.

"So you're getting hard to handle."

"Point noted. Is there more of this lecture? I hope not,
because I'm already bored. And not that it's any of your
business, but I only drink at night." He glanced at the
clock and a muscle twitched along his jaw. Three fifty p.m.
"Today's an exception," he muttered. Seeing the same men
again had brought back the horror of their last meeting,
when Katherine had seen the disastrous e-mail with the
licentious photos of him with other women and everything
had gone into the tank. "As for drinking alone," he said with
biting sarcasm, "it's never too late to learn."

Max sighed softly. "The lecture's over. How you choose
to go to hell is your own business. But try not to use that
snarky tone with Lillibet. She's new, she's an excellent ana-
lyst, and I wouldn't want to lose her because you're an asshole."

Dominic lifted his glass to Max. "Consider me warned.
Lillibet will be treated with extreme deference. Is she some
politician's daughter? Just asking."

"No."

"Thank God. Politicians can be demanding." Dominic
smiled tightly. "Now, if you'll excuse me." He drained his
glass, reached for the bottle, and shot a look at Max, who
hadn't moved. "Do you mind? I'm busy." Uncorking the bot-

tle, Dominic poured himself another drink, leaned back in his chair, and put the glass to his mouth. He didn't hear the door shut because he was calculating how much liquor it would take tonight to erase the memory of Katherine's tears when she'd looked up from his laptop that day in Hong Kong.

He was still there after the office had gone dark, another opened bottle in hand. The wall of muted TV screens opposite his desk was the only illumination in the room, and his eyes were half shut against the glare.

The door slowly opened and a beautiful, leggy blonde quietly entered the room, shut the door behind her, and leaned back against it. "I'm the last one here, Mr. Knight," she said in softly accented English. "I was wondering if you needed anything before I leave."

Innuendo was thick enough to cut with a knife.

Explicit enough to penetrate the layers of Dominic's despair.

He automatically looked up at the familiar tone of voice and crooked his finger. "What's your name?"

"Tatiana," she said, moving toward his desk.

"Surname?" He'd loosened his tie and collar, his attire otherwise unaltered since the meeting, his white shirt a vivid contrast to his dark suit in the heavily shadowed room.

"Ismay."

No relation to a politician he knew, nor a family of his acquaintance. That didn't make it necessarily safe, but safer. "How long have you worked here, Tatiana?" he gently queried, instinctively surveying the lovely young woman. Max had good taste.

"A year, sir."

"Have we met?"

"Twice, sir."

"And what do you do for us?"

"I'm one of your attorneys."

"And you were wondering if I needed anything?" he murmured.

"Yes, sir."

His gaze narrowed at that third *sir* and he wondered if they'd met somewhere other than the office. Or were his vices common knowledge? "Why did you think I might need something?"

"You were all alone in the dark." Opaque glass panels framed the door.

"Drinking."

"I see that."

"Would you like a drink?" A gratuitous impulse or perhaps a mechanical prompt in a situation like this.

"If you wouldn't mind."

He shut his eyes, the bittersweet phrase like a punch in the gut: he'd said it to Katherine during their first breakfast together at the Garden House, and again after the cocktail party in Hong Kong, both occasions lush with memory. "Actually, I *would* mind," he said, his voice suddenly crisp as he shoved himself upright from his lazy sprawl. "I'm sorry, Miss Ismay." He smiled politely. "I'm too drunk to be good company. Although I appreciate your concern. It was a pleasure to meet you"—he dipped his head—"again. Have a pleasant evening." He grabbed the bottle, pulled out the cork, and thought about offering an additional apology when she didn't move. But he stared at her instead until she did move because he had no intention of fucking her. Now or ever.

After a slow five count, she turned away.

Jesus, he thought glumly, watching the door shut on Miss Ismay; he couldn't even accept a beautiful woman's offer of sex. He was seriously fucked up. Then a highly unpleasant thought surfaced. There wasn't a chance in hell Katherine was going without sex—not with her libido. And for a fraction of a second he thought about calling Tatiana back. But he didn't want her; he wanted only Katherine— who could never get enough fucking, who was always ready, who was so incredibly responsive he had only to touch her and she was wet for him.

He swore under his breath, then out loud.

Christ, it was like going through withdrawal, his cravings so intense he couldn't function normally. He was edgy, couldn't sleep; he was drinking alone when he never did. At least he wasn't hallucinating yet. Then he swore again. Katherine was on his mind constantly, her image stamped on his brain, and if that wasn't hallucinating it was only a matter of interpretation.

He shoved the bottle away, then the glass.

An addiction could be overcome.

He'd dealt with worse problems in his life.

And it wasn't as though he didn't have countless women willing to spread their legs for him. A shame he felt no pleasure at the thought; not necessarily a rare feeling—that lack of pleasure in his life. But it was infinitely worse now after having climbed to the top of the mountain with Katherine and witnessed the great beauty of the world.

He probably shouldn't have bolted; perhaps a less fucked-up person would have stayed.

But she'd left too.

So the riddles of the universe remained.

He absently glanced at the clock as though to confirm his location in time and space in the more prosaic world, then turned to the windows and registered brief surprise. It was completely dark. With a weary sigh, he reached for his phone, punched in a number, and spoke rapidly in French. "I'll be down in ten minutes, Henri. No, I don't think so. No, I'm not hungry. Just home, and then you're free for the night."

Pushing himself to his feet, he switched off the TVs, found his way to the door in the light from the windows facing the Quai d'Orsay, and checked the hallway in the event Miss Ismay hadn't taken her dismissal to heart. He was grateful to find himself alone.

It would have been a huge effort to be courteous even for as long as it would take to get to the entrance doors downstairs. He wasn't in the mood for polite conversation.

FOUR

In the next few weeks, Max and the entire staff in the Paris office were on guard around Dominic. His moodiness was undiminished, his temper volatile, his patience nonexistent.

Max had delayed going home; with his demons back in full force, Dominic needed a babysitter. But Max was finally leaving for Hong Kong and in an effort to safeguard the office staff in his absence, he broached the subject of Dominic's ill humor. "While I'm gone," he said, "maybe you could rachet down your temper. No one dares talk back to you except me. So take a break for a week. Okay?"

Dominic put down his pen, leaned back in his desk chair, and flexed his lips in an unpleasant smile. "You sound like my mother. And I don't like my mother. So back off. Now, have you heard from Ross on that Amalfi Coast hotel?"

"Not yet."

A marginal scowl. "And why the hell is that?"

"Maybe you should just go fuck her," Max snapped. "You've become impossible to deal with."

"And maybe you should shut your fucking mouth," Dominic snapped back, a dangerous gleam in his eyes.

"Jesus, Nick, lighten up. Not only did you practically tell the investors on the rare earth project to go screw themselves, but everyone in the office has been walking on eggshells every day wondering whom you're going to savage next."

"They get paid enough," Dominic growled. "It goes with the territory."

"Look, do you want me to say I was wrong about Katherine? Because I'd be more than happy to do that if it would put you in a better mood."

Dominic gave him a venomous look. "I don't want you to say anything about Katherine *ever.*"

Max shrugged; he was done playing therapist. "Fine. Suit yourself. I'll be back in a week. Do you want anything from Hong Kong?"

"Bring Leo and Danny back with you."

"Because of the Romanian rumors? You think the Balkan mafia threat is real? Are Gora's in-laws really going to want that twenty million back that they stole from you?"

"Who knows? Possibly." Dominic blew out a breath. "And I apologize."

Max smiled faintly. "Apology accepted."

Dominic ran his fingers through his hair and let his hands drop, restlessly flexing his fingers. "I was thinking too," he slowly said, "with the rumors out there, Katherine should have some security. Would you round up a crew and send them to Singapore?"

"She's in Singapore?"

"So I've been told."

"By whom?"

"I doubt you know them."

He knew everyone Nick knew, including Justin, who'd casually asked about Katherine. "I see," Max said blandly. "Have you talked to her?"

Dominic shook his head.

"Are you going to talk to her?"

"It's none of your concern whether I do or not."

Max sighed. "I suppose you can't get any worse."

Dominic's mouth twitched. "I'm pleased to have your approval such as it is."

"As if you need it. Care to tell me why she's in Singapore?"

"No."

If Dominic hadn't been involved, he would have said so. "Staying at Raffles, is she?" Max inquired coolly.

"I believe so."

"In the Cathay Suite?"

"She might be."

Then Dominic had put her there. It was his favorite. "For long?"

A cool blue gaze. "That I don't know."

"I'm surprised. It sounds as though you have everything under control."

Dominic leaned forward, carefully aligned the pen on his desk, then looked up and smiled tightly. "There are limits to what I can do."

Max laughed. "That's exactly why she intrigues you. You didn't just leave her, she left you, didn't she?"

"Is there no privacy in the world?" Dominic drolly remarked.

"Not a whole lot. When are you leaving for Singapore?"

"Tonight."

"Staying long?"

"I doubt it."

FIVE

Kate was sitting with a male colleague at a table in Raffles Bar and Billiard Room when Dominic walked through the broad doorway and came to a stop. He wore a dark polo shirt, dark slacks, a dun-colored sports jacket, and he looked cool and collected and beautiful as sin.

She went still, her heart grabbed at her ribs, hot desire dive-bombed her brain. Left her breathless.

Even at a glance, Dominic's shocking physical beauty, the raw energy spilling from him, the arresting, electric blue of his eyes, pushed all her buttons, switched on every playing-with-fire impulse, made her suddenly conscious of all she'd missed.

He stood utterly motionless, his stance deceptively easy as he surveyed the room, a dominant lion contemplating his kingdom.

Every eye in the room was trained on him—on the unequivocal power beneath the careless pose, the hard-edged swell of muscle beneath the fine tailoring, the extraordinary beauty, the quiet confidence. Even the bartenders stopped their work. You could have heard a pin drop.

Dominic appeared immune to the hush.

Then he saw her, smiled faintly, and advanced into the room.

When he came to a stop at their table, he said pleasantly, "How nice to see you, Miss Hart. What brings you to Singapore?"

"Work."

"Ah." He smiled. "I should have known. Can I buy you and your companion a drink?"

"No." She'd only just managed to put all the pieces of herself back together. She refused to unravel her hard-won normalcy.

"We'd be honored!" Her companion spoke at the same time, his expression one of wide-eyed awe.

The disparate answers broadened Dominic's smile. "Why don't we go with the yes. Another round of the same?" He half turned, nodded, and a waiter appeared as though by magic. After a quiet exchange, Dominic turned back to the table and took a seat, thrusting out his hand to Kate's companion. "Dominic Knight. Pleasure to meet you."

"Johnny Chen. I know who you are." Beaming from ear to ear, Kate's young associate vigorously pumped Dominic's hand. "My family's from Hong Kong."

Dominic spoke to him in fluent Cantonese, Johnny replied, both men laughed, and Kate fumed. Damn him, Dominic was going to charm the hell out of Johnny, who'd been an amiable, good-natured colleague during her time at CX Capital, and she was going to have to pretend some minimum courtesy. She wasn't sure she was capable of speech let alone politesse, with her heart beating like a drum and her libido doing the happy dance. *Jesus, do you mind?* she scolded herself, bitch-slapping her libido. *This is the man who walked out on you.* Johnny explained that they were celebrating the completion of the project they'd worked on together.

Dominic urbanely replied, "I'd say that calls for champagne." As though on cue, the two bottles of champagne he'd ordered were carried over.

Kate knew what Dominic was doing and watched in silent exasperation as he kept refilling everyone's glasses and gently persuading Johnny to talk about their project at length. Johnny explained how he and Kate had worked together all night at times, how they'd worked on weekends too when they were on the trail of something good, how he'd learned so much from her.

Dominic's jaw clenched whenever Johnny pronounced Kate's name with puppy-dog adoration. Then he'd reach over, top off Johnny's glass, and politely ask another question.

Four bottles later, Johnny was slurring his words, swaying in his chair, and regularly losing his train of thought. Coming to his feet, Dominic beckoned a waiter over for assistance, then leaned over and spoke to Kate under his breath. "Stay where you are. I'll be right back."

She should have left. Really, any sensible woman would have. She wasn't mentally or emotionally ready to deal with Dominic. Everything was still too raw, her feelings not up to the challenge. It was also insulting—how he casually trespassed into her life uninvited. Zero for five. She ordered a sandwich. Or maybe her hotspur libido did the ordering. *If you don't want to stay, I will,* her little voice whispered. *A month with only your vibrator is long enough.*

"Some people can't hold their liquor," Dominic said on his return, sitting down and smiling at Kate. "Nice kid though. I know his uncle."

Just because her libido had no boundaries didn't mean Kate was willing to cave. "That was masterful to watch," she said. "I'm impressed."

"Apparently Johnny was impressed with you as well." Dominic leaned back in his chair, gave her a nod. "Did you fuck him?"

"I really couldn't say. Have you been fucking anyone interesting?"

"Actually, I've been abstinent. My friends think I'm dying of something."

Fortunately her sandwich arrived just then because she was speechless. Either Dominic was lying or...She was speechless.

Dominic smiled a thank-you to the waiter, then pointed at the sandwich as the man walked away. "We can do better than that. Dinner somewhere? What would you like to eat?"

The phrase hung in the air. Potent. Lush with possibility.

She flushed, feeling an unwanted desire leap inside her and forcibly tamping it down.

"I really *haven't* fucked anyone since you left," he said quietly.

"Since *you* left."

"We could argue the point. We both left."

"Speaking for myself, for good reason."

He wasn't touching that. "I missed you."

She valiantly resisted the urge to reply in kind; she

wouldn't so easily succumb to hope. "You knew I was here," she said instead, narrow-eyed and accusing. "How?"

"Someone I know saw you in the lobby a few days ago. I decided to take a chance. Could we please not argue? You look wonderful." His sudden grin was sexy and sweet. "I could show you a good time, Miss Hart. After thirty-six days of no sex, I think I could last all night and the next day and"—his grin widened—"however long you want."

"That's it?" she said coolly. "I'm just supposed to say yes and forget you and those women, your leaving, and everything that—"

"I'd like that, yeah."

"I suppose you would," she said tightly. "Just move past the train wreck and keep on fucking."

"Jesus, Katherine, I'm ten kinds of sorry, if it helps. Everything was moving too fast. I couldn't handle it. I wish I'd done things differently, but I didn't. And you were leaving too, so don't pretend you were looking for some long-term relationship. You even put it in writing, babe. Never do that. It's always a mistake."

A cocked brow. "Advice from an expert?"

He started to say something, then stopped himself. "I don't know. But I do know my fucked-up life isn't yours. You're not one of those people who deliberately hurt someone just for the hell of it. And your reasons for leaving"—he ran a hand over his hair, sighed—"well, I'd probably do the same. But I don't want you mad at me. I'm doing my pathetic best to apologize. So stop glaring and talk to me. Let's work this out. I'm not a complete prick."

A tiny smile formed on Kate's lips, half rueful, half real.

The tightness in her shoulders eased. That was major con-ciliation. "You look tired," she said.

"No shit. I've barely slept in weeks."

A small silence. A slow exhalation. Her first impulse was to say: *Come, I'll hold you; sleep.* But she'd suffered too much heartache in the past weeks, cried too many tears. "I suppose now that you've gotten rid of Johnny I might as well have dinner with you," she said, not entirely sure she was doing the right thing. Not entirely sure about anything, with Dominic close enough to touch.

His smile was instant, the dazzling one that always made her feel like the luckiest woman in the world.

"Would you like dinner at the trading station? Or any-where. Literally. My plane is ready to go."

"Jesus, Dominic, you could turn a girl's head."

"If it's yours, I'm good. Otherwise, I don't give a damn. And I mean it about going anywhere you want." He took a small breath, started to say something, thought better of it, stopped, and said instead, "It's really nice to be with you." He shifted slightly in his chair, a quick up-glance, the blue of his eyes shot with happiness. "Really, really nice."

She could barely breathe. Everything she wanted was hers for the asking. Weeks of wretchedness erased if she only said yes to the blissful fantasy he offered. She'd live happily ever after if she said yes. Or more likely the dream would bleed away and the world would turn cold when he left again. Because he surely would.

He leaned forward, his butane-blue eyes suddenly dead serious. "Could we go somewhere else? Anywhere else."

She tried to rearrange the chaos in her brain but her

overtaxed mind had slowed to a crawl. She said, "Where?" When she didn't mean it. Her subconscious had rashly spoken. He reached for her hand; she jerked it back.

"Sor—" He stopped himself; she'd accused him of meaningless apologies the night of the party in Hong Kong. "We could go"—a flick of his finger—"you name it. I don't care where it is. We'll just talk. No strings, no agenda, you can tell me to go to hell and I'll listen."

"How about we stay here."

She hadn't told him to go to hell. Things were looking up. "Fine. Dinner here then."

"I've missed a few of my birth control pills lately so I'm really not available for anything but dinner," she said, giving him an expressionless green stare, needing to ink in the boundaries for her own peace of mind.

His bland gaze hid the bombshell exploding in his head. "Not a problem. Dinner's fine. I had no expectations."

"Of course you did."

Of course he did. And he'd heard of condoms even if she hadn't. "Let's not argue. Would you like to have dinner in the bar or in the dining room?"

She suddenly smiled. "I like when you're being nice."

"Then I'll see that I'm on my best behavior for you."

A sudden, treacherous rush of affection warmed her senses. She almost said, *I don't want dinner, I want you.* "Super," she said. "And the dining room will be fine."

There was no question Dominic was on his best behavior at dinner. She was tempted to take notes. His manners were so polished, his conversation so agreeable, she marveled at such brilliant composure. It wasn't until they were having after-dinner drinks that she began feeling guilty. Regardless of his motivation, Dominic was truly sweet and attentive, careful not to make any moves on her, never mentioning their meltdown in Hong Kong. She felt as though she were taking advantage of him and his kindness when she'd decided in the past few weeks that if she just kept on keeping on eventually her life would return to normal. And as much as she wished it weren't true, she knew that no matter how sweet Dominic was tonight, he would only bring heartache in the end.

Setting down her port glass, she mentally braced herself, then said, "I don't want to lead you on. I'm not good at pretense. I appreciate your"—she gestured at the largely untouched food on the table, a combination of nerves and desire having stolen their appetites—"hospitality, but you and I are looking for different things. You want me wrapped up neatly, tied with a bow, packaged up, and shipped to you whenever you feel like screwing me. I can't do that. Sometimes I wish I could. You're far superior to my vibrator. But I can't. Understand?"

No, because if he was honest, that's what he wanted. Drinking his port, he set down the glass and pushed it out of the way before looking up. "Would you be interested in an exclusivity contract? Your terms."

Her jaw dropped. "You can't be serious."

"That sounds like a no," he said calmly, already moving his next chess piece, too smart to take offense.

"I cried too much and too long after Hong Kong," she said, the misery still raw. "Why would I want to relive that?"

"I drank too much and slept too little after Hong Kong. I'm trying to reach some compromise with you so neither of us has to relive the last month."

"So you propose a compromise about sex?" She tried to keep the rebuke from her tone; after all, she'd been a willing participant in Dominic's sexual games.

"Partly," he said, careful not to respond to the unmistakable censure in her voice.

"And the other part?"

He merely shrugged. "I don't know. You have to admit, after knowing each other only a few days, full clarity wasn't likely. At least for me."

"So you ran," she said, each word bitter and metallic.

There was a hard flash in his eyes. "Don't start. You ran too."

He had new hollows under his cheekbones, faint shadows under his eyes, a coiled restlessness beneath his disciplined façade. Was it possible he'd been as wretched as she? That he really had been celibate? She was suddenly drained of anger, as if a timer had run down on some monumental struggle and she was left weak but alive. "Have you really not slept with anyone since Hong Kong?"

He shook his head. "I haven't."

"I don't know if I can believe you." But the most amazing wave of endorphins washed over her like a fresh breath of sea air.

"Believe me. Ask Max. I've been a total ass to everyone at our Paris office."

"Because you missed me."

"Like crazy." That at least was true; all the rest was pure anarchy.

The word *crazy* bulldozed away the entire devastating wreckage left behind from those photos, the bloodlust for vengeance, the flood of sadness that had swamped her life. It characterized the turbo-charged intensity of their relationship. "How crazy," she whispered.

He smiled, knowing what she meant. "Almost—but not quite—that crazy. We'll buy some condoms."

"I haven't said yes yet." But her breath was coming fast.

He saw it, heard it, saw as well her bright green eyes that held the sunshine missing from his world, her lush red mouth that offered the promise of pleasure he'd come half-way around the globe to possess, the beauty of her pale face that had filled his dreams. He leaned forward, reached across the small table, and took her hand. "Say it." A low, hushed command. "Say yes."

She pulled her hand away, his touch electric, her body responding like Pavlov's dogs. Her mind, fortunately, was still partially open for business. "Tell me what you mean by exclusivity," she said, with a willful jut to her chin.

He sat back, gratified and relieved, understanding that it was just a matter of negotiation now. "It means anything you want it to mean."

"Then I want a mutual exclusivity. One that either of us can revoke by e-mail."

A soundless whistle. "That's cold."

Low-stoked anger glowed in her eyes. "You'd know about cold."

So not interested in renewing the argument of who left whom, his voice was smooth as silk. "We should be able to manage that."

"I should hope so. What's the point otherwise? You do

what you want and I wait for you? That would be stupid of me."

He smiled. "Agreed."

"This isn't amusing, Dominic. I'm not even sure I believe you can follow your own terms," she said crabbily. "So if this is all just bullshit so you can get me into bed, I'd rather not play this game."

"Forgive me. I'm dead serious. Have security follow me. I'll pay for it."

She gave him a pointed look. "Why would I trust them when you're paying them?"

"I'll give you the money," he offered, quickly adapting. "Hire whomever you want."

"I don't want your money."

"If you have a better idea, I'm listening." Unruffled, accommodating to infinity.

She grimaced. "You're missing the point. I don't think you can change." She was no prude, but Dominic had no scruples when it came to kink. It was a major part of his life.

"I told you I'd give up all that. I did."

"For me? Oh, hell, bleep that. I've been drinking."

"No, that's okay. It *was* mostly for you, although maybe it was just time to shut it down. Don't ask me to understand. I don't. I just know I've missed you."

Maybe he'd pushed all her pity buttons. More likely she'd been delusional in thinking she could withstand temptation when he was so close and so beautiful it made her heart ache. "I missed you too," Kate said softly. "The Johnny Chens of the world just don't cut it."

"Did you fuck him?" A sudden edge entered his voice.

"No. Tell me about your love life," she said, equally acerbic.

"Fair enough. The only time I even came close to a woman was when a friend in Paris asked me out for dinner. Way before the meal was over, I knew I'd made a mistake. I gave her some excuse and had my driver take her home. That's it." He didn't mention Tatiana because it was meaningless. "Otherwise I jacked off and drank at night. Now, tell me about *your* love life. Was there someone other than Johnny Chen trying to get in your pants?" That hard edge to his voice again.

"Not really. I couldn't go through with it." Missoula had been a huge mistake. She cringed every time she thought about it.

"Go through with what?" A narrow-eyed steely look.

"My roommate set me up. I thought I could forget you if I slept with someone else."

A visible tick flickered across his jaw. "You *slept* with someone?"

"No, I only kissed him."

"Him? What's his name?" To be filed away for possible reprisals.

"Ben."

"Last name," he said curtly.

"I have no idea. I was just doing it to do it." A touch of sarcasm entered her voice. "Surely, you know the feeling."

He dragged in a breath; he was well acquainted with casual sex. "Did Ben *touch* you?" He kept the fury from his tone by sheer will.

"Don't, Dominic. It was nothing. I burst into tears and

locked myself in the bathroom. Okay? It was totally embarrassing."

"And he just left? He didn't try and talk you into anything?"

"Unlike you," she said pointedly, "some men understand
a refusal."

His lips firmed. "I see," he said tersely.

"I doubt you do. Now tell me about your dinner date,"
she said with the same green-eyed jealousy.

"There's nothing to tell. We ate dinner, my driver took
her home."

"What's her name?"

A brief pause, instinctive male wariness. "Why?"

"Maybe I could introduce her to Ben," Kate sardonically
murmured.

Dominic softly exhaled. "Her name's Victoria Melbury."

"That doesn't sound French."

"It isn't."

"Where's she from?"

He sighed. "Does it matter?"

"Only if you don't tell me."

An eye roll. "Jesus, she's from London. She's in the phone
book but I hope like hell you don't call her because she
doesn't matter. Now, could we talk about something else?"

"My, you're testy."

"Like I'm testy about Johnny Chen slobbering all over
you and probably Ben too. I should punch them out."

"Please don't. And I won't call Victoria. Deal?"

"Deal." He suddenly grinned. "I suppose it wouldn't be
you unless we were arguing over useless shit. Could we

get the hell out of here?" He nodded at her drink. "Are you done?"

"Yes, sir."

"There. Finally." He made a writing gesture to the waiter keeping an eye on their table from a discreet distance. "That makes my twelve hour flight worthwhile."

"Speaking of worthwhile," she said, "what are we going to do about condoms?"

The waiter who'd arrived at the table pretended not to hear, but Kate blushed red to her hairline.

Dominic didn't care if he heard or not. "Send the charges to my trading station," he politely said to the man. "And have my car brought up."

He took one look at Kate and murmured as the waiter walked away, "I'm sure the man has heard the word *condom* before, Katherine." Slipping a bill from the money in his pocket, he left the tip on the table, looked up, and smiled. "But I do enjoy your modesty. Not quite as much as I enjoy your lack of modesty in private."

"Please," she whispered. "People might hear."

His nostrils flared. "Christ, don't blush like that or I'll fuck you right here."

"Dominic!" A more forceful whisper laced with alarm.

Coming to his feet, he walked around the table to pull out her chair and, bending low, murmured in her ear, "There's a quiet hallway not twenty feet away where I could fuck you if you promise not to scream."

"Don't you dare!" she hissed. But her body was instantly engaged, eager and willing, the impetuous pulsing between her legs sending out hard-core signals of availability.

"Don't challenge me, Katherine," he said quietly, then stood upright, eased back her chair, and held out his hand. "That always has predictable results."

"I'm not touching you until you promise to behave," she said as quietly, looking up at him, not moving.

"Don't be silly. You don't like me to behave. We've always agreed on that, if nothing else. Now take my hand. People are beginning to stare. I don't care, but I know you do. Or would you like to be the center of attention? I could start undressing you if you like. I could have them clear the room"—he smiled wickedly—"or not if you're in an exhibitionist mood. I could fuck you on the table." He glanced around and smiled at all the staring faces before returning his gaze to Kate. "What do you say, baby? Round one here or are you going to take my hand?"

"I'll make you pay for this later," she said fretfully, placing her hand in his, aglow with lust after Dominic's provocative offer of exhibitionist sex. "After I've come a few times."

He pulled her to her feet with a knowing grin. "Sounds like fun times ahead. We can discuss your agenda in the car."

SIX

O nce they were in the car, he asked, "Where to?"
    "A pharmacy first."

He grinned. "Is that all I mean to you? A hard dick?"

She ran her hand over the bulge in his crotch, enjoyed his quick intake of breath, then flashed him a grin of her own. "Let's just say it's priority numbers one through twenty at the moment. I think I wore out my vibrator—or actually, *your* vibrator. Thanks by the way, it *was* better than mine. I won't ask how you knew that because I do have an agenda. Afterward you can explain."

"Maybe there won't be an afterward. Maybe I'll just keep fucking you."

She briefly shut her eyes, then smiled up at him. "Right now that sounds absolutely heavenly. This has been a very *long* month."

"Thirty-six days," he muttered, looking grim for a split second. Then he turned and hit the switch for the intercom. "A pharmacy, Chu. The first one you see."

As the car pulled away from the hotel entrance, he debated what to tell her about the security risks they faced. He had no intention of revealing how dangerous it could be—it would only scare her. So he decided to avoid any reference to the Balkan mafia. "Would my place suit you? I don't mean to alarm you, but it might be safer. We're having slight problems with a business competitor," he improvised. "A matter of industrial espionage on our research lab here. They might be doing some surveillance."

She shot him a look. "Were they following me today? I had a creepy feeling someone was watching Johnny and me when we left work. I can't imagine what I'd have to do with your research lab though."

"No, of course not. Perhaps it was some of our security people." He pulled out his phone. "Give me a minute. Max will know."

His conversation was circumspect after Max said his men weren't in place yet, Dominic's speech deliberately guarded. After ending his call, he turned back to Kate, his expression neutral. "Max said he'd talk to our men. If you saw them they weren't doing their job. You should be fine now." His comment was only half a lie because she *would* be fine as of tomorrow morning. "So no more creeping you out," he added with a smile.

"Just out of curiosity"—a quick grin—"are you stalking me?"

"Maybe a little."

"So no one actually saw me in the lobby at Raffles."

"Not really." That got him off the hook about CX Capital; better she thought he was keeping tabs on her. And of course, he was; he'd known her assignment was closing down before he'd left Paris.

"You've been monitoring my activities."

He smiled. "It's become a habit."

"That leaves me somewhere between pissed off and flattered."

"Hold that thought." Chu was stopping at the curb outside a small shop with a green neon pharmacy sign. "Let me take care of this first."

"Wait," she ordered, putting her hand on his arm. Faced with the danger of becoming involved with Dominic again, she wavered. "Why am I doing this," she whispered, "when I promised myself I wouldn't?"

"For the same reason I flew halfway around the world. What's between us defies reason. We're obsessed, infatuated—"

"Probably deranged," she muttered.

"But in a good way, babe." Leaning over, he kissed her, quickly, heatedly, then softly sighed and sat up. "It's going to be fine. I promise."

"Easy for you to say. You'll get on your plane and—"

"And nothing. We're both in the same place. It's no easier for me than for you. If it were, I wouldn't be here. I'd be—"

"Sleeping with some bitch in Paris."

"Right. So obviously this is something we have to deal with, although if you don't mind, I'd like to do it in five minutes." He dipped his head. "Someone else might buy all their condoms and neither one of us wants that."

"We could go to another pharmacy."

"Or we could be at my place fucking."

She grinned. "When you put it like that."

"You always were eager," he said with an answering grin.

"I was thinking *reasonable*."

He bit back his critical dissent and smiled. "I couldn't

have said it better. Now be a sweetheart and let me get out of this car." He glanced at his watch. "They might close soon."

She watched him lope across the sidewalk, stiff arm the door open, and stride to the back of the small shop. He walked right up to the counter and said something to the elderly customer the clerk was serving, giving them both a dazzling smile. The elderly man laughed and stepped aside. The salesclerk fluffed her hair as she listened to Dominic's instructions, her eyes wide, clearly caught in his force field. Dominic pointed and chatted with the elderly man while the clerk cleared her display of condoms, then he helped her shove the boxes into two bags.

Leaving a bill on the counter, Dominic waved and bolted for the door.

"Nice old guy," he said, entering the car, pulling the door shut, and dropping the bags on the floor. "The clerk was a little slow, but hey"—he held up his thumb—"success."

"Do you have enough?" she inquired sardonically.

He grinned. "Don't want to run out. Remember, I've seen you in action, babe. More, more, and more is your motto."

"I hope you're not complaining."

"No way. Thrilled, excited, champing-at-the-bit enthusiastic. How's that for an uncritical endorsement of your sexual appetite?"

"That's better."

"You haven't even seen better yet." Leaning forward he rapped on the privacy glass and the car immediately picked up speed. Falling back against the seat, he pulled Kate into his arms. "Have I mentioned how much I missed you?"

"Once or twice."

"In about ten minutes, I'm going to *show* you how much I missed you."

"We don't *have* to wait."

"Yeah, we do," he whispered, bending his head, kissing her forehead lightly. "I have plans."

"Good. Because now that my assignment is done at CX Capital, I'm on vacation."

His dick really liked the sound of the word *vacation*.

She noticed his surging erection and pleasure flooded her senses. Reaching over, she cupped his balls, gently squeezed, and watched the burgeoning swell beneath his linen trousers. "I don't want to wait," she whispered, moving her hand to his zipper.

"You never do." He lifted her hand away. "Luckily, I can help you out." He eased her back on the seat.

"I want *you* though," she pouted.

He smiled and, leaning over, nibbled on her bottom lip. "I'm yours, baby. But ten minutes isn't long enough for me. Not after I've waited so long. So let me help you relax a little. Something simple, quick"—he bit her lip—"satisfying. Don't say no." He stopped her with a finger on her mouth. "You know I don't like that word."

Jesus, he only had to look at her like that, talk to her in that softly threatening way and she turned liquid inside, was instantly primed and quivering.

"Just say yes, baby. And I'll make you feel good."

She nodded.

His brows rose.

"Yes," she said and watched him smile.

After a quick glance out the window, gauging their progress, estimating their time to the trading station, he slipped off her shoes, unzipped her slacks, and eased them down her hips and legs, along with her panties. Kneeling on the car floor, he spread her legs and bent his head. As his tongue slid over her swollen clit, he heard her breathy little sigh and smiled.

Jesus Christ, she made him happy.

Kate slid her fingers through his silky hair and with a low, throaty groan, wholeheartedly gave herself up to the ravishing, unequivocal pleasure. To the delight, contentment, and seething lust that was all wrapped up in one vital, indispensible man.

Then Dominic slipped two fingers deep inside her, found her precious nerve center, and measured it with his fingertips with such delicacy she thought surely she would expire with bliss. But he made it even better, like he always did, fiercely better, flame hot, sensationally better. Until finally, desperate for release, she uttered a wild, frenzied cry and climaxed with the hot, gloating, over-the-top pleasure only Dominic conferred.

SEVEN

When they reached the trading station, Dominic helped Kate with her clothes, escorted her into the main house, and came to a halt in the entrance hall. "Tan will show you to the conservatory," he said with a glance at the young man who'd opened the door for them. "Give me a minute to clear up a few things."

She shot him a spiking glance, tinged with suspicion. "I hope that doesn't mean you have to hustle some woman out of your bedroom," she said under her breath, not as cavalier as Dominic when it came to staff who were close enough to hear.

"Ye of little faith," he said with a full smile. "It's business." He'd deliberately not immediately escorted her to his bedroom as a matter of courtesy. Tact and conciliation—that was his plan.

"Don't keep me waiting too long."

Whether it was a threat or a plea he understood the message. "Literally, two minutes." He brushed her cheek with a kiss. "Don't get too comfortable."

But of course it wasn't two minutes. It was closer to fifteen minutes by the time Dominic had seen that his security understood the newest mafia threat in the city and he was assured that the trading station was securely locked down. Tan's relatives would be summoned as well. His family came from a warrior culture slightly tamed by modern legalities, but not entirely pacified.

When he walked into the conservatory—home to a superb collection of orchids—he glanced at the coffee service on the table and the cup in Kate's hand and grinned. "Coffee? Am I expected to be up all night?"

"You are." She gave him a happy smile buttressed by her recent orgasm and some delicious chocolate petit fours. "Otherwise, I'd be wasting my time."

"We certainly wouldn't want that," he said, taking a seat opposite her, stretching his legs out, and making himself comfortable on the cushioned rattan chair.

She pointed at the silver pot. "Coffee?"

"I'm good, thanks. My adrenaline is pumping big time."

"How nice for me," she murmured, setting her cup down.

"And me. Now all you have to do is tell me what you want. I'm going to be really careful not to cross any red lines tonight, so the agenda's entirely up to you."

"Well, first I want to come again. I don't care how."

His lashes lowered infinitesimally. "You'd better watch your choice of words, Katherine."

"How about the usual then?"

A flicker of a smile. "Your usual or mine?"

"I'll take potluck."

His smile broadened. "Here I'm trying to be a good boy, and you're breaking the game wide open. You sure?"

"With that look—probably not."

An extravagant shrug. "So we're back at square one."

"Not necessarily," she said, a teasing light in her eyes.

He exhaled softly. "Now you're just fucking with me."

"You're better at this than me. If you're doing something I don't like, I'll just say no." She drew in a small breath. "That's probably not going to happen."

The raw need in her voice was like a drug to an addict, the elixir that stole through his senses and made him feel as though, for this moment in time, the world was perfect. "Why don't we begin with something simple," he murmured, "and we'll go on from there. Open your blouse for me." She was wearing her own clothes—not the clothes he'd bought for her in Amsterdam—the army green slacks he'd seen at her first interview, a plain white blouse, no jewelry, tan lace-up shoes.

A small start. "Here?"

"Yes, here."

"Your staff," she said nervously.

He dipped his head faintly. "Just do it, Katherine."

She hesitated, quickly scanned the plant-filled conservatory, the colorful orchids spilling down the trunks of trees, the open door to the terrace and the tropical night.

"None of it's a problem," he said gently, watching her quick survey of the nineteenth-century glass house. "I thought you wanted to come again," he prompted, his lounging pose unaltered, his voice mild. "Open your blouse and we'll get started."

"Please, Dominic," she whispered, shifting slightly in her chair. "There are people around."

"I don't see anyone."

"They might come in any minute."

"Not unless you call them. Would you like some company?"

"God, no." But perversely, a lustful jolt shuddered through her and she clenched her thighs together.

"Really, Katherine," he said with a faint smile. "You're getting wet, aren't you? Does the thought of performing in public appeal to you?"

"Absolutely not!"

"Should I check?"

"No, stay away," she said tensely.

"Me—stay away?" His voice was soft with insolence. "Would you prefer Johnny Chen? I'm sure he'd be happy to fuck you, although I don't think you'd enjoy him. I'm guessing he'd come in two seconds and then what would you do?"

"And I suppose you wouldn't?" She knew it was stupid even as she said it, but Dominic's unfettered arrogance never failed to get a rise out of her.

"If you're going to be argumentative, at least be reasonable," he said amiably. "No, I wouldn't come in two seconds, as you well know. So take off your blouse." He smiled. "Pretty please?"

She blew out a breath. "I don't know how you're always so restrained, when I'm falling apart." She tried to suppress her libido, reminding herself how she disliked Dominic's corrupting power, how she disapproved of docilely yielding to him. That she'd left Dominic in order to avoid relinquishing her freedom.

"I like that in you," he said pleasantly, immune to issues of power when he wielded incomparable authority. "I like your irrepressible passion. Please don't change."

She sighed, smiling faintly. "As if I could."

"Lucky me," he said. "You're not wearing a bra," he added in a cooler tone, jealous of every man who came near her. "You must have made Johnny Chen very happy."

"Everyone's not like you, Dominic."

"Any man likes big tits," he murmured. "You must have given Johnny a hard-on a dozen times a day. Whenever you're ready, Katherine." He opened his sports coat slightly to expose his prominent erection. *Maybe power wasn't irrelevant after all, maybe the thought of Johnny Chen looking at his tits required payback.*

She dragged in a breath, flushed rosy pink.

"You can have this as soon as you get undressed." His voice was blunt, exacting.

"I shouldn't." An automatic response when Dominic spoke as though he owned the world and everyone in it.

"Just so we're clear, Katherine. I play this game only because you like it."

"*You* do too."

He shrugged faintly. "I don't *dislike* it, but I like lots of things. It doesn't have to be this."

"So I could choose something else?" Her lips twitched impudently. "I could tell *you* what to do?"

"Perhaps." Had Johnny Chen seen that impudent grin? Had she been playful or flirtatious with him?

"That sounds like perhaps *not*," she said with a flicker of a smile.

"Did he touch you?"

A look of surprise. "You mean Johnny?"

"Unless there were more men you'd like to tell me about," he said gruffly, the blue of his eyes suddenly cold.

"Stop it, Dominic. Right *now*."

"Did *anyone* touch you?" he asked, ignoring her, jealous for the first time in his life. Not entirely sure he knew how to deal with it civilly.

"You don't own me, Dominic," she quietly replied. "We've been through this before. If that's what you want, I'm leaving."

"Not tonight you're not. It's too dangerous."

"Jesus, Dominic," she muttered. "You haven't changed one single bit. I'm here whether I want to be or not? You're in charge of every goddamn thing. Orders every fucking second."

"And you're still fighting me every inch of the way," he retorted brusquely. "So tell me, which one of us hasn't changed?" He shut his eyes for a second, slid down on his spine, then blew out a breath and looked at her from under his long lashes. "I told myself I wouldn't do this—piss you off, argue, lose my temper. But I'm jealous of every man who looks at you. *Every. Single. One.* I wish I didn't give a damn. I wish it didn't matter to me. I wish you weren't in my thoughts and dreams every minute of the day and night. So don't tell me to stop feeling the way I do," he growled. "I *can't.*"

"And you wish you could." She grimaced. "I know the feeling."

"We are truly fucked," Dominic said with a sigh. "On the other hand, you're here, I can see you and touch you"— he smiled—"maybe. So things could be worse." He slid upright again. "At least I don't feel like drinking every minute. That's good."

"And I don't feel like crying every minute." Kate smiled back. "That's a relief. Still," she said with a little flutter of her fingers, "do you think the sex is worth all the angst?"

"You're kidding—right? The sex is fantastic. Fuck the angst." The warmth in his eyes could have illuminated Singapore for a decade. "You make the world livable, Katherine. And at the risk of pissing you off again, I should know. Look," he said gently, "we're not going to solve the riddles of the universe tonight or maybe ever. All I know is I'm happy when I'm with you and miserable when I'm not. That's gotta mean something."

"I suppose," Kate murmured. "I've never felt so rotten before either."

"So fuck it. Who cares if we're clueless about the reasons. How about I make you happy now?"

"And I'll make you happy back."

"Sounds like a plan."

He was suddenly tired of talking, but then he had a one-track mind when it came to Katherine. And his flight across the world to get here had only increased the anticipation of touching her, tasting her, possessing her. "It's been a long month for both of us," he said, rising from his chair in a smooth, supple, deceptively easy motion. "It's about time we had some fun." Closing the distance between them in three strides, he lifted the table with the silver coffee service aside while her heart drummed in her ears, the hard, steady pulsing between her legs beat a wild, welcoming tattoo, and her frenzied carnal cravings reminded her that it *had* been a very long month.

Shrugging out of his jacket, he dropped it on the white

marble floor and gracefully knelt at her feet. "Let me help you with your buttons, then with another orgasm. After that we can debate our options." Without waiting for a reply, he gently spread her legs, leaned forward, and unclasped the first pearl button on her blouse.

Issues of submission and independence, of temptation and willingness, were no longer relevant. Dominic was impossible to resist. And at the moment, with lust hammering her brain, with sharp-set desire ravishing her body, she was willing to do anything to feel him inside her. She reached for the zipper on her slacks.

He stopped her hand. "I'll do that. I've played this film in my head a thousand times the last few weeks." He slid the second button free, then the third, his slender fingers deft and quick. After he opened the fourth button, he unclasped the hook on her waistband, slid the zipper down, freed her blouse tails from her slacks, and slowly opened the plain white linen as if he were unveiling the Venus de Milo, the *Mona Lisa*, and all the wonders of the world.

He softly exhaled as her pale flesh was fully revealed— remembering how her skin felt, the silken warmth, the softness; how she always responded to his touch with eagerness, wild for sensation—for him. The déjà vu triggers were almost overwhelming. He sucked in a shaky breath.

"Are you remembering?" she whispered, as though she could read his mind, as though they were watching the same movie, listening to the same song.

He looked up and nodded. "I've replayed every breath, every heartbeat, every good thing that happened to us."

"Along with every mind-blowing orgasm," she said with a small smile.

"Oh, yeah, those most of all. So you're not going anywhere this time."

"Is that a fact?"

"Fucking A. Hell can do without me for a while. And I'm going to make you feel so good you won't even think about leaving."

"What if I have to work?"

"You don't have to work."

"What if I *want* to work?"

"Then I'll see what I can do about working you," he said with a grin.

"Sex fiend."

"Uh-uh. I'm just trying to keep up, babe. You're the one who sets the wicked pace."

"I hope you're not looking for an apology."

"No way. I'm thanking my lucky stars you fell into my life. And now that you have, I'm locking the door behind you."

"So I'm your captive?"

"Something like that. You're also the best thing that's happened to me in a very long time and I'm not stupid enough to let you go."

"What if I want to go?"

He smiled. "Then I wouldn't be doing my job." His smile faded. "Look, if and when that happens, we'll talk about it."

She sniffed. "You're impossible. But I want you anyway."

"Good, because this is new times, better times, baby. We're not going to screw this one up. So let's see what we can do about making each other feel good for the foreseeable future. Okay?" He smiled. "Gimme a yes."

"Yes, sir," she said, smiling back.

He grinned. "There you go, baby. You're playin' my song."

He slid the blouse off her shoulders, down her arms, over her hands, then pulled it aside and let it drop from his fingers. "Now what do we have here?" he whispered.

His erection answered first, surging higher.

She took notice. "He likes me," she murmured.

He held her gaze, his flame-hot. "He's missed you—and these," he murmured, sliding a fingertip over the pale swell of her breasts. Her sumptuous tits were more beautiful than he'd remembered, ripe, plump, her nipples already hard and peaked, waiting to be kissed. He gently touched one taut crest then the other, the pad of his finger feather light—a grazing caress, delicate.

Riveting. She sucked in a breath, moaned, spiking pleasure melting downward in a warm, blissful flood.

He was instantly overcome with jealousy at the familiar sound, at her hair-trigger arousal, at her lack of restraint. "No one's seen these since Hong Kong—right?" His dark brows were angled in a frown. "Humor me, baby. This is a whole new world for me."

"I should say no," she whispered, wishing that in the past month some other man could have made her feel this explosive lust and free her from her inconvenient, burning desire for the elusive Dominic Knight.

His anger instantly drained away, his gut-tightening jealousy faded. "No you shouldn't," he said gently, his fingertip gossamer light on her nipple. "Because I want these to be mine." Then he cupped her chin and raised her face so their eyes met, so he saw her smoldering desire and she his unflinching resolve. "Tell me they're mine," he said quietly. "And I'll let you come."

"Sorry, too late." Her green gaze was playful, the flush of arousal pinking her skin. "I don't think I actually *need* you."

He laughed. "Goddamn, I've missed you, baby. But..." he softly said, bending his head, giving her a quick glance from under his lashes, "maybe I can change your mind." His mouth closed gently over the tender tip of her nipple and he set about showing her who needed whom.

As the warmth of his mouth drew in her nipple, she felt her body open in welcome, as though he had only to make that first small overture, delicately touch her sensitive crest with the tip of his tongue, and every combustible sexual nerve she possessed instantly ignited. It was one of his many accomplishments—his incredible tactile finesse. And if she weren't feeling the delicious heat sliding downward from his mouth to her quivering, throbbing sex, she might take issue and allow her jealousy full rein.

But he was nibbling now, his teeth leaving little jolts in their wake that tingled at first, then stung, then ravished her senses and stole her reason and reminded her of the nipple clips in Hong Kong so violently that she cried out in a frenzy of need.

He lifted his head, the air suddenly cool on her nipple. "Soon, baby. Try to relax."

"I can't!"

"Sure you can." He touched her cheek. "Try." Then he dipped his head and gently bit her other nipple.

It was no contest; it never was.

He could make her feel so fine it didn't matter if she was needy or self-willed, free or not, when the pleasure was so flat-out wondrous.

He teased first one nipple then the other, carefully gauging her response as he deftly brought her to the explosive brink before releasing the pressure of his mouth and letting her hysteria slowly wane. Then beginning again, sucking gently at first then not gently at all, masterfully restoking her arousal.

Saturated with prodigal sensation, wallowing in bliss, dizzy with pleasure, Kate forgave Dominic all his transgressions. She forgave him for all her weeks of misery because only he had the gift to make her feel this good: glowing, insatiable, deep in love. She didn't even care that he flinched at the word *love*. She was beyond reason and logic, her body tingling, pulsing, melting inside, slick, liquid, desperate. "Dominic, please," she said on a suffocated breath, pushing his head away. "You win. I want you, I need you. *Now, this instant.*"

He took her face between his hands, his gaze close. "We need each other, baby. Give me a few seconds. Okay?"

She nodded, or tried, his fingers unyielding.

"I don't want to miss this. So hang on. Please?"

She loved him contrite, although she loved him every possible way. "Maybe, probably, hurry..."

His fingers slid away from her face and he pulled off her shoes, slacks, and panties in one fell swoop. Coming to his feet, he picked her up as though she were weightless and carried her to a chaise, where he deposited her with a super polite, "I'll be right with you."

He stripped off his clothes with astonishing speed. Then he took the condom he'd pulled from his pants pocket and put between his teeth, ripped the foil open, and rolled the condom down his erection. *He was like a fucking professional*, she thought. "You're awfully good at that," she said, grudging irritation in her voice.

He looked up at the umbrage in her tone. "At what?"

"Putting on that condom."

"Is there some reason I shouldn't be? Don't answer that. I don't have time to argue." Suddenly he was towering over her. "Would you like to spread your legs or should I do it? You're not the only one in a hurry."

"Do I have a choice?"

He suddenly laughed. "You don't really want a choice do you?"

"I suppose not, with that really fabulous dick about to make me happy."

"Smart girl." He put one knee on the chaise, she opened her thighs, and a moment later, he was positioning himself between her legs. "A word of warning. This first time isn't going to break any records for endurance. As soon as you start coming, I'm right behind you." He didn't wait for an answer; she was panting and so slick with longing, he glided in with only the slightest resistance.

She climaxed almost instantly, he quickly followed, and after an oppressive thirty-six days of estrangement the brute force of their tempestuous orgasms, the sheer, blinding pleasure, left them momentarily stunned.

Was it possible to actually have an out-of-body experience? Empirical evidence was making Dominic a believer.

Was it possible to fall hopelessly, head over heels in love again, with a man who didn't want to be loved, because of an outrageously grandiose orgasm? Kate wondered.

The mind-boggling affirmation was direct, razor sharp, and terrifying to them both.

He should withdraw, he thought with alarm—to Paris or beyond.

She should politely say "thank you" as if none of this were out of the ordinary, she nervously reflected, and take the first plane home.

But neither one moved. "I'm losing it," he said half under his breath, his eyes slits as though to contain the raging turbulence within.

"We should—stop," she said, gasping.

"Later."

"When?" Someone had to be rational.

"Talk to me in a year."

She went rigid in his arms despite the heady mix of wistful, fervent devotion. "Impossible!"

"Try me," he growled.

"Damn it, Dominic, you can't just—"

He covered her mouth with his, defiant of reason, heedless to all but his own selfish desire, his ravaging kiss ignoring her resistance, the brute force marking her with an inexplicable stamp of ownership—like Attila the Hun with a new concubine.

As rash as he, she shamelessly capitulated, gave herself up to his plundering mouth and tongue, wanting what he wanted, wanting more. Wanting his love; wanting what she could never have.

As her resistance melted away, she responded with her familiar tempestuous passion, recklessly matched his fevered kisses with a wildness of her own, impulsively bit his lip. He sucked in a breath, then bit her back with the same seething fury. They were both out of control, their nerve endings on fire, their cravings so intense they could taste it, their need for each other irrepressible.

And where Dominic had been uncertain about his plans—actually, he'd had no plans—suddenly his roadmap to the future was clear. He lifted his head marginally and smiled at her, feeling as though truth and goodness and all the virtues of the world were within his grasp. "You make me insanely happy, baby, but bite me that hard again," he said with a grin, licking the blood off his bottom lip, "and you'll get the spanking of your life."

"Then it might be worth it," she whispered, stretching upward; his bite having been more restrained, only teeth marks reddened her lip.

Shoving her back down, he circled her wrists with his fingers. "You'll have another chance later," he said lightly, dropping a kiss on the bridge of her nose. "Right now, I have a semiserious proposition. So don't say no right away."

"I wouldn't dream of saying no to you after that dyna-mite orgasm." She smiled faintly. "Does this have anything to do with my next orgasm? Please say yes."

He smiled back. "Yes. But give me a minute first. I hate these things." Withdrawing from her body, he sat on the edge of the chaise, yanked off the condom, and tossed it in the jungle of plants. "Don't lecture me," he warned her. "My staff doesn't give a shit."

"I wouldn't think of it," she murmured.

Her reply was so amenable, his gaze narrowed. "Is that sarcasm? Forget it," he said quickly. "I don't care, as long as you're not getting up to leave."

Her green-eyed gaze was balmy with contentment. "I don't feel like leaving just yet."

"Perfect. Because I have something that will make the sex even better."

"You have my full attention, Mr. Knight," she purred.

He laughed. "I thought I might." But he drew in a quick breath and said warily, "Listen, don't shoot me down until you hear me out, okay?"

She grinned. "It must be super kinky."

He gave her a flinty look.

She mimed a locking motion across her mouth.

"Now, first, I'm perfectly willing to use condoms for as long as you want, but with the multiple orgasms you prefer, along with, shall we say, the marathon fucking sessions you like, condoms would be a real pain in the ass. So"—he took a quick breath—"if you're interested I have an alternative. Since your period is just ending—"

Shock and surprise instantly gave way to indignation.

"Don't give me that look. There's no such thing as privacy anymore. I read the interview brief on you in Hong Kong and remembered because it mattered to me at the time. Am I right about your period?"

"Jeez. Is that kind of invasive detail actually legal?"

"I never asked. So am I right or not?"

She made a face, then nodded.

He smiled. "Since when did you get shy?"

"That's kinda personal."

"Unlike fucking. So can I get back to my plan?"

She wrinkled her nose in a little bunny twitch.

"I'll take that as a yes. One more thing and don't be squeamish. It's just a simple question. Is this the fifth day of your period?"

Her brows flew up. "How the hell did you know that?"

"I told you, I read the brief. I have a good memory; once I see something, it's here." He tapped his head. "Anyway, the timing couldn't be better for a contraceptive shot. The shot would be effective immediately."

She glowered. "How would you know that?"

"General information. Don't get pissed. I read about it."

"Why?" Her glare was undiminished, her jealously unreasonable but stubbornly persistent.

"Because it happened to be on *The Times* Health page I was reading," he said, keeping his voice super calm. "And birth control impacts me. Okay?"

"Yeah, I've heard that."

"Come on, babe, I'd like to say I was a virgin when I met you, but I can't. I told you I haven't been with a woman since Hong Kong. And that's major for me."

"I suppose," she grumbled.

"You better suppose," he grumbled back. "It's in the category of moving mountains with my history." He briefly shut his eyes as though reconfiguring his past against the present, then looked at her and smiled. "This is a whole new wonderland, babe."

"Thank you," she said softly.

"No problem," he said as softly. "It was worth it." He leaned forward and bushed a kiss across her mouth. "So what do you say?"

"Okay."

He sat back. "Just like that—okay?"

"Yup."

"That blindsided me," he said with a grin. "No argument?"

"Actually I'm a little allergic to latex and a lot allergic to the lubed ones, and honestly, I like to feel you."

Taking issue with any condom use on her part, he wanted to grill and cross-examine her on the history of her latex allergies. But understanding that argument was counterproductive, he stifled his resentments and reached for his sports jacket instead. "Let me call my doctor," he said, pulling his cell phone from his coat pocket.

"You can get a doctor this time of night?"

"I can get a doctor anytime. He works for me."

She scowled. "I hope you're not going to tell me he gives these shots to all the women you entertain here."

"I don't bring women here. It's my home."

She gave him a dirty look. "You brought them to the Garden House."

"I don't consider that my home," he very carefully replied, his voice gentle, his expression completely blank. "If my mother hadn't been at the house when we got there, we would have stayed on the Peak. And before you jump to conclusions, I don't bring women to my home on the Peak either. You were the first."

"Maybe this doctor gives these shots for you somewhere else," she said, ignoring his momentous admission because she was jealous of every woman he'd ever looked at and her jealousy was an irresistible force.

"I've never asked him to do this for me before. Please, Katherine. I don't want to talk about the past. It's over. And if you'll agree to an exclusivity pact, there's no one but you."

"What if I don't agree?"

He exhaled softly. "What do you want me to say?"

"How about the truth?"

"Then I'll be fucking someone else. Satisfied?"

It was amazing how much it hurt to hear him say that. To think of him with another woman. To consider life without him now that he'd returned to her.

"Hey," he whispered, taking her hand in his, gently squeezing it. "I don't want anyone but you. But it's not as though I'm eighty, okay? So let's get together on this. I want only you. No one else. It's been a hellish month, let's not fight about how much I want you. There's no measure large enough or high enough or deep enough. I'm on the verge of begging you, baby, and that's fucking scary." His smile was inexpressibly tender. "So give me a break. Say yes before I embarrass myself completely. We'll hammer out the details later about where and when, how often"—he grinned—"and what you want for toys."

She smiled. "I think I missed the begging part. You sound pretty assured."

"I am about the toys."

"You always were arrogant."

"And you always resist me."

She gave him a look from under her lashes.

He grinned. "Well, sometimes you do."

She sighed softly, not sure whether she was giving in to him or whether life without him was insupportable. "So—do I need an attorney?"

In a flash, he lifted her onto his lap, wrapped his arms around her, and dazzled her with a smile. "I'm so freaking happy," he whispered, kissing her gently. "And if you want an attorney, we'll get you one. I don't really care, so long as I know you're mine."

"Hey!" She poked him in the chest.

"Let me reword that," he said with a grin. "So long as you know I'm yours. Is that better? Should we send out announcements?"

"Very funny."

He gave her a small considering look. "Actually, I wouldn't mind. It would get other—er—people...off my back. My PR people could publicize our relationship, formalize it as it were. What do you say?"

"I don't like publicity."

He frowned. "You don't want people to know we're together?"

"Dominic, please, this is all very sweet, but you can't sustain it—not for long anyway. Then I'd have to parlay all the stupid questions, my privacy would be shot to hell, and, at the end of the day, I'd be crying in public instead of in private. If I agree not to see anyone else, I won't. Personally, I don't think you can do it, but we can try because you make me happy too." She kissed him lightly. "In every imaginable way."

He knew when to take a break from negotiations. "You'll find out I can do it," he said softly. "You're my world, baby." He lifted one brow. "So?" He held up his phone. "Do I have your okay to call the doctor?"

EIGHT

Dominic and Kate waited for the doctor in Dominic's bedroom, the large space dominated by a four-poster bed contemporary with the nineteenth-century building. Constructed of teakwood to withstand the tropical heat and humidity, the wood had mellowed over the centuries to a warm ochre, the aged finish burnished to a silken gloss. Folding doors, closed now, led out to a veranda; central air kept the heat at bay along with an overhead fan gently revolving in the high raftered ceiling. The bed, chairs, and sofa were all covered in a pale, natural linen, simply tailored and unembellished. The floor was polished teak, the two dressers and desk as well. It was a masculine room.

Dominic had found them robes, Kate dwarfed by one of his that was sizes too large. They were seated side by side on his enormous bed, where they'd just demolished an assortment of sandwiches, cookies, and milk that Dominic had ordered for Kate, along with beer and some Malay street food he favored. He didn't coax her to try any of it because he was determined to be polite rather than controlling.

"Christ, it feels good to be hungry again," he said with a sigh of contentment, lifting the snack tray away. "I've barely eaten since Hong Kong." Offering Kate the last cookie, he gestured at the empty plates. "Should I order more?"

"Probably not"—she arched her brows—"with *your* doctor on his way."

He understood the message loud and clear. "Ask him when he gets here. Yash will tell you you're the only one. He doesn't ordinarily do this for me."

"Oh God..." She sighed. "I wish I wasn't so—"

"Jealous. Don't feel alone. I didn't even know what the word meant until I met you." His gaze was unwavering, a barely there smile on his lips. "I'm charting new territory with you, babe. No question."

"Everything about you, this, us—is new for me too. I feel confused, jealous, insanely horny. Like some infatuated teenager with no sense of proportion."

"I'm sorry," he said coolly. "You didn't actually *date* anyone in high school did you?"

A mocking glance. "And you didn't either."

"Course not."

She laughed. "Just so long as we never stray from this fantasy world, everything will be copacetic."

"Indeed."

His smile was a thing of beauty—killer, drop-dead gorgeous, tender, with just enough king of the jungle to make her pulse rate spike. "You said that before dinner in Amsterdam in the same hot, sexy way. I almost threw myself at you and promised you anything."

"Personally, I wanted to drag you upstairs that night and fuck you until I couldn't move."

She grinned. "Where did we go wrong when we were both on the same speeding freight train?"

He shrugged, the gray silk of his robe shimmering in the lamplight. "It just took you a while. You were skittish."

"Is that what I was?"

He crooked an eyebrow. "Or you were fighting me off. Take your pick."

"Your reputation *was* daunting."

"That's all over."

His voice was husky and low, touchingly earnest. She looked up, held his gaze. "So everything's good now?" she whispered.

He bent and kissed her cheek. "You have my word, babe," he said gently. "Nothing's going wrong this time. Not one goddamn thing. So give me a smile and half that cookie. We'll order more once Yash leaves."

He was deliberately recasting the conversation. She wasn't surprised. He avoided emotional drama. Breaking the peanut butter cookie in two, she held it out and smiled. "I'll follow orders just this once."

He grinned. "Hey, once is better than nothing; I'll take what I can get." He plucked the cookie from her fingers, then lifted her glass of milk from the tray and offered it to her. "I'll see that you have chocolate milk tomorrow."

"I'm good. White milk is perfect with cookies." She dipped her cookie in the milk.

"Right now *everything's* perfect," he said, lightly brushing her cheek with his knuckles. "And it's gonna stay that way. We deserve it after a month of misery." He slid the half cookie into his mouth.

"I've already forgotten all that. This is heaven. Seriously."

"No kidding," he murmured, chewing. But even as he spoke, he was struck with a small, niggling doubt. Katherine was his benchmark for all that was good in his life. Yet their first meeting had been such a random act of fate, like winning the lottery, that he worried the old adage—*the only sure thing about luck was that it would change*—might be true.

"Hey—Earth to Dominic."

He swallowed, then grinned. "Sorry, dozing off," he lied. "I haven't slept much lately."

"After the doctor's gone, sleep," she offered, handing the glass back. "I'm not going anywhere."

I'm not going anywhere. Her sweet assurance was like rain after a ten-year drought, or food to a starving man, or deliverance from a life of despair. "Thanks, I might." He spoke with a perceptible reserve, patterns of a lifetime were difficult to change, his new-found sense of hope too fragile to risk.

The knock on the door was a relief. Not accustomed to dealing with personal feelings, his brain was reaching overload tonight. He set the glass aside. "That's Yash." Dominic slid off the bed.

"You're staying, right?" Mild trepidation underscored her words. "I'm not doing this without you."

Dominic shot her a look over his shoulder. "As if I'd leave you alone with another man."

"Oh good. I like that I'm not the only one who's jealous."

He swung around, looking grim for a moment before he remembered his manners and wiped away his scowl.

"Jealous doesn't even begin to describe my intolerance of you with other men," he said quietly. "Fair warning, babe, you're mine. Clear?" He held her gaze. Waited.

"I suppose." A small, frugal compliance.

He shook his head, the movement so slight as to be infinitesimal. "Wrong answer. Come on, babe, humor me."

"Oh, very well. Yes, then. But not always, Dominic. Not every time."

"We'll see."

"Dominic!"

"Sorry."

"No you're not."

"Give me credit for trying at least," he grumbled. "It feels like I'm maneuvering through a fucking minefield. I'm never sure what's going to set you off." He dipped his head in a small conciliatory gesture, shifted his stance. "Look, I'll get the hang of it. It'll just take a while. Could we discuss jealousy and boundaries later? Please, baby? Yash is waiting."

He was incredibly appealing, restless, that small worried crease between his brows. She smiled. "Sure."

He exhaled. "Thanks." Turning, he strode to the door, opened it. "Evening, Yash. Come on in. Meet my girl."

My girl. Such warm, fuzzy, beautiful words. Kate felt like some fourteen-year-old with her first crush. A moment later the men were at the bedside. Dominic made introductions, then turned to their visitor and grinned. "Isn't she adorable?"

Yash concealed his shock. Dominic as stud he knew, but enamored? It boggled the mind. "Absolutely," he smoothly replied, turning to the beautiful redhead with a smile. "A pleasure to meet you, Miss Hart." She'd blushed at Dominic's compliment—which really *was* adorable. She was also small and delicate in Dominic's oversized robe— part of her novelty no doubt. Dominic had always been drawn to tall, sleek, glamorous women.

"Call me Kate—please." Returning his smile, she con- templated the handsome young man casually dressed in jeans and a white polo shirt, his ethnicity an amalgam of Singapore's multicultural Chinese, Malay, and Indian popu- lation. "And I apologize. Dominic shouldn't have called you out so late at night."

Another moment of shock. *Dominic chastised by a woman? Surely a first.*

"I told her it wasn't a problem. Tell her it isn't, Yash"— Dominic grinned—"or I'll have to listen to her bitch at me."

Yash had never seen Dominic acquiesce to a woman. "It's not a problem," he replied politely. "Dominic and I have known each other for years." *Often in circumstances that could only be characterized as licentious.*

"We met in London." Dominic turned to his friend. "Probably—what…four, five years ago? Yash was celebrat- ing his medical degree from Cambridge and I was trying to drink the club dry."

"A memorable night as I recall." At Dominic's warning glance, Yash quickly said, "Now how may I help?"

Dominic pointed at the leather bag on Yash's shoulder. "You brought the shot?"

He nodded. "I have a few routine questions first. Just protocol. There can be side effects with some women." A

short time later, after Kate had answered no to all his que-
ries, Yash explained how the drug worked immediately
within the perimeters of a woman's period, its safety and
effectiveness, the duration of its coverage, possible side
effects. "Any questions?"

"What does immediate mean?" Kate raised her brows.
"Realistically."

"There's no rush," Dominic interposed. "It doesn't matter."

Another spike of her brows. "Speak for yourself."

"Apparently there's a rush," Dominic said blandly,
turning to Yash. "What kind of time frame are we talking
about—hours, minutes?"

"The literature uses the words *immediately* or *right
away*, and while the drug function is clear, every woman's
reaction varies. In fact, studies show three out of a hundred
women get pregnant even while on the drug."

Those were good percentages. Dominic smiled at Kate.
"Your call, babe."

"Three out of a hundred. Uh-uh, that's your call."

He shrugged. "Not a problem."

"Sure?" A teasing light illuminated the brilliant green of
her eyes. "Last chance to escape."

Christ, Yash thought. He'd seen everything now if
Dominic was seriously considering possible fatherhood
with this young woman.

Dominic's smile lit up the room. "Why would I want to
escape?"

Yash choked down a gasp.

"Okay then. I'm sure too...I think." Kate paused, glancing up at Dominic, who was watching her with an indul-

gent smile. "Yes—yes...let's do it." She turned to Yash with a faint grimace. "Is everyone so uncertain?"

With Dominic's casual reply still bouncing around in his brain, it took him a fraction of a second to answer. And another fraction of a second to figure out how to answer, since Dominic funded his research lab. He didn't actually have patients.

"Tell her everyone is uncertain, Yash, or she'll keep quizzing you. Don't give me that look, babe; you know you overanalyze every goddamn thing."

Kate's brows rose. "Yash can answer for himself, Dominic."

"It's a big decision." Yash replied, tamping down his surprise at this situation. "You're not alone in wanting to be sure."

"There. See?" Dominic turned to Yash and gave him a nod of thanks. "So now what, Doctor?"

Yash directed his attention to Kate. "If you'd like to roll up your sleeve, I'll get the syringe."

"Let me do that for you, baby." Dominic quickly closed the small distance to the bed. "Hold out your arm."

"Dominic, for heaven's sake. I can roll up my own sleeve."

"I didn't say you couldn't. Let me help though, okay? Shots can be a bitch. Speaking of which," he added, turning back to the doctor as he shoved the blue silk sleeve aside and held it out of the way. "Will Katherine's arm be sore?"

"It's hard to say." Yash held the syringe up. "Shots affect people differently."

Dominic frowned. "Maybe you should stay till morning. Just in case."

"If you like—certainly."

"Really, Dominic, don't make him waste his night. It's only a shot. I'll be fine."

"Why take a chance? Yash doesn't mind." Dominic gave the doctor a significant look not open to interpretation. "Tan will take care of you. Have that single malt you like for a nightcap. Now shut your eyes, baby. Here we go."

Afterward, Dominic walked with Yash out into the hall.

"I may need you stateside for a week or so," Dominic said. "Will your schedule allow?"

"Sure. Although if you're worried about the lady's reaction to the shot, you needn't be."

"Good. It's not that though." Dominic took Yash's arm and moved him away from the door. "Leo and Danny are coming in from Hong Kong. They should be here in a couple hours. There's a possibility the Balkan mafia are in town looking for Katherine."

"Don't tell me she's not what she seems?"

Dominic grinned. "Jesus, wouldn't that be something out of a fucking movie." Then his smile faded, a rueful note entered his voice. "No, actually she did some work for me that may have put her in jeopardy."

"Does she know that?"

"No and I want to keep it that way. She's"—Dominic pursed his mouth—"let's just say having the mafia on her tail might freak her out. So send for whatever you need for the usual emergencies. We'll fly out early in the morning and hopefully avoid complications."

Yash had served as trauma surgeon when Dominic and his crew traveled to the outbacks of the world. Venture capital routinely pursued natural resources in some of the more violent regions of the planet. So risk and security as well as ransom were major issues. In fact, ransom took the form of a business model in some third world countries; even wearing an expensive watch could be fatal.

"Why is the Balkan mafia pissed?"

"Katherine found twenty million dollars of my money that had been pirated out of a factory I own in Bucharest and circuitously shipped to an account in Singapore. They lost it and we got it back. And they don't like to lose twenty million."

"No shit. They'd kill you for a thousand."

"Pretty much. So I'm going to make them an offer they'd be wise to accept, but in the meantime…"

"You're getting out of town."

Dominic nodded. "The States are relatively safe. Between major profiling and stringent visa requirements, only the professionals get in."

"And these aren't professionals?"

Dominic shook his head. "Small-time wannabes."

"It'll take me about an hour to get my kit and return."

"Thanks. I'll see you in the morning, unless Katherine suffers some side effect from the shot."

"Slim to nil on that."

"Regardless, I don't want to take any chances."

"I noticed. She's important to you."

"I've barely slept the last month without her. We're back together as of"—Dominic glanced at his watch—"three hours, twenty minutes ago and life's worth living again. So, yeah, she's important." An unreadable look, then a smile. "Give my regards to Leo and Danny."

"Yash is settled in," Dominic said, as he reentered the bedroom. "Everything still good? Nothing hurts?"

"Everything's good now that you're back." She smiled. "We were apart too long."

He shut his eyes briefly, shaking away the memory of the last month. "I'm thinking about handcuffing you to my wrist—no joke."

"You say the sweetest things," she cooed.

He laughed and took a deep breath, his voice dropping to a whisper. "Just don't leave my sight—okay?"

Tears suddenly choking her, she nodded.

Swinging up onto the bed, Dominic scooped her up in his arms, settled her on his lap, and held her close. "We're going to make this work. I promise. Come hell or high water, floods, earthquakes, fucking acts of God. My word on it."

A hiccupy little smile. "Thanks."

Brushing her tears from her cheeks with his thumb, he dipped his head and kissed her softly. "We're on the yellow brick road this time, baby. All the bad witches are gone."

Her eyes widened in delight. "You watched *The Wizard of Oz* too?"

"I had to. My sister, Melanie, luuuuved it."

Kate giggled. "I can't imagine you as a kid."

"Just as well. I was hell on wheels."

"And you're not now?" she teased.

"Depends who's judging I suppose," he said with a lecherous grin. "You've been known to like hell on wheels on occasion."

"Speaking of which," she murmured.

He softly exhaled. "Why don't we wait until morning?"

She wrinkled her nose. "I don't want to wait."

"You never do." He sighed. "But this is different. Maybe *immediately* doesn't mean immediately. You heard Yash."

"Then use a condom."

"You're allergic. Let's just wait till morning."

"How about I get off myself," she offered with a flirty smile. "You can watch. Give me tips."

"Tempting, baby, but I don't think it's possible."

"Me getting off or you just watching?"

"Guess," he said drily.

"Can I be selfish then? I think this shot is amping me."

A lift of his brows. "Everything amps you."

"Only when you're around. Word of God," she said to his skeptical look.

"I find that hard to believe. But thanks."

"Hey, I mean it." She wrapped her arms around his neck and kissed him. "You can bet your bank account on that," she said, sitting back and smiling up at him.

"Good news," he said softly, rather than respond with the cynicism nourished by his upbringing. Bending his head, he kissed her lush pink mouth and hoped the world really was all sweetness and light.

"So...are you coming along for the ride or not?" she said a few moments later, even more impatient; his kiss could have brought a corpse to life.

He shook his head. "Not this time. I'll help you though."

Her smile was sunny. "You're such a dear. Unselfish. Magnanimous. Altruistic."

"Sensible. Practical. Not looking for trouble."

She grinned. "That too."

"You're sure nothing hurts now?"

"I'll scream if something hurts."

"That's worthless," he drawled. "You always scream."

"I'll scream *It hurts!* How about that?"

"Simple enough." His blue gaze was lead-us-into-temptation enticing. "Would you like to play a little first?"

"Give me a minute to decide, yes." She slid her fingers through his sleek hair, tugged his head down for a kiss. "Yes, yes, yes...yes."

"God, it's good to have you back, baby," he whispered, his heart in his eyes, his old flawed world locked away. "It's fucking heaven on earth..."

NINE

One slow, stirring, hot and heavy kiss later—Kate was whimpering, Dominic was thinking, *Screw waiting,* when a tiny, still-functioning portion of his brain screamed, "HAVE YOU LOST YOUR MOTHER-FUCKING MIND?" The sound was faint and distant, however, almost drowned out by reckless, dare-devil I-don't-give-a-shit horniness. But Dominic's hard-wired fight or flight reflex heard it, hit the panic button, and alarm bells blasted through his lust-addled mind. Sweeping Kate from his lap with dizzying speed, he dropped her on the bed, rolled away in a flash and lay on his back—eyes shut, breathing hard, bathed in a sudden cold sweat.

"I won't…hold you…responsible," Kate gasped, feverish, impatient, insatiable desire a hard, throbbing ache deep inside. She turned to look at him, her eyes half-lidded, passion-hazed. "Please, Dominic…don't *do* this to me!"

He wouldn't look at her, his self-control stretched to the limit. What if he listened to her, pleased her, pleased himself and his raging libido? What then? Every possible outcome raced through his mind—none of them advantageous, all of them pushing the 3 percent odds he was willing to accept. Dragging in a breath, he first raised his head, then sat up in a ripple of rock-hard abs. "I'll find you…something else." His voice was a harsh rasp, every muscle in his body taut with restraint.

"I don't want something else! I want you!" Quivering with frustration, Kate grabbed for his dick.

Catching her hand midair, then her other hand, which was intent on the same target, he hauled her upright and held her at arm's length. "Forgive me, baby," he whispered. *God, he felt like shit turning her down.* "I promise I'll make it up to you tomorrow."

"No, now!" Trembling with need, heedless to reason, she struggled to free herself, twisting in his grasp. "Please, I can't wait! I can't talk myself out of coming like you! Dominic—have *pity*!"

His nostrils flared; a voice was goading him, *It's only once....Come on.* And she was so goddamn small and defenseless, so needy, his old, hard-core impulses were urging him to ram it home. His erection surged at the thought.

"See—you want to too!" Her gaze on his engorged dick swelling even larger before her eyes, Kate jerked against his constraining grip. "Dominic, just once more! Once more can't matter," she pleaded.

He shook away the brute image filling his mind, but it took him a second more to completely repress his savage impulses, keep his libido in check, and another second to remind himself that the last thing he wanted right now was to frighten Kate away. "Baby—listen to reason," he said more calmly than he was feeling. "You don't need my dick to come. We'll do something else. And in a few hours everything's wide open again—okay?"

"No, it's not okay," she muttered, flushed and overwrought, so close to orgasm that logic and reason were no longer functioning. "I thought this was about me, not you, but you're always in charge, aren't you—every freaking minute." She tried to wrench free. "Just let me go."

His grip was unyielding, his voice, in contrast, gentle. "You don't have to wait because I do, baby. There's a hundred other things I can do to help you out." *Oh shit.* Her gaze had instantly turned from flame-hot to arctic.

"Only a hundred?" Ice a mile high in her voice.

"It was an expression." *He knew better than to prolong a lie by explaining too much.*

A taut silence fell.

Kate was trying to deal with that hundred number like a rational adult.

Dominic was thinking how much easier it was to deal with women who wanted only his money.

"Fuck this," she muttered. "I don't even care anymore. You're right. I'm wrong." She tried to twist free. "Let go will you?"

"In a minute."

Tension rippled through the air.

"Do you mind?" Kate tautly murmured, glancing at his hands pinioning hers, twitching in his grip.

"I'm waiting for you to relax."

Her gaze came up like a laser. "Are you afraid I'll hurt you?"

Laughter flickered in his eyes. "Should I be worried?"

She sniffed, then sighed. "God, I hate when you're so bloody calm and sane."

"One of us has to be." In the interest of detente he didn't mention he knew who that was.

"Maybe I can be calm too."

"Good. Tell me when and I'll let you go."

"Jesus." She half smiled. "Why do I always feel like an unruly child when you're acting so—well...adult."

"It's probably just that I'm older. And—"

"You've been fucking way longer."

His lashes dipped in acknowledgment. "Maybe that's it."

"I suppose you've done this a couple thousand times," she said with a small grimace. "I try not to think about that too much."

"I wish you wouldn't think about it at all. Although," he said with a small smile, "it's better that we're not both beginners." A flash of amusement lit his gaze. "At least I know how to entertain you—right?"

He smiled at her reluctant nod.

"And seriously, baby, I really like your go-for-broke personality. I'm not knocking it. I'm just trying to keep our problems to a minimum. Okay?"

Another grudging nod.

Dominic dipped his head and held her gaze. "So are we done with this tug of war?"

"As long as this isn't one of your games, Mr. I'm-in-Charge," she said fretfully.

"I wish it were. I'm just being practical."

"As always. Isn't that your motto with women?"

"Not with you—never with you...which is the problem. Look, it's only a few hours and admit it, you don't want—well...unintended consequences any more than I do. Right?"

She didn't immediately answer. "I suppose," she finally said with a rueful grimace. Then she sighed softly. "Yeah,

you're right," she added, flushing slightly as she acknowledged his good judgment. "And I don't mean as usual so
don't get a big head."

He smiled. "Thank you. I won't." Dropping a kiss on her
knuckles, he released her hands. "Now let me find something to get you through the night."

A lift of her brows. "You have toys here? Why didn't you
say so before and we could have avoided all this bullshit?"

This wasn't the time to point out to her that he *had*
offered her alternatives. "Because I don't have toys here,
that's why," he said instead.

"Really?"

"Really." He didn't elaborate because he didn't want any
discussion of toys that might bring up memories of the Garden House video. "I should be able to manage a substitute
of some kind to make you happy."

Her sudden smile was the familiar one he remembered
from their many arguments. The wide-open, cloudless smile
that instantly beguiled. She never held grudges; she didn't
even much care whether she won or lost once the contro-
versy was over. "How do you do it?" she murmured, running her finger along his jaw in a small possessive gesture
he would have found objectionable in any other woman.
"You're always stay überreasonable when I'm freaking out.
Thanks too—about well—the unintended consequences
issue. Really. I'm grateful."

"You're not alone in being unreasonable." He smiled.
"I have my moments too." *Like monitoring her activities the
last month.* "Now, can you wait a few minutes while I scope
out some toys?"

"What's a few minutes?" She grinned. "No pressure."

He smiled. "You tell me."

"Five."

"Ten. This is a big house."

"Eight."

"Nine."

She glanced at the bedside clock. "And counting."

"Do I get a prize if I come in under the limit?" But he was already halfway to the door.

"I'll think about it."

"Do that or maybe I won't give you a choice, maybe you'll have to—" Whether promise or threat, the door shut on the rest of his sentence.

Dominic returned in record time to find an empty bedroom. The doors to the veranda hadn't been opened. Katherine wasn't likely to be playing hide and seek; the corridor had been empty. That left his dressing room. Dropping the items he'd found on the bed, he strode toward the closed door.

Quietly opening it, he stood on the threshold of his dressing room and felt a chill run up his spine. Kate was halfway down his wardrobe wall, several doors left open behind her; she was currently flipping through his neatly hung shirts. "Could I help you with something?" His voice was ultrasoft.

She swung around, his long robe brushing the floor. "Sure you could," she said softly, smiling.

"I meant could I help you with something in here." *He'd never considered himself gullible. This might be a first.*

Another smile. "Here's fine."

He didn't smile back. "What are you looking for?"

"Women's things. With your track record at the Garden House, I'm inclined to trust but verify. Maybe you're not the only one with control issues."

He felt his muscles relax, felt a profound sense of relief—dicey issues of trust resolved. "You—controlling? That could be interesting."

She shot a quick glance over her shoulder as she turned back to the wall of closets. "Call it morbid curiosity if you like; this is what I do in my line of work. Look for things: clues, patterns, details that don't make sense in the grand scheme of the universe."

He leaned against the door jamb. "Curiosity killed the cat, baby. Just kidding," he quickly said as she spun around. "Look all night. You won't find anything. I'm a monk here."

"That must make up for you not being a monk anywhere else," she murmured.

He shrugged. "I'm moving on to better times."

"With me."

She was the only woman he'd allow such unreserved presumption and he wondered whether it was because she was the only woman who'd ever left him. But more interested in the present, he pleasantly said, "That's the plan. You and me. Good times, happy times. Sunshine and fucking roses from now on." He gestured toward the wardrobe with a flick of his finger. "Come on, you're wasting your time. Let me entertain you instead."

She grinned. "I'll hurry. How's that?"

He rolled his eyes and she went back to opening doors and flicking through his clothes. "Christ, you have lots of, well...everything," she said.

"I do." His voice was mild; he had no intention of arguing.

"How can you possibly wear all this?" She began systematically opening and shutting drawers in a built-in bureau.

"Three hundred sixty-five days a year times two or three years before most clothes go out of style. You do the math."

"It's still seriously plutocratic."

"I'm sorry if it offends you."

"No you're not." Shutting a drawer full of blue socks, she opened another filled with black socks.

"I fund several charitable foundations if that helps," he said, his voice scrupulously neutral. "I could show them to you if you like."

She turned. "Would you?"

"Certainly. Later. I thought you wanted to play."

"Are you trying to change the subject?"

"No, just the schedule of events. You won't find anything but my clothes in here because I've never had a woman in this house." He briefly raised his hand. "Scout's honor—not even my mother. She prefers shopping in Hong Kong. And I apologize for my wealth, but making it helps keep me sane." A faint smile. "I consider that a good cause too. Now, I found a few things you might like. Could these policy issues wait?"

"No women ever?" *She wasn't so easily diverted.*

"Only you last month when you came to talk to the bankers."

"No female staff?" She smiled. "You see I'm incredibly jealous."

"None. I'm incredibly careful."

She grinned. "So there's a possibility I could take you to court and wring some money from you if I play my cards right?"

"You could try," he murmured, although he'd gladly give her whatever she wanted for the pleasure she afforded him.

"I suppose you have phalanxes of attorneys guarding you and your assets."

"Yes. Offices full."

She smiled sweetly. "But not from me."

She knew. "But not from you," he quietly agreed.

"I have no defenses against you either." She swallowed hard so she wouldn't cry. "Not a single one." Her eyes were suddenly wet with tears.

He was at her side before the first tear spilled over and, drawing her into his arms, he held her close. "We're both helpless against our feelings," he whispered, wiping the wetness from her cheeks with his fingers. "But happy too, right?"

She nodded and stretched up on her toes to kiss him.

Dipping his head, he met her lips, and whether fate or destiny, accident or chance, had brought them together, they understood that what they had was an astonishing gift.

Actually a goddamn miracle, Dominic reflected, inured as he was to the concept of benevolence. *A miracle he intended to preserve.*

TEN

A short time later, Kate was reclining against a mass of pillows, nude, her arms raised over her head, her wrists tied to the bedposts with the belts from their robes.

"Now look, baby," Dominic said, sitting back on his heels after securing the last tie, pointing above her head. "Those are slip knots, the belts are tethered to the bed loosely so there's a lot of give. You can reach the ends with either hand. Pull them free whenever you want...if you want. Okay? I told you before, the agenda's yours tonight. I'm just here to help." Picking up his discarded robe, he shoved it out of his way.

"So you're entirely unselfish."

A twitch of his lips. "Not entirely. But my control issues work both ways. I'm generally pretty well disciplined."

Her gaze flicked downward to his monstrous erection, hard against his stomach. "I don't know. He looks restless."

"We're working on that. You first, then we'll see."

"But I don't get him until morning?"

His eyelids fell fractionally. "Think of it this way. Tomorrow he's yours for the duration."

"Meaning?"

"Meaning, we're completely at your service."

No commitment timeline but what did she expect from a man who was interested in an exclusivity contact?

Rather than continue a conversation that wasn't going

anywhere he wanted it to go, Dominic smiled and said, "So—in the interim, how do you feel about this?" He held up a small Asian cucumber. "Or this?" He picked up a miniature lavender Japanese eggplant. "Or these?" Dropping the vegetables, he wiggled his fingers and stuck out his tongue.

There was no point turning down orgasms because he wasn't willing to name a wedding date. He wasn't Prince Charming, she wasn't Cinderella; this wasn't a fairy tale. "Okay," she said.

His smile broadened. "All at once?"

"No, not all at once, wiseass. It's not humanly possible."

"You sure?"

"Funny."

"I'm not being funny."

"Now you're making me nervous."

"You can say no—anytime."

"Then no thanks."

He shrugged.

A flush rose on her cheeks. "I suppose they always say yes."

"I wouldn't know. I don't do ad hoc sex games. Someone's always paid to provide the equipment. There's no need for me to go out on search missions. Oh, shit, now you're mad about that. Look, let's just live in the Zen moment. I'll take care of you tonight. All you have to do is tell me when to stop." His voice drifted lower. "Or not."

"Arrogant man." But her voice was velvet soft too. "If I wasn't tied up, I'd hit you."

"Untie yourself." He held his arms out wide, dipped his handsome head. "Hit me."

"Now you're just showing off." He was the picture of strength, sitting cross-legged on the bed in an easy quasi yoga pose, all brute power and machismo, his lean, muscled body flexing beautifully from abs to pecs to biceps when he'd lifted his arms.

"Speaking of showing off," he murmured, dropping his arms and reaching out to gently tug on her peaked nipples, watching them swell under his fingers. "You'll win that contest. I remember saying I was going to fuck these fantastic tits that first night in Hong Kong, but I never did. Tonight might be the night," he said softly.

"If I let you."

His sharp glance was shot through with surprise for a flashing moment before a polite shield fell into place. "I can only hope then," he drawled, releasing her nipples and leaning back on his hands. "Are we done talking? Just asking. Does your pussy like it when I tug on your nipples?"

"A little."

He smiled. "Want more?"

"Don't say it like that, Dominic. I'm not asking or begging tonight. You said the agenda's mine. So make me feel good."

"With pleasure." He leaned to his right, stretched out his arm, and picked up the small, gleaming eggplant he'd placed on the bed. "All washed and clean—I soaped and rinsed it twice. Apparently, protocol requires a condom on it—not that I'd know personally so you don't have to scowl. But since condoms are a problem for you"—he smiled—"we went to plan B."

"We?"

"The royal we," he blandly lied, not about to disclose

the staff's aid in his search for objects to satisfy Kate. She didn't understand the concept of personal retainers. They were well paid to see that his life ran smoothly. Tan had even come up with some silver ben wa balls, still new in the box, that he'd intended as a gift for his wife. "Now, lie back, relax, and we'll see about making you happy." He reached out again, picked up the last two items, set the Asian cucumber next to the eggplant, and opened the small red silk-covered box. "Have you tried these before?" He held up the ben wa balls, scrupulously washed, and shook them so she could hear the little bells inside.

She made a moue. "That's not exactly improvising. Where did you get them?"

Since the truth was awkward—for her, not him—he resorted to another lie. "I found them in the room where Danny stays when he's in town. I figured if anyone was likely to have playthings, he would."

"So he has women here but you don't?"

He shrugged. "When I'm not here he can do as he pleases."

"You really *are* careful."

"It saves time, money, and lawsuits."

"So the drawbridge is always up?"

"Basically. Could we talk about something else? My life isn't that interesting."

"More interesting than mine, but"—she glanced up briefly at her fettered wrists and smiled—"not at the moment. Especially since you probably know what to do with"—she dipped her head in the direction of the ben wa balls resting on his palm—"those pretty silver things."

He smiled, lifted his palm marginally, and said, "Why don't we just say I'm here to make *your* life more interesting. Once these are in place I'll be able to hear you when you move or walk. Or when you climax, because these little trinkets will keep you hot and wet and horny. I'll take you shopping some day or out for dinner and see how long you last before I have to find somewhere to fuck you. Would you like that?" he asked softly, sliding one of the silver balls up her slick, pulsing cleft.

She shook her head.

"Sure you would."

"No, Dominic." But her voice caught at the last because he slipped the second silver sphere upward where it struck the first and the faint ringing sound was adjunct to the most delicious ripple of pure, unspoiled pleasure. A soft, involuntary moan issued from her mouth in a breathy shimmer of sound.

"See you were wrong." A matter-of-fact observation. "Now let's see where else you're wrong. Not humanly possible you said." He forced the ben wa balls deeper, which arrested her dissent and gave rise to a tantalizing little purr instead. "Don't worry, this is small," he needlessly said with her attention internally focused and hot desire swiftly rising unchecked in spiraling ripples to every trembling nerve in her body. He spread her pouty sex with his thumb and forefinger, eased in the convex end of the cylinder-shaped eggplant, and gently pushed until a third of it disappeared; he glanced up. "Good so far?"

Her eyes were shut, her nipples taut, stiff peaks, her breathing erratic, the rosy flush rising up her neck and face manifest arousal.

"Answer me, baby. Are we good?" He didn't require an answer; he just wanted one.

She recognized the small gruffness in his voice. She could have refused to answer, but swamped in blissful delight, she was more than willing to appease him. Her lashes lifted slightly, she held his cool blue gaze and smiled. "Everything's perfect."

"Right," he said. Shoving the smooth lavender object deeper, he watched her face. "How's that? *More* perfect?"

She gasped as the pressure on her G-spot intensified and the invading mock dildo nudged the ben wa balls deeper so they slid titillating and smooth as silk along the rich network of seething, skittish nerves that were switched on to hot and horny. Greedy for more of that exquisite, carnal jolt, wildly impatient, she flexed her hips, reaching for the next flame-hot, explosive thrill—the tinkle of bells marking her restless urgency.

"You like that?" he whispered, neither expecting a reply nor requiring one. It was her playtime. He was only the means to that end.

Placing the heel of his palm just above the cusp of her pubic bone, he pressed gently, and was gratified when she instantly went still. It wasn't that he'd doubted her abstinence the month past—or at least not much—but her swift response soothed any niggling suspicions. She was hungry for sex, her orgasmic trigger rocket ready.

Oh Christ. Since when did he micro-manage a woman's personal sex life?

Then the first small orgasmic ripple flared through Kate's

long-deprived, Dominic-famished senses and she gasped, "Sorry...I can't wait."

He smiled. *Some things never change.* "Don't be sorry, baby; that's why I'm here. So you don't have to wait." And his uneasy thoughts gave way to more immediate issues. Increasing the pressure of his palm on the immovable object solidly submerged in Katherine's lush sex, he gently massaged her sweet spot, fully aware of her breath-held, eyes-shut, on-the-brink tremors. Her back was arched, her body taut, the slight, irresistible quiver signaling her imminent climax fluttering under his palm. "Need a little help?" A whisper soft rhetorical question he answered himself. "Try this." Slipping his other hand between her legs, he gently eased his middle finger between the make-shift dildo and her swollen clit, and delicately stroked the sleek, distended nub. Listening to her tiny, vaporous whimpers quicken as her arousal began peaking, he softly caressed her clit with a well-practiced facileness, and enchanted with her complete lack of control, he watched her wild, headlong, careening race to climax.

Then, moments later, as she hurtled over the edge, he smiled indulgently, pleased with the degree and intensity of the powerful, roiling orgasmic tidal wave engulfing her.

He calmly waited for her inevitable scream.

But Kate was holding her breath against the sheer, stunning ecstasy melting through her body, instinctively preserving what she had so long missed—the fathomless splendor, the incomprehensible rapture, the hot, hot, hot delirium.

Until ultimately her lungs rebelled.

She gasped for air.

Taking advantage of the momentary pause, Dominic placed the tip of the slender cucumber where his finger had been, forced the additional dildo deeper, gently jammed it against both her clit and G-spot, then nudged it an infinitesimal distance more. "Is it too much?" he murmured just before he placed his palm against the portion still visible and pushed.

Her scream shattered the stillness, her entire body went still, and a second tempestuous orgasm overtook her in a scorching explosion of pleasure piled upon seething pleasure that lasted and lasted...

Dominic was technically adept when it came to sustaining orgasmic sensation and particularly interested in pleasing the beautiful young woman who'd sabotaged his entire way of life, reconfigured his notions of personal freedom, and, in artless compensation, given him inexplicable happiness.

This was his version of welcoming her back.

Sometime later, Kate felt the world return by slow degrees: sound, marginal perception, smell—*God she loved Dominic's shampoo. Musky and sweet, with a faint undertone of cedar that reminded her of home.* She opened her eyes.

"Did you enjoy yourself?"

She gazed up into Dominic's handsome face and his amused blue gaze. "You feel smug, don't you?" But her voice was languorous, soft with contentment.

He shook his head, the faint movement dislodging a sweep of black hair he'd shoved behind his ear. "Just useful."

Her smile was serene. "Modest too."

He shrugged. "You're always easy. You know that."

Knowing just how wrong that statement was with anyone but him, she chose to change the subject. He was
the least likely man to appreciate her confession. He had
women falling all over him. She expected he always had.
"Your hair's longer," she said, redirecting her thoughts and
the conversation.

"I was too lazy to have it cut." *And too indifferent when
his life had been totally fucked.*

"I like it." She reached up and slipped the errant tress
behind his ear.

"I like everything about you," he said simply.

"Good, because you've become my drug of choice,
my addiction, my greatest pleasure." She gave him a shaky
smile. "You can't leave this time," she whispered.

"I won't." He didn't even question his promise or debate
who had left whom. In fact, he was seriously considering
locking up Katherine and throwing away the key.

"Oh, Lord." She made a face. "Feel free to jerk me back
to reality when I get too demanding. I shouldn't have said
that."

"Say whatever you want. I mean it. Most of the world
tells me what they think I want to hear. You're different."
He touched her cheek gently. "In every imaginable way."

"And I like your world-class orgasms that delight me
in every imaginable way," she said with a lift of her brows,
determined to restore the playful dynamic between them.
"Really, I can't thank you enough."

His practiced smile was instant and effortless. "So, we
did good?" He smoothly slid the provisional dildos free.

Her smile in response was angelic.

"It was a thousand times better than good." She lazily stretched as though recalling every lush sensation. "God, I missed you—and all this...the defenseless desire, the insatiable need"—she smiled—"the mind-blowing happy endings."

While he found his overwhelming need for one woman bewildering, he understood with unequivocal clarity the incredibly intense sex they shared...He'd missed that too. "I'm not going anywhere," he said quietly.

Her smile was wobbly again, his earnestness affecting her tenuous hold on good judgment. "I'll probably drive you away I'm so crazy needy."

"I like your crazy." Bending low, his dark hair falling forward to frame his face, he brushed a kiss down the fine bridge of her nose. "I have from the first. So you won't drive me away." He arched one brow. "And just so we're clear, you won't be leaving any time soon either."

"I can't." She ran her fingers down his arm and said in a breathy little hiccup, "I'm truly addicted."

He grinned. "You just like to fuck."

"I hope that's not a problem." Her voice was teasing again; there were certain rules to this game.

"I hope it's not a problem when I fuck you twenty-four/seven." A purposeful statement without a hint of teasing.

A flicker of unease in her eyes. "You're kidding."

"Uh-uh." He reached for the tie on her left wrist, pulled it free, then reached for the second tie.

"You can't mean it." Her apprehension was plain.

"I do." He pulled the second tie loose and shot her a blank look. "You're my constant wet dream, baby." Revealing his emotions was a radical departure best managed in small doses. He'd admitted more of his feelings in the last few minutes than he had in his lifetime. He preferred the familiar world of sex and more sex. That was his comfort zone.

"If you didn't sound so scary, I'd say, thank you."

"Believe me, I should be thanking you. I've never been so horny. Come on," he said, picking her up and putting her on his lap. "Let's see if those ben wa balls turn you on when you walk. And then I'm thinking a couple of orgasms. Yours first, of course, because I'm not stupid." He slid his index finger inside her for a quick check; nothing distracted her like sex. And he'd had enough talk for one night.

She caught her breath, uttered a small throaty moan on cue. Then another, as he slid off the bed, the pressure of his forearm on her bottom wedging the silver spheres deeper. "You okay?" he said, setting her on her feet.

"Not really." She drew in a breath; her knees had gone weak and a high-wattage delirium was jolting her senses in a tumultuous frenzy.

He politely held her upright until her agitation diminished. Then he said, "Good now?" as though understanding perfectly the finite pitch and measure of her arousal.

She nodded.

He dropped his hands. "Now don't move"—he began to say and caught himself. "Just relax for a minute."

She smiled faintly. "Good save."

"I'm walking a damned tight rope tonight, baby," he murmured with a lazy smile. "No question."

"Consider it a learning experience," she purred.

His gaze was suddenly blast furnace hot. "Maybe for us

both," he said with exaggerated courtesy. Then he turned away, walked across the bedroom to a linen-covered sofa set against the wall, and sat, facing her. Stretching out his arms along the sofa back, he slid down on his spine, spread his legs slightly, his perfectly formed erection fucking beautiful, Kate thought like a genuine, grade A addict. "Okay, baby." He crooked his finger. "See if you can make it this far."

She shook her head. "I don't think so."

"Those ben wa balls are small." He spoke softly. "You can do it."

"What do you mean small?" She could feel them with every feverish nerve; she was creamy wet and antsy.

"As in not large," he said with a flicker of a smile. "You can take more. You know you can. We don't have to argue about that. Now, come to daddy, baby. Move slowly. One step, then two." He pointed to the floor before his feet, then looked up. "Got it?"

"I hope that's not an order."

"Would that be a problem?" he silkily inquired.

"Maybe. Why don't you come here and fuck me instead."

"Because that's not the way it works." His voice was patently tolerant, as though explaining particle physics to a novice.

"You said—"

"Trust me, baby. I know what you want. If I keep this up, you'll come just standing there. You like orders."

"So do you."

He smiled. "Then we're good. I give the orders, you take them, and you'll climax all night long. Tomorrow too, although—" There was time enough to mention San Francisco when they were on the way to the airport. Right now, he had more important things on his mind. He was about to explode; self-control had its limits.

"What about tomorrow?"

"I'm going to be fucking you tomorrow. Did I not say that?"

"Finally," she said. "I won't have to beg for your dick."

His gaze was laser sharp. "You still don't have any god-damn patience," he said coolly.

"And you still know how to be a prick," she said in a voice that would have cut glass.

The distance between them was suddenly acrid with spleen.

The silence equally caustic.

Five seconds later, Dominic's small sigh barely rippled the air. Sliding upright in a silken flow of bronzed muscle, he raked his fingers through his hair, dropped his hands, and flicked a finger in Kate's direction. "Have it your way then. There're condoms in the drawer behind you. If you don't care about your latex allergy, I don't see why I should."

When she turned, her gasp brought him to his feet in a flash, and a second later he was holding her upright, two of his fingers deep inside her, pulling out the ben wa balls. Tossing them on the bed, he dipped his head and whispered in her ear, "I warn you, I'm doing this only once with a condom. I have long-range plans and they don't include you being out of commission with some latex allergy. So no argument. Agreed?" Lifting her, he seated her on the edge of the bed and frowned. "I need an answer."

"Do I have a choice?"

"You always have a choice," he said, clipped and curt.

She gave in to his cool stare and nodded.

"Christ, dealing with you is like rewriting the fucking *Art of War*," he grumbled, leaning over and pulling open the drawer on the bedside table. Grabbing a foil-wrapped condom, he ripped it open.

"Don't use that. Okay?"

About to toss away the foil, he shot her a startled look.

"I don't mean to be difficult."

"You could've fooled me."

She was all huge, pleading eyes. "Just don't. Please?"

He stared at her. "You're killing me, babe." His jaw twitched, he swallowed hard—twice—the silence between them suffocating. Then he swore softly and tossed the packet and condom back in the drawer. "I suppose if this is makeup sex, you get to make the rules," he said gruffly.

"Thank you."

He rolled his eyes. "Hold the thanks. This might not take more than thirty seconds the way I'm feeling."

"I hope not. Sorry," she quickly added.

"You better be. You're the girl who never even came with Andrew or what's-his-name. Don't expect me to be on a time clock."

"Sorry. Really. You're always wonderful."

He finally smiled. "Polite humility? I'm impressed."

"And I'm grateful."

"You're just grateful I'm better than Andrew."

"In a thousand different ways," she said sweetly. "Although speaking of Andrew, I have a question."

"Could it wait?" If he was actually participating in a

game of Russian roulette, he'd prefer a quick orgasm to compensate for the sword of Damocles hanging over his head. Shoving her into the middle of the bed, he pushed her down.

"Andy tells me he's in Greenland," Kate said, ignoring Dominic's question, gazing up at him with a lift of her brows. "Did you do that?"

"Maybe." Placing his hands, palms down, on either side of her arms, Dominic leaned over, swung his legs up, and settled between her thighs in a smooth reverse push-up that showcased his swelling biceps. He nudged her legs wider.

"He has a girlfriend there. Did you do that too?"

Guiding his erection to her slick, glossy sex, he stopped and looked up. "Shit. I wish I'd thought of that."

"So you really are managing my life?"

Intent on getting off, he eased the head of his dick forward just far enough to make his point. "What happens if I say yes?" His deep voice was silken, assured. "Are you going to cut me off?"

"Damn you," she whispered, stirring her hips faintly, so he slipped in deeper, so the delicious flesh-to-flesh friction burned away minor resentments. "As if I could."

"Okay then, yes." After which he effectively ended the conversation by plunging hilt deep into Kate's ripe, welcoming body with a businesslike combination of finesse, authority, and a seriously spectacular hard-on.

Dominic's carnal groan was gut-deep and brute; Kate whimpered at the head-banger hysteria electrifying her senses.

A long simmering silence fell.

"You're sure you don't mind my insisting...on no condom?" Kate's voice, softly apologetic, broke the stillness.

Discarding a number of rude replies, Dominic reminded himself that he was currently snugly engulfed in paradise and capable of a few seconds of politeness. "Of course I mind." *Like he minded this conversation.* "But my dick has trouble saying no to you."

Kate smiled up at him. "That's sweet."

He sighed softly. "Look, babe, fucking you isn't a real imposition, although we might be paying somewhere down the line for this goddamn gamble."

"You were willing to gamble last time," she reminded him. "How about I have a turn?"

"It's okay to make mistakes so long as they're new ones. We keep making this same one, baby, we're going to be in trouble."

"I *am* an accountant. I can crunch numbers."

"Could we talk about this later?" he said. "I'm having trouble focusing on more than one thing right now." Smoothly flexing his legs, he marginally withdrew, then swung his hips forward again and drove into her until he filled her completely and she sighed in bliss. "Later's good."

"Jesus Christ." He laughed. And from that point on, he made sure that she no longer had breath to speak.

But she felt each slow, gliding, perfectly measured invasion and gasped at the plunging depth of each powerful downstroke, the ravishing ripples spreading outward in a sumptuous wave of ecstasy, offering her consecutive glimpses of shining nirvana. She clung to him, his back muscles flexing and moving beneath her wide-spread fingers, the musky fragrance of his hair teasing her senses, the warmth of his body comforting after weeks of deprivation. Trembling and needy, impatient, she whimpered for release.

Her breath was warm on his shoulder, her impatient moans a potent drug to his senses, stiffening his already rock-hard dick, powering his next plunging thrust, and the next and next as he forced himself deeper, buried himself in her velvety warmth, his sense of pleasure so clean and pure, he could have lasted forever.

But only moments later, quivering, nearly unstrung, flushed with passion, Kate looked up, her gaze half-lidded, and begged, "Please, please..."

His eyes wide and clear, he dipped his head, kissed her rosy cheek, and whispered, "Anytime, baby." Then he smoothly took her over the edge in a billowing, sweet-scented delirium, following her in his own surging climax, spilling freely into her succulent sex.

Then, while Kate was still floating and aglow, he dipped his head, kissed the hollow behind her ear, and in the grip of some manic lust said in a warm hum against her skin, "I'm going to use your tits. You don't have to move. This one's for me."

In one smooth motion he withdrew, rested his weight on his hands, swung his legs up and knelt, straddling her waist.

Just watching the easy, coordinated power, his muscles tense and flex, his lean athletic body move into position with such single-minded intent, triggered an insurgent fascination deep in some evolutionary female reflex. Not only was his visual splendor arresting, Kate thought, but his determined willfulness kindled a sharp, primal response that jolted her senses. Her nipples swelled on cue, hot desire blazed through her body, her sex throbbed in wistful longing, and she softly moaned. Shameless in her greed.

Dominic smiled faintly. This *was* going to be short and sweet, no games, a purely selfish climax. Maybe next time. "You want some of this, baby?" He gently stroked her taut nipples. "It looks like it." Effortlessly balancing a hair's breadth above her ribs, years of surfing forging enviable leg muscles, Dominic drew his erection away from his belly, forced it down between her breasts, and said, "Hold it there."

As her fingers closed hard around the swollen crest of his dick, he sucked in a breath. "Easy, easy, or this is going to be over in a hurry." Capturing the outer flare of her breasts in his palms, he pressed his hands together and her soft, resilient flesh framed his rigid length. "I got it now," he murmured.

His hair had fallen forward, obscuring most of his face, although with high pressure sensation beginning to surge through his brain, he may not have seen her anyway. As the feel of her hands slipped away, he murmured, "Do you want my cum all over you?" A second later, he added under his breath, "That's not actually a question." Then his lashes drifted downward, shutting out the world, and without waiting for an answer, he gently thrust into the cushiony silk of her flamboyant cleavage, eased back as the head of his dick touched her neck, swung forward again, and with a soft sigh settled into a highly gratifying rhythm.

But the sound of Katherine's frenzied breathing soon registered in the small portion of his brain not completely consumed by feverish sensation and he remembered that he wasn't alone in his unremitting horniness. He didn't sigh, although he would have liked to. Instead, he summoned his manners—or perhaps he cared enough about Katherine to summon them. "Here, baby," he said indulgently, taking her hands and positioning them. "You hold your tits. There, tight, like that, so I can feel it. That's the way. Now you can come along for the ride." Gently squeezing a nipple with one hand, he reached back with the other, found her swollen clit, slid his finger deeper, targeted her soft, cushy G-spot, and murmured, "How's that? Feel good?"

Her wispy sigh ended in a soft, low groan. Beyond words at the moment, she nodded.

He got the message and slid in a second finger.

And she suddenly understood, as though the incomprehensible now had meaning, that feeling this intense pleasure had nothing to do with free will but with the willfulness of one Dominic Knight—who held her in thrall. He moved his fingers just then in delicious, lazy circles over her throbbing G-spot, and reflection gave way to a sharp-set, hurtling thrill that tore through her sex, raced up her spine and exploded in a sharp high cry.

Check off one, Dominic thought.

Then, since the game had changed and speed was no longer the issue, he moved his hips in long, slow strokes, taking his time. Indulging himself and her, bringing her up again, skillfully teasing her hard, pink crests, leaning down occasionally on his back stroke to suck on her engorged nipples, continuing to massage her swollen clit and G-spot, slowly, delicately, gently drawing one orgasm after another from her slick, throbbing sex. Until, his benevolence exhausted, he finally said breathlessly, "That's it," covered her hands with his, exerted additional pressure, and climaxed in a powerful, protracted, strung-out-to-the-max orgasm that rocked his world.

When his breathing was semirestored and he knew where the fuck he was again, he flipped his hair out of his face, smiled down on Kate, and stroked her tousled curls in gratitude. "Christ, it's good to have you back, baby. Better than anything. Really." He shook his head; a quick reality check that this was still about sex. "Now how big a mess did I make?" He reached for a towel, then looked back and grinned. "Sorry about that." He wiped her cheek.

"Not a problem," she said, returning his smile, beginning to recognize his leaps back from the edge. "You were good to me. I have no complaints."

"There you go. Two people with common interests. It must be karma."

"Or random fate," she purred, not knowing how long her personal paradise would last, but intent on enjoying every minute while it did. "Either way we win."

ELEVEN

Nick's phone is turned off. What the fuck is going on?"
Max squinted at the bedside clock, quickly rolled out of bed. "Jesus, keep it down. You'll wake Liv."

"Well, where the *fuck* is he?" Roscoe, Dominic's CFO back in San Francisco, roared, in only a slightly less strident tone.

"You woke me up at two in the morning to ask me that?" Max muttered, striding away from the bed, not wishing to interrupt his wife's sleep.

"Nick always answers his phone. Is he dead and no one told me?" Roscoe growled.

"He's in love," Max said, moving toward the bathroom.

"So he can't talk on his phone?" The notion of Dominic in love was too preposterous to believe.

"I'm guessing he's busy fucking his sweetheart."

"Nick doesn't have sweethearts. He doesn't even understand the meaning of the word. So what's he really doing?"

"I'm serious. He has a sweetheart—or at least the equivalent of a sweetheart in Dominic-speak. Although I wouldn't bet he's not learning a little about the language of love. What do you think of that?" Max grabbed his robe from the hook on the bathroom door.

"I think you're fucking *crazy*."

"I'm not but Nick might be…at least for the moment."

Crossing the white marble floor Max opened the connecting door to his office. "He's in Singapore pursuing his dream girl. Now, granted," Max added, shrugging into his robe and making his way to a chair by the windows, "this lust or lovesickness or whatever might not last. But long story, short," Max said bluntly, dropping into the chair, "our hard-nosed, pragmatic, emotionally distant CEO is currently way the hell over the edge. And I'm not exaggerating. Justin says Nick had him set up a job for Katherine in Singapore and he's paying for it all, including her princely salary."

"Jeez, what the hell does she have that the other thousand didn't?"

"What she has is—she's not like the other thousand. She's not an ornament or a mountain-climbing companion. She's a beautiful, sexy, small-town girl with a brain who doesn't care about his money. *And* she walked away from him in Hong Kong."

"So it's the bloody challenge," Roscoe said with disgust. "He can't ever pass up a challenge. If there's a mountain to climb, he'll fucking climb it."

"That's my guess."

"Then once he has her, he's reached the summit and it's over. Hopefully that will be soon because I need my phone calls answered."

"Maybe," Max said in a warning tone, squinting at the brilliant silver moon over Hong Kong harbor. "But Nick hasn't touched a woman in a month. No sex clubs, no call girls, Vicky kept phoning in Paris and I had to tell her he was on safari and out of cell range. So I'm not completely sure where this is going. He's not playing to past history."

"Christ, is he sick?" Roscoe's stridency gentled to a genuine concern. "You're not saying that, are you?"

"No, no...Nick's health is fine. Although one of our Paris attorneys who hit on him and was rejected was spreading a different story in the office. I had a talk with her the minute I heard, and shut it down. We don't need any rumors about Nick being sick. It doesn't affect our stock price since Knight Enterprises is privately held, but gossip like that can be dangerous in terms of the company's long-range plans."

Roscoe's sigh echoed down the wire. "We really don't need this bullshit now. We've got a dozen new projects on the books. Jesus Christ, tell me this will be over soon. Lie if necessary."

"I wish I could."

Another sonorous sigh. "Okay, it's not as though I have a choice. If he's off the grid, he's off it. I'll do my best to calm down the manager at our aerospace facility who needs some goddamn special fuel yesterday. But if you talk to Nick, have him call me. This company doesn't run without him. It never has."

"Tell me about it. I had that conversation with him when he was derailing in Hong Kong. It didn't last long, as you can see. But then living a life like his, where you can have anything, buy anything, coerce anyone, ruthlessly bend the world to your will—well, he's hard to stop."

"Not always a bad thing," Roscoe murmured, single-minded like Dominic in the art of the deal, "when it comes to making money at least."

"Katherine isn't about making money though. That's

only one of her unorthodox qualities. She's not his stereo-typical playmate and I'm guessing that's her allure."

"But she's still a playmate," Roscoe brusquely said. "So what are you thinking? A week or two before he comes to his senses?"

"I really couldn't say. This could be different."

"Fuck it," Roscoe grumbled. "You're not telling me anything I want to hear."

The phone went dead.

Max pushed himself out of the chair, walked back to the bedroom, dropped his robe, and climbed back into bed. There was nothing he could do or say to control the situation. Nick did as he pleased. He always had.

So Max might as well sleep.

Liv had a family picnic planned for tomorrow. A smile touched his lips as he thought about his son's shriek of excitement when they'd told him. For some reason, his little angel liked outdoor picnics, even in winter.

TWELVE

At the sound of the soft click of the bedroom door latch, Dominic came awake and glanced at the lighted numbers on the clock: 3:21 a.m.

Shaking off the first few hours of peaceful sleep he'd had in more than a month, he looked up as Leo's shadowed form approached. "I'm up."

"We should go."

Both men spoke in an undertone.

"Raffles?"

"Cleared out and on the plane."

Dominic carefully slid Katherine from under his arm and rolled off the bed. "How many men?" He strode toward his dressing room, Leo keeping pace beside him.

"Eight."

"Jesus. Gora's serious. And we have?"

"Ten. But we'll be in the air before they can muster a full crew."

Dominic softly closed the dressing room door once they were inside and flicked on a light. "Okay, fill me in while I dress."

Leo ticked off the positions of each of Gora's men, where they'd picked up their arms, who in Dominic's security crew was watching whom. "The chambermaid at Raffles packed up Katherine's things and sent her luggage out in a laundry cart," he said. "One of Tan's men picked it up on the loading dock and Gora's guy sitting at the bar was none the wiser."

Having pulled on a pair of jeans and slipped his feet into sandals, Dominic slid a T-shirt over his head and checked the time on his watch. "The plane's ready?"

"On the tarmac."

"We'll meet you outside. And thank everyone."

A few minutes later Kate sleepily mumbled, "What are you doing?" as Dominic wrapped her in a quilt.

"A slight change of plans." And he explained that slight change in such a soothing whisper that she drifted back to sleep before he had to lie too much. Lifting her from the bed, he stood motionless, watching her for a second in case the movement woke her up again. She was like a child in sleep—angelic, manageable, her willfulness temporarily vanquished. He smiled. Not that a few orgasms didn't play a part in her tranquility.

Here's to hoping she would remain that tranquil, even with the assassination squad on their trail. He turned and walked away from the bed.

Moments later, having traveled the length of the house, Dominic approached the front door, which was quickly thrown open by one of his houseboys.

Tan stood there, waiting for Dominic, and nodded. "Have a safe journey," he said in Malay.

"That's the plan. You, on the other hand, have to consider yourself under siege. They'll come here when they can't find her." He spoke softly back in Malay in the event Kate wasn't sleeping deeply.

"We're locked down tight." Tan spoke as quietly. "And up to strength. My relatives came in an hour ago."

Dominic smiled. "So the army's in place."

Tan shrugged. "Since clan warfare's frowned upon, they don't get a chance to have much fun anymore. Everyone's happy."

"Give them my thanks. You know what to do if—"

"We know how to dispose of bodies."

"Then thank you again. Leo tells me eight men were sent out." Dominic arched a brow. "For one woman."

"Barbarian overkill." Tan grinned. "No offense."

"None taken." Dominic was perfectly aware that Europeans had been referred to as barbarians since they first set foot on the Asian continent seven hundred years ago.

Tan lifted his chin toward the drive. "Leo's pacing. You'd better go."

Dominic glanced out, then back. "Stay in touch. And seriously, no bloodshed if it's avoidable."

"Everyone knows that, boss."

"Jesus, don't smile when you say that."

"Yes, *sir*, boss."

Dominic rolled his eyes. "Deference from you makes me nervous. Stay out of the courts at least—okay?"

"Sure thing, boss."

Dominic sighed. "I give up. Call Leo if you need anything." He dipped his head, smiled faintly, murmured, "Good-bye" in Malay, and moved out into the sultry night.

The moment Dominic appeared on the porch, Leo stopped pacing, swung around, and walked to a gray sedan idling in the courtyard.

In front and behind the gray Mercedes were two black Mercedes SUVs, all three cars armor-plated at the factory, all with bullet-proof glass and tires, all with professional drivers at the wheel. The three-car formation was standard for travel in dangerous situations. Dominic had had the cars flown in by one of his transport planes; he also had vehicles permanently at his homes in London and Rome. These had come from Hong Kong with Leo and Danny.

On reaching Leo, Dominic said under his breath, "Tan seems to have things in hand."

"No shit." Leo opened the sedan's back door. "It's like party time in there."

"They know what they're doing though," Dominic noted, bending his head to step into the car.

"Understatement."

Leo shut the door once Dominic was inside, took his place up front in the passenger seat, and gave Jake, the driver, a thumbs-up.

Jake flicked his lights, the lead SUV moved off, the heavy timber, iron-strapped gates began sliding open, and seconds later, three cars issued from the compound, maintaining a tight car's length between them, traveling fast.

Danny rode shotgun in the lead car, with a man in back, the same configuration employed in the vehicle following the sedan. Two of Dominic's crew were guarding his plane. Everyone was armed to the teeth.

Dominic was settled in the back of the sedan with Kate in his arms, pleased that she hadn't required a detailed explanation for their precipitous departure. The less she knew the better. He'd resolve the mafia issue. All it took was money and enough muscle, persuasion, and ruthless-ness to strike a bargain with his adversaries. He wasn't wor-ried. After a decade in a pitiless business, he'd mastered the art of arbitrary power.

At that time of night traffic wasn't an issue. Also, accord-ing to Leo, the Balkan mafia wasn't fully mobilized yet. The seventh and eighth man had just arrived in Singapore that evening; the advantage was still theirs.

The cavalcade moved at high speed down the city streets until it reached the freeway, where the drivers promptly accelerated, sinking the speedometer gauge into the red zone. One brief moment of concern arose when two trucks entered the freeway at the last entrance ramp before the airport. But the drivers simply swerved around the trucks as though they were standing still and moments later brought their cars careening through the gates of the private plane terminal in a trail of smoking rubber.

The SUVs took up defensive positions on the tarmac between Dominic's waiting plane and the gate while the sedan rolled up to the ramp of the 747-8. Two armed guards stood on either side of the ramp as Dominic quickly mounted the stairway with Kate. Once he was inside, all the men save the drivers came on board. The aircraft door was shut, one of the drivers pulled the ramp away, and seconds later, the plane was cleared for takeoff and taxiing down the runway to the low throttle roar of GEnx-2B67 engines.

Just as Dominic was putting Kate to bed, the plane lifted off in a scream of jet engines. "It's takeoff, that's all, baby. Everything's good," he soothed as she came awake with a start. Tucking the quilt under her chin, he lowered his head and gently kissed her. "We're in the air for fifteen hours, so sleep as long as you can. You're not missing a thing."

"Are you coming to bed?" Her voice was thick and syrupy.

"In a few minutes."

"Hurry..." she said, the word trailing off.

Her eyelids slowly shut as she spoke, but he sat with her until her breathing deepened into full REM sleep before leaving the bedroom. Moving through his office next door, his mind on logistics and scheduling, on all he had to clear up before landing, he entered the outside corridor that ran the length of the 251-foot fuselage. Swiftly making his way past the six bedrooms with twin beds, he came to a skidding stop at the kitchen doorway when he saw his cook putting away supplies. "You don't have to stay up, Sese. We won't need anything until breakfast."

The big Tongan turned from the cupboard and smiled. "You sure? Those guys upstairs are smokin' kif. That means the munchies."

"They can eat snacks—chips, cold cuts, whatever. I'll tell them they're on their own. You're off the clock."

"You want anything special for the lady's breakfast?"

Dominic looked at a loss for a moment. "Do we have chocolate milk?"

"You bet. I heard the lady enjoyed her chocolate milk the last time."

Dominic smiled. "Efficient."

"Did you think I wasn't? And since you don't seem to be on top of this, I'll see that I have some bacon sandwiches on hand just in case. Leo told me to talk to Deshi, so I'm

clued in. And I know your tastes. Although, if there's anything else you want in the morning, just ask."

"Sounds like you're ahead of the game," Dominic said
pleasantly.

Sese gave a little bow. "I'm guessing you have to keep
up your strength. As for the lady's wishes, I'm all ears."

"We'll let you know. With the time zone changes"—
Dominic shrugged—"I don't know when she'll wake."

"Not a problem. Leo tells me I have a couple days off to
visit my relatives once we land in San Francisco."

"I'm thinking a week."

"Sweet."

"I couldn't agree more. Now get some sleep."

Dominic had hired Sese from a restaurant in Jakarta
after eating the best beef rendang he'd ever had. That the
young chef handled himself superbly in a bar fight later
that night had further clinched the deal; it had also estab-
lished immediate rapport with the members of Dominic's
personal security. In addition, the huge Polynesian could
outdrink anyone on the crew, a feat of some consequence
in the peer group that saw to Dominic's safety.

Although Sese didn't take orders well from anyone but
Dominic, the other men had learned to ask politely if they
wanted him to cook them something special.

Passing the dining room, exercise room, and small
library, Dominic reached the circular staircase that led up
to the lounge.

Leo raised his glass and smiled as Dominic came into
view at the top of the stairs. "Safe and sound," he drawled.
"Fuck the Balkan mafia."

"Temporarily," Dominic reminded him, walking over to the bar and pouring himself three fingers of whiskey. "But thanks everyone." He surveyed the group of hard-bodied, battle-scarred veterans relaxing in green leather club chairs with drinks in their hands, the pungent smell of kif in the air. "Katherine's safe. I'm pleased." Dropping into a vacant chair, he drank half his whiskey, rested the glass on the chair arm, leaned back, and softly exhaled. "She's going to wonder why we're traveling with so much security though. I'll have to come up with some logical explanation. I just don't want to scare her needlessly."

"You're good at that, Nick. Telling women what they want to hear." A flash of a grin, an Australian accent, a glass lifted in salute.

"I think that's your department, Clive." Dominic smiled. "You'll have to give me pointers."

The handsome young man with a permanent Aussie tan, the neck of a weight lifter, and hair so blond it was white offered up a look of fake surprise. "You talkin' to me, mate?"

"Yeah, you. Anyone who can escape their own wedding and leave the bride smiling is what I'd call fucking persuasive."

"We were friends. It helped." Clive shrugged. "That's not your style, Nick." He gave Dominic a lopsided grin. "Not that your style doesn't get results."

"Better results now," Dominic said, very, very softly. "Katherine's a rare gift. I'm not sure I deserve her."

An awkward silence fell. They'd never heard Dominic speak of a woman with such tenderness.

"Do you think they'll follow us?" one of the men asked to break the disquieting hush.

Dominic looked blank for a moment, then he spoke in his normal, easy drawl that still held faint hints of California surfer. "Most of the mafia foot soldiers can't make it through U.S. customs. A few might, but not the entire roster that came into Singapore. Which reminds me." He turned to Leo. "Have you gotten in touch with Gora?"

"An envoy's en route from Sofia. I'll know something in a day or so."

"I need a week before I meet with him."

"I guess I don't have to ask why?"

Dominic gave him a cool stare. "I understand sooner is better, but it's not going to happen. A week minimum. After that anywhere, anytime—I'm ready to parley."

"It's going to cost you."

"We'll see. Gora has a family that makes him vulnerable. Also a barely legal mistress in Rome he can't stay away from for long. I'm thinking she's our best chess piece."

"Can you trust him?" Danny asked, holding his breath after a big drag from the bong.

Dominic shrugged. "Hard to say. He's been reliable in the past, but regardless of his trustworthiness, Katherine is going to need security."

"What kind of security?" Leo asked, his voice measured.

"My kind."

Eyebrows went up around the lounge, but no one voiced their thoughts. They'd all been with Dominic since he'd first met Max, Leo, Danny, and the others in a Cape Town bar where everyone had been drinking their breakfast before a day of surfing. As an employer Dominic paid premium wages, gave generous travel allowances, footed the bills for homes or apartments, and allowed flexible schedules that offered time for families. Any of them would take a bullet for him even if it wasn't their job.

Leo's face was expressionless. "How soon do you want Katherine's security in place?"

"Starting now. Make whatever adjustments you need. Bring in whomever you need. Do it quietly. Katherine's not to know of the added surveillance. I won't have her life disrupted by Gora or anyone else." Dominic suddenly grinned. "Don't look so surprised. She's an incredible woman. I'm not about to put her in jeopardy." He dipped his head. "For purely selfish reasons. Is that better? Less shocking?"

"You have to admit, Nick," Danny said, flipping a dreadlock out of his eyes, "you with a woman for more than a few hours *is* shocking."

"Get used to it." Dominic grinned again. "And so will I."

Dominic's phone suddenly pinged. Pulling it out from his jacket pocket, he glanced at the display. Coming to his feet, he set his glass aside and said, "Get some sleep while you can. I'm not sure what our schedule will be in San Francisco. See you when we land." Moving away, he hit the answer bar. "Give me a minute to get to my office, Justin. How's the family?"

THIRTEEN

The family's great," Justin said. "Mandy's at her book club. The baby's in bed—not that Adam will be the baby long with Mandy due in three months. I'm having a drink and watching Manchester United get creamed."

"How old is Adam?"

It took a fraction of a second for Justin to answer. The Nick he knew wasn't interested in children. "Adam's nineteen months—this coming Thursday as a matter of fact."

"Is he blond like Mandy or dark like you?"

Justin wanted to say, What're you smokin'? "He has my coloring. Needless to say, my parents were pleased."

"I imagine. Is it going to be a girl or boy this time?"

Seriously, Nick must be high. "A girl."

"And Mandy's out buying frilly pink things, I suppose."

"Yeah, for months. I hope we're not under surveillance," Justin said drolly. "Frilly pink things? Not in your usual vocabulary."

"My sister has six kids. I've seen it all."

And never mentioned it before. "So you're an uncle."

"Yeah. They're great kids. In fact, we're on our way to San Francisco now for my sister's birthday."

"We?"

"Max said you called him," Dominic said. "So I'm guessing you know who 'we' is."

"Just checking. Actually, that's why I called you. Bill McCormick raved about Miss Hart's white hat hacker skills. He has another job for her but I thought I'd better check with you first. I figured you'd want to know."

"What's the assignment?"

"Something in London. Your lady's a real hotshot and apparently in great demand. Strictly in a business sense, okay? Cool down. I can smell the smoke coming out of your ears from here."

Dominic frowned at the accuracy of Justin's gibe, then asked in a deliberately neutral tone, "Do you have details?"

Justin explained what he knew of the project as described to him by Bill McCormick. Someone was doing proprietary trading on their own; not much yet, but CX Capital was concerned after the big whale at J.P. Morgan London had cost the bank six billion. "Or at least that's the amount J.P. Morgan acknowledged," Justin added drily.

"Or detected," Dominic drawled.

"Which is why CX Capital is anxious to have your clever Miss Hart on board. Although a word of warning, they'd like her for a six-month consult."

"Tell McCormick it's probably a go. I can't speak for Katherine. She has a mind of her own. But either way, he has to wait a week. We're on vacation."

"You're kidding! *You're* on vacation?"

"I am," Dominic said coolly. "Any more questions?"

"Nope." *Not with that don't-get-too-personal tone.* "I'll tell Bill to contact Miss Hart in a week."

"Have him text her a proposal now. That way I can get back to you once I know Katherine's feelings on the subject. I'm guessing she'll want the assignment. If that's the case, I'd appreciate your help in buying a flat for her. Something near my house in Eaton Place. You can explain to her, should she accept, that you have a sublet available. Put the lease in the name of one of my fringe companies so it's not recognizable. Talk to Roscoe. He'll help you out. Clear?"

"Any special price range?"

"I don't care. Something nice."

"Everything's nice in that area."

"Why don't you look for a two-bedroom? Anything bigger, Katherine might get suspicious. Ask Mandy for her opinion. She has a good eye. And if she doesn't mind or even has the inclination, I'd like her to furnish the place. I understand it's asking a lot considering the limited time and her condition, so I expect her to invoice me accordingly for her assistance. Tell Mandy to hire a decorator either to help or do most or all the work; I'll set up an account in her name at your bank. I'll see that Katherine understands there's a possibility that the flat is for sale at a fire sale price. Some lowball number that might entice her. She's making good money now."

"Not enough for a flat in Belgravia."

"That's where I come in," Dominic said with exquisite understatement.

"To explain that a five-million-dollar flat actually costs—"

"Five hundred thousand, because someone died in it and wasn't discovered for two weeks. Also, I'm willing to be her banker. So don't worry about the explanation. I'll handle it."

"Don't bite my head off now, but I gotta say, she must be something special. You're the guy who sends his driver to pick up his dinner date. And nine times out of ten, gets to the restaurant an hour late, if at all. What am I missing?"

"You'll see if Katherine comes to London. She doesn't fit into any of the normal boxes. She talks back to me all the fucking time, a precedent-setting event for which I have no reasonable explanation. So don't ask."

"Now you've really intrigued the hell out of me."

"Keep your distance. She intrigued the hell out of me first."

"You don't have to warn me off, Nick. I don't even look at other women anymore. No joke. Who woulda thought?"

"Certainly not me. But congratulations. Happiness is a rare thing."

"Sounds like you're starting down that road."

"Maybe. It's too early to tell. I'll call you in two, three days with an update on Katherine's decision."

Dominic had just ended the phone call with Justin and turned on his computer when his brother-in-law called.

"I didn't forget." Dominic leaned back in his chair. "I'm on my way."

"Just checking," Matt said. "I know your schedule is tight."

"Never that tight."

"Melanie worries that's all. I'll reassure her you're alive and well and on your way home."

"Tell her I'm bringing a guest."

The cheer in Dominic's voice was startling. "Anyone she knows?" Matt asked, curious as hell.

"A girl...actually a woman I hired as a consultant a month or so ago. She worked for me for two weeks. I just bumped into her in Singapore. You'll like her."

"Good. Looking forward to meeting her."

"Her name's Katherine Hart."

"I'll tell Melanie."

"Mother met her in Hong Kong. Tell Melanie that too."

"I think she might have already heard of her." When Dominic mentioned Letitia and Hong Kong, Matt suddenly recalled his mother-in-law's vulgar comments.

"No surprise there, I suppose. But Mother was so fuck-ing rude in Hong Kong it still pisses me off."

"Just in Hong Kong?" Matt's voice was amused.

"Yeah, right. What was I thinking? By the way, I have that jade you wanted for Melanie," Dominic said, dismissing issues of his mother's impossible behavior.

"I was just going to ask."

"Sis will love it. Seventeenth century. One of those mountain slash hermit pieces. The craftsmanship is unbe-lievable." His sister collected jade objets d'art. And Matt was rich enough to indulge her; his family construction firm was one of the oldest and largest in the Bay Area. "So, eight tomorrow?"

"Come earlier. We're having a family celebration at six with just us and the kids."

"Tell the kids I brought some good stuff."

"You always bring good stuff."

"That's why they like me," Dominic said lightly.

"Not true, Nick. They like you 'cause you actually listen to them."

"I listen to them because they're interesting. So we'll see you at six."

"Sounds good. I'll show you my new cruiser."

"Another one?" Matt restored vintage Chris-Crafts.

"This one's a beauty. I've tons of before and after photos."

"Looking forward to it. Give Melanie a kiss from me."

Dominic spent another hour dealing with his most pressing e-mails. He didn't even want to think about the havoc a week's vacation would cause. Roscoe was already freaking out because Max was also on leave.

Dominic called Roscoe in an effort to soothe his panic and after patiently listening to his CFO complain about the impossibility of leaving all the decision making to him for an *entire* week, Dominic politely acknowledged his concerns. "It's a lot to ask, I know. Delegate more. It's not as though we don't have several tiers of qualified management. And you know damned well I've never taken a real vacation since we started this company. You could always reach me online or by phone. So I'm not apologizing for taking time off. I'll still be available for emergencies. But only if they're real emergencies. Everything else can wait."

"Everything's a fucking emergency!" Roscoe roared, as if Dominic hadn't politely indicated his feelings on the subject. "You gotta answer your phone!"

Since Roscoe spoke at a full volume most of the time, Dominic was inured. And in this case indifferent to Roscoe's frustration. "Not this week, Roscoe." Dominic's voice was brusque. "There's no such thing as an emergency unless I'm losing every penny I have. That's my only red line, okay? Nothing else fucking qualifies. Not. One. God-damn. Thing."

"Jesus Christ, who the hell ever thought you'd fall in love," Roscoe grumbled.

Dominic went silent for a moment. "That's not germane, Roscoe. And it's none of your business anyway."

"Sorry, Dominic." Roscoe's chastened tone was only marginally lower than a bellow. "You're handing me a real shitload of work on short notice, that's all."

"I apologize. But this is important to me."

Roscoe sighed. Even after two divorces, he still didn't totally discount the notion of love. And in Roscoe's opinion, Dominic had never even come close before. His marriage to Julia had been a friends-with-benefits relationship. Julia shared Dominic's love of extreme sports, their bond deep and intimate, but in Roscoe's estimation, curiously platonic. "Okay, kid, I understand. Forget what I said. Everything's copacetic. Have a nice vacation."

"Thanks, Roscoe." The warmth was back in Dominic's voice. "I owe you."

"Damn right you do," Roscoe gruffly replied. "One week though? Can I count on you being up to speed after that? Just asking."

"Count on it," Dominic said, smiling at Roscoe's soft-spoken query. "See you in a week."

But Roscoe's comment about love was doing a number on Dominic. He must have heard that from Max. Jesus, was that what Max thought? *That this was about love?* Fuck no. *No!* It was just pure, unadulterated lust.

Sex with Katherine was fantastic; she was fearless, eager, impatient.

And she wanted only him.

There was a concept.

He relaxed and felt the tension in his shoulders melt away.

Felt his old familiar world of sexual play restored.

No longer in the mood to work, he turned off his computer and pushed away from his desk.

But he stood outside the bedroom door for a long time before he finally went in. Then he stood by the bed watching Katherine sleep. Was there a chance in hell he knew what he was doing? Where this was going? Did he even want it to go anywhere? Could it be possible that it was more than sex?

Sensing his presence, Kate's eyes fluttered open. "Come hold me," she murmured, her voice soft with sleep.

"I'll be right with you."

She smiled at the familiar phrase, then pursed her lips in a reply that didn't quite make it past her drowsy senses.

Dominic battled the magnetic pull of her soft pink lips. He wanted to grab a fistful of her hair, tip her head back, make use of her mouth, conquer her, possess her. Mark his territory.

He beat back the reckless impulse, reminding himself she'd only just returned to him. Backing away from his violent urges as if from fire, he took a deep breath, then reached up, pulled his T-shirt over his head, and dropped it on the floor.

By the time he climbed into bed and drew her close, she was deep in sleep once again. Her breath was a faint whiffle across his chest, her silken curls tickled his throat, the slow rhythm of her heart against his ribs oddly tranquilizing.

He felt strangely divorced from the desolation of his life: his unfortunate history and unforgiving memories, old resentments and older family drama. And the world around him shrank to this bed on this plane with this woman in his arms. The wasteland of his memories faded and he decided that if feeling a little unbalanced about love and intimacy was the price he had to pay for this sweet, invisible peace, he'd pay the fare without complaint.

And tip the mythical gods to boot.

He inhaled deeply. The flowery scent that rose from Katherine's skin was weirdly therapeutic. Like aroma therapy, he decided with a smile. Calming.

Delicious.

He closed his eyes and slept.

FOURTEEN

He thought he was dreaming. Then he realized he was inside her. He didn't know how long the boundaries of dream and real life had merged, but his dick was rock hard, buried deep, and Katherine was softly purring as he lazily moved in a smooth, silken drift, in, out, in…oh fuck—that was so intense it made his jaw ache. Pulling her closer, he wrapped his arm around her waist as she lay curled against him, her back to his chest. Splaying his fingers over her stomach, he tugged her into his erection, drove in a fraction more, and smiled as her sleepy purr turned into a breathy little gluttonous gasp.

Moving his hand upward, he ran his palm slowly over the soft curve of her breast, filled his hand, then flexed his fingers and gently squeezed. The moan coming from deep in her throat was unbound pleasure. "Feel that little ripple slide down to my dick?" he whispered, thrusting his long, rigid length deeper, then deeper still.

"Ummm….ummm—oh God…don't move, don't move…"

"What if I do?"

"I'll die," she breathed.

"We can't have that." The amusement in his voice was unmistakable. "It would ruin our vacation." Slipping his hand downward, he gently stroked the pressure cooker of her clit with extraordinary delicacy and subtlety, the pad of his finger almost weightless.

Her response was immediate and predictable: breath held, coiled and shaking.

Dominic moved then, but in a good way, in a way that sent a thrilling little frisson up her spine, jolted every strung-out pulsing nerve, brought her in brief, trembling moments to the hovering brink of climax, and when his massive arousal cleared a path to that perfect zero spot, she gasped, then screamed as orgasmic bliss exploded.

"Happy vacation," he whispered against her ear, flooding her sex with a spiritually attuned white-hot river of cum. It was near enough to morning to no longer worry about unintended consequences. Immune from liabilities now, he was free to fuck to his heart's content.

When Kate's last bone-melting, heart-pounding spasm waned, she sleepily breathed, "I don't know if that was a dream, but it was super nice..."

"Ummm..." he agreeably murmured, not entirely awake either after a month with little sleep. Lifting the hair on the back of her neck, he gently kissed her nape and tugged her closer, still partially erect inside her. "Go to sleep, baby. I'm here..."

Hours later, coming out of a dead sleep, Dominic squinted at the light edging the window blinds.

"Are you awake?"

"Getting there," he mumbled, the soft demand in her voice dragging him up from the depths of slumber.

She wiggled her bottom in a little undulating rotation.

He sucked in a breath as his dick surged in size and

length. "That'll do it," he said in a normal tone of voice. "I'm up."

Then she reached between her legs, found one of his testicles with her fingertips, and gently tugged on the sensitive flesh at the same time she pushed her little ass backward and whispered, "I need you. Deeper."

"You've got us, baby," he murmured. "We're *all* up." And following instructions, he drove forward with a thrust that *really* woke him up and resulted in Katherine's high-pitched gluttonous cry, which always added inches to his dick. As if her ravishment ramped up his libido. As if her wanting him with equal recklessness was their justification and intent, the razzle-dazzle splendor that shaped their willful desires.

It was over soon and she gasped, "I hope—you don't mind—but I'm going to be making up—for lost time tonight or morning—or whatever hour it is. My apologies—in advance."

"No need to apologize, baby." He kissed her shoulder. "I'm not going anywhere." He shifted his hips slightly. "I like it here."

FIFTEEN

It was raining lightly when they landed, the cloud cover heavy and dense, not a star visible, even the moon completely shrouded. Dominic carried Kate to the waiting car and left her in the warmth of the backseat while he spoke to a customs official outside.

Dominic entered the car a few minutes later and quietly asked, "Awake?"

"Sorta."

"We're almost there," he said as someone shut the car door behind him. "Fifteen minutes or so."

"I should have dressed." Dominic had wrapped her in a gray cashmere blanket.

"I didn't want to wake you. Pete knows me. I've been flying in and out of this airport for years. He checked you and your passport when I carried you out." Dominic smiled. "He thought you were beautiful." Leaning over, he kissed her lightly. "I couldn't agree more." Resting back against the seat, he glanced out the window as the car sped down the service road. "Christ, it's good to be home. It's been a while."

"You didn't like Paris?"

"It sucked without you." He turned his head and smiled. "Now I know the meaning of an epiphany."

"A neural blast to your brain's circuit board?"

"No, baby." He touched her cheek with the backs of his fingers. "I don't have an IT mind. It means life sucks when you're gone." He took her hand, slid lower on the seat, stretched out his legs. "Now this I like," he said, squeezing her hand. She wished she could speak as casually, but she was so deep in love *her* brain's circuit board *was* shorting out, burning away reason, shaking her confidence. She was sure to make a muddle of any reply and then he'd look at her—confused, or worse, alarmed. So she just tightened her grip on his hand in acknowledgment.

He didn't notice her silence, female acquiescence a given in his life. And he was distracted in any event, mentally running through his diminished work schedule. Realistically, he was never completely off the clock—unprecedented vacation or not.

Between leaving a number of time zones behind and erratically sleeping on the plane, Kate dozed off, sluggishly coming awake after the car came to a stop. Gradually opening her eyes, she saw Dominic leaning forward and talking quietly to the driver, the cadence of his voice softly definitive, the driver nodding in reply or answering in monosyllables. She turned her attention to her surroundings and surveyed the quiet, perfectly manicured neighborhood, the quiet, elegant street dense with villas on ocean-front lots with spectacular views—the scent of serious money in the air.

When she pushed herself up into a sitting position, Dominic quickly finished his conversation and turned with a smile. "How are you feeling? We just pulled up."

"I'm fine," she said drowsily. "What time is it?"

"Almost midnight."

The back door curb-side opened.

"Evening, Nick." A young, ponytailed man holding an umbrella leaned in. "Welcome home."

"Thanks, Eddy. It's good to be back. Is this an all-night rain?"

"That's what they're saying. No wind though, a weak front up from the south."

"So we won't be getting any waves?" Dominic asked, turning back to Kate, tucking the blanket around her like a sarong, leaving an end to throw around her shoulders.

"No. Maybe by the end of the week."

"Possibilities then." Picking up Kate, Dominic effortlessly slid out of the car.

Her stomach always did a little flip at such blatant physical strength. Some emotional regression to caveman days, she decided with an inner smile.

With Eddy holding a huge umbrella in his slack wrist protecting them from the rain, Dominic observed the courtesies. "Eddy, Katherine Hart, Katherine, my old friend Eddy O'Brian."

Kate smiled. "Pleased to meet you." Fortunately her blush was masked by the night. She wasn't as capable of ignoring her state of undress as the two men.

"Pleasure's mine," Eddy said in his slow drawl. "Nick doesn't get many visitors. Nice to have you here." He turned to Dominic. "Patty's been cooking up a storm since you called."

"That's why I called." Dominic gave Eddy an oblique look. "Jet lag," he said. "I'll talk to you later."

The tall, lanky young man smoothly stepped aside, then followed them up the path to the house, holding the umbrella. At the entrance, he nodded. "Door's open. Get some rest."

Kate's gaze slid up the pale gray limestone-sheathed, three-story house, each level punctuated with large sash windows framed in white stone, a delicate French look to the exterior.

"Home sweet home, baby," Dominic murmured, nudging the door open with his foot.

Then Kate experienced one of those kick-ass Hollywood movie moments because Dominic carried her over the threshold, shoved the door shut with his shoulder, came to a stop, and gently kissed her. "Good?" he whispered, as he raised his head.

"Super good." *As in stealing her heart good.* "It always is with you," she added in a flirty lilt.

"Ain't it just," he teasingly drawled. Then he set her on her feet and raised his brows. "Do you want the grand tour now or in the morning?" He touched the soft cashmere. "Warm enough?"

"Plenty warm." She wiggled her toes. "Do you have heated floors everywhere?"

"Probably. Are you hungry?"

"I'm always hungry."

"That must be why we get along."

"Not the only reason."

He laughed. "True. There's that raging addiction of ours. But hold that thought until I show you the place."

Kate had a tour of the main floor rooms: living room,

dining room, kitchen, office, a maid's room with an empty glass and a bottle of twenty-five-year-old Macallan on the bedside table. All the furniture in the house looked lived in, not decorator magazine pristine, the big kitchen gleaming stainless steel with appliances for serious cooking.

"Impressive stove." She waved her hand at the red enamel restaurant-size stove. "Not for you, I assume."

"Uh-uh. That's Patty's. You'll meet her later."

The empty glass and whiskey. "She's here?"

"No. She's mostly eight to five."

"So she'll be here eight to five?"

"Still not used to staff are you, baby?" He took her face in his hands. "If you don't want her around, she won't be around," he said gently, holding her gaze. "But Patty's been with me for a helluva long time. We get along. So think about it." His hands slid away and he stood back.

Dominic's casual view of hired help was light-years away from Kate's comfort zone. "She won't mind company like me?"

He smiled. "We'll have to ask her. You're the first."

"You always say that. I don't know if I believe you."

He saw the blush pink her cheeks and knew what it meant. But he wanted to clear up any misunderstandings, so he said, "Believe me. You're the first I've invited into any of my homes for more than a cup of coffee. Okay?"

As doubt still lingered in her eyes, he murmured, "Are you clear on your position in my life? You're not entertainment. Not even close. You're my girl."

"So you're telling me to calm down."

"Pretty much." A smile in his eyes, he leaned in close. "If a further explanation is required, let me know."

Prey as always to his heart-tripping beauty, her breath caught in her throat. "That'll do," she murmured, having located her voice. She didn't actually want things spelled out anyway, when her dreams were vastly different from his—just like his interpretation of *my girl* was probably less meaningful than hers.

He eased back, held out his hand. "Next floor then?"

She followed him downstairs to a level that was completely dedicated to exercise. She saw every imaginable machine, every free weight—most of which she couldn't have lifted—a lap pool and a mirrored tai chi studio he only waved to in passing. But he did say, "The tai chi studio's just for me, okay?"

When she didn't respond, he pulled her to a stop. "That's the truth."

Heart pounding, she only blinked and nodded, those jarring Christmas photos forever etched on her psyche.

He didn't elaborate. He knew better. "I'll show you the upstairs, then we'll find something to eat."

Four bathrooms, four bedrooms, a smaller office, his large bedroom overlooking the ocean conspicuously filled with boy's things: baseball caps, footballs and soccer balls, a dirt bike shoved in a corner, three PlayStations, two iPods, a pair of skis, two surfboards, a guitar, a bong. Surfing photos everywhere.

She made a slow turn in the middle of the room, taking in the memorabilia of his youth. "You've been here awhile."

He hadn't moved from the door. "Quite a while. I don't like change. Or at least not here."

"I can tell."

He ran a slow hand through his hair. "Yeah, well, some change is nice. Like having you here." He spoke with a kind of muffled reluctance, his clear eyes on her. He opened his mouth to speak, shut it, stood there broad shouldered and lean under his faded North Coast T-shirt, narrow-hipped in his jeans, his brooding gaze fixed on her. Then without a word, he covered the distance between them, this man in a boy's room, strong and powerful now, ruthless and logical, never possessive, *never, never, never*—except with her. He slid his hand around the back of her head, cupped it in his large palm, slowly pulled her up against the sleek, hard length of his body, and lowered his mouth to hers. "I need to be inside you."

His low, soft growl reminded her of how defenseless she was against his casual commands, how she felt with him inside her, how he could make her forget everything but pleasure. And her body stirred as it always did when he looked at her like that, his intentions clear. "How far inside?" she purred in a soft throaty contralto, her green gaze feline and sultry, deliberately provocative.

"Stop it." His voice was cool, his gaze suddenly distant, like an abrupt downshift in a transmission, her sex kitten come-on a jarring flash of déjà vu, the number of women who'd offered themselves to him infinite. "I'm not paying you by the hour." There was an acid pause before he spoke again. "Frankly, you don't have the skills."

Her arm shot out, her eyes hot with spleen.

He caught her palm before it hit his face, held it lightly in further insult as she struggled to break free. "Careful," he said, unbalanced by the flashback, wondering for the first time whether he was being played. "You might get hurt."

"Are you threatening me?" She cocked her head as though they were actually having a conversation, as if the dripping sarcasm in her voice was honey; ignoring the fact that he was towering over her, his eyes like flint. "Are you going to bring out the whips?"

He stared at her so long, his gaze unflinching, that she wondered if she'd finally stepped over some invisible mark, if she'd shot her mouth off one too many times and something unpleasant was going to happen. Then his unblinking stare disappeared as quickly as it had arrived and he was back in her time and space.

"Relax." Dominic smiled slowly. "You wouldn't know what to do if I brought out a whip." And whether he was being played or not was irrelevant to his immediate plans. "All I need from you, baby, is for you to spread your legs. You know how to do that."

Her temper instantly shot back up to a full boil. *"Let go!"* she said through her teeth.

Her eyes were free of fear. He'd always liked that about her. "If I were to let go"—he took a moment to sort through the clutter in his brain: the resentment at the great upheavals she'd made in his life, the goddamn horniness that never went away, and perhaps most, the unsettling trauma of having her in this room—"you can't leave."

"Don't say *can't* Dominic," she said, staring at him stonily. "You really aren't paying me by the hour. In fact, we don't have by-the-hour playmates where I come from."

"I wouldn't be so sure about that." But he dropped her hand and opened his arms wide; the brilliant negotiator complying. "I take back the *can't*. Your move, baby."

"That's such bullshit."

He smiled, weirdly pleased with her defiance. "I know. Come fuck me."

"I'm not in the mood," she said icily.

"Pity," said the man who had gone out and conquered the world. "Maybe next time." And reaching out, he placed his hands on her hips, hauled her close despite her curses and squirming, dipped his head, and stopped her swearing with a hard, punishing kiss. Ramming his tongue down her throat to make his point about who was in charge, he took advantage of her choking surprise to slide his hands under her arms and, holding her at arm's length, moved toward the bed—ignoring her wild punches, her kicking feet, as if contentious sex were the norm in his life. *Oh, that's right, it was.* Reaching the queen-size bed covered in a brilliant blue and green psychedelic silk-screen quilt, he tossed her in its general direction, then dragged his T-shirt over the back of his head and let it drop.

"Goddamn it," Kate gasped, her breath knocked out of her. "Have you…no fucking…respect?"

"Respect?" Dominic looked at her with amusement. "What are you—some Southern belle for Christ's sake?" His voice was mellow. "No one gives a shit about that. Unless you'd like to respect *my* wishes and spread your legs," he added with soft mockery. "Although I'm guessing that's not what you had in mind." Leaning down, he jerked the blanket off her with one hand and unzipped his jeans with his other. Then, in the process of freeing the button on his waistband, he suddenly lunged for the bed.

Catching Kate's ankle before she could scramble away,

he dragged her back and flipped her over. "You're making this harder than it has to be, Katherine," he said mildly, ignoring the fire in her eyes. "You know you like to fuck. That's pretty well documented. What's your problem?"

"You're my problem. You're fucking crazy."

The words rang out in the quiet room.

His eyes widened a little; otherwise he was absolutely still. "What?"

"You heard me. You need a fucking therapist."

There was a short silence.

"Don't forget you're in my house. I'd watch your mouth if I were you."

She ignored the implicit threat in his voice, the small insistent twitch along his jaw. "I've been in lots of your houses."

"But not *this* house," he said darkly.

"Meaning?"

He looked at her steadily. "Meaning I'm not sure you should be here." He uncurled his fingers from her ankle, placed her foot back on the bed with unnecessary care, and struggled with his chaotic feelings, wanting and not wanting her in his house, this room. In his life.

"Mind telling me why?" She was no psychologist, but this room was a time capsule.

His look was unreadable for a moment, then he shrugged. *He wasn't going to say this room had always been his last barricade against the world, his sanctuary and refuge. Or that he didn't deal well with emotion. Or with personal relationships.* "Let's just say it feels different."

She tuned in to the restraint in his quiet declaration,

the unexpected underlying tumult, the sudden desolation. "Maybe this isn't a good time for you."

He looked at her lying pale and nude and voluptuous on his bed, glanced down at his rock-hard dick, then back at her. "I wouldn't say that."

Her mouth firmed at the casual indifference in his tone. "Maybe it's not a good time for me."

"I'm not sure that matters."

"Jesus, that master of the universe never goes away, does he?"

"What the hell do you expect?" he said, his voice no longer mellow or casual or weary in his mildly contemptuous way, but suddenly razor sharp. "You think I'm going to change? You think that hot sex with you is going to alter my life? Burn away thirty-two fucking years of encoded distrust and the poisonous shadow of my parents? I've got news for you, baby. It ain't gonna happen. So just get the fuck out. This is my room."

"Your last defense you mean."

His eyes were searing blue. "Yeah, it is and you're not supposed to be here."

She swung up out of bed, stood well away from him, faint color rising on her cheeks. "I need my clothes."

He stared at her, at her redhead's pale translucent skin, at her pulse-quickening beauty, at her extravagant tits and her soft, curvaceous body that fit his like a glove. "Later," he said.

She straightened her spine at his words, drew herself up to her full height, which still fell short of his by a foot, forced herself to meet his implacable gaze. "I'm not going to let you walk all over me, Dominic. I'm not afraid of you. Jesus, will you stop? Don't look at me like that. Like you're doing a cost analysis and your dick has the final vote."

"My dick always has the final vote with you, baby. And the first and tenth and hundredth."

"It's nice to know you care," she said, her lips compressed, unfiltered animosity in her eyes. "This is a real Hallmark moment."

"Don't get all worked up," he said, as if he weren't standing there with a major hard-on behind his open zipper. "Maybe that's how I show I care. Maybe that's the only way. Maybe I don't know any other way."

"Jesus, you are so fucked."

"Uh-uh—you are." He moved in a blur, picked her up, tossed her back on the bed, kicked off his sandals, and, standing at the side of the bed, freed the metal button at the waistband of his jeans. Sliding his fingers into his open fly, he shoved his boxers down enough to draw out his heavy cock.

She glared at him. "You're such a child."

"I was never a child, Katherine," he said with a small sigh. "Not within memory. Tell me you want this. That's not too difficult, is it?" His mind fuck aside, there was no way he wasn't going to screw her.

She tried not to look, but his massive erection was defying gravity, starkly upright, the swollen head reaching past his navel.

"He's not insulted by bitchy women, baby." The faintest of smiles flickered across Dominic's face. "But we need you to get with the program. You know how it works: I give the orders. You follow them."

"Go to hell," Kate snapped.

Something tightened in his jaw; his smile disappeared. "I'm not playing this game anymore," he said, cool and seamless, the billionaire CEO reinstated. "I've been kissing your ass since Singapore. I don't kiss ass." He gazed at her across endless years of hard living and taking what he wanted. "I'm done with this bullshit."

"Excuse me? Is that what this is?"

"I don't feel like excusing you right now." His voice was grating, deadly, her second question dismissed. "Just do what you're told." He ran his closed fingers up the length of his pulsing dick, took a deep breath as the pleasure streaked up his spine. "Now tell me you want this deep inside you."

She should tell him to fuck off. Better yet, she should get up and leave this infuriating man with his invisible world he was battling; she should turn her back on this impossible relationship that wasn't a relationship at all, unless nonstop fucking qualified. Perhaps she might even have followed through if his eyes hadn't been fixed knowingly on hers, if he hadn't run his finger all the way up his monstrous dick so slowly she could see the fresh blood pouring into the network of distended veins feeding his arousal.

A sudden spike of shimmering desire raced through her body, recklessly vaulted over judicious thought, left her quivering. Instant recall of the consequences of Dominic's brusque orders flooded her senses: the wild hysteria, the seething need, the soul-stirring ecstasy; how he could make the pleasure last.

"You're pissing me off Katherine. Talk to me or fuck it; I'll turn on some porn and take care of myself." He circled his erection with his fingers, slid his hand down to the base of the thick shaft, tipped his towering dick in her direction, and arched his brows.

"Will you be starring in the porn?" Bile spilling from her tongue.

He gave a small shrug. "Not necessarily. Would it interest you if I were?"

She blushed furiously, and for what seemed an ice age she was under the gaze of a silent observer who had the power to overlook the ordinary constraints of life. Who had the power to make her ache for him.

"The porn can wait," he said quietly, as if he could read her mind. "But I need you to answer me. Politely. You must, Katherine."

She flinched at the steel edge in his voice, called herself every kind of fool for trembling at his free-of-apology demand. Had she learned nothing in the month past about personal freedom and choices? "Okay, then, yes," she said, as though she had no will of her own, as though she were on some carnal autopilot.

"Okay?" he said silkily, because he'd been walking a bloody tightrope since Raffles trying to please a woman for the first time in his life and he needed some serious payback. "That doesn't sound very enthusiastic. You can do better than that."

"I want..." Her voice was shaky under his burning stare. "I want you—that." She pointed at his engorged dick, which he was holding lightly in the curve of his fingers. "When I shouldn't. When I should walk away and leave you and your dick behind."

"But you're not going to, are you?" His voice was smooth and dangerous.

She looked up, her eyes large, a current of distrust shimmering through her senses. "I should," she whispered.

"I wouldn't let you anyway." A languid rise of his hand, a flick of his index finger. "Show me, Katherine. I want to see if you're wet." He frowned when she didn't move. "This isn't about what you want, Katherine. It's about what I want. You know the rules."

She suddenly felt cold under that still blue gaze; her hands started trembling.

"Jesus." His voice was soft. "You're scared?" He looked at her, his face rigid, his jaw tense. "This is too fucked up." He nodded, his gaze infinitely weary. "There's the door. Get out. I'm sure someone has carried in your luggage by now."

A heartbeat later, she shoved herself up on her elbows, met his gaze straight on. "I'm not scared of you." There was that faint air of defiance, as if she were daring him to throw her out. "Just stop being a prick. Enter the human race."

He smiled faintly. "Easy to say."

"Well, dial it down a notch. Can you do that? I'm not going to piss all over your boyhood mementos. I'm here for only a few days."

"You never know," he said, because deference was unnatural to him, especially with sex. "It might be more than a few days."

"Oh, I know all right," she said, unblinking, deference equally meaningless to her. "Now, can we get this show on the road?" She pointed at his dick.

"Not a problem." His smile was brilliant. "Any more

directions? I wouldn't want to make any blunders," he murmured, his voice softly insolent.

"One last direction," she unwisely said. "Make me feel—"

Hot with temper, he was on top of her before she'd finished speaking, slamming into her because she could piss him off damn near better than anyone.

Stunned, she sucked in a breath. "What the *hell* are you doing?"

His erection barely past the entrance to her body, her taut, unyielding flesh strangling the head of his dick, he gazed down at her, his lips curled in an icy smile. "I'm trying to fuck you, baby. I'm not getting much help. Should I order in some lube?"

"Get. Off. Me," she said, tight and angry. *"Right now."*

"No way." His reasons for refusing were enigmatic and territorial. The territorial part he understood; that was the part where he fucked her.

"How about some minimum recognition of who you're screwing then?" She spoke with cold intensity, because he hadn't moved and it didn't look like he would, the head of his erection pulsing against her tense flesh.

"I know who you are." He shut his eyes, blew out a breath. "You want an apology? I apologize."

"How about a real apology? You know, one that isn't completely devoid of feeling."

He stared at her sullenly. "You don't want much, do you?"

"Jesus fucking CHRIST!" she cried in full revolt. "I'm not doing this with a man who doesn't give a shit who's in his bed. Get OFF me!"

He raised his brows. "Calm the hell down. Take a deep breath. You want a better apology? Is that what you want? I've been apologizing left and right lately, so one more can't matter," he said. "Not that it seems to have done much good." His gaze dropped, then lifted again. "When I'm getting this kind of resistance."

She could feel him studying her and wondered in the ripening silence if she'd ever reconcile her mindless longing with rational judgment when it came to Dominic, if she ever could say no and mean it, if she ever could look at his dark, brooding beauty and not want him. "Give me a minute," she said. *To see the error of my ways, to regain my sanity.* "In the meantime I'll take that apology."

When he didn't answer, she surveyed the beautiful face with the critical gaze, the rigid line of his jaw. "Who's resisting now?"

"I apologize, Katherine." His voice was drained of emotion.

"You're not good at this are you?"

He sighed. "You're a fucking witch." He wasn't even sure why he was engaging in this skirmish other than the fact that Katherine had upended his perfectly comfortable, thoroughly selfish life—the one where he didn't deal with his feelings.

She smiled sweetly. "Thank you. You're equally appealing."

"So can we close down this lesson on manners?" he asked very quietly, using every ounce of self-control he possessed after seeing that smug smile.

"Certainly." Another sugar-sweet smile.

Fuck it. He thrust in fast and hard, as if he were furious or crazed or under so much accumulated pressure he was blind to the critical nuances of the most minimum courtesy, as if issues of forgiveness and apology had never been mentioned. As if violence alone wiped away smug smiles, rebalanced the power equation, burned away his perpetual hard-on.

Kate's shriek rang out in a piercing wail.

It hit him like a stun gun.

He jerked back and hung suspended above her, every muscle tense. "Oh fuck." He shook his head, blinked as though returning to the world.

Kate had tears in her eyes.

"Oh Christ," he said. "I'll stop. I can stop."

"It's all right." It was amazing how she was willing to relinquish her self-respect to please him, how the chemistry, the physical attraction, his body, had become her happiness and curse. Judgment suspended, her world. "You surprised me, that's all."

But she winced as he accidentally shifted positions and he looked at her, his gaze brooding. "I'm such an asshole." He blew the hair out of his eyes. "I have no fucking control with you." But his erection swelled and expanded independent of his remorse and he shot a flickering glance downward. "Seriously, you should kick the shit out of him."

"I don't know," she said, her heart pounding, unarmed in a battle she couldn't win. "He *has* been really good to me."

Dominic looked up, stared at her as though he were trying to decipher the chaos of the universe, as if only she could stabilize the dangerous drift into the abyss. "And?" A whisper of a question, soft as silk, warm, tender, the blue of his eyes without the habitual arrogance.

"And I need you inside me, if I'm saying that properly?"

His smile was swift. "Very properly. Thank you."

"And I'm fine, really." She shifted slightly to try to accommodate his size, wanting to please him for any number of reasons: for the unforgettable pleasure he offered in and out of bed, for the reward of his smile, for his moments of tenderness, for the really incredible fucks—let's not forget those.

"You sure?" Other than his surging dick, he was motionless.

Gazing up she saw the raw worry in his eyes. "Maybe slow it down a little."

He nodded. "I can do that." He grinned. "I'm not fucking fourteen. I can do it. But let me deal with this zipper first so it doesn't rip your skin." Alternating impressive one-armed push-ups as he lay between her legs, he peeled himself out of his jeans and boxers, kicked them away, then took her hand, closed her fingers into a fist, and placed it against his chest. "Punch me here if I'm hurting you. I'll stop. Okay?"

"Yup."

"Good to go?"

Without waiting for an answer, he entered her with excruciating slowness and an economy of movement thanks to muscles honed to impeccable standards of strength. And when, after languorous, endless moments of sumptuous friction and snug, velvety yielding, he reached the ultimate, maximum depth, she was panting and quivering.

"Better?" he whispered.

Kate nodded. Luckily she didn't have breath to speak

or she might have told him she loved him because she was drugged with bliss, glowing with love and on fire. Everything below her skin was heated, stirring, a tempest in her blood, the feel of him inside her, filling her completely, melting her heart, making her tremble. She looked up to see his eyes fixed on her, clear blue, a worry line between his brows. "You know what to do if I'm hurting you. Right?"

"Yes." A barely audible whisper.

"I don't want to hurt you. I'm sorry as hell I did."

How could he talk so calmly, like he was ordering a coffee? "I know," she said half under her breath, so he had to lean in to hear her.

"I want you"—his nostrils flared—"way too fucking much. Shut me down if—"

She slid her finger over his mouth.

He grinned. "Done talking?"

She nodded, ran her hands down his arms, and softly sighed as he withdrew with a fluid indolence.

Then he paused at the extremity of his backstroke and murmured, light and teasing, "What if I make you wait?"

"Don't you dare." She grabbed his hips hard.

He didn't move; she was slippery wet now, drenched, desperate. "Just for the record," he said gruffly, "you fuck only me. Right?"

Frantic to feel him, she breathlessly agreed. "Yes, yes, yes."

"Yes what?"

"Only you, Dominic! For God's sake, Dominic, I don't want anyone else!"

His monstrous jealousy assuaged by her fierce reply, he

smiled. "That's what I want to hear, baby." Pushing back in, unhurried, his mouth on hers, breathing her in, his dick swelling larger and harder as he penetrated more deeply, he came to rest at last where everything becomes meaningless except for the unimaginable pleasure.

Then with masterful patience, he waited motionless inside her as her body pulsed and throbbed around him, as her senses leveraged themselves up to a seething frenzy with the speed and violence he'd come to recognize. His Katherine was never cool and dispassionate, always wildly unbridled. And when he began slowly moving, in and out, smoothly, carefully, watching her keenly for any sign of discomfort, maneuvering his dick with practiced versatility into all the right places, just hard enough to make her sigh or groan, concentrating on her G-spot nerves, meeting her undulating hips with practiced skill, he felt a deep-seated pleasure. As if she belonged here in his private hermitage.

Kate felt as though she were flushed with wonder, filled with joy, every heartbeat vibrating with love, her senses racing toward delirium thanks to Dominic's sweet, unselfish indulgence. It was his genius and talent to be generous like now...like that—oh God. She sank her nails into his arms as that first unquestionable ripple slid up her throbbing sex; she sucked in her breath, shut her eyes, and went still.

Recognizing the cues, understanding Katherine's preference for a full-stop climax, he thrust in slowly to the mouth of her womb, heard her gasp, forced himself a fraction deeper, then dropped his head, let his mouth open over hers, and tasted her sweet, keening cry.

Their orgasms rolled through their senses in spectacular, searing waves, Dominic's powerful body covering her, gorging her, pumping into her, pinning her to the bed while astonishing, adrenaline-high, nuclear-level climaxes pushed sensation into the stratosphere.

A flame-hot, Dominic-fueled orgasm that left her throat raw and her nerves quivering.

An unimaginable Katherine-induced blast of madness and triumph that left him with a smile on his face.

Dominic did apologize afterward, not grudgingly, but with fond kisses, his body resting lightly on hers, his erection still gently throbbing inside her. "I'm going to control my dick and my temper from now on. I promise."

Her arms twined around his neck, she smiled up at him. "Just so you know, I get all sexed up when you're demanding and moody."

He had a pretty good idea already that she did, considering their time in Hong Kong, but he only said, ultrapolitely, "Thanks for the data point. I'll keep it in mind. Now, what do you want to do?"

"Really? My choice?"

He hesitated only a second before he said, "Your choice, babe. I owe you."

She pointed at the bookshelf. "Show me some of the books you liked to read when you were young."

Having anticipated a sexual request, he did a double take.

She gave him a wide-eyed look of innocence. "I'd like to know. Start with your favorite."

"Grant's memoirs." He slid off the bed and moved toward the shelf. "It's a fucking good read." And coming back to the bed, he described his favorite scenes, the reasons he liked them, how he'd first discovered the books when he was eleven.

She tried not to appear openly adoring, and asked questions with a nominal neutrality. She might have even succeeded in concealing her doting affection because after a time, he turned his head on his pillow, his gaze open and warm, and said, "Tell me about your favorite book."

He ignored the fact that he'd never asked a woman that question, never even considered a conversation about books relevant to male-female discourse.

When Kate said, "Tolkien's *Lord of the Rings*," he smiled and said, "Of course."

And when she'd finished explaining her love of the story, she sat up and said softly, "Are you okay with me here? Just asking."

There was a long pause while he stared at her, then he let out a small breath. "I want you with me. I'll deal with it."

"Is there anything I can do to help?"

His lips formed a little smile. "Baby, that's too big a job even for your self-confidence. I don't know how many therapists have tried and failed." His eyes glittered suddenly with suppressed rage and he dragged in a long, slow breath.

A crackling static shot through the room, as if forked lightning had hit. All the air seemed to disappear. Kate's voice was faint. "How many?"

He took another deep breath, raised his eyes to the ceiling. "I lost count." He paused, then looked at her and smiled. "You're being incredibly well behaved. Don't worry. I'm perfectly sane."

"You're saner than anyone I know, Dominic," she said quietly. "Really."

He looked at her from under the dark fan of his lashes and swallowed. "You sure you want to hear this?"

"I like when you talk to me. I like to hear you talk." *I like everything about you.*

He nodded in resignation or weariness.

She didn't dare breathe, fearful he'd change his mind and shrug himself back into his inaccessible habitat.

"Don't say I didn't warn you," he said with a scowl.

She wanted to say there's nothing you can tell me that will change the way I feel about you. But she only shook her head. "I won't."

"When I was a child," he began softly, a small frown settling between his brows, "my mother took pleasure in emotionally harassing me for some goddamn reason. I fought back. So she was under the impression I wanted to kill her. Not that I was going to, although...there were definitely times..." he said, his voice trailing off. He took a breath. "Anyway, starting at age six, she sent me to one psychiatrist after another. When they each, in turn, realized she was most of the problem, she'd cancel my appointments and find another shrink. And so on and so on. I can't tell you how many kind, or incompetent, or downright dangerous therapists I saw, how many thousands of pills I didn't swallow. You get good at it. I could hold a pill in my mouth for however long it took before I was able to spit it out. Even if I had to open my mouth for them. Even if I had to drink a fucking glass of water in front of them."

"Jeez. Is that even legal? Giving drugs to a six-year-old? Especially like that?"

He raised an eyebrow. "It is until you get old enough to find a way out. What I learned early on, though, was how to shut down in under three seconds. How to survive in a hostile world. Both have come in handy in my business." He smiled grimly. "Making lemonade out of lemons, right? And my sister, Melanie, was always there when I got home. She knew how to make me feel better, calm me down."

Kate's heart was thumping in her chest. She was speechless.

He gave her a sideways look. "Hey, it's not so bad. And it was a long time ago. I rarely see either of my parents; the war's pretty much over. Very little radioactive fallout." But the faint bitterness in his voice was apparent.

"I'm so sorry," she whispered.

"Don't be. It was a long time ago." Something tightened in his jaw, then he raised one of his heart-stopping smiles and held out his hand. "Come on, baby, you're here, so I don't think about any of that shit. Tell me one of your stories about growing up with Gramps and Nana. Tell me something good."

Her hand in his, she began talking, chattering, rambling on, making jokes, telling him about Nana's vodka still with the detail of a scientist because he seemed interested. Then about Gramps's gun collection, which had him asking questions. After that, stories about her dog and cat, about summer camps. Wanting to make him happy, wanting him to forget the frightened six-year-old at the psychiatrist, wanting him to smile and lose that strained look he'd had talking about his childhood.

Before long, the furrow between his brows disappeared and he seemed relaxed, almost content. He half lifted his head on the pillow, then sat up in the graceful flow of muscle that never ceased to electrify her senses, took her by the shoulders, dropped back down, and pulled her into the warmth of his body. "You're helping me more than you know, Katherine." There was no sharpness to his voice now, no edge, just a quiet softness. "You'll have to send me a bill for therapy services," he murmured, closing his eyes.

She inhaled the scent of him, the sweet musk and cedar, took pleasure in the warmth of his skin under her cheek, the taut, supple muscle beneath the bronzed flesh— a body disciplined by a hard, disciplined mind. And she felt like crying for the little boy who hadn't swallowed all those pills, for the child victimized by the cruelty of adults who owed him love and failed him. Who hadn't just failed him but mistreated him.

They slept for a time and when they woke, they indulged their senses in amorous play, then, prompted by a jet-lag lethargy, napped again. Eventually, Dominic coaxed Kate into the shower with promises of sex, then afterward, driven by hunger, he found them robes so they could go downstairs. Dominic, Kate at his side, peered into a commercial-size fridge, contemplating the provisions within. Four of the shelves held covered dishes, each labeled with instructions for heating or not.

Kate pointed at a Saran-wrapped salad that was marked:

Do Not Microwave. "She's not sure you know not to heat a salad?"

Dominic rolled his eyes. "I did once and Patty's never forgotten. That I was stoned out of my mind at the time apparently wasn't excuse enough for her." He pulled out a dish of enchiladas, one of Mongolian beef, and then the salad. "Take out that rice pudding, will you?" He pointed with the enchilada dish. "You have to taste the best pudding in the world."

"There's modest praise," she teased.

"I kid you not, baby. It's world class. Patty flew to New York and coaxed the recipe from a chef who'd refused my request. It's an Afghani recipe with pistachios, cardamom, and some other stuff. Anyway, I'm eternally grateful to Patty. And for those less enthusiastic," he said with a smile, nodding at a ceramic cookie jar in the shape of Darth Vader, "cookies?" His smile widened. "Silly question. I ordered chocolate milk too. Unless you want a beer or a drink."

After heating up the dishes in the microwave, they carried their smorgasbord upstairs and spread it out on the bed, along with beer for Dominic and chocolate milk for Kate. Then they fed each other Patty's best efforts like lovers do.

It was a day of pleasure, of small bewitchments, and of off-the-charts rapture. But Dominic kept an eye on the clock and the time finally arrived when he gave Kate a kiss, climbed out of bed, and said over his shoulder as he walked away, "We have to get dressed for Melanie's party. I had some clothes delivered for you. So don't sulk, okay?"

Kate gave him a dirty look anyway—or tried to at

least. She mostly just stared at him, because he was standing splendidly nude across the room at the entrance to his walk-in closet and looking incredibly yummy. Damn, if she was going to make a reasonable case for her independence, she really had to ignore all that stunning maleness.

"You never quit, do you," she said. Then sighed. "Am I some toy for you to dress? Or are you ashamed to be seen with me in my ordinary clothes?"

He swung around to face her in a torque of sleek, tensile muscle and restive impatience. "Neither. Come *on*, baby" he grumbled. "Didn't anyone ever give you presents? Maybe we *should* see some crazy therapist so he can tell you to knock it off."

"Or *she* could tell you to knock it off. Cuz I'm right," she said, keeping her voice light.

His eyes suddenly creased with amusement.

"What?"

"Therapists don't use words like *right* and *wrong*. They prefer gray, equivocal words. Repeat-what-you-just-heard-me-say compromises that aren't really compromises but a form of apathy. Obviously, you've never been to one."

"No. Although I'd like someone to tell *you* that you can't order people around twenty-four/seven."

"You may have noticed I'm having a little trouble with you," he said drily.

She slid down lower on the pillows, made a motorboat sound with her lips, studied her painted toenails. "I'm probably overreacting to your gifts," she said evenly, still looking at her toes. "So I give up. Happy now?"

"Let me get this straight. You're saying you'll wear some

of these clothes? Hey, look at me." She looked up with calculated slowness so he didn't think she was giving in on every little thing. "If you must know, you've exhausted me into capitulation."

"I like that word, *capitulation*," he said with a twitch of his lips.

"Don't get used to it," she muttered.

He quickly put up his hands in surrender. "Understood."

She gave him a faint smile. "You really are on your best behavior."

"Yeah, well"—a teasing grin—"I have plans."

"I think we both do." She was like ten times, maybe a thousand times, more susceptible to Dominic's magnetism, to his charisma and allure in this bedroom, where so much of his childhood and youth were on display: in the photos on the walls, the trophies on the shelves, the collection of tin soldiers in the glass cabinet, the shelves of well-read books. He'd allowed her into his life, into his home, casually offered up his sister's friendship. Not that he wasn't staking ownership as well, she understood—but with a slightly pained expression and a polite smile that only made him more lovable. She wasn't sure her independence would survive against the full onslaught of his willfulness.

But she loved him—anyway and every way.

Dominic wasn't the only one who subscribed to a *what the fuck* philosophy.

Looking up, she took in Dominic's raised eyebrows. He must have asked her something.

"I'm done. Is that what you wanted to know? I'll wear whatever you want."

"That's not sarcasm?"

She shook her head.

"Good. So first—thank you. I really like to buy you things. I like to show you off. I can't help it." He smiled. "Really, thanks."

She felt weirdly pleased when she shouldn't, when the phrase *show you off* was seriously retro and against all her feminist convictions. "I understand feeling helpless." She half-lifted her hand, searching for the right words. "I tell myself not to get involved. Yet here I am—involved. I'm letting you talk me into these clothes too. How's that for helpless?"

With Kate in an accommodating mood, Dominic decided to push his luck. "Could we put that in our exclusivity contract—that I can buy you stuff when we're together?"

Her green-eyed gaze turned guarded. "What stuff?"

"Just gifts."

"This argument's never going away, is it?"

"It's a stupid argument," he said quietly.

"Oh hell." A sigh, a little bunny twitch of her nose, a grimace. "No jewelry, though."

"Why not?"

"It's too expensive."

"We'll toss a coin."

She gave him a jaundiced look.

"You don't trust me?"

"Not exactly. I've got a pile of luggage full of clothes and jewelry in my living room in Boston as we speak."

"We'll talk about it later."

"Ohmygod!" she exclaimed, sitting up and jabbing a finger at him. "You already bought me jewelry!"

"Nothing grand."

"Anything that's not from Walmart is grand to me."

"You have to broaden your horizons, baby. No shit." Then he changed the subject because he was willing to settle for one victory at a time. He'd talk her into the jewelry later. When they were having sex.

She was a pushover after a few orgasms.

And some of the jewelry *was* for sex games.

He smiled a few moments later when she answered his question with categorical, left-brain indifference. "You decide what you want me to wear. I don't care."

"Now you're talking. And by the way, it's a real turn-on dressing you."

"Ditto." If his spending vast sums of money on her could be ignored, the hands-on activity of him dressing her *was* flagrantly arousing.

Her smile was really hot and sexy. He almost gave in to temptation, until he glanced at the clock. "Are you going to get out of bed or should I come get you?"

She patted the bed. "Why don't you come here."

He reluctantly shook his head. "No can do. We don't have that kind of time."

"When do we have to be there?"

"In fifteen minutes."

"You mean we could have been making ourselves happy in bed instead of arguing? Why didn't you say something?"

"It's hard to read you sometimes, baby. I'm doing my best."

"Hmmph."

"We'll be back in a couple hours. Or if you get hard up we can go into one of Melanie's bathrooms and lock the door."

A wide-eyed look. "I don't think so."

"Just saying."

"I hope you're not saying you've done that before at your sister's."

His face was impassive. "I'm just trying to be helpful."

"It might be more helpful if you put on some clothes. You look too damn scrumptious standing there."

He dressed in under three minutes like he always did, pulling on boxers and black jeans, shrugging into a black cashmere V-neck sweater, then jerking on socks and black suede lace-up boots, smoothly tying them with a few economical twists of his fingers.

She didn't know if a dressed Dominic was any better. It was almost impossible not to drool at such sexiness. He was extraordinarily handsome dressed all in black, dark, intense, sensual, a graphic novel kind of hero, unequivocally hard-edged and powerful. His longer hair was the same style he wore in most of the surfing photos that cluttered the room. One huge, colored photo covered an entire wall. Dominic was in the pocket of a powerful wave, riding the face in a fluid turn, the white-capped lip so high it dwarfed him, and even from a distance, even racing against the thundering blast of water churning behind him, you could see his beautiful, wide smile.

"You surf much?" she asked, pointing to the photo. "Or is that in the past?"

"I do when I have time. But that was one of my more

awesome days," he said, grinning. "In Hawaii. The beach had been blackballed because the waves were so dangerous. But that just means you have to ride the wave hard core, no fear. Everyone crashed that day except me. I iced that kamikaze wave, Gerry caught me on camera, and there it is. One of my better memories."

"You look young."

He pursed his lips for a second. "I must have been fifteen or sixteen—no, sixteen—I was living here already. I bought this place so I could be near Melanie. I helped babysit her first two kids before I went to college."

"Can you do that?"

"What?"

"Live on your own at sixteen."

He shrugged. "I never asked. Melanie signed for me. It worked out."

As Kate bit back the dozen prying questions crowding her brain, Dominic tapped his watch. "Enough memory lane shit," he said. "We should get you dressed." He held out the clothes draped over his arm. "Although, if you want, there's still enough time for me to give you a little prize for being so nice."

She smiled. "Am I nice?"

"Nicer than anyone I know," he said softly, his eyes half-lidded, a ghost of a smile on his lips.

A hot current of need ran up her spine. She'd seen that look before. "Tell me I don't have to talk to your mother," she said quickly, rising from the bed, her heart fluttering against her ribs. She refused to melt into a puddle of lust on cue.

"Don't worry," he said calmly, as if he hadn't registered her reaction. "I don't *want* you talking to my mother. She's troublesome," he added dryly.

Coming to a stop before him, Kate tipped her head back and grinned. "You're way too good to me. Life's strange isn't it?" Her voice went soft. "How we met, how I can't live without you"—she smiled—"at least for long."

"It's good strange, babe. And it's the same for me . . . your absence tears me up." He almost said, *You have to sign the exclusivity contract*, but caught himself. Time enough in the morning to begin that battle. "Lift your arms now. We're on the clock."

Loss of control aside, when it came to pure gratification, she had to admit that having Dominic dress her was right up there with Venezuelan chocolate and winning the lottery. The act itself was tender, affectionate, impossibly erotic. And in her current mood of complete, utter adoration, Kate glanced at the shimmering midnight-green-velvet long-sleeved, scoop-neck blouse Dominic was holding and said, "Should I wear a bra?"

"I wasn't going to ask."

"Should I?"

"You might be more comfortable."

"It's not about me being comfortable." She smiled. "Are you worried about your mother?"

He shook his head. "That's useless. There's no pleasing her. But I don't like other men looking at my tits. You know that."

"Yours?" Her voice was teasing.

"Yes. Mine." Not a scintilla of teasing in either word.

She shouldn't feel a hot, sexy rush flood through her senses when he spoke like he owned her. Taking a small breath to tamp down her desire, she tried to speak in a normal tone. "I suppose you have some bras here."

"I suppose I do."

She waved her hand at the walk-in closet, a great variety of women's clothes visible on the racks. "How do you do this on short notice?"

"Phone." From Paris. But he left that unsaid.

"And everyone scurries."

"They don't mind. They're paid well."

"I suppose you have a bra in a matching color."

"I expect so. Should we look?"

He found a dark green lace bra in a drawer of bras and held it out for her while she slid in her arms and turned her back to him.

Reaching around her, he slipped her breasts into the lacy cups, slid his fingers up the straps to smooth them over her shoulders, hooked the bra, and bent to kiss her shoulder. "Maybe you won't need a maid. Maybe I'll always dress you," he whispered, his fully clothed body pressing into her back, his fingers slipping over her shoulders and downward to the swell of her breasts. "Would you like that?"

Suffused with desire, Dominic's powerful body and gentle touch stirring her senses, his sweet comments affecting her susceptible heart, she leaned back into his solid warmth and nodded because tears were welling in her throat.

"Hey, baby. We can't have you crying," he whispered, beginning to recognize her moments of silence. He turned her in his arms. "You'll mess up your nonexistent mascara."

She giggled.

"That's my girl," he grinned. "We gotta get moving," he said, stepping back. "Oh Christ." He almost took her bra off again she looked so goddamn sexy with her pale breasts in high plump mounds above the scalloped cups. He almost gave in to temptation and had the clock not inopportunely chimed the quarter hour, he would have. Instead, he sucked in a breath, grabbed the velvet top, and quickly slid it over her head and down her arms. Adjusting the scoop neckline bordered in beaded glitter, he smoothed the delicate velvet down her rib cage.

"I can't decide about panties," he said.

"I can tell it's a family party."

"You're right. Panties tonight." He leaned over and smoothly slid two fingers into her succulent sex. "But I promised you one for the road. Interested?" When she didn't answer other than to clutch his shoulders, he whispered, "That must be a yes." Gracefully dropping to his knees, he spread her legs wider with a little nudge of his free hand, then leaned forward and added his tongue to his fingers, licking and sucking her clit while he lazily stroked her pulsing tissue, deep and slow, in a gentle ebb and flow, or side to side, or more forcefully and compellingly at times—his virtuoso skills well honed. Practice makes perfect was not just an idle phrase for Dominic Knight.

Kate's world narrowed to soft, lambent sensation, to touch and feel, to the exquisite cadence and rhythm of Dominic's fingers, to the benevolent performance of his mouth and tongue. To a simmering, seething, increasingly frantic delirium as he scissored his fingers open inside her for better access, reached for her G-spot, and licked it like a lollipop.

She captured his head in a viselike grip, wanting to preserve the intoxicating pressure, the wild, fierce glory, whimpering as flame-hot rapture ravished her senses, spiked through her core, left her quivering in limbo.

He drew his head back fractionally. "Ready, babe?"

Did she have to answer? Could she find the breath to answer? What if she couldn't? She struggled to speak.

"It's okay, Katherine," he said gently. "I've got this." Carefully forcing in a third finger, he slowly slid it in palm deep, until she was gorged, until every sleek bit of tissue was stirred and stretched, throbbing in time to the frantic beat of her heart. Then he dipped his head, recaptured the small nub of her clit, and sucked with tender, exquisite restraint.

She instantly climaxed with a familiar unbridled scream.

He smiled; there was no faking it with Katherine. Careful not to move his fingers, he waited until she slowly opened her eyes. "Satisfactory?" He glanced up from under his lashes.

She sighed and unflexed her fingers clamped in his hair. "As in completely mind-blowing, Mr. Knight."

"Good to hear, Miss Hart," he replied politely, sliding his fingers out, coming to his feet, touching his fingertips to his mouth. "Ummm...nice. If we weren't going out, I'd leave your mark on me, but"—he gestured at a comfortable chair—"sit for a minute. I'll be right back."

Dropping into the soft, cushiony chair upholstered in a sunny, surfing motif fabric, Kate basked in a warm post-orgasmic haze while the sound of running water echoed from the bathroom. Even when Dominic returned, she didn't move. "Sorry," she murmured. "I'm on pause." She smiled at him. "My body's in overload."

"You'll have time to wind down at the party. Then you'll be ready again." He grinned. "Because we're on vacation."

"Is that what a vacation means? Nonstop screwing?"

"I've never taken a vacation before. But nonstop screwing is definitely on my agenda with you. I hope you don't mind?"

"And if I did?"

He glanced at her, flashed a smile. "I'd have to change your mind."

"Oh, God," she groaned, instantly tight and hot with longing, the undeniable power of his soft intimidation frightening—and recklessly compelling. "How do you do it? I've never been like this before, insatiable, constantly horny, seriously oversexed."

"There's no such thing as oversexed."

Her brows shot up. "For you maybe."

He smiled. "Then I can teach you. But not right now." There were very few people in his life he chose to please, but Melanie had always been at the top of his list. "We gotta get out of here in the next few minutes." Squatting between her legs with the effortless ease of killer muscles in perfect harmony, he wiped her sex with a washcloth, threw the wet cloth into the bathroom, then slipped on her a scrap of green lace that functioned as panties and a pair of black, skinny, cropped-leg jeans. That she was still in a minor trance didn't deter him; he lifted her effortlessly, zipped and buttoned, said, "Perfect," softly once, giving her a pat on her knee, then stood and disappeared into the closet.

"Open your eyes, babe."

Jeez, had she dozed off? Although after countless orgasms in bed and her recent one for the road, maybe she had an excuse.

A calm, measured look. "Do you want coffee?"

She shook her head, forced herself into the present. "I'll have a rum and Coke later. If your sister has rum."

"I'm sure she does. So?" Dominic held up two pairs of shoes. "You chose."

She smiled. "Really. You think I can handle it?"

He grinned. "A limited choice, baby. Your fashion sense is appalling."

"I believe I've said this before. I don't care. Either one."

"These then." He swung a pair of black suede, ankle-strap shoes with gold studs down the chunky heels. "Unless you'd rather not wear heels."

"Those are fucking high."

"Depends how much you drink."

She lifted her brows.

"Something less elevated then." He dropped the ankle-strap shoes, knelt at her feet, and slipped on a pair of black glittery ballet flats. "These are safer. As I recall in Amsterdam, you weren't too steady in spike heels." Smoothly coming to his feet, he took her hands and pulled her up.

She looked up and grinned. "Maybe I was just hitting on you."

"Lucky me." He pulled some earrings out of his pocket—small gold hoops with single emerald teardrops. He'd told his jeweler to keep it simple.

"I probably *was* hitting on you," she conceded. "Sub-consciously at least."

"While I was fully conscious of wanting to nail you on the spot." He slipped on one earring, since he hadn't gotten any grief.

"That would have raised a few eyebrows."

"I doubt it. I pay their salaries." He slipped on the other earring.

"Whoa...two things. First—not an image I want in my head. And second—don't do that I'm-master-of-the-universe crap. It pisses me off."

"Naturally, I apologize."

She gave him a squinty-eyed look. "As if."

He shook his head. "Haven't you noticed yet, babe? My recent freak-out aside, I pretty much do whatever you want. You're calling the shots. I'm just here to serve and assist." He held out his hand. "We really have to go. I'll introduce you to the part of my family I care about. You okay with your hair—need a brush?"

"You tell me."

"Nah—that FF look is hot."

"FF?"

He smiled. "Freshly fucked."

"And you're saying it's okay in public?"

"We call it messy curls or artful disarray in public. You're good. Let me get you a jacket. It's trying to rain again tonight."

She clamped her mouth shut when he walked out of his closet with a flower print, short, swingy, silk raincoat, the

background green, multicolored flowers in every color of
the rainbow lighting up the fabric—the kind of making-a-
statement raincoat you saw only on Paris runways.

"Arms out, babe. Ah...perfect. Now that's a good fit,"
he said calmly, as if none of the other clothes had fit. "Jeez,
have you shrunk?" He sliced the air above her head, then
drew the edge of his hand to his chest. "Must be the shoes."
He grinned. "Stay close. I'm going to have to keep you from
being trampled tonight."

It was impossible to be angry with him. Why was she
even putting up a fight? All too soon, she'd be missing him.
So smell the roses while you can.

"Do you like the coat?"

He was smiling at her. "It's perfect. Thanks."

"Melanie's going to love you, baby. Come on." He
grabbed her hand. "I can hardly wait to show you off."

She put up her hand. "I'm not your newest toy. You
know that—right?"

"Jesus, I don't *want* you to be." His voice dropped low.
"I just want you to be *mine.*"

Something in his voice at the end made her nervous.
"No scenes, okay?"

Mild puzzlement. "As in?"

"As in you getting hot about the men I talked to in Hong
Kong."

"Then don't talk to other men." A blunt, uncompromising command.

She raised an eyebrow. "You're kidding."

Seeing the flush flood her cheeks, he quickly rectified
his error. "I was out of line. Sorry." He blew out a small

breath. "I'm just so fucking jealous. I wish I weren't. But"—
he smiled faintly—"since I'm a control freak, I should be
able to exercise a little self-control. So no scenes. I promise."

Sometimes she caught a glimpse of the boy inside the
mighty, overachieving, hard-ass global magnate. "Thanks,"
Kate said. "I appreciate your understanding. And I'd rather
be with you than anyone else, so there. We're both on the
same page."

The warmth in his eyes brought a lump to her throat.

He dipped his head and lightly touched her lips. "It feels
as though all the stars are aligned tonight," he whispered
against her mouth. "The first time ever for me." He raised
his head and smiled. "Crazy—hey?"

"Everything we do is crazy." Aware of the shift in his
tone, she was careful to keep her voice light. "Why stop
now?"

They left Dominic's home and walked outside to the
sidewalk, where he pulled her to a stop. "Just a minute," he
murmured.

A second later, Leo, Danny, and two other men came
out of the shadows of the adjacent yard—the houses separated only by their driveways.

Kate glanced up at Dominic. "They stay next door?"

"I like my privacy."

"Is security really necessary?"

"It's just a precaution."

"What does that mean?"

"Just what I said. Evening, guys. How's everyone?"

After greetings were exchanged, Leo and Danny took

up positions in front of them, the other two men fell in behind. Taking Kate's hand in his, Dominic started walking east.

"You have to explain these four guys to me," she hissed.

"There's nothing to explain. I generally travel with security."

"There wasn't anyone with us in Hong Kong or Singapore."

"We're only walking a block tonight. It's kinda hard for them to stay out of sight."

"That's it?"

"That's all there is to it. There's Melanie's place up ahead," he said, wanting to shut down this conversation. "Don't feel as though you have to remember all the children's names. They don't care."

SIXTEEN

When they reached Melanie's, Dominic and Kate went inside while the security crew checked out the perimeter of the house before coming in.

Dominic hung up Kate's coat in the entrance hall closet, picked up the shopping bag that had been brought down from his house earlier, and gestured in the direction of distant voices. "We'll find them in the kitchen. Family birthdays at Melanie's are pizza since the kids got old enough to holler. It's good pizza though. But save some room. The adult party has a better menu."

When they reached the large kitchen at the back of the house, a wild whoop went up the moment they appeared in the archway. And a second later a wave of screaming young children powered toward them.

"Hey, hey, watch it, guys," Dominic warned. "I have a guest tonight. Don't knock her over."

All but the youngest girl came to a skidding stop in time. The little blond toddler with curly hair grabbed Dominic's leg and tried to climb up, shrieking, "Unka Nicky, Unka Nicky, hold me!"

Dropping the shopping bag, he swung her up in his arms and gave her a kiss on her chubby cheek. "Ummm...peanut butter."

"We got a puppy! We got a puppy!" The little girl banged

on his shoulder with her half-eaten peanut butter and jelly sandwich. "Wanna see?"

"Give me a sec, sweetie. Eat your sandwich. I want to introduce my girlfriend."

By this time, Melanie and Matt had come up, along with a stout, five-foot-nothing older woman who was smiling broadly enough for her kohled eyes to crinkle at the corners. With Birkenstocks on her feet, tie-dyed pajama pants, and brilliant henna-colored hair, she was, head to toe, a member of the hippie generation.

"Hi, Mrs. B." Dominic moved forward to kiss her cheek, holding the sandwich-wielding toddler well away. "Are you keeping the ship running smoothly?"

"Of course." She squinted at him with her snappy black eyes as he stepped back. "Are you still being a bad boy?"

"Uh-uh. I've got myself a girl. She's keeping me in line." He took Kate's hand. "Katherine this is Mrs. B. She's been helping around here for, what?"

"Seventeen years. Pleased to meet you, Miss Kate. You've got your hands full with him, I'll tell you that."

"I've noticed." Kate glanced up at Dominic, her gaze mischievous. "We're working on his manners."

The housekeeper gave Dominic an approving smile. "She's not afraid of you, Nicky. That's good."

Dominic dropped his head and gave her a quick grin. "I'm afraid of *her*, Mrs. B. Katherine's one tough cookie."

"It's about time you're afraid of someone." She surveyed him with an examining gaze as good as any psych-ops interrogator's. "Don't want you to think you really do own the world."

"As long as I have you to slap some sense into me that won't happen."

"Good thing I'm here then." Her delivery was blunt, but she looked at him with tenderness.

"Still on your mission from God?" A half smile, a lift of one brow. "Who's winning, Mrs. B?"

She snorted. "Have you ever seen me lose? Another thing," she briskly added. "Tell your people to leave my kitchen spotless when they go. Last time I had to clean up after them."

"You won't even know they were here, Mrs. B," Dominic said with a respectful dip of his head. "They got the message."

She started untying her apron. "You kids have fun then. Nice to meet you, Miss Kate. I'll see the rest of you in the morning." Whipping off her apron, she smoothed her Grateful Dead T-shirt over her generous bosom, handed her apron to Melanie, and walked away like she was a member of the Olympic power walking team.

Kate found it fascinating that everyone deferred to the housekeeper, including Dominic. Even the little toddler had viewed the conversation in silence.

"Now that the warden's gone," Dominic said under his breath, a smile in his voice as he turned to Kate, "let me introduce everyone." Holding Kate's hand, he ran through the names: Melanie, Matt, Nicole, Isabelle, Keir, Dante, Rafe, and Ellie, who waved what was left of her sandwich when she heard her name. Melanie gave Kate a big hug, Matt did too, and all the children smiled warmly. "I told Katherine she doesn't have to remember all your names right away,"

Dominic added, with a nod at the children. "So be polite, okay?"

"Can we see our presents now?"

The young girl Kate had seen at Dominic's office in Palo Alto was speaking. Nicole was dark like Dominic and very beautiful, while Dominic's sister was blond, delicate, warm, and welcoming, a younger, friendlier version of their mother, Letitia.

Dominic gave Melanie and Matt a sideways look. "It's up to your parents."

Melanie briefly surveyed her young brood. "As long as you remember your manners."

Dominic grinned. "A few years too late for that."

"At least they have *some* manners, unlike you."

"You got me there, sis," Dominic noted blandly. "Although Katherine's trying to whip me into shape—aren't you baby?"

Kate turned bright red.

"She blushes," Dominic said with his best bad-boy grin. "Isn't that sweet?" he said like a botanist might, showing off a newly discovered orchid from the deepest jungles of Indonesia. Leaning over, he pulled her close, even though Kate was giving him warning glances. "And while Katherine's trying to teach me manners, I'm trying to teach her not to give such a shit about what people think. We've got a little work to go there though"—another teasing glance—"right, babe?"

"Good God, Nicky, stop," Melanie ordered. "She won't want to stay. Ignore him, Katherine. He can be spectacularly impudent. Go," Melanie said, pointing in the direction

of the family room. "Get out of here, Nick. Katherine's staying with me."

Dropping a swift kiss on Kate's cheek, Dominic turned
to the sea of expectant, youthful faces. "Come on, kids, I'll
show you what I found in Singapore." Bending to pick up
the shopping bag, he glanced at Kate. "You okay if I leave?"

"Of course she is." Melanie took Kate's hand and looked
at her brother with a twinkle in her eyes. "I'm going to
entertain her, tell her all your deep, dark secrets."

Coming upright, Dominic's eyes held a brief unease,
quickly stifled. "Don't believe anything she says, baby.
And if you scare her off"—Dominic gave his sister a mock
threatening look—"you'd better run."

Melanie patted Dominic's arm. "Now why would I want
to do that when you've found someone so nice?"

His sister's conciliatory response, her gentle hand on his
arm, softened the set of Dominic's mouth and Kate understood what a moderating influence she was in his life. Kate
was grateful he had her. Dominic was, in so many ways, a
man alone. Private, withdrawn, living an isolated life within
the narrow confines of his privileged world.

"The pizza will be done in fifteen minutes though,"
Melanie cautioned, giving her husband a warning look.
"Show Nick your boat pictures later. Mrs. B won't forgive us
if we let her pizzas burn."

"Don't worry, sis. Your kids can rip open packages in
no time flat. We'll be done in plenty of time for pizza."
Dominic shot a look at his restless nieces and nephews,
who were trying to control their impatience. "Ready, kids?"
He nodded toward the family room. "Come on, Matt, you

can help me gear up some of this stuff." A grin for the children. "First one seated has a chance to beat me at chess later tonight."

As the thundering herd raced off, Melanie waved Kate toward a seating area off the kitchen. "Would you like a drink?"

"I would. I can make it though." Kate could see a small bar against the far wall.

"Please, sit. I'll get it. What would you like?"

"I'd like a rum and Coke, lime if you have it."

"That sounds good. I'll make two."

A few minutes later Melanie carried over two ice-filled glasses, handed one to Kate, and dropped onto the sofa with Kate.

"Lovely view." Kate indicated the window wall, lights sparkling on the other side of the bay.

"It is lovely, isn't it?" Casually dressed in a pastel blue sweater and jeans, Melanie kicked off her shoes, tucked her legs under her, and leaned back against the arm rest. "Matt found the house for us before Nicole was born."

"You have a wonderful family. Dominic's lucky to live nearby. He was telling me he helped babysit Nicole and Isabelle when they were young."

"He did. He's great with kids. All the children absolutely adore him. He spoils them, of course, but I don't mind. He needs family in his life." Melanie smiled. "To remind him there's another world beyond making deals. Although you seem to have coaxed him away for a few days, at least. Roscoe tells me Dominic is actually on vacation. I'm pleased you were able to do that. He's never taken a vacation before. You must tell me your secret."

"I'm afraid I didn't have anything to do with his decision. Dominic doesn't ask for advice—at least not from me.
I ran into him in Singapore and the next thing I knew, we
were on a plane, coming here."

"Say what you will," Melanie said with a cheerful lilt to
her voice, "if not for you, I very much doubt Dominic would
have cleared his calendar. You didn't know that? Roscoe
called me to see if I could talk some sense into Nick. I told
him, 'Not on your life.'" Melanie paused and gave Kate a
warm smile. "I can tell he likes you."

"He's very likable as well," Kate said, blushing, then
quickly changed the subject. She wasn't about say that
Dominic was the most wonderful thing that had ever happened to her. "I hope I'm not imposing tonight. Dominic says
no, but then he tends to overlook other people's opinions."

Melanie laughed. "You've noticed. I could pretend
Nick's presumption is a result of his success in business,
but"—her mouth twitched into a lopsided smile—"Nicky's
been telling people what to do most of his life. I just ignore
him. I suggest you do the same. As for imposing—you're
not in the least. It's a pleasure to have you join us. Nick has
never brought a friend over to any family occasion." Her
smile faded and, looking down, she ran a finger around
the rim of her glass. A brief silence fell before she looked
up. "Do you mind me asking you how you feel about Nick,
other than liking him? Forgive me," she softly added, seeing Kate's sudden unease. "I know I'm overprotective. But I
worry about Nick. He's been through a lot."

Kate hesitated a moment then said, "The death of his
wife you mean."

"Yes, that too."

Melanie glanced away, lost for a moment in the obscure misery of Dominic's youth. Then she blinked and reclaimed the present. "I can't help but notice," she said, then stopped. "Well—how Nick's so cheerful with you, vital—even joyful. I'm so grateful to see him like that, smiling, happy. You see, Nick normally doesn't relate well to people...with any intimacy, I mean. Although," she added with a small smile, "he can be very charming if he wishes."

"I know," Kate said, indelibly conscious of Dominic's many virtues. "I've seen Dominic's charm in action...in Amsterdam and again at a charity event in Hong Kong. He's amazingly charismatic. Every woman was captivated, and the men liked him as well. He raised a lot of money for Max's wife that night."

"How nice for Liv. I haven't seen her since Conall was born." Melanie paused, as though debating her next remark, before she said, "I understand you met my mother when you were in Hong Kong. You may have noticed that she and Dominic lack...er—a certain—rapport."

That was a nice way to put it. Since Melanie had brought up the subject of their mother, Kate gave in to her morbid curiosity about the life and times of Dominic Knight. "Dominic told me a little about his childhood." She watched Melanie's face in the event it was a forbidden topic. "He mentioned the therapists."

Melanie's head jerked up. "He did?"

"Forgive me," Kate said quickly. "I shouldn't have brought it up. Really, it's none of my business."

"No, please, it's not that. I'm just surprised." Melanie

was barely breathing, visibly pale. "Nick never speaks of those days."

"I may have pressed him...just a little," Kate replied, softly apologetic. "Although he didn't seem to mind."

"Obviously, if he told you what he did." Melanie gave her head a little shake, as if settling the dust from those undecipherable years. "It seemed like the nightmare would never end," she said so softly it was barely audible. "Although it was so much worse for Nick." She dragged in a breath. "It was really hateful."

"I can imagine...actually I can't," Kate said bluntly. "He was so young. I can't fathom...all those years of"—she didn't know where to look when she wanted to say, *All those years of torture.*

Melanie sighed, set her glass aside, clasped her hands together, and kept her gaze on her tightly clenched fingers. "I was too young to do more than offer him comfort. I wish I could have done more. I felt so helpless." She looked up, unclenched her fingers, smiled a tiny desolate smile. "But Nick wasn't completely defenseless even then. He was always very strong. Iron-willed. Determined."

"I don't know how strong you can be at six. I mean...six, Jesus—oh, hell, sorry. It's not your fault."

"You're right to be appalled," Melanie said, her voice very small, her brows drawn together as though recalling the anguish. "I've always felt that Nick should have been born into a different family where...well—just a different family. One that celebrates independent children." Her sudden smile was fragile, strangely touched with humor. "Although, from the very beginning, Nicky was remarkably...active, actually activist—like a one-baby revolt. He was unbelievably demanding. He never cooed or gurgled, he screamed the house down through four nurses and two au pairs. I was the only one who could hold him, make him smile, silence his screams. I'd sit beside him and read to him while the nurses fed him or he wouldn't eat. So I was taken out of school and privately tutored until Nick entered preschool at three."

"Jeez."

She laughed softly. "You see what you're in for? Nick's always been very willful. It's how he survived. And since he had so little control as a child, his need for control now is huge. He treats my family as a special case—as his special dispensation. But in general"—she rolled her eyes—"watch out." A smile flickered across her face. "Now I hope I haven't frightened you away. Really, Nicky has very nice manners."

"I've noticed. And don't worry, he doesn't frighten me. But I have no expectations," Kate said. "I'm just enjoying his company."

Melanie picked up her drink and took a sip, as though giving herself time to find the right words. "You may or may not know this," she finally said, "but you're the only woman who seems to have gotten through to him. Just the fact that you're staying at Nick's house—*that* house, and he brought you to my birthday tonight is really…unprecedented. So I worry that you may be able to hurt him," she said, her gaze that same clear blue as Dominic's. "He has vulnerabilities."

"I doubt I *can* hurt Dominic. If anyone's going to be hurt, it'll be me. His track record with women"—Kate shrugged—"isn't reassuring. But honestly, I don't know what he wants. We've known each other for only such a short time." It was easier to be objective with Dominic out of sight; his physical presence stripped her of her clarity.

"But you like him."

"Who wouldn't like him? He's an amazing man."

Melanie smiled. "I think so too."

Then curiosity overcame practicalities, perhaps even politesse. "May I ask *you* a question, and if you feel I'm out of line, just tell me." Kate ran her finger down the condensation on her glass. "Dominic's house...that is—in the house...there's no evidence of his wife anywhere."

"That's because Julia preferred their apartment on Russian Hill. She called that house Dominic's surfing museum. Nothing much has changed there since he bought it. He likes it that way. Don't get me wrong, Julia was very good for him. The best friend he ever had. Maybe the only real friend he ever had. They went everywhere together, to the most dangerous and amazing places. I think she offered him constant distraction beyond the machinations of the business world. Nick isn't good alone. He surrounds himself with people and constant activity. He always has. With the exception of his reading. You probably saw his books. Did he show you the room over the garage that he calls his library?"

"No, I'd like to see it. I saw the books in his room."

"I don't think Julia shared that interest. She was a complete extrovert; she belonged to any number of charities, sat on the boards of several. But, most important, Julia was completely loyal and in Dominic's cutthroat world, that kind of loyalty is rare." Melanie paused for a moment. "Julia's death left a huge black hole in Dominic's life."

"I've heard." And now she knew why. Julia was a paragon of womanhood.

"Although you seem to have changed the recent course of Dominic's life." Melanie smiled. "I don't wish to offend you, so I'm trying to delicately skirt the subject of your and Dominic's relationship."

Kate lifted her brows faintly. "I'm not sure we have a relationship."

"I disagree," Melanie softly countered. "And that's why I'm pressing you when I've barely met you. But you see, Nicky has never brought anyone other than Julia over to our house. A woman, I mean. And he gave us all orders to be especially nice to you." Melanie smiled. "He just doesn't do things like that." She laughed. "So I'm really wondering if you cast some spell over him."

"If anyone's cast a spell over anyone, it's the other way around. I'm trying to keep my feet on the ground in a world I've never known. Dominic's wealth is overwhelming. He deals with it casually, tells me to do the same, but I can't. It's intimidating, he's intimidating at times. He doesn't take no for an answer." Another shrug. "But I'm deeply unhappy without him. He tells me he feels the same way, although honestly, I can't imagine someone like Dominic sustaining a 'relationship' for long." Kate made a sweeping gesture with her free hand. "There. All my cards are on the table."

"I like your honesty." Melanie leaned over and patted Kate's knee. "And I'm relieved. Most women are attracted to Dominic's wealth."

"He's aware of that, actually cynical about it. I'm not

sure he understands that money or not, he'd have women chasing him."

"Apparently his cynicism outweighs logic." Well aware of her brother's history with women, Melanie deliberately changed the subject. "Will you be traveling with Dominic?" she asked. "He never stays anywhere for long."

"No. We're on this vacation of his and then I have to go back to work."

"He said you won't work for him."

Kate took a small breath, debated how much to say, and chose discretion. "I wouldn't be comfortable working for him."

"Because?"

I'm jealous of every women he talks to—a real deterrent to harmony in the workplace. "It's just a personal preference."

"I'm sorry," Melanie quickly said, taking note of the embarrassment pinking Kate's cheeks. "I've really pried haven't I? But he's my baby brother."

"It's not a problem. I understand."

"Well, I'm pleased you like him," Melanie said. "And I'm pleased he brought you to visit and I'll keep my fingers crossed that you both get what you want."

"May I ask one more question? Dominic said your mother would be here tonight."

"Ask anything you like. As for Mother"—she paused—"I try to include her in family occasions as a courtesy."

"I don't know if you heard, but I met your mother in Hong Kong. At the time I wasn't aware of the therapists and—er—resentments. Now that I know some of what went on, I'm surprised Dominic was so—"

"Tolerant of her?" Melanie interposed. "That's because there's nothing Mother can do or say that touches him anymore. I'm not sure there ever really was. It was always just a struggle for supremacy and Nick won that war." Melanie grimaced faintly. "Although in the way of a preemptive apology, please don't take anything Mother says to heart tonight."

Kate smiled. "I won't."

"And if Mother does offend you, I'm sure Dominic will step in."

"Oh dear."

"No, no, you're not to blame. It's just that Mother takes pleasure in annoying Nick. He has no problem defending himself. He's really quite surefooted after all these years."

"He did seem impervious to her remarks that day in Hong Kong."

"He escaped home at thirteen and came to live with us. Since then, he's been irrepressibly independent. Mother is no more than an annoying asterisk in his life."

"Thirteen? Wow. He didn't mention that. He only said that he'd bought the house down the street when he was sixteen and that you signed for him."

"He was able to buy the house because our uncle left his business to him in a trust Nick could claim when he turned sixteen. Jordan had always been fond of Nick, often had him down to LA to visit, took him sailing. Uncle Jordan built racing yachts."

"*That's* where Dominic learned to love sailing."

Melanie nodded. "Jordan died at thirty, washed overboard in a storm at sea. Nick was thirteen. It was devastating for him. But thanks to Jordan, Nick was able to gain independence at a young age. Remind me to show you a photo of our uncle. He and Nick could have been twins. He was my father's brother," she added in explanation. "But Jordan didn't get along with my father any more than Nick did. That might have been part of their bond, although they had much more in common: surfing, sailing, their guitars, a nonconformist mind-set."

"I think I saw a photo of him in Dominic's bedroom," Kate said. "I thought it was Dominic in a masquerade costume: slicked-back hair, a white dinner jacket, a cigarette in one hand, a martini glass in the other, palm trees in the background. The image was pure playboy."

"No, that's Jordan. He *was* a playboy." Melanie smiled. "And apparently genetic imprinting is holding true in Nicky's case. But we're seeing a different side of him tonight with you," Melanie quickly added.

Kate blushed. "Thank you, but I'm remaining pragmatic about our—er—friendship. When I was researching Knight Enterprises before my interview, I read about all the women who have passed through his life. At the time I wondered if he ever slept?"

It was Melanie's turn to blush. "Not as much as he should. I wasn't going to mention it, but since you have— there have *always* been women," she said gently. "With the exception of his marriage, during which he was completely faithful, I'm not sure he's ever turned a woman down. But Nick seems very different with you. I mean it—genuinely different. Considerate, affectionate, happy." She grinned. "Roscoe's afraid Nick's sick because he's lost his laser focus on business. Have you met Roscoe?"

Kate shook her head. "I just know who he is."

"I assured Roscoe that Nick was fine. That maybe you were the sickness, as in love sickness," Melanie said with a little smile.

Wouldn't that be heavenly. "I doubt it," Kate said with a little shake of her head. "In fact, I'm determined to keep my feet firmly on the ground when it comes to anything even smacking of romance with Dominic. His dealings with women are casual and cursory." She raised her glass. "So here's to sanity." Putting the glass to her mouth, she drained it.

Melanie sighed. "I suppose that's sensible. Still"—she grinned—"I've always been a romantic. So fingers crossed. Ah—there's the timer on the ovens. Would you mind calling everyone in to dinner?" Coming to her feet, Melanie turned back to Kate. "And if there's ever anything I can do to help...if you ever have any questions about Dominic, please let me know. I think you're good for him," she finished politely. "Take it from me, Nick could use a little grounding."

The dinner table was noisy and festive. The children had all made simple birthday gifts for their mother. Dominic said, "You can open mine later. It's for your collection." Matt had given his gift before the party. Melanie blew out the thirty-eight candles on her cake with the help of her younger children and Mrs. B's pizza was fabulous. Dominic teased and joked with all the children, they clearly adored him; all of them sported dinosaur watches that Dominic had brought them, along with electronic, handheld games and Nicole's special gift of pearl earrings and a necklace.

Seated beside Kate, one arm on the back of her chair,

Dominic kissed her from time to time as if eight pairs of eyes weren't watching. She blushed each and every time. Melanie would nudge Matt and cast him knowing looks, the children pointed and giggled or, in the case of the young boys—eyes wide in horror—they'd moan, *"Ewww."*

To which Dominic would nonchalantly reply to their moans in variations on a theme. "Just wait. You'll find a girl you'll want to kiss someday. And Katherine tastes like pizza. Good pizza. So she's worth kissing."

During the course of the dinner, Dominic also coaxed Kate to relate some of her stories about Gramps's canoe business. He knew Matt and the boys would be interested. In fact, Matt wrote down the number of Hart Canoe Outfitters and promised the boys a trip to the Boundary Waters next summer.

"You should come too, Nick," he said.

"I might. I've never been there."

Kate shot him a look.

Dominic smiled. "You could be my guide. You must know the area."

"Blindfolded."

He lowered his mouth to her ear. "Speaking of blindfolds," he whispered.

She blushed even brighter red, her heart pumping overtime.

Melanie gave Dominic a reproachful look. "That's enough, Nick. Stop embarrassing the poor girl. She's going to get up from the table in a minute and leave you."

"We can't have that." He put up his hands. "I'll behave."

"You have my permission to kick him, Kate."

"Mom!" six-year-old Rafe exclaimed. "You said no kicking!"

"Your mom's just kidding, Rafe. Kicking's *wrong*," Dominic said, grinning at his sister.

"So is embarrassing someone," she said sharply. "Now, who wants cake?"

After the cake had been demolished, the children went to their rooms and the adults had time for a drink before the party guests arrived.

Dominic took a seat in one of the chairs by the windows, pulled Kate down on his lap, drew her back against his chest, and wrapped his arms around her. Matt and Melanie sat side by side on the sofa, Melanie tucked against Matt, his arm draped over her shoulder.

A small quiet descended in the aftermath of the dinner hubbub, only the sound of waves washing up on shore soft background noise.

Dominic smiled. "Really nice party, sis. Too bad all the others have to show up. Maybe we could turn out the lights?"

"You like some of the guests, Nick."

"I don't know about *like*."

"Inhospitable crank," she teased.

"Hey, all I do is deal with people twenty-four/seven. It's nice to take a break. We might not stay long." He dipped his head toward Kate. "Unless you want to, babe."

"It's up to you." Kate was being polite; her greatest pleasure was having Dominic to herself.

"Fair warning, sis, if you don't see us around. By the way, my staff from Lucia will make sure the kitchen is clean as an operating room before they leave since Mrs. B got on their case last time." Dominic glanced at his watch. "They should be here soon. My security crew will be coming and going once everyone arrives." *He didn't mention the added force that had arrived after them to patrol the perimeter.* "Leo's a fanatic. Sorry."

"Not a problem," Matt replied. Dominic had explained the situation to him when the children were busy with their presents. Neither man wanted the women to know the extent of the threat. "Guys with global empires need security," Matt added with a grin. "Unlike local contractors."

"Speaking of local contractors." Dominic pointed west. "Leo saw security at one of the houses they were remodeling up the block. They were checking the workers' IDs before they let them into the yard. Do we have a Russian oligarch in the neighborhood?"

Melanie lifted her brows. "A talk radio notable."

"With enemies?"

Matt grinned. "Or paranoia."

"Hmm, a different kind of enemy," Dominic murmured. "I hear the food trucks driving up." He whispered to Kate, lifted her from his lap, slid her to one side, and rose from the chair. "I'll get the door. I haven't seen Rudy or Slim for a while."

Kate discovered that Dominic owned one of the city's celebrated restaurants and Lucia catered Melanie's birthday each year. Soon the kitchen was bustling with chefs and servers, delicious aromas were beginning to waft through the house, and Dominic returned, carrying a tray of martini glasses.

He offered drinks to Melanie and Matt first, then set the tray on a table by Kate's chair. Lifting her up, he sat back down with her in his lap, handed her a glass, took his, and raised it in a toast. "This is a drink Katherine and I had our first night in Hong Kong compliments of Po at the Ritz-Carlton. To good memories." After they drank some of the martini, Dominic turned to Kate, kissed her cheek, and whispered, "The best memories, baby. Are you my girl?"

She nodded, too choked up to speak.

"You better be. You really look nice tonight," he added softly. "I always have the most beautiful girl at the party." Then put his mouth against her ear. "How's the bra?"

"Uncomfortable."

"I'll take it off later and kiss my tits, one by one, for suffering on my behalf." His voice dropped lower. "I suppose your nipples are all squished under that green lace. They're going to need some consolation. I'll suck on them until they're happy again. And when your nipples are stiff and throbbing, I'll spread your legs and put my hard dick inside you so slowly you'll be begging me for more. But I won't, I'll make you wait until I give you permission to come. And if you're very—"

"God, Dominic, don't...please—your sister." She dragged in a shaky breath as her body liquefied, melted, instantly keyed up into do-me mode.

"Sis can't hear. Do you want me buried deep inside you? Just nod," he softly teased.

"Jesus, stop," she hissed, the fierce ache between her legs ratcheting up. "I mean it, Dominic! We're not alone!"

"I can fix that, baby."

"No! Jesus, no!" she hoarsely whispered, raw desire spiraling outward from her core, streaking up her spine.

"Can you feel me?" His breath was warm against her

ear, his swelling erection nudging her bottom. "You'd like to feel me inside you, wouldn't you? Come on baby, say yes. There's plenty of time."

"Absolutely not!"

He grinned. "Now *that* they heard. God, I love when you blush. Do it for me again. They're looking at us. Tell me how many times you'd like to come. Two, three? We might even have time for four."

Her cheeks were aflame, her face glowing hot, her arousal visible for all to see. Jesus. She desperately tried to calm her breathing, glared at Dominic, struggled to keep from panting, and failed. "I...am...not doing this...at your...sister's house."

"Sure you are," Dominic whispered, recognizing the tremulous quiver underlying her words. "You like to come, baby. Lucky I'm here. No thanks, Matt, I still have part of my drink," he said calmly, answering his brother-in-law's query. "No, Katherine's good too. You like the flavor? I thought you would. Max was kind enough to get the recipe for me." Dominic shifted his position slightly to allow more room for his erection and was gratified to hear Katherine stifle a gasp. "Ah—you've seen the view then." He smiled at Matt. "I was trying to impress Katherine. You liked the view from the bar at the Ritz-Carlton, didn't you baby?" he said, as if he were asking if she preferred one lump or two for her tea.

"Yes, very much."

Awkwardly, her voice was no more than a whisper.

Dominic ignored the slightly stunned expressions on his sister's and brother-in-law's faces. Setting their glasses aside, he smoothly came to his feet with Kate in his arms, and pleasantly said, "I'm going to let Katherine freshen up before the guests arrive. We'll see you in five. Maybe ten," he added over his shoulder as he walked away.

"Take your time," Melanie called out cheerfully. "We still have twenty minutes before the guests arrive. And you certainly don't have to be here to greet them."

Matt grinned at his wife as Dominic walked away. "Why not just offer them our bedroom?"

"Nick's probably going there without an invitation."

"Jesus. Does the man have no boundaries?"

Melanie gave her husband one of those are-you-kidding-me looks.

"Okay, okay. But Nick actually seems to have feelings for Katherine. Unlike his usual arm candy who serve a purely sexual function. Definitely a first for him," Matt said drily.

"And truly awesome." Melanie's glance was bright, gloating. "He can't keep his hands off her. I've never seen Nick like that."

"Don't get your hopes up, honey. Nick's the least likely guy to go off the deep end over a woman. He just doesn't do that. Never has. You saw his marriage. They were fuck buddies, deep sea diving buddies, mountain climbing buddies. Need I go on?"

"I don't care what you say. Something's different this time. I'm a woman, I'm his sister. I can tell."

"I just don't want you to be disappointed when he walks away from her like he's walked away from the other five hundred. Think about it—okay? That's what he does. By the grace of God you came out of your screwed-up family in one piece. Dominic didn't."

SEVENTEEN

Kate slammed her fist into Dominic's chest. "Damn it, I am not doing this! Do you hear me! God only knows who might see us."

He didn't break stride. "Relax. I'm not going to fuck you in the hallway."

She snorted. "Oh, good, then there's no problem."

"Exactly," he said, ignoring her sarcasm.

"Goddamn it, Dominic. You can't just get up when we're having drinks with your sister and her husband and carry me away for a fuck."

"Baby, they don't care."

"I do!" she said, punching him with all her might. "I *fucking* do!"

She practically broke her hand and he didn't even flinch.

"Keep it down," he said, his voice as smooth as his stride, "or we'll have a pack of kids on us. And that *will* be a problem."

"So let me get this straight." Suppressed fury in her voice, her eyes, in the hot edge to her voice. "I have nothing to say about this? What I want or don't want doesn't matter?"

He shot her a quick, mild-as-hell look. "Jesus, don't give me that shit. You're wet and horny and you know it. This won't take long. We'll both come, you probably a few more times than me, then we'll go back and greet all the guests who I don't give a rat's ass about, you don't know, and neither of us wants to talk to. At least we'll both be in a fucking good mood. Think of it that way."

"Put it in such romantic terms, who wouldn't be delighted to join you in this escapade?"

He tried to repress his grin. "*Escapade?* Should I be wearing tights and a sword?"

"Asshole."

"Come on, baby, don't give me shit about whether this is romantic or not. If you had a choice between a Hallmark card and an orgasm, I know which one you'd chose."

She released a gusty sigh. "I'm not arguing the merits of coming, I'm arguing the venue."

"And I'm telling you the venue is fine." He stopped in front of a door, glanced up and down the hall, then leaned down, turned the knob, and kicked open the door.

Kate's eyes widened in shock at the photos of Dominic's nieces and nephews lining the walls. "Stop or I'll scream! I swear I will!"

Kate's muffled shriek ringing in his ears, Dominic came to an abrupt halt a foot into his sister's bedroom. "It's private," he said casually. "Isn't that what you wanted?"

She gave him a cold-eyed stare. "What I want is to be back in the kitchen drinking my drink."

"Bull."

"Well, I'm not doing it here, that's for sure."

At least the doing it part was no longer at issue. Softly exhaling, he swiveled around, surveyed the direction from which they'd come, then turned left and walked down another corridor. After passing two closed doors, he stopped, scanned left and right, then pressed the levered handle with his knee, pushed the door open with his foot, and stepped inside a green marble bathroom. Setting Kate down, he locked the door, turned back to her, and smiled. "Private enough?"

He watched her survey the large, luxurious room: marble walls and floor, decorative fixtures in crystal, a tub large enough for a family, a glass shower stall that overlooked a private courtyard, the whitest towels and rugs she'd ever seen.

She swung back to him, her lips pursed. "Whose bathroom is this? It's too far away to be your sister's, it's too palatial to be the children's."

The pause was less than a blink in time. "It's just an extra."

"Don't lie to me."

It was vaguely irritating—her peculiar way of looking at him sideways. Although it was obscenely sexy too, as if she were offering something besides her opinionated judgment. "It's Mrs. B's."

She groaned. "You should have lied."

"Christ," he said, "give me a hint if that's what you want. I'm trying to be a fucking Boy Scout so you don't get pissed."

She smiled up at him, looking triumphant. "I thought you said you wouldn't be doing any more ass-kissing."

He grinned back. "Sometimes ass-kissing is useful."

"Manipulative bastard."

"Whatever it takes, baby. You keep changing; the game

plan keeps changing." But he liked when she smiled like that—all dew-fresh sweetness so natural it should have a sell-by date on it. "I'm open to suggestions. We have twenty minutes. More if you want. There isn't one single party guest who interests me. The only person I want to see is right here," he said quietly, reaching out, curling his fingers around her shoulders, pulling her into his body. Bending his head, he touched her lips with his in a barely there sensation.

A young boy's kiss, she thought, her romantic sensibilities not entirely abandoned. Then he colored her romantic vision in pastel shades of perfect when he whispered, "You're the only person I ever want to see—in the morning, at night, and all the hours between."

"Good," she whispered back, because if she said any more, if she said what she really felt, his expression would turn blank, he'd shut down, and her vacation would be over.

Good? He bares his soul and he gets, *Good?* It struck him suddenly that her reasons for leaving him in Hong Kong could still be an issue, that his screwing around in the past had come back to bite him. God knows she wasn't like other women who would have swooned at his feet if he'd said as much to them. But he wanted what he wanted; he always had. So he raised his head and said with unprecedented sincerity, "I can make it better than good, Katherine. I can make it anything you want."

She smiled, understanding she was gambling with her life just being there, understanding as well the quiet power of her addiction. "I know. You're my Svengali. You can do anything."

That was better. He didn't realize how much it mat-

tered that she smiled like that—like she had on the Glory Girl. Maybe the time had come to retract his cardinal rule against emotional entanglement; admit his obsession with Katherine might be more than a temporary affair. He took a small steadying breath before he relinquished everything that made him feel comfortable, and he couldn't quite disguise the reluctance in his voice. "My doing anything includes waking up with you, seeing you at breakfast, knowing you're beside me during the day, holding you close at night." His voice dropped to a hush. "Come live with me, work for me if you like. Or, better yet, just be with me, don't work, make me happy."

She wanted to stop this moment in time. His reluctance aside, Dominic had offered her paradise. An unthinkable paradise, unfortunately, for mere mortals who didn't live in Dominic's rarified world. For people who couldn't just reach out and take whatever they wanted. For people like her. "Could we leave the big decisions for later and just make each other happy now?" she asked with forced calm.

He half smiled. "This bathroom's not romantic enough for you?"

"I'm just kinda shaky right now—that's a big agenda." *And a huge gamble for someone who wasn't a complete risk taker.* She wasn't a master of the universe who had the world at her feet. She had wanted this more than anything, but the fact that Dominic had left more women behind than she could count was a scary reality. "Could we talk about it later?" Intent on ending a conversation that was likely to end in heartbreak for her, she slid her hand to his zipper and began opening his fly.

Sex was their unambiguous connection, safe from scru-
ple or doubt.

Dominic almost insisted on a better answer because
he *was* a master of the universe, who fought for what he
wanted. But before he could take issue with her response,
his voice of reason whispered: *She just saved you from
yourself, dude.* Then any further thoughts were eradicated
from his mind when Kate pressed her warm palm against
the gap in his unzipped jeans and his erection spiked. Automatically moving his hands down Kate's back, he grasped
the hem of her blouse and lifted.

"No!" She shoved at his arms, panic banishing the
tumult in her brain. "We don't have time for that."

He flicked a glance at her hands on his upper arms.
"Let go."

Her fingers instantly slid away as though programmed
to obey his gruff tone. Then a heartbeat later, her rebellious
instincts kicked in. "If this is Mrs. B's bathroom, I don't
want to make a mess. Let's do something simple, minimum
undressing, nothing to clean up. Although," she added with
a small smile, "there might be an upside if I get to watch
you cleaning the bathroom." Her smile widened. "That
would be priceless."

"Or you on your hands and knees cleaning while I fuck
you," he said, drawing her hands to his chest, looking down
at her with amusement. "Now that's what I call priceless.
And don't worry about Mrs. B. She's not a problem."

Kate gave him a sharp look. "Don't you dare say
because you do this all the time in here."

"Okay."

"That's not the answer I want."

A lift of his brows. "Is this a lie or no lie situation? Give me a clue."

She scowled, tried to pull away. "Fucker."

"I just met you six weeks ago, baby," he said with inexhaustible patience and a steely grip. "I can't change the past."

"In sharp contrast, I don't have a past," she said huffily.

"One of your many charms," he said calmly, a ghost of a smile on his lips. "All that sexy innocence. It makes me crazy. I should lock you away. Or shackle you to my bed."

She shot him a look of pure incredulity. "That is so fucked up."

"Too unromantic?" he said with a straight face.

An eye roll, a delicate hiss to her voice when she spoke. "I've got news for you, Kemosabe. Check your calendar. We've moved past the dawn of time."

"I have a news flash for you," he said with the authority conferred by zero obligations and unlimited wealth. "I can do either one of those things. No problem."

Her eyes suddenly lit up with temper. "I'd fight you."

He smiled. "Even better."

"Jesus, you're a disrespectful shit." Each word was a hard, pugnacious zap.

He glanced down at the prominent bulge in his unzipped jeans. "Take it out," he said smoothly, "and we can discuss my being a disrespectful shit and your liking it. Come on." His voice was soft as he dropped her hands and unclasped the metal button on his waistband. Opening his fly wider, he shoved his boxers out of the way. "Slow and easy now. Watch the zipper."

She didn't move.

He softly exhaled, ignored her filthy look. "I have all night, hell—a week if you want. You're the one concerned about my sister. Should I turn on the TV while you're trying to make up your mind if you want to fuck or not?" he asked mildly, as if he didn't have a mammoth hard-on, as if he could control his dick like he controlled everything else in his world. "There's an NBA game I wouldn't mind watching." He reached for the remote on the two-sink vanity.

The bathroom was as big as her living room; even the TV was pretty huge for a bathroom—and placed conveniently on the wall at the foot of the marble tub. She shot a quick glance over her shoulder as he flicked on the TV and clicked on ESPN.

"Goddamn it," she spat. "Do you ever give an inch?"

He shifted his gaze from the TV to her. "You have no idea," he said drily. "We're not talking inches, we're talking miles, fucking continents. So stop breaking my balls."

"Really?"

"Yeah, really."

It was part grumble, part annoyance. It was also sweeter than hell because underneath he was saying he couldn't stay away. "I'm done breaking your balls." Her smile was filled with possibility. "I apologize for any inconvenience."

He laughed. "Thanks. I feel better now about you totally fucking up my life."

"Maybe I could make it up to you."

He hadn't heard that pure, clear willingness before, the unquestioning consent and permission. He didn't even think twice. He went for it. "Maybe you could take a look at my whips."

Her gaze came up swift and hot. "That doesn't do anything for me."

After a lifetime of docile women, he didn't actually mind her intransigence. He liked the challenge. But then he was on the distant shore of fucked up. "Let me file that away," he sardonically murmured, "for future reference. Right now, I'm waiting. He's waiting. Move."

"Watch it," she snapped. "Or your dick might suffer."

"You watch it. Or I might carry you out naked past all the gawking guests and screw you at home."

Her eyes were huge. "You wouldn't."

"I wouldn't take the gamble if I were you." His gaze flicked downward, then up, his brows faintly raised.

Her cheeks flushed, her mouth firmed, but she slid her hand down his stomach, curled her fingers around his erection, and carefully worked it up past his zipper.

"There's a good girl," he said pleasantly, as if he hadn't baldly coerced her. "Get on your knees, give him a little taste of your mouth, and then we'll decide how we're going to fuck. Your way or mine."

She shot him a poisonous look.

"If only looks could kill, Katherine," he drawled, his smile wicked. "I suggest you do what you're told, or a helluva lot of people will be seeing your amazingly fuckable body."

She lowered herself to her knees under his smug gaze, took his pulsing dick in her hands, and pulled it away from his body. His erection was hard as nails, she could feel the torque in her wrists as she hauled him downward to her mouth and licked a path up the velvety flesh.

He groaned softly, gripped her shoulders. "Slowly now," he murmured. "It's not a race."

She instinctively complied to his soft command, as though her senses were trained to respond, as though her body understood the rewards for compliance. Her nipples instantly peaked, her sex turned liquid, sybaritic anticipation coiled deep inside—ignoring all her unresolved resentments.

But his threat was real and whether she loved or hated his authority—either she did what he wanted or he'd carry her naked past all the guests.

She didn't, for a second, question his audacity.

Straightening her spine, she stretched to fully accommodate him with her mouth. Then, dipping her head, she readjusted her grip on his rigid dick, sliding her fingers upward slightly to guide his swollen crest to her mouth. Her jaw strained as she opened wide to ease what she could of the huge erection past her lips, her sex fluttering, warmth spreading between her legs as she selfishly wished his mouth were doing her, or better yet his dick.

"Deeper," he grunted, tapping her cheek.

If her mouth weren't full, she would have sworn at him. On the other hand, if she wanted to feel him inside her soon, if a selfish quid pro quo was on her agenda, she'd do well not to offend. In fact, might he oblige her now if she asked? She began to pull away to do just that when his hand cupped her head, dragged her back, and the broad, smooth head of his dick hit the back of her throat. He exhaled in a hoarse groan and as his quads gently flexed against her forearms, he breathed, "Jesus fucking Christ."

His strained expletive echoed hotly in her aching core. She felt her breathing quicken, heard Dominic's muted groans as he began to move again, and she experienced a small moment of triumph knowing she could do that to him. The ruthless master of the universe was vulnerable after all. She glanced up. His eyes were shut, his hands pressed against the door, his breathing ragged.

Sliding his fingers through her hair, he growled, "Don't stop," and forced the rhythm again—half choking her for a second until she grabbed one of his balls in warning. He swore, but his grip loosened. "Watch it, baby." He spoke in a rasp. "It's your toy too." Brushing the pad of his finger over the verge of her upper lip, he watched his dick slide in, dragged in a sharp breath at the fantastic rush, and then guided the motion more benevolently. Slowly in, her mouth warm and wet, her lips tensile slick as she sucked him in, the explosive jolt as the head of his dick prodded the back of her throat, so staggering each time his reflexes were momentarily numbed and he forgot to breathe. *Jesus fuck.* Then he'd come around, start breathing again, restlessly watch his dick slide out of her mouth, and wait for the next incredible head-banger kick.

It was unhurried splendor; Dominic wanted it to last. With both feet in the grave he'd still remember these moments, he thought, his low, muffled grunts calibrating the insane bliss, validating Katherine's truly fuckable mouth.

Dominic's deep, guttural intonations, his hoarse pleasure

sounds, reverberated with primal intensity through Kate's vulnerable senses, wildly provoked and aroused, as if her body were blindly in sync, as if her carnal passions automatically responded to his voiceless grunts, as if on some Darwinian level she was responding to Dominic as dominant male.

Her nipples were tight and hard, the throbbing deep inside audacious, her impatience for him, for sex, frenzied. He had only to exert his authority, insist on obedience, and she yielded with shameless anticipation. As if her body had been trained to recognize his cues, to submit without question, to uncompromisingly please him.

"Stop." A blunt, grating command, quickly effected, his palms pressing hard against her face, holding her in place, his dick filling her mouth.

Startled, her gaze came up in alarm.

"You okay? I'm not hurting you am I?"

His hands were warm on her cheeks, his fingers gently massaging his erection through her skin. She tried to shake her head in answer.

Whether he understood or her response didn't matter, he smiled. "Do you like when I have this much power over you? Do you like to service me, baby? I sure as hell like it," he murmured, clearly not requiring an answer. "Move now," he said softly, releasing his grip. "Slowly. Oh, fuck...that's good. You're learning, baby." He slowly exhaled, gently flexed his hips, shut his eyes briefly as she gasped, took him deeper, and the world went still for a second. "You're getting good at this," he breathed a moment later when his brain started up again. "Maybe we could teach you to *like* it rough. Maybe with enough repetition—you'll learn to like it any way I want." Grabbing her chin, he abruptly withdrew his dick, forced her head up. "What do you say, baby? You always like to come. You're willing to do just about anything for that, aren't you? So you'll learn, won't you? Answer me, baby." His fingers were leaving marks on her face; she couldn't move her head. "Blink for yes."

She dragged in a breath, tried to ignore the hard pulsing between her legs, the powerful raging lust screaming through her senses. A second passed, his fingers bit deeper. She blinked.

He smiled faintly. "Good girl. But then you have a real appetite for fucking, don't you?" he said, low-pitched, a strange steely undertone to his comment. Releasing her chin, he smoothed his fingertips over the angry red marks in a considering gesture, as though reviewing his options. Then he leaned over, slid his hands under her arms, lifted her to her feet. "Maybe it's time to teach you some useful skills. Undress for me. Leave your bra on. I like to see my tits bound. Clear?" Each word was clipped and brusque, uncompromising. "Speak, Katherine." He dipped his head, his smile wicked. "Or blink if you prefer. I'll get the message."

"You're such a prick," she hissed, even as every shimmering nerve ramped up for action, even as the moist ache of desire was making her desperate.

"But you want it anyway, don't you, baby?" he said gently, as if he had X-ray vision and could see her brain waves, her pulsing core. "Answer. You're wasting valuable fucking time."

She hated herself for wanting him, deep down and visceral, she really did. And for a flashing moment she wondered if she could refuse him. But she wasn't that self-sacrificing and he wouldn't let her anyway.

"Yes, you son of a bitch."

"You swear a lot. We're going to have to clean up your mouth."

"Fuck you."

His thousand-watt smile was instant and insolent. "Moody, but a recognizable verb. As soon as you're undressed, baby, we'll work on the fucking lessons."

Damn his breathtaking good looks and hard-ass body, his outrageous sex appeal and gigantic dick. Had a woman ever said no to him?

He lightly tapped her bottom lip in a flagrant gesture of possession. "I appreciate your interest, but get rid of the clothes." He swept a fingertip along the underside of one breast. "Remember, leave the bra on."

Lounging against the door, he watched her, his gaze half lidded while she slid off her shoes, unzipped her jeans, wiggled out of them. He looked amused as she folded her jeans and set them on the vanity. Then, slipping off her lace panties, she placed them on her jeans and turned to face him.

"Jesus Christ, Katherine." His voice was heated, his gaze in contrast, cool, assessing, an obscure emotion shimmering in its depths as he surveyed her standing there, small, shapely, her pubic hair gleaming damply between her legs, her big tits straining the fine lace. She looked even more naked with the dark green lace in sharp contrast to her pale skin, the half-undressed image blatantly erotic. The fact that she was standing there on his orders was messed up as hell and incalculably lurid.

And not just for him.

She shouldn't respond so predictably to his orders—so readily, so shamelessly. She shouldn't instantly capitulate just because he was too beautiful for words, or because some inexplicable crash of endorphins and pheromones spiked through her brain. She should have more sense. But he had only to look at her with that predatory gleam and she was flooded with sharp set desire, her body dissolved into a lustful puddle of want. And nothing else mattered.

"You look fantastic, baby. Your big tits locked in tight and everything else open for business." He went absolutely still. "Although with your randy pussy, maybe we should lock that up when I'm not around...Get you a chastity belt." His mouth pursed. "I don't suppose there's much call for those anymore. I'd like to have one made."

"Jesus, time out, freak." But her voice turned wispy at the end as a hot lewd jolt coiled like a pinwheel in her wetter than wet sex, making her dizzy with longing.

He gave her a knowing smile. "You like that? I thought you might. Gold or silver for your chastity belt, baby? We should probably put my name on it just to remind you who you belong to, who owns you. Because coercion turns you on, doesn't it? You like to be ordered to fuck me, don't you?"

"No." The single syllable was shaky.

He laughed. "That's a helluva needy sound, baby. You don't really mean no, do you?"

She wouldn't meet his gaze.

"Of course you don't," he said, answering for her. "A little discipline makes you cream your pussy. We both know that. Look at me, Katherine. I need an answer."

Her gaze came up, her nostrils flared. "Maybe."

His smile was wicked. "And maybe if I fuck the hell out of you we'll find out for sure." He pointed at his boots. "Kneel. Unlace them. This could take a while."

"Dominic, please. Everyone will know. Your sister." But even as she spoke, her body, her quivering senses, were begging him to fuck her.

"What about my sister?" he said, frost in his voice. "Kneel, baby." He pointed again. "Do it."

His expression was cold and ruthless; the man who gave orders that others obeyed. Not just here, but everywhere in the world.

"Dominic...please." She opened her mouth, hesitated under his chill gaze, moved closer instead, put her hand on his powerful arm, looked up. "Could the boots wait? I'm not saying no. I wish I could," she whispered. "But we shouldn't stay here too long."

He didn't move, his body held in check.

She rested her forehead on his chest. "Please?"

He was rigid at first, silent and unyielding at first, then he shifted slightly, slowly exhaled, and she felt the first stirring of hope. A split second passed, or it might have been years, then he looped his arms around her, ran his thumbs lightly up and down her spine, and brought his chin down on the top of her head. "Sorry, baby," he whispered. "I want you too much. It makes me crazy." He sounded tired.

"Me too," she said into his sweater, wishing that she

didn't want him so badly. That he wasn't so beautiful and strong and perfect. That she didn't have to lose her independence every single time he smiled at her.

If she hadn't had a month to recognize how powerfully she craved him, if she hadn't realized in Missoula that sex with just any man wasn't enough, if she didn't know that a month from now, or a week or even less than that, she might never see him again, she might have had more pride. Instead, she raised her face to him. "I'll unlace your boots, but let's not stay here long. If that's all right with you," she added, so deferentially he quickly scanned her face to see if she was taunting him.

Then she slid down onto her knees, which effectively answered that question.

"Ten, fifteen minutes," he said. "How's that?"

It was her turn to study his face.

Their eyes met.

"I just want to fuck you, baby," he said gently. "I don't want to fight. And look," he added with a sigh, lifting her to her feet. "I can undress myself." He ran his palms over her mounded, lace-covered breasts, slowly smiled. "But keep that on."

"Control freak." But she was smiling too, because she was astonishingly happy when he smiled like that, when she knew he wanted her as much as she wanted him.

"Yeah. No shit."

"I might *want* to undress you though." She held his gaze, touched the soft cashmere sweater. "Maybe I won't *let* you undress yourself."

He smiled. "Go for it, baby. Either way I win."

"We can argue about who wins the most later," she said, feeling purely forgiven and recklessly happy. She slid her hands under his sweater, up his ripped abs and taut rib cage, past his hard muscular pecs. Then he helped her pull the sweater off because she couldn't reach high enough even after he'd dipped his head.

He stood perfectly still after that, with the exception of his erection, which had a mind of its own. And he watched with pleasure as she knelt at his feet, unlaced his boots, tapped first one ankle then the other, and slipped them off. He raised his feet again so she could take off his socks. And he sucked in his breath when her hand brushed his dick as she slid his jeans and boxers down his hips.

She lifted her gaze, smiled at him. "I really wish we were home."

She'd said home. He couldn't remember ever feeling this good. "Same here," he said. "We won't stay long." Then he took her hand, led her to the chaise that overlooked the courtyard, sat, and pulled her down so she straddled his legs, adjusted his palms over the taut lace covering her creamy breasts, and said, "Tell me when you've had enough. Then it's my turn and we're out of here."

She placed her hands over his and said in a very small voice because she was beginning to tremble, "How long do we have to stay at the party?"

"An hour at the most...less," he said when he saw her pout. "I promised Nicole a chess game and if the game's over in ten minutes, she'll know it's bogus. Come watch me."

"I suppose I can't be completely selfish." Leaning in, she

took his face in her hands and kissed him because he was ridiculously beautiful and she couldn't resist.

He smiled when she sat back, wanting to give her the world when she kissed him like that. "Except for your orgasms," he said, knowing he could give her that right now. "You can be selfish there, baby."

"You're so sweet."

He laughed. "Let me get that in writing for the next argument." Placing his hands on her waist, he gently raised her, his twitching dick pretty much done with talking. And when she slowly lowered herself down his stiff cock, when they felt the fucking earth move, when they shut their eyes against the stark, raw, incredulous pleasure, they both wondered how one person could so completely and utterly change the world.

Once she was brim full and he was maxed out, and the warm, sumptuous pressure was sliding up their spines like velvet heat, he grabbed her bottom, flexed his fingers, held her firmly in place, and rolled his hips upward hard.

She gasped. "Again." A breathy, suffocated, muted sound.

Only audible to the man who was watching her like a hawk, feeling her quicken around him, knowing her hot-headed impatience. "Sure, baby."

Harder that time because he really wasn't sweet.

Her sharp cry added inches to his dick.

She was shaking.

"Too much?" he whispered, moving his hands up her back, gently stroking the dip of her spine. "Rest a minute?"

She dragged in a breath, nodded, and he lowered his

head and kissed her lips, softly, softly, soothing her jittery nerves. Then he bent his knees to offer her a support, eased her back, and traced her compressed nipples through the confining lace in slow, circular motions, his fingers exerting enough pressure for her to flinch.

He stopped. "Does it hurt?"

"Not very much."

He breathed in hard. "Jesus Christ, Katherine." His words emerged in a strangled rush of air, edgy, a white-knuckled voice. "No one else can have you." He rested his thumbs on her nipples. "What do you think of that?"

She looked up at him from under her lashes, the green of her eyes equatorial. "I don't want anyone else, Dominic."

He'd never heard his name spoken so beautifully. With challenge in every whispered syllable. And an undertone of possession as unfettered and unconditional as his.

"Thank you."

She took a small breath and he felt his thumbs slide over lace. "Pleasure's all mine," she whispered, her gaze flickering downward.

Slipping his thumbs under the rim of lace, he pried her nipples free, added his index fingers, and gently squeezed. "Tell me if I should ease up."

Her eyes were shut, her breathing shallow, the world dissolving from view.

"Or not," he said under his breath and, flexing his hips, he thrust upward, jacking his erection with ruthless intent at the same time he brutally compressed the soft flesh of her nipples.

She shrieked, then panted in explosive little bursts, then

moaned, low and whisper-soft as the most shocking pleasure battered her senses.

Dominic waited for his brain to stop detonating.

He didn't ask again after that.

He drove into her hot, slick sex over and over again,
then harder still, holding her captive, his fingers
ed on her nipples, not caring at first who came when
rst until he heard the familiar gasping sound she made
st prior to orgasm, felt her tense around his dick, and he
dragged himself out of the savage fantasy swirling like a
hurricane through his brain.

He paid careful attention to those small preorgasmic
whimpers he'd replayed over and over in his dreams that
month in Paris, the same ones he'd heard for real the past
two days, the sights and sounds that were etched so deeply
in his psyche that they'd probably be the last thing he'd
think of before he kissed off.

He smiled at the thought.

Then her high, thin wail began.

"Here, baby, we're here," he whispered, moving his
hands to her hips, locking his fingers hard to hold her
in place, arching his back and giving her everything she
needed. Holding himself where she wanted him most, feeling her convulsions ripple up his dick, watching her, gratified and content, as she climaxed with her usual unmuzzled,
free-wheeling abandon.

With Dominic her orgasmic pleasure was so ungodly
intense that she always came down off her high harboring the
faintest melancholy, knowing he'd always be her gold standard for pleasure, knowing he'd be impossible to replace.

Knowing she'd be without him someday.

And bereft.

But a moment later, with the warm, shimmering tremors still cutting a rapturous swath through her senses, she
dismissed her pensive thoughts. She had Dominic now,
tomorrow, perhaps longer. So carpe diem—until sh
out of road.

"That was fabulous as usual," she said with a grati
sigh. "But you know that, don't you, Mr. Knight."

"I didn't," he lied, his smile radiant enough to bathe th
entire world in sunshine. "Thank you, Miss Hart."

Her lashes drifted lower. "So," she whispered.

"Your call, baby." He moved inside, delicately, slowly.

She sucked in a breath. "Goddamn."

"You like?"

His expertise was the result of years of flagrant lechery
and an innate talent for fucking and while she might resent
the reasons for his expertise, she definitely benefitted from
them. So she really had no right to take issue. No more than
she had the right to sulkily murmur, "Sometimes I wish you
were a virgin."

"I feel the same way about you," he said, his voice suddenly razor sharp, his jealousy limitless.

"From now on, ours is an entirely monogamous relationship. My attorney will have the exclusivity contract
ready for us to sign tomorrow."

"You're serious."

"Did you think I wasn't? Did you think I ask just any
fucking woman to sign an exclusivity agreement with me?"

He was glaring. "Sorry," she breathed.

"You'd better fucking be sorry. Jesus, Katherine, when the hell are you going to get it? I'm not screwing around here. This is for real."

"I'm sorry," she whispered. "I understand."

"It's about fucking time you do." He dropped his head back against the chaise with a thud. Shut his eyes. Counted to ten enough times not to frighten her. Then he opened his eyes and said quietly, "Sometimes you're really stupid for a genius hacker."

"And sometimes you don't understand that I'm looking at a man who hasn't been serious about a woman since—when—how many years, Dominic? What the hell do you expect? Why would I think you've changed?" She gasped. "Jesus, does he ever go limp?"

"Not with you around. You're signing those papers tomorrow. End of discussion. Now, how many more times do you want to come?"

"I don't want to come at all when you're talking like—oh God...Jesus." She shut her eyes against the exquisite, spiking ecstasy. "Oh fuck." Pleasure lit up her brain as he thrust deep inside her again, rapture flared like wildfire through her body, melted hot and lustful through her sex, made her weak with longing and insatiable with desire and reduced her to a sordid mass of horniness.

"Change your mind, baby?" he murmured, straightening his legs, pulling her up so she was straddling his thighs, ruthlessly changing the subject, selfishly changing the subject, making sure Katherine would accommodate him now, on the contract tomorrow, always.

Fully aware of her taste for wild, audacious sex, when

she was panting hard and flushed and glowing, he said, sharply so she'd hear him through her frenzy, "First, you have to make me come, Katherine. That's an order. Don't you dare come first. Open your eyes, tell me you understand."

She struggled to open her eyes. "I don't know...if I can...wait."

"Of course you can. Because you know what will happen if you don't?"

Her eyes flared wide. "No, please."

"Yes, Katherine. Do it or I won't let you come for a week. Only a week this time, Katherine. That's not as bad as a year. Now, I know you can do it if you try. You learned how to wait in Hong Kong, didn't you? I need an answer."

"I'll try."

"That's not good enough, Katherine."

She took in a deep breath. "I won't come."

"There you go, baby. I knew you could do it. Now take your time. I'm not in a rush to climax. Jesus, Katherine, don't get all pissy. Don't I get a turn?"

But two minutes later, when it was obvious she wasn't going to be able to stem her orgasmic momentum, he slid his finger along the top of his erection, found her clit, pressed gently, and whispered, "Here, baby, let me help you."

She tensed, shook her head.

"No rules, baby. I'll come with you, okay?"

Throwing her arms around his neck, she dropped her head into the hollow of his throat, whispered, "Thank you, thank you, thank you," and began shuddering.

"Everything's good, baby," he whispered, feeling her spasms begin. "We'll go together." Holding her hips, his fingers splayed wide, her orgasmic screams echoing in his ears, he forced her thighs wider and drove deeper into her. He grunted with each powerful thrust and quickly came like he'd never come before, like he'd been starved for sex, like there was nothing in the world but need, sensation, then spectacular, fission-level relief.

For a man who'd had enough orgasms for ten lifetimes, he knew he was operating outside the normal perimeters of his life with Katherine. All he could think about was screwing her again. Wanting more. Right now. This second.

But she was shaking, so he caressed her shoulders, her back, comforting her, stroking her, soothing her. He kissed her lightly on the top of her head, her temples, on the curve of her cheek, until her tremors stopped. Then he turned her face up to him and kissed her mouth, gently, then deeper when he shouldn't, when they should get dressed and join the party.

She started to tremble again.

His cue to be sensible. He raised his head and sighed softly.

"We better make an appearance."

She groaned. "Do we have to?"

"I wish we didn't." He ran his hand through his hair, stared out the glass door to the darkened courtyard. Frowned. "Come on, baby." He sat up a little straighter, lifted her away from his shoulder, smiled faintly, and kissed her once on her pouty lips. "We'll make our excuses and leave as soon as we can. I promise."

EIGHTEEN

They were backing out of the bathroom kissing when they heard a disgusted, "Euuwww! Kissing again!" Quickly disengaging, they found six children staring at them: the two older girls smirking, the boys clearly revolted, and Ellie wide-eyed in her pajamas, clutching a teddy bear.

"Ready to play chess?" Nicole said with a world-class grin.

Dominic wanted to ask, *How long have you been here?* but he didn't really want to know. "Give me a couple minutes, Nicole. We have to check in with your mother."

"How long?" Nicole did a teenage eye roll that was part sass and part know-it-all. "We've been waiting *quite* a while."

He gave her a bland look. "I'll be up in five minutes. Now go back upstairs. You shouldn't be here in the first place."

"Mom didn't know where you went so we looked for you, that's all."

No shit. Stop grinning. "Fine, good. Set up the board. I'll be there soon."

As the children disappeared down the hall, Kate muttered, "Please, tell me that was a mirage and they really weren't here."

"Relax. Nicole's the only one old enough to know anything. The others are too young."

"Oh, good, that makes me feel better. Only one child knows we were fucking."

"You worry too much," he said casually, taking her hand and moving away. "Come on. Let's get this over with. The sooner we make an appearance the sooner we can leave. And the sooner I have you in my bedroom"—he grinned— "doing things for me."

"If you want me to do things for you," she said, giving him an unblinking stare, "I'm going to need a time frame for departure."

"Um—that sounds grumpy." He flashed her a smile. "Am I doing penance for something?"

"If you hadn't walked away from your sister, we wouldn't be in this mess."

"I'd be happy to take the blame," he said. "But you can't tell me you didn't enjoy yourself." He shot her a teasing look. "Or are you a better actress than I thought?"

"Shut up," she grumbled. "And I could have waited."

"No, you couldn't. You should be thanking me," he said blandly, dipping his head and kissing her lightly on the cheek. "I showed you a good time."

"You're impossible," she muttered.

"Just trying to keep up with you, baby. I've never met a more impossible woman—and I mean that in the nicest way," he dulcetly said.

She sighed softly. "I've just never been outed like that before."

Get used to it baby. His life was the National Enquirer *on steroids.* Dominic glanced at his watch. "We should be able to leave by nine. How's that?"

"It's fine as long as no one makes any remarks about—well . . . you know—us disappearing. Because that would be totally embarrassing."

"Just stay next to me," he said, squeezing her hand. "No one will say a word to you. And we'll be walking out the door at nine—I promise. Now give me a smile. Forty minutes and we're out of here."

They stopped in the kitchen first, ordered two of Po's martinis from the bartender, and while Kate was watching the bartender make the drinks so she'd know how to do it herself, Melanie came up behind Dominic and touched his arm.

He turned with a frown, his gaze on a sleek blonde beyond the kitchen lifting a champagne glass to her mouth. "Why is she here?" he asked in an undertone, lifting his chin slightly in her direction.

"Mother invited her." Melanie spoke as softly.

"I wonder what Mother promised her?"

"Really? I don't wonder for a second."

Dominic shot his sister a black look. "She never fucking quits, does she?"

"Not this side of the grave."

Dominic snorted softly. "Incentive to stay healthy and outlive her."

"Or turn saintly."

"That's for people like you, sis. People like me wouldn't recognize a saint if her halo was hitting me over the head."

"Mother's meddling aside, it looks like Charlie will be wasting her time tonight."

"Tonight or any night. I took her out a couple times, that's it. Why she's never given up is beyond me."

"You must have shown her a really good time."

Dominic glowered at his sister.

"You could have told Julia not to hire her. You should have," Melanie added firmly.

"Julia's NGO was her business. I never interfered."

"Except to fund it."

He shrugged. "It made her happy."

"You're too nice, Dominic. You should fire Charlie. Or have someone in your organization fire her. She doesn't have to work. She's just hoping to get her claws into you and she's willing to play her role as concerned citizen of the world while she's waiting to snare your fine ass."

"Good luck with that." He glanced over his shoulder at Kate, waited to catch her eye, then blew her a kiss.

Melanie gave her brother a teasing look. "You must have had fun with all your *freshening* up."

He turned back. "Off the charts. I'm a very lucky man."

"Lucky about what?" Kate asked, coming up, carrying their drinks.

"Lucky that I found you, baby." Taking his drink, he leaned in and kissed her. "I was just telling sis that we're not staying long. After the chess game with Nicole we're escaping."

"You should say hi to Roscoe," Melanie said. "He came in a few minutes ago."

"I will before we leave. I'll bring him one of these." Lifting the glass to his mouth, Dominic drained it and handed it to a passing server.

Melanie said, "I'd like to steal Katherine for a short time so she can meet Gretchen. She's my dearest friend," she added, smiling at Kate. "Dominic, tell Katherine she'll like Gretchen."

Kate looked at Dominic, pretended to smile.

"You'll like her. Really," he gently said, putting his arm around Kate's shoulder. "Gretchen's a partner in a cyber security firm. Stay with me if you like, but you might enjoy talking with her. She was ahead of you at MIT." He turned to his sister. "Gretchen's closer to my age than yours, right?"

"She's a year older than you. Give me five minutes," Melanie coaxed Kate, recognizing her reluctance. "Just come say a quick hi."

Putting his mouth to Kate's ear, Dominic murmured, "I'll expect you upstairs in five minutes." Then he turned Kate slightly and kissed her under everyone's fascinated gazes.

A small hiss ran through the crowd at the spectacle, because Dominic never engaged in open displays of affection. Caught up in the glow of the moment, bathed in happiness, Kate didn't hear the soft whisper of sound resonating around the room. She only delighted in Dominic's tender kiss—different from hot desire, sweet, almost wistful. "Okay," she whispered when his mouth lifted from hers, "I'll see you in five minutes."

"I'll be waiting." He glanced at his sister. "Don't keep Katherine too long." Then he smiled at Kate. "Follow the noise when you get upstairs. They're not a quiet bunch."

Melanie led Kate through the crowd, avoiding all the guests who were interested in meeting her after Dominic's very public kiss. Melanie merely nodded or smiled in passing, not slowing down to chat. "Most of these people won't be of interest to you," she murmured, waving at a couple who were openly staring. "Some are neighbors who'd be offended if they weren't invited, some are my friends, some are Matt's friends from work or play—he's a sports fanatic. There isn't a sport he doesn't play. Dominic's not much better. Then there are some of Mother's friends whom I try to avoid, ah—there's Gretchen." Melanie drew Kate to a young woman who was standing at the windows, gazing at the lights of a ship coming into the bay. She wore a pantsuit, as if she'd come from work, her dark hair expensively cut so it swung in a sleek, ebony wave when she turned at Melanie's greeting. A smile lit up her eyes. "Great party, Mel." She held up her flute. "Great bubbly."

"And why not? It's your vineyard," Melanie replied with a grin. "I'd like you to meet Katherine. She's Dominic's friend. Katherine Hart, Gretchen Calder."

After courtesies had been exchanged, Melanie offered a brief account of Kate's activities for Knight Enterprises. "Katherine did some consulting work for Dominic and tracked down a good deal of money that had been stolen from Knight Enterprises. Thanks to her expertise, it was returned. She's from your alma mater; you might have had professors in common. I think you'll be more interested in each other than anyone else here tonight. Refills anyone? No...then, I'll leave you two alone."

"Melanie should be a cruise director," Gretchen said as Dominic's sister walked away. "But she's right. Most of these people here are incredibly boring." She grinned. "How rude is that? Tell me about the stolen money."

Kate explained the Bucharest issue in broad terms and answered a few more detailed questions; the two women compared notes on illicit banking and the dark market. Both spoke the same obscure language, worked in the same free-wheeling, tech-savvy world where unhindered creativity was the bible and code vulnerabilities and encrypted operating systems were chapter and verse. In fact, they got along so famously, Kate readily accepted an invitation to lunch. "I'll give you a call when I know Dominic's schedule," she said.

"Anytime. I'll show you my operation." Gretchen smiled. "And my baby. I bring her to work with me."

"Sweet. The modern workplace in action."

"It helps when you're part owner."

They spoke for a few more minutes about Gretchen's baby girl, who was eight months old and already recognized pictures and words on the computer screen. Then when two other women joined them, Kate chatted for a few minutes more before excusing herself.

Dominic was right. When she reached the top of the stairs, the children's high-pitched voices echoed down the hallway. Following the sound, Kate came to a stop in the open doorway of what was obviously a young girl's room. Decorated in soft pink and apple green, a large canopied bed held center stage, framed posters dotted the walls, clothes were strewn everywhere, and a noisy game of chess was in progress.

Kate's gaze zeroed in on the women seated on either side of Dominic. The trio was on the bed, the women framing Dominic like matching bookends. Both blond, one with a tawny mane of hair, the other with frothy curls the color of pale dandelion down, their long-legged, elegant bodies were smoothed into wool slacks and tiny cashmere sweaters that showcased their perfect boobs, not too big, not too small—like they were special ordered to accommodate their form-fitting sweaters. Large diamond studs sparkled in their ears and the scent of their perfume was heady even at a distance.

They were as perfect as first-rate orthodontists, personal trainers, and cosmetologists could conceive, both women resplendently artificial with almost a plastic quality to their collective improvements. That they could have been clones for a thousand other expensively put together women was a bitchy judgment call, but nevertheless true. Neither woman had the smallest spark of vitality.

Ah—except for that.

One of the women was staring at her with squinty-eyed menace.

Whether that belligerent glance came with an audible sidebar or whether some random protective instinct kicked in, Dominic suddenly looked up.

He smiled. "Hi, baby. Come on in." He patted his knee. "Sit with me."

The chess table had been drawn up to the bed, Dominic and the women on one side, Nicole sitting opposite on a pink frilly chair, the other children either sitting or standing around the table, watching and kibitzing.

Dominic politely said, "Excuse me," to the woman on his left, indicating that she move, then raised his arms to Kate as she approached.

The tawny-haired blonde moved a minimum of six inches; Dominic frowned slightly, but didn't speak other than to whisper, "Missed you, baby," as he pulled Kate onto his lap.

"And you are?" the sleek blonde said, scowling at Kate.

"Katherine, this is Charlie and"—Dominic nodded to his right—"Angela."

"Don't ask," Charlie said, her smile cool. "It's a family name."

That wasn't what she was going to ask. Kate was going to ask what she thought she was doing sitting so close to Dominic she was giving him friction burns. But Nana wouldn't approve if she was openly rude so she said, "Nice name," and smiled instead.

"Are you from around here?" Angela's gaze was arctic.

Kate shook her head. "No."

A pursed mouth, a calculating up and down look. "Where *are* you from?"

Kate debated for a second, tempted to say Mars. "Minnesota and Boston mostly."

Angela raised one perfectly plucked and dyed eyebrow. "Harvard?"

"No."

"I didn't think so," the frothy blonde said with a jeering smile. "What *do* you *do*?"

"I work in IT."

"Is that how you know Dominic? You *worked* for him?" Angela's emphasis on the verb suggested that work was for those poor souls without substantial trust funds.

Really, Nana, do I have to be nice? Kate inwardly sighed. "Yes, I worked on a project for him."

Dominic glanced up from the chess board while Nicole

was deciding on her next move and put an end to the rude interrogation. "I'd like Katherine to become involved in the company full time, but she won't. She wants to be independent. Isn't that so, baby?" He brushed her cheek with his fingers in a small reverential gesture. "I'm trying to talk her out of it. I'd like her to stay with me and make me happy instead. So far, no luck. But I'm not giving up."

If that wasn't pure heaven, it was only a cloud away, Kate decided. How sweet of Dominic to stake his claim in such a public way. She couldn't have scripted a better response if she'd tried and the blondes' shock and indignation was just the icing on the cake.

At the sight of the women's gaping mouths, Dominic tugged Kate closer and turned his attention back to the game. Clearly his message had gotten through. "Hey, Nicole, just a sec. Sure you want to do that? My bishop's just sitting out here"—he pointed to the edge of the board—"waiting for your hand to lift from that rook. Come on, think."

Nicole moved her rook out of danger.

"Good girl. That's better. Now I'm going to move my knight and he's always a threat. So pay attention. Katherine's a good chess player. She could give you a few pointers. She beat me in Hong Kong."

"She did?" A chorus of voices, six youthful pairs of eyes swung to Kate.

"Yup," Dominic said.

The six pairs of eyes swung back to Dominic. "For real?"

"Darn right. Katherine's really good. She knows what she's doing. Here, help Nicole and we'll show them."

Dominic dipped his head a little and smiled at Kate. "Feel like helping?"

After his kick-ass defense of her, Kate was willing to do just about anything for Dominic, his words still warming her world by a couple hundred degrees. "Sure. No problem." She smiled at Nicole. "Let's see if we can take your uncle down. Okay?"

"Julia used to play chess with you, didn't she, Dominic?" Charlie snidely interposed. "I remember her saying what a good player you were."

"She didn't actually play much," Dominic said coolly. "She was trying to learn." He turned to Kate and smiled. "Ready to take me on, baby?"

At which point, two glowering, seriously frustrated women melted into the background.

Dominic and Kate played for blood as usual—both averse to failure.

Since the children had been playing with Dominic for years, they were all heatedly involved in the game, giving advice, shouting instructions, jumping up and down when someone made a slick move. Even Ellie understood when something good happened and she'd smile around her teddy bear's wet ear and the thumb in her mouth.

Toward the end Kate and Nicole were playing keep away with their king and one knight, with Dominic aggressively in pursuit. They were staying out of trouble, but it was only a matter of time before Dominic finally checkmated them.

"Took you long enough," Kate said, smiling.

He grinned. "You're a real pain in the butt to catch. I

was wondering how long you were going to keep your king on that safe square." He wasn't really. He knew she'd make a break for it. Katherine never played safe for long.

"Another game, another game!" the children screamed.

"We can't," Dominic said. "I promised Katherine a walk on the beach tonight. We'll play some other time."

"Tomorrow! Early!" A clamor of shouting that was satisfied only after a glance passed between Dominic and Kate.

"Tomorrow, but not early," Dominic warned. "We'll text you." Lifting Kate to her feet, he rose from the bed and politely glanced at the two pouting women. "Good to see you again," he said, then turned back to the children. "Okay, kids, practice on your own. We'll see who wins tomorrow."

"Hug, hug!" Ellie squealed, jumping up and down on the chair where she and her teddy bear had viewed the game.

Bending down, Dominic picked up the toddler, hugged her, gave her a kiss, and set her down. "Anyone else?" he said, surveying the other children with a faint smile.

They all wanted hugs, even the boys, who were trying to be grown up.

Even Nicole, who hung back at first until Dominic winked at her and she rushed into his open arms.

"Nicole's almost past the hug stage. She's growing up so fast," Dominic said a moment later as he and Kate moved down the hallway. "I remember when she was born."

"They're great kids. Do you think you should have let Nicole win?"

"Did you want me to?"

She shrugged. "I can't decide."

"Did Gramps let you win?"

"I think he might have every once in a while."

"Give me a look then next time. I can do that. See, you're making me a better person."

"You're doing pretty well on your own. The children all love you."

The sudden silence was awkward, the word *love* suddenly lighting up their brains.

They both started talking at once.

"You first," Dominic said, cautious in the face of danger.

"I was just going to say you left two very disappointed women behind," Kate said, sensibly dismissing notions of love. "I think they were hopeful."

"They shouldn't be."

"They're both lovely." *Truthfully they were. Perfect in a plastic sort of way.*

He shrugged. "If you say so."

"How well do you know them? Forget it. You don't have to tell me. Really, I don't know why I asked."

"Yeah, you do. Because you're jealous like me. And I hate it," he muttered. "It's driving me nuts as much as you are. Look, I took them out a few times years ago. That's it."

"Jesus. Hope springs eternal then. Or are they recently divorced or something?"

"Haven't a clue. They're not on my radar."

"Friends of Melanie's?"

"More or less." He blew out a small breath. "Women like Charlie and Angela are attracted to my money. They don't know how boring I am. Work, work, and more work. That's all I do."

"Maybe they like your dick too." That kind of hard-eyed, determined possessiveness she'd just witnessed wasn't just about money.

"Let's not go there," he said softly, holding out his hand for her as they reached the top of the stairs. "It doesn't matter what they like. Let's talk about something else."

"Are we really going for a walk on the beach?"

He smiled. "Thank you. Your tact is admirable. And yes, if you don't mind. I'd like to show you my bridge."

"Your bridge?" she said drolly, flirtation always safer than actual emotion.

He grinned. "It is when I'm home. And I want you to see it. Now, let me find Roscoe," he said when they came to the bottom of the stairs. "I'll say a few words and we can leave"—he glanced at his Santos watch—"right on schedule."

Roscoe didn't look at all like Kate had imagined. She knew he was older, so she'd anticipated someone overweight, bald or graying, a few wrinkles.

He was dressed in jeans and a gray silk long-sleeved shirt buttoned at the neck, his blond hair long like Dominic's, his lean face tanned, and either he'd had some good cosmetic surgery or he had good genes. He didn't look a day over forty.

"So you're the sorceress," he said gruffly when Dominic introduced her.

"Uh-uh, Roscoe, Katherine's my good luck charm. Life's been much better since I met her. So be nice." Although he was already; Roscoe's voice was perfectly modulated rather than his usual wake-the-dead volume.

Roscoe smiled. "Thanks for bringing in the twenty mil."

Dominic had said Roscoe had been married twice. She could see how women would like him. That was a very nice smile. "My pleasure."

"You should work for us."

"I'd rather not, but thank you."

He lifted his brows to Dominic. "What the hell's wrong with you Nick? Can't you make her an offer she can't refuse?"

"I'm trying, Roscoe. But she doesn't care about money. How do you deal with that?"

"I'm sure you'll think of something," Roscoe murmured. "If you have a minute, I'd like to talk about a couple things."

Dominic gave Kate a searching glance. "Do you mind, baby? Five minutes?"

"I'll go find Gretchen. Come get me when you're finished."

"See, Roscoe? Is she perfect or what?" He took Kate by the shoulders and spun her around. "There's Gretchen. Five minutes, I'll come get you."

Kate went to the kitchen first because Po's martini was like the nectar of the gods and she was addicted. She'd find Gretchen once she had her drink.

But she'd just reached the counter where the bartender was working and ordered her drink, when a man's voice close to her ear, said, "Dominic has excellent taste as usual."

She turned to find a tall, tanned, fair-haired man smiling at her and wondered if all Dominic's friends looked like California surfers.

"Kip Watson," he said with a dip of his head. "I can't tell

you how pleased I am to meet you." His voice was soft and low, a playful twinkle in his eyes.

"Katherine Hart. Nice to meet you."

"You're not from around here." He grinned. "Fargo?"

"Everyone says that. And I don't think I have an accent."

"It's charming. Don't change it. Can I get you a drink?"

"I've ordered, thanks."

"Will you be around long?" His gaze slowly raked her figure before returning to her face. "I'm saying a little prayer here. Tell me yes," he said, his smile slow and easy.

"I'm not sure." She shrugged faintly.

"That's better than a no. May I take you to dinner some night?"

"No, you can't," Dominic said, coming up and slipping his arm around Kate's shoulder. "She's mine."

"Mine?" Kip lazily arched his brows. "What the hell does that mean?"

"It means back off, Kip, or I'll break your neck," Dominic said with the same lazy arch of his brows.

Kip's smile was smug, a little swagger in his voice. "You're not a teenager on the beach intimidating some rogue surfer, Nick. Those days are long gone."

"I know exactly where and who I am," Dominic said quietly, his glittering blue gaze squarely focused on Kip.

"So you're not going to do anything to me."

"I wouldn't count on it."

"Here? In Mel's house? Who the hell are you kidding?"

"Did I say I'd do it here? I don't remember saying that. But I remember saying I'll break your neck"—Dominic drew in a small breath—"if you get anywhere near Katherine." He leaned forward slightly, aggression straining every nerve, his quiet voice deadly. "And that's a promise. So stay the fuck away from her."

Slack-jawed, fear passed over Kip's features with hurtling speed—like a movie clip in double time.

"Now get the hell out," Dominic said, very, very softly.

Terror-stricken, Kip looked like a deer in the headlights.

"Would you like help?"

The whispered words acted like the crack of a whip.

Kip leaped back, spun around, and fled.

"How's that?" Dominic nuzzled Kate's cheek. "No scene. I didn't even raise my voice."

She turned and looked up. "Break his neck. Really?" she said, with mild surprise. "Do you think you might have overreacted just a tad?"

Dominic frowned. "Kip's an asshole on his best day. You don't know him like I do. It wasn't really a dinner invitation."

"I wouldn't have said yes."

"He had no right asking," Dominic said curtly.

"You can't threaten everyone who comes near me."

He could and he would. "Sorry, babe." He lightened his tone. "Maybe Kip just got to me."

She gave him one of her sidelong looks. "Did you fight a lot when you were young?"

It took him a moment to answer, his teenage years fully engaged: school, sports, sex, surfing. He was busy. "I don't know about *a lot* of fights. But between seething hostility over family issues and raging hormones"—he shrugged—"I had a fight or two. I wasn't the only one. Teenage boys, what can I say? It seemed as though there was always some dude on the beach who was trying to prove something. And I played football, so I knocked a few heads around there, but nothing out of the ordinary. I played baseball too, but that's not a contact sport." No way he was going to mention the endless sex—which *was* a contact sport. "I didn't sit around much, but I never went looking for a fight. If that's what you were wondering." He smiled his most charming smile, the one that salved female peevishness and displeasure; the one that had gotten a helluva lot of use. "Are we good now? Am I normal enough not to make you nervous? Can we get out of here?"

But it took them another half hour to reach the door because everyone wanted to talk to Dominic or get a closer look at the woman everyone was so curious to meet.

Those who wanted to talk to Dominic were almost entirely women, but he side-stepped most of them with a smile and a few brief words, until one woman grabbed his arm and wouldn't let go.

She was like so many of the women here tonight: elegant, slender, well-dressed, well-coiffed, beautiful.

"Come for coffee sometime," she said, breathy and soft. "Anytime."

"I'll check with Katherine," Dominic said, gently freeing himself from her grip. "She's running our schedule. How are Joe and the kids?"

The woman didn't seem to hear or comprehend. "I really miss you," she whispered.

"Thanks, Bets. I'm sorry," he softly said, backing away toward the door, "but we're on our way out."

Before Kate could fall prey to the realization that the scene she just witnessed might well be her shortly, her melancholy thought was swept aside by the sound of a sharp, familiar voice.

"You should get a haircut, Dominic."

Letitia Knight was standing stiffly between them and the door, a sneer on her perfect face, her pink manicured fingers clasped at her waist in a pose reminiscent of the queen on a walkabout. Only the purse was missing.

Dominic came to a stop. "If I wanted a haircut, Mother, I'd get one."

She sniffed. "You're not a surfer any longer."

"What makes you think that?" he said pleasantly.

A quick condescending glance Kate's way. "I see Miss Hart is still keeping you company."

"Yes, she is. I feel very fortunate. Is there something on your mind?"

"Charlie said you were dismissive of her, actually rude to her."

"And that's of interest to you because?"

"Because her mother is a dear friend of mine. I expect you to be more courteous."

"Don't expect anything from me, Mother. That ship sailed years ago. Now, if you'll excuse us, we're leaving." When she didn't move, Dominic dropped Kate's hand, walked up to his mother, and said very quietly, "Please move, Mother." He dipped his head, his gaze completely blank. "You're in my way."

She moved.

"Wise choice," he murmured. Then he turned, walked

to the closet, took out Kate's raincoat, helped her on with it under Letitia's gelid gaze, and without further communication with his mother, guided Kate to the door.

A moment later, they stood outside.

"Sorry about that," he said with a small sigh. "I was hoping to avoid her."

"Don't be sorry. She's of no significance to me."

He smiled. "Another area of agreement for us." He looked up. "Hi, Leo. Everything quiet?"

Leo came out of the shadows. "Everything's fine."

"It was a nice party but we'd both rather be home."

"Don't blame you."

Dominic took Kate's hand and started walking. "Let's take a rain check on the bridge tonight," he said quietly, trying to shake away his mother's confrontation, wondering why she'd irritated him more than usual tonight. "Suddenly, home is more appealing."

"You don't have to convince me to stay in. I like being alone with you."

He softly exhaled. "Same here, baby. We're both tapping into the same good vibe."

His mother had gotten to him, she thought. And why wouldn't she? It was all fine and good to sweep all that misery under the rug, but it surfaced from time to time. Or it was deliberately provoked by Letitia Knight.

The cold-hearted bitch had been waiting for him.

NINETEEN

I left our phones charging next door," Dominic said as they entered his bedroom. "Be right back."

In a few moments, he returned through the connecting door to his small office, barefoot now. Moving to the bed, he held out Kate's phone. "Roscoe said I have some e-mails I should look at. He's been deleting what he can. Maybe Nana left you a message. Did you tell her you were here?"

"Not yet." Kate turned on her cell.

He grinned. "Or ever?"

She did an eye roll. "I'm thinking about it."

"Let me know if I should say hi if you call her," he teased, dropping onto the bed, pulling some pillows behind his head, stretching out beside Kate, and scrolling through his remaining e-mails. He'd deleted the one from Leo with the time and place for his meeting with Gora.

"Jeez! I have another job offer! Wow!" Kate quickly sat up, stared at the screen, read the entire e-mail, then handed it to Dominic. "CX Capital liked my work in Singapore."

"And why wouldn't they?" he said with an approving smile. "You're the cyber wizard who can always find the missing loot." Setting down his phone, he took hers and read the message he'd been waiting for. "Congratulations." He handed her phone back. "The money's not bad either."

"It's huge! Well, not compared to your idea of money,"

she said with a small smile, leaning over and placing her phone on the bedside table. "But some of us are used to living on scholarships and ramen noodles. Did you see they have a sublet apartment available for me?"

"They really want you, baby. Although you could stay at my place in London if you like."

"Don't be mad if I say no. Okay?"

He smiled. "I won't be, Miss Independent. See, I'm learning. So, does the job sound like something you'd like to do?"

"Does it ever! They have some major security vulnerabilities they need closed. Is that fun or what?"

Dominic laughed. "Apparently."

"I don't have to be there until next week," she said softly. "I'm glad."

"Me too. We still have a few days then." He reached out and pulled her on top of him. "Just us." He lifted his head from the pillow, kissed her, and, dropping back, said quietly, "I'm happy for you, baby."

"Thanks. I love what I do."

"It's a good feeling, isn't it?" He smiled. "I'll fly you to London. Tell them you don't need a plane ticket. Once you're settled in, I have to go to Rome. Business," he added. His meeting with Gora was scheduled for Tuesday.

"Because you've put everything on hold for a week."

He nodded. "Things can wait. I'd rather be with you while I can. Especially if you're going to be working again."

The words *I'd rather be with you while I can* triggered all her insecurities about time, or rather their lack of time, exclusivity contract or not. There were enormous dangers in loving someone like Dominic Knight. No matter what he said, the pattern of his relationships was a huge red flag. As were all the women he'd politely evaded at the party tonight. And her jealousy was like a fire-breathing beast— not even close to tame. So even though she should have left well enough alone, accepted her place in the manifold ranks of women who'd passed through Dominic's life, and counted her goddamn blessings, she said, "Who's Bets?"

"Why?" His clear gaze was on her, his voice mellow.

"Because she seemed to really miss you, that's why."

"*You* don't have to miss me," he said, ignoring her question. "You're already welcome in my life." He reached up and touched her cheek with his palm. "I don't know how many times I have to tell you that."

"You didn't answer. Who is she?"

"Bets is someone who needs someone," he said, the quiet affirmation in his voice not meant to persuade but to confirm.

"Not just any someone. You."

"I can't help that. She can't have me." He ran a slow hand through her tousled hair. "You can have me if you like."

She took a small breath, rolled off him, sat up, and gave him a shaky smile.

He suddenly wished like hell they'd never gone to the party. Or that Betsy hadn't gone to the party. Or that he could think of some excuse that would placate Katherine. His mind was blank; he must be more tired than he thought.

"I know I'm supposed to be coy and not rock the boat with a big-time player like you," Kate said, her voice very quiet despite the determined look on her face.

Not good, he thought. *Katherine determined.*

"But I've never been coy or cautious, so here goes. I love you. You don't have to love me back. You probably couldn't even if I wanted you to. But it's all I can think of— even when I know how colossally stupid it is to love someone like you. It's on my mind all the time, every minute, every second, so I'm telling you."

It wasn't about Bets. That would have been easier.

The silence lengthened.

"Say something."

His gaze was shuttered. "What do you want me to say?"

"I think I've heard that line before. But this isn't a multiple choice question. Tell me what you're thinking."

He smiled faintly. "I'm thinking that I wish you weren't asking me to tell you what I was thinking."

"Why?"

"Because I don't want to piss you off."

This time she smiled just a little. "That bad, hey?"

"No, it's not bad. Nothing about you is bad. It's just that I don't know what I'm thinking. My brain doesn't work like that."

"Are you uncomfortable? Uncertain?" She grinned, feeling elated now that she'd made her confession; all the pressure of not talking about her feelings was gone. "Are you wishing I'd shut up?"

"Yes."

Her brows rose. She'd rather know than not know. And it wasn't as though she seriously expected Dominic to hand her a ring.

"Yes to all that." An almost inaudible sigh, then his lashes lifted and he gave her a long critical look. "Look, baby, you don't understand," he said softly, his blue eyes surprisingly open now. "No one ever asks me what I'm feeling. And even if they did, I'm guessing those doors were closed and locked long ago. I don't sort out my feelings, I don't know how. In any case, they're irrelevant to the actions I take. My activities are based on pragmatic decisions."

"Am I a pragmatic decision?"

"I knew you were going to say that," he grumbled, raking his hand through his hair, hitting his knuckles on the headboard and wincing. He rubbed his knuckles, dropped his hand on the bed. "I don't know what you are. I don't know what fucking day it is when I'm screwing you or waiting to screw you and just finished screwing you. You've made my life a total take-no-prisoners clusterfuck. This is the second time I've walked away from my world for you, because of you...because of my obsession with you. So you might be in love, I don't know what that means, but I'm fucking *involved*, if that's what you're wondering—in ways I've never been before." He scowled at her. "But that's all I know. Don't expect me to know what love is. I don't."

"Even with your wife you didn't know about love?" She shouldn't have said it; she knew she shouldn't have even before his whole body went completely rigid.

"I'm not talking about Julia," he said tightly.

"But I want to know," she said bluntly, staring him down. "So you might as well tell me."

He didn't say anything for a long time.

"I can outlast you," she whispered. "Or maybe I should

start undressing." She gave him an impudent smile. "That always gets your attention."

He gave her a nasty look. "I don't know why the fuck I put up with you."

"Because I don't roll over like the rest of them. I make you work for it. So tell me."

She saw him flex his hands into fists, saw him stretch his fingers wide, figured he was trying to decide how little to tell her.

He looked at her with visible unease and when he finally spoke, his voice was so soft she had to lean in slightly to hear him. "I thought I knew what wanting someone meant. Being with them, doing things together, liking the same people, the same activities, never arguing. I never knew it could be like this, like it is with you." He took a breath before he went on. "Julia was my best friend, my companion. You're my obsession, my craziness, my waking dream. So if you're wondering how I feel? I'm here. When I could be a thousand other places." A muscle twitched along his jaw. "What I don't know is how long these feelings will last, whether this—us—will last. Whether we'll feel the same way about each other at the same time—now, tomorrow...whenever. That's all unknown and I don't deal well with unknowns. Also, you're very young. You haven't lived much, while I've stretched the limits of excess, lived an unchecked and incorrigible life. And while I'm not completely altruistic, your innocence is a consideration. The fact that I might be taking advantage of that innocence is a consideration. You should have choices. And I'm not sure I want to give you those choices."

"Done now?"

He shrugged. "I guess."

"Okay. A couple things. First, I don't love you kindly, like some Jane Austen heroine who's going to pine away if you leave me. Or at least I won't pine forever. I'll find someone else. Everyone does. But right now, right this minute, I love you like I'm on fire, or in the eye of a hurricane; I love you wildly, maybe even violently. I'm not a Bets, whatever her deal is. Don't get me wrong. I'd miss you like hell. I did last time. But I wouldn't have come after you. I just wouldn't. If you don't want me, I figure it's your loss." She grinned. "Arrogant bitch, hey? But then you know about arrogance, don't you?"

"Probably." He smiled faintly. "It sounds as if you've got this pretty well covered?"

"I've been thinking about telling you for a while. And watching all those women tonight, wanting you to notice them, talk to them, give them a smile, made it super clear that if you didn't want me, I couldn't make you want me." Her lashes dipped slightly. "See—maybe I'm pragmatic too."

"As for the second thing," she said matter-of-factly, "I figure we have what, three, four more days to enjoy ourselves. So I'm willing to put aside the loving stuff if you tell me what you're going to do for me"—she fluttered her lashes in flirtatious parody—"*right this minute.*"

He laughed, rolled up, grabbed her, and swung her back on top of his long, lean, powerful body. "I've got a few things in mind," he murmured. "Interested?"

"Hell, yeah. I'm like you. I prefer fucking to talking." She grinned. "But I just wanted to clear the air, reconcile the tumult in my brain, put that long-burning fuse out before the powder blows. And now," she playfully purred, "are you going to entertain me?"

"We'll do our best, baby." He gave her a quick kiss, lifted her away, dropped her on the bed. "Be right back," he said, feeling like he could climb ten mountains and still keep going, feeling invincible. "By the way, I'm in a possessive mood," he added over his shoulder. "Just sayin'."

"Sounds intriguing."

"Glad to hear it. Because you don't have a choice."

When he walked back into the bedroom, Kate put up her arm and grinned. "Just stand there. I can come just looking at you." Wearing only black jeans, Dominic was broad-shouldered, hard-muscled eye candy.

He held out his cupped hands to show her what he had and kept walking. "You're going to come even better with these." Reaching the bed, he sat beside her. "Here're the accessories for the evening." He tipped his palms and dropped several items on the bed. "You can rate them for me later."

"Jeez, I don't know if I should be excited or nervous."

Ignoring her comment, he gestured at the tumbled pile on the bed. "Need a rundown?"

She took a small breath. "Just those." She pointed at the three pieces of jewelry. The silk scarf, soft brush, rubber dildo, and lube didn't need explanation. The two bracelets just looked like bracelets, and the pearl necklace was equally innocuous.

He picked up one of the three-quarter-inch wide gold cuff bracelets, snapped open the hinge, gave a half twist to the diamond clasp, and gently drew out a four-inch gold chain. Repeating the process with the second bracelet, he screwed the two diamond clasps together, stretched out the now eight-inch chain, folded the hinges to close the bracelets, and held up a pair of very expensive handcuffs. He smiled faintly. "Function clear?"

She ran her finger inside one bracelet. *Property of Dominic Knight* was engraved in a large font. She glanced up and said wryly, "Vanity or arrogance?" *Return for Reward* was in a smaller script but easily visible too. "And is the reward for the return of the bracelets or me?"

He shrugged. "I'm just protecting my interests," he said ambiguously. "I told you I was possessive."

"Jesus, do you mind? That's a mile or so past possessive."

"It's never been a problem for you before." His voice was deliberately bland.

"I've never seen this degree of presumption before."

"I'll keep that in mind."

"And I'll keep in mind that I get to say no."

"If you want to." He smiled. "Maybe you won't."

He said that way too confidently. "So tell me, Mr. Property of. How many of these have you bought before?"

"There's no before, baby. Just these. That's it You're my holy grail."

A faint lift of her brows. "You'll forgive me if I don't believe you."

"You're forgiven. But it's the truth." In the past, he was supplied with marketplace equipment for his sexual amusements, just like he was supplied with the women. He'd never bought anything himself before.

Briefly silenced by the frankness of his tone, she stole a look at him while strange, quixotic emotions washed over her, some beautiful, some exciting, the scent of him suddenly filling her senses. She felt her skin prickle, her palms dampen, and vaguely uncomfortable with the compromises her body was so quickly making, she gestured at the necklace. "Leaving our differences aside, what's that for?"

Picking up the thin gold chain, he ran his fingers down a pendant comprised of five pearls separated with smaller pearls, then twisted the pendant to demonstrate its flexibility. He smiled. "These pearls are for your virgin ass."

She shook her head furiously. "Uh-uh. Save those for someone else."

"But I had them made for you."

"Return them then." She glared at him. "That's definitely a no. You're mistaking me for one of your paid ladies."

"Not likely baby," he said with a grin. "They don't talk back." Then he gave her a look that suggested she must have been locked away in the convent for the last twenty years without a pearl necklace because even there they knew about virgin asses. "You should try it," he said, smooth as silk. "You might like it. Remember, I've heard you say no before just prior to screaming the house down with a climax."

"Don't look so smug." But her heart was beginning to pound because that was a real cocky smile. "This is way different."

He stared at her. "I could make you do it. You like it when I make you do things."

The deep tenor of his voice and the heated memory in

his words was ramping up her libido. She could feel herself getting wet. "Jesus, don't look at me like that," she said, trying not to sound breathless. "I don't *want* to, okay? There're plenty of other things I *like* to do."

He grinned, thinking how lucky he was to have her, how goddamn fuckable she was. "Open your mind, baby."

"I'll do that just as soon you open your mind about your feelings. *Comprende?*" she said, a familiar edge creeping into her voice. She catapulted out of bed and walked to the bathroom, slammed the door, and locked it. A few seconds later he was pounding on the bathroom door. But it wasn't loud or violent; it was a low, steady pounding, like drums beating a message through the dark, hissing jungle. Like he knew the message would get through. Like he knew it was just a matter of time before she opened the door.

When she finally did, he was standing there.

"Hey." He smiled, slow and sexy and knowing.

The small sound vibrated through her body.

"Compromise?"

She nodded.

He held out his hand and she went to him.

He drew her to the bed, where they sat, his warm fingers twined with hers, their side-by-side poses like *American Gothic*, bedroom version.

She let out a small breath and he glanced at her.

"You first," she said.

"Give me five minutes with the pearls."

"Then I get five minutes with what I want?"

He nodded.

"You're not going to ask what?"

"Should I?"

"It's not sex."

He sat there a moment. "I don't suppose I have to wonder what it is?"

"Not if you were listening when I jumped out of bed a few minutes ago."

"Oh, what the hell," he said with amusement. "How hard can it be?"

But he made it clear that his five minutes didn't include anything else but the pearls. Because, although he didn't mention it, he had to make sure that Katherine was so sexed up, so wet and horny, so aching with need and near climax that she wouldn't back out.

He had her stand between his legs where he slowly undressed her, lifting off her blouse, unzipping her jeans, slipping them and the lacy wisp of panties down her hips and legs. "Now this uncomfortable bra," he said with a smile, reaching behind her and unclasping the hooks. "My long-suffering tits need consoling."

She softly exhaled as her breasts were freed, and gently stretched her spine.

"You really don't like bras, do you?"

"No more than you'd like your dick strangled in a jock strap."

He laughed. "So I should be more understanding."

"My boobs would appreciate it."

"Spoilsport," he murmured, his mouth twitching. "But I suppose I should apologize to my tits." Taking her by the waist, he pulled her closer. "I'll kiss them all better," he whispered, sitting up straighter so his breath warmed her nipple, then the warmth of his tongue followed and, wrapping his hands around her breast, he tugged her lower, took her nipple into his mouth, and sucked for long endless moments. Until her breasts felt swollen and engorged and every small suction of his mouth, no matter how gentle, slid down her quivering nerve endings, heated and delicious to the deep, powerful ache pulsing between her legs.

Kate groaned, moved her hips in frenzied need, laced her fingers through Dominic's hair, clutching his head to her breast, wanting more, wanting him deep inside her. But he slid the dildo into her dewy cleft instead and she whimpered in craving, in disappointment, overwhelmed by sensation, feeling punished and pleasured in equal measure.

But seconds short of her orgasm, when she could already feel herself starting to peak, he dropped his hands and sat back. "Intermission, baby," he said calmly. "Act two coming up."

"I'm going to kill you," she spat, reaching down for the dildo.

He stopped her. "Kill me later," he said, grabbing her wrists, pulling them together over her stomach, and holding them immobile in one hand. "When it's your turn." Reaching for a gold bracelet, he snapped first one, then the other on her wrists, checked that the chain was clasped together before releasing her. "Prologue to act two, baby. Does being my captive turn you on? It sure as hell does me." He reached up and stroked her swollen nipples. "Feel good?" he said unnecessarily, as she softly groaned.

She was warm and tingling everywhere with the dildo buried deep; feverish and flushed and so damned close to being where she wanted to be, she could almost measure the distance to carnal release. But that satisfaction was eluding her, quivering just out of reach, the wild craving shuddering through her body, agonizing, intoxicating, beyond any former memory of need.

But Dominic was in control as usual.

Once her breathing calmed, he pushed the dildo deeper, then deeper still, carefully monitoring her response, her moans, whimpers, how she moved her hips into his thrust, how the mounting tension was building in her body. "Having fun?" he asked, a small smile playing across his mouth.

She didn't hear him at first, so he stilled his hand.

Her eyes widened in surprise.

"I was wondering if everything was fine so far," he said gently, circling the nub of her clitoris with his index finger.

Her whole body jerked, pleasure swamped her senses, and she softly moaned.

"You want to come don't you?" he murmured, pressing her pulsing clit in little perfectly placed tap, tap, taps.

Instantly, the first ripples of preorgasm spread through her belly, slid up her spine, tightened her sex, and she pressed into his hand.

"Not yet, baby," Dominic said, placing a restraining hand on her hip. "You're not quite ready."

"I can't wait," she breathed, shivering with desire.

"Of course you can."

And he pulled the dildo out.

She squealed in frustration, glared at him, and said through her teeth, "You son of a bitch."

He smiled. "True, but we won't let that get in our way."

Coming up off the bed, he kissed her tenderly in apology and whispered, "It gets better, baby." He held her close, her naked body pressed to his, her cuffed hands a potent reminder of her submission, of his control, of the riveting dynamic that held them both in thrall. Sliding his hand downward, he pulled her bound hands up and framed his denim-covered dick with her fingers. "Rub me," he said, taut and low. "Hard." Lowering his mouth again, he slowly slid his tongue past her lips, shifted his hips forward, and kissed her slowly, deeply.

Softly panting into his mouth, desperate for release, she traced the length of his erection with her fingers as ordered, rubbed her palms over the rigid swell of his dick. Inhaled his soft groan and deliberately bit his tongue. Just to remind him that she had a say in this game.

Swallowing the taste of blood, he drew back, held her challenging gaze. "Are we doing this rough, baby? Just asking."

"I'd like to just do it," she hissed, "sometime this fucking year."

He broke into a grin. "Will you ever learn patience?"

"About the same time you learn there's a word called *love*."

He went utterly still.

She laughed. "Jesus, Dominic, is it really that fucking scary? You can always change your mind, you know."

His voice went soft. "You like to jerk my chain, don't you?"

"You're jerking mine. I want to come and you're giving me shit."

"Then let's get to it, baby." He picked her up and seated her on the bed.

She looked up. "Don't forget, I get my five minutes."

"I haven't forgotten." His smile was wicked. "Right after me." Taking her shackled wrists, he slid his other hand down her back and eased her down on the bed. Then he rolled her on her side facing him, placed her cuffed hands across her waist, put a pillow under her head, and surveyed her with a faint smile. "Very nice, baby. Are you comfortable? Everything good?"

"You're having fun, aren't you?"

He grinned. "Not yet, but I'm guessing I will."

"Don't forget, there's a time limit."

"Don't worry, you won't have to wait a year."

"That's not what I meant."

"You're not really in the position to give orders, baby." He gave her a lazy wink. "I'll be doing that."

Instantly, her nerve endings began to twitch, an insistent throbbing pulsed inside her, as if Dominic had only to look at her with that casual absolutism her body perceived as the sweetest of tyrannies and she melted.

He smiled. "You're going to thank me soon, baby. I can tell."

She tried to ignore the rippling pleasure warming her senses, was both horrified and aroused at the power he exerted over her. "I may not," she said, trying to speak in a normal tone, "depending on what you do."

"Don't worry, baby," he said pleasantly, watching the flush pink her cheeks. "You will." Dropping to his knees beside the bed, he gently kissed her, then sat back and looked at her for a moment, his mouth slightly pursed.

Her breathing picked up. He was making her nervous. "It better not hurt," she warned.

The silence stretched and she was about to tell him no way, when Dominic blinked. "You look amazing, baby," he said softly. "And I won't hurt you. I'd never do that." He brushed her cheek with his fingers. "We'll try some conventional foreplay first. Take it easy. You okay with that?"

Her heart was racing; she bit her lip.

He didn't move, although one eyebrow lifted faintly.

"Okay," she whispered.

His smile was improbably sweet and a bit relieved. "Thank you." Then his mouth quirked into his more familiar killer smile. "*You* can thank me later." Picking up the dildo, he slid his finger down her slick sex and glanced up. "I guess we can save the lube for later."

She took a breath before she answered, the imprint of his gliding finger still shivering through her body. "Is that a problem?"

He looked amused. "Certainly not. It's one of your many charms, baby." Sliding the dildo into her sleek cleft, he waited for her to catch her breath and open her eyes before he moved his hand. Then he slowly drew the dildo out, pushed it in again, watching her as she softly moaned and rode the rhythm—in and out, side to side, deliberately focusing on her G-spot for lingering moments. Very soon, she was panting again. "So far, so good?" He raised her chin with one finger, held her gaze, and gave her a smart-ass grin. "Nod if you don't feel like talking."

"Don't...forget L-O-V-E," she panted, locking her gaze with his, fully capable of keeping up with smart-ass grins. "Although—I'll expect—actual words. A nod won't—"

He'd made a small adjustment so the dildo was lodged

firmly against her G-spot and he watched her shudder. "Don't talk," he said. "Now shut your eyes."

"You don't like me glaring at you?"

He smiled. "Jesus, what don't you understand about don't talk?"

She stuck her tongue out.

"Anytime, baby." He put his hand on his zipper.

She held up her cuffs. "I'm a little—busy right—now."

He bent to kiss her. "That's the way I like you," he said against her mouth. "This is my kind of busy." He shoved the dildo deeper and as she lay quivering, he slipped the black silk scarf over her eyes and tied it behind her head. "Tell me if you feel things more intensely now."

"I still feel like killing you." But her voice was wispy, and tiny pearly rivulets were sliding down her thighs.

Goddamn, that was one lush centerfold. In another life, he would have ravaged her without compunction. With old habits hammering at his brain, he dragged in a breath of restraint and did a slow ten count to tamp down the worst of his impulses. "Give me a minute, baby. I'll change your mind," he said softly, easing the dildo a modicum deeper and tapping it in place. "I'm good at this."

While she whimpered with ecstasy flaring through her senses, Dominic pushed her plump breasts up and out, until they were perfectly framed by her arms and her nipples were fully accessible. Then he dipped the brush into the jasmine scented lube and ran the sleek sable tip around and around her nipples, watching her crests swell and peak, taking his time, pushing her back down as she arched her spine, tense and greedy, begging for more. "You always rush, baby." He slid the brush over the heavy swell of one breast, down the deep valley of her cleavage, heard her gasp, and whispered, "Relax. It gets better."

Restless and frustrated, aching, frantic for release, she violently shook her head, "Let me come," she whimpered. "You don't have to do anything for me after. You don't have to talk about anything. Please, Dominic! Oh God, please!"

"It's too soon, baby," he murmured, pinching one nipple until she cried out before releasing it. "Trust me."

She moaned as the blood coursed through her nipple again, and the pain was replaced by a rush of pleasure, every sensation more intense with her eyes covered, every craving more explosive. She pressed her legs together, trying to bring on her own orgasm.

"No you don't." Forcing her legs open, Dominic lifted her ankle over his left arm and, leaning in, used his other hand to brush the slippery sable tip over her taut flesh framing the dildo. Up and down, around and around, while she writhed and whimpered and her whole body began to quake. Then, without warning, he lifted her ankle from his arm and placed her foot on the bed. "Think of something soothing, baby."

"I can't," she sobbed.

"Try that om thing."

"Fuck you," she gasped, so overwrought and feverish a thin sheen of perspiration filmed her body.

"All in due time," he said. "But not yet." Gripping her nipples between his thumbs and forefingers, he stretched them gently outward until she squealed. "Too much?" He opened his fingers, watched the taut flesh contract, heard her little feverish whimper, and cupped her big breasts in his palms. "Your tits are swollen and heavy." He leaned in and nipped her ear. "But your body's not completely pre-pared," he whispered, "for maximum pleasure. When you get there, baby, you'll be ready for anything."

She never thought she'd allow him unconditional license. And yet, she was so over-the-top horny now, so utterly consumed by lust, his words sounded like a prom-ise of pleasure rather than a threat. And a moment later, when he slid his finger past the dildo to expose her clit, then lightly skimmed the tip of the brush teasingly over her greedy nub in slow twirling spirals, half-delirious, trem-bling all over, she cried out. "Please, Dominic. Don't make me wait. I'm ready now for whatever you want to do."

How many times, how many hours and days, weeks, months, and years had he played these carnal games? And yet, when Katherine fully, eagerly offered herself up to him, all those former vice-ridden amusements faded into oblivion. Bending low, he gently kissed her trembling lips. "I'm going to go very slowly," he whispered. "We'll take our time." Glazing the pearls with lube from the brush, he added, velvet soft, "You'll feel the brush first."

Sliding his hand under her right knee, he lifted it, then set her foot on the bed to allow him better access. Dip-ping the brush in the scented lube, he slid the sleek tip in slow circles over and around, up and down her virgin entrance while he eased the dildo in and out, slowly, gently, targeting her G-spot for brief moments, then shifting away, knowing the pearls would put added pressure on the dildo and her favorite sweet spot. And when she was delirious with pleasure, panting, needy, the flush of arousal spreading up her chest and throat, he slipped the first lubed pearl past the sensitive opening, heard her helpless whimper turn to a low, lush moan, and seconds later slowly eased in the next pearl...and then the next. Another and another. Until all five were snuggly inside.

She was filled as she'd never been filled before, the forbidden pressure exquisitely arousing, the dildo moving on one side, the pearls flexing on the other. Writhing under the overwhelming invasion, uttering little keening cries, the flush rose hot pink up her throat to her face, signaling her imminent orgasm.

Recognizing how she was trembling on the brink, Dominic slipped off her blindfold, took her face in his hands, leaned in close, and whispered, "I own you, baby. Every breath. Every heartbeat. Every precious part of you."

She shook her head, formed the word *no*, but was so near climax, so ravenous with lust, she couldn't find breath to speak.

He leaned back, ran his finger over her mouth. "I need a yes, baby. You know that don't you."

He didn't have to say, *Or else.* She tensed.

"You're mine, baby—property of Dominic Knight." His fingers brushed her cheek. "Aren't you?"

She nodded.

He smiled. "There you go, baby. Time to rock and roll." Sliding his hand between her legs, knowing that at this stage of her arousal if he pulled out a pearl, the incredible rush would kick-start her climax—he did just that.

He wound the thin gold chain around his finger—and pulled.

Her orgasm exploded on cue, wildly, loudly, her scream shattering the silence. And as he slowly pulled out each additional pearl, her nerves, already fiercely convulsing, were further goaded and pleasure amplified, magnified, into a seething, tumbling, unrestrained cascade of maxed-out, unparalleled sensation that continued so long and with such unremitting intensity that she was left pale and trembling.

Only when her last spasm died away did he slide the dildo out. Then, lifting her into his arms, he cradled her on his lap and gently kissed her until she stopped shaking. "You're incredible, Katherine," he whispered, his breath warm on her cheek, feeling as though all his senses were heightened, as though he'd had the orgasm himself.

It was both unnerving and fantastic.

Like so much of their relationship.

He came out of his reverie when she tapped his chest with the cuffs.

Unclasping the bracelets, he dropped them on the bed. "Are you okay?" He dipped his head, met her gaze. "Nothing damaged?"

Her smile was slow and lush. "Everything's fine. That was intense. You really are Svengali. I hate you and love you at the same time." She suddenly grinned. "But you know what's coming next, don't you?" Sliding off his lap, she moved to the foot of the bed, and sitting cross-legged, tried not to smirk. "My turn."

He was feeling so fine that he didn't even grumble,

although he knew what was coming. Especially when she'd casually mentioned love. He turned to face her, slid up against the headboard, settled back, and stretched out his legs. "Do your worst, baby."

"Tell me about Julia."

His surprise showed; he'd expected a quiz on his feelings.

"It's just that she seemed like such a remarkable woman, selfless, brave, compassionate. Like some superwoman."

"She *was* remarkable," he said, finding it easier to talk about Julia, not knowing why exactly, wondering if his fabulous nonorgasm was the cause. "But what you and I have is different." There was a short silence, as though he were searching for the right words. "It's chaotic, volatile, occasionally mind-blowing." He smiled. "You're my reminder that life comes in many shades of beautiful.

"I met Julia on Everest," he went on, as if she'd asked. "She was climbing with a group raising money for some charity she was involved in. She was amazing. Nothing stopped her. Only five of us made it to the summit that spring. And we nearly didn't. The weather was fierce. Rare storms. There shouldn't have been any that time of year." He shrugged. "It's funny how life is overshadowed by chance so often. How you meet someone. Or maybe you don't. And an opportunity passes you by." His voice had gone soft at the end. "Do you ever think how we almost didn't meet? I do." He seemed to gather himself, his mouth twitched into a grin. "It damn near makes me think about going to church if I had a church to go to."

"I'm more a gypsy fate person. Although," Kate said

with a little dip of her head and the dazzling smile that always made him feel like the most fortunate man on the face of the earth, "I'm not above thanking Lady Luck or whomever for this—us—you, me, whatever. So tell me," she said abruptly, changing the subject back because she had a limited time to ask her questions and Dominic's late wife was a major enigma. "Julia's charity offers microloans to women, right?"

"Actually, the charity was something Roscoe's first wife started and when that marriage folded, Julia took over."

"I suppose there were too many grateful women wanting to show their gratitude for you or Roscoe to handle."

He looked up startled, then nodded, and said, "Some. Enough."

"Julia kept them at bay."

He shrugged. "I don't know. I never interfered. And Charlie was with Julia almost from the start. They'd met in a marketing class at Stanford. I didn't know either one of them then. They were younger, not in my field and the school's"—another shrug—"big. Not that I'm interested in talking about Charlie."

"That makes two of us."

He grinned. "And my five minutes are almost up."

"Were you timing mine?"

He laughed. "You never take long, baby. But fast or slow, I just want you to know you're rocking my world in a really nice way."

"Then maybe I could ask you a favor."

"My answer is yes." He smiled. "I know that look."

"Then you don't mind?"

"Not while my heart is still beating."

"I just want it simple. I like to feel you over me. I like to feel you slowly fill me. I like the warmth of your body on mine."

"You got it, baby."

They made love gently, slowly, without drama or fireworks. Once, then once again when she said, "I just love coming when you do." And one more time because he liked coming with her. She fell asleep first. He lay awake for a time, reflecting on the phrase *making love* from an entirely different point of view. But soon he dozed off too. It had been a long, busy, physically taxing three days.

TWENTY

Dominic awoke with a start, his mind racing. He glanced at the windows—still dark—then at the clock. Six. Carefully easing out of bed, he grabbed his jeans, walked out into the hall, stepped into them, and quickly descended the stairs. Entering his office, he shut the door, powered up his laptop and sent a quick e-mail to Justin: *It's a go. Find a flat. Talk to Roscoe. Will touch base later.* Then he sent an e-mail to Roscoe: *Justin needs an account set up. Give him whatever he wants.* Shutting down his laptop, he raised his head and listened for a moment.

No sounds from upstairs. He picked up the phone.

"Sorry to wake you," he said.

"Anytime, Nick," a sleepy voice said. "What's up?"

Dominic could hear the rustle of bed sheets. "I need a codicil to my will. Nothing complicated. I want to split my assets between my sister and a Miss Katherine Hart. If you need her social security number or address, check with Roscoe." A door shut and his attorney's voice was suddenly crisp.

"Are you sure? Just an attorney question, but that's a fucking lot of money."

"Melanie won't mind sharing. She and Matt are comfortable."

"Jesus, you're not dying of something?"

"No, my health is fine. I have a meeting on Tuesday that could be difficult. In the event things don't go well, I'd like Miss Hart to be taken care of."

"What do you mean don't go well?" Chris Robbins's voice shot up.

"It's just business. But the people I'm dealing with are, let's say, unpredictable."

"Seriously?" Another spiking rise in tone.

"Don't worry about it. I'm sure everything will be fine. This is just insurance."

"Okay, okay. But why haven't I heard of this woman?"

"Because you're my attorney, not my keeper."

"Are you gonna marry her?"

"I haven't thought about it. So if I had to give you an answer right now, I'd say no."

"But you have decided to give her half your fortune. Any special reason for that?" Chris Robbins carefully articulated.

"Not that reason," Dominic said with amusement. "But I have plenty of money. She might as well have some."

"Jesus, you're not high are you?"

"Nope, and she's not blackmailing me. So you've done your fiduciary duty, Chris. I know what I'm doing. Bring the codicil with you when you come at ten. I'll leave my desk drawer open. Just put the papers in there."

"Last time. You're of sound mind and all that shit."

"Better than usual. Actually, much better. See you at ten."

Returning to bed, taking care not to wake Katherine, Dominic slid under the covers. He was pleasantly exhausted; Katherine had worn him out last night. But he couldn't be happier. Turning his head on the pillow, he looked at her lying on her back, deep in sleep, and was reminded, as always, how young she looked in slumber. Rosy-cheeked, her eyelids faintly smudged with vestiges of last night's eye shadow, her long lashes resting on her pale, silken skin. So smooth and soft, it was like a baby's skin. Her full lips were a natural pink, her lipstick long gone, the shape of her mouth picture perfect, tempting. The back of one hand lay curved against her temple, the other rested on the upper swell of one breast, the pink aureole slightly covered.

Her nipple fully erect.

That was truly tempting.

Fresh-faced and dewy-skinned though she might be, she was all woman in every other sense and he could feel his erection coming to life, exhausted or not. Roscoe calling her a sorceress was not entirely without merit. Perhaps Roscoe understood that better than anyone, since he'd seen Knight Enterprises without a CEO twice in as many months.

Unprecedented actions for a man who'd worked nonstop for the last twelve years. Then Katherine came awake and smiled at him, and nothing else mattered. Not work, not the last twelve years, not the last twelve minutes. They had a few more days together. He wasn't going to spoil them by thinking too much. Leaning over, he kissed her good morning. "How are you feeling?" His brows lifted faintly. "Sore?"

"A teeny bit."

"I'm sorry."

"It's nothing really."

"That's good, but I do apologize. Would you like me to run a bath for you?"

"Not right now. And you can stop apologizing." She smiled. "Because your five minutes were radically fine, I had my five minutes too, and they were excellent."

He smiled. "You're a tough negotiator." He pointed at the remote on her side of the bed, deliberately changing the subject. In the clear light of day, he wasn't about to open up any further discussions about his feelings.

"What are those two *Sesame Street* words?" Kate archly inquired, a mischievous light in her eyes.

The merest flicker of a frown, quickly gone. "The remote. Please. *And* thank you."

She handed it to him.

He clicked on the TV, tossed the quilt aside, and threw the remote at his feet. Before she could utter another syllable, he flipped her so her head was near the foot of the bed, rolled over her, settling between her legs all in one smooth, kinetic flow of brute force and muscle. "Just so you don't forget who gives the orders here," he murmured as he flipped through channels. "Although you've done a very nice job of keeping my dick up the last three days." He dropped a kiss on her nose. "We *both* thank you, even though you wore us out."

Kate shifted her lower body slightly against his erection. "He doesn't seem worn out."

"That's a relative term with you, baby. Anything this side of last rites is a go, so we're good." His gaze was on the TV. "So what can we do for you this morning?"

"Oh, I don't know. I was thinking about maybe an orgasm to start the day."

"Only one?"

"Hey, do you mind?" She tapped his cheek.

He glanced down at her. "Really? They're rewiring the electrical system in an old Camaro. I can do two things at once."

She glared at him.

"Okay, okay." He hit Record, then clicked off the TV. "There." He smiled at her. "Here we are, baby. Full concentration."

Taking her face between his hands, he slowly kissed her and even more slowly entered her, knowing exactly where she wanted him, how deep, and how high.

"I need to feel you inside me and over me, touching me," Kate whispered, lifting her mouth for a kiss as Dominic languidly slid inside her. "Always..."

"That works out then," Dominic murmured, smiling as he kissed her. "Because we have this insatiable craving for you." But she was swollen, tight. "Tell me if I'm hurting you." He stopped to rest, waited for her flesh to relax. "You sure you're okay with this?"

Her green-eyed gaze was sleepy. "You feel good," she whispered. "Big."

No shit. Because she was super tight. He gently flexed his legs, advanced a fraction more, felt like a fucking explorer mapping new territory. But her sleek tissue slowly turned supple, yielding, and ultimately he reached his goal. "Is that too far?"

"Ummmm—no...umm," she groaned. "Oh God—do...that again."

He always felt absurdly pleased when he could give her pleasure, as if he were placed on earth to indulge her; a bizarre thought always quickly forgotten after sex. "Like this?" He barely moved, but he shifted his hips enough to exert a tenuous pressure on her favorite sweet spot.

"Oh, God, Jesus, Dominic," she panted. "You can't ever leave..."

"Just a little," he murmured, withdrawing enough to add friction to the pressure when he thrust in again.

Her protest died in her throat, altered to a low, rapturous moan. Then she jerked his head down hard and hissed, "You're perfect, damn it. I hate you for it. Now do that again."

He did, several times and in several different ways, until she'd come, he had, she had, until much later she finally punched him hard in the chest.

"Sure?" he said with a faint smile.

"We're not all machines," she gasped.

"You're the boss, baby."

She rolled her eyes.

"You don't have a clue," he said with a smile, having altered his entire life for her. "But no complaints." He kissed her lightly. "Time for a soak in the tub?"

She almost said, *How do you know that's exactly what I want at this exact moment?* But after all those lovely, gentle, balmy morning orgasms, she wasn't in the mood to ask any questions she might not really want to know the answers to.

They were in the tub when Patty arrived, the kitchen

noises drifting up the stairway an indication that she was setting up for the day.

"Hungry?"

Kate was sitting between Dominic's legs, her back against his chest, her head on his shoulder, half asleep. She nodded.

"Want breakfast in bed or downstairs?"

"Whatever you want."

"Can you stay awake to eat?"

"Coffee," she murmured.

"Coming right up, baby. Don't move. I'll be right back." Easing out from behind her, he stepped out of the tub, saw that she was resting comfortably against the tub back, and turned on the faucet to warm the water while he threw on a pair of sweats.

Semidressed, his wet hair dripping on his shoulders, he flicked off the tap and frowned; Katherine's eyes were shut, her breathing slow. "Should I lift you out? I wouldn't want you to drown in your sleep."

"I won't drown," she whispered. "Hurry."

He was in the kitchen moments later, rubbing his hair with a towel. "Morning, Patty. I need coffee five minutes ago."

"She must be hot. You don't fetch and carry." Flicking her blond braids over her shoulder, Patty pulled out a tray and set two large cups and two spoons on it.

"She is." Dominic grinned, tossing the towel on the white marble counter. "So I fetch and carry. Some pastry?"

"Warm chocolate croissants?" The coffee was poured, sugar and cream added to the tray.

"You're a saint."

"We already determined that years ago." Patty took two

288   C. C. Gibbs

croissants out of a warming oven drawer and placed them in a napkin-lined basket. "Have your special friend tell you what she wants for breakfast. I'll see what I can do. Or maybe," she said with her usual cheek, "I'll just cook what I want."

Dominic gave her a look. "Maybe you'll cook what Katherine wants today."

"Whoa...did I really hear that?"

"Just be nice, Patty, okay? Do that for me?"

"Sure, Nicky. No problem." Folding the napkin ends over the croissants, she handed the tray to Dominic. "But I'm expecting to meet a goddess after seeing you actually move your ass for a woman," she said with a wink.

He swore at her, and she grinned. "Just for starters I'll make French toast with caramelized bananas and crème fraîche. But I'm open to orders, boss. You know that."

He didn't, of course, because Patty hadn't taken an order in the sixteen years she'd worked for him. But she cooked like she surfed, perfect form, and to-die-for creativity, so he'd never complained. And she was looking serious and sincere, which was a hopeful sign. "Thanks, Patty. Now be nice to Katherine. I like her."

No shit, Patty thought, watching Dominic's retreating form. *Let me mark this day on the never-thought-it-would-happen calendar.*

When Kate and Dominic came down to breakfast, Kate did a quick double take because Patty was close to Dominic's age, blond and beautiful in a cool Nordic way, and in great shape, and she wondered if they were more than employer/employee. But she reminded herself that

Dominic had been relatively open with her last night...or as capable as he was of openness—so she had to give him the benefit of the doubt.

Dominic introduced the women.

"Nice to meet you," Patty said, taking in Kate's cuff bracelets without expression.

"Same here." Kate smiled, ignoring Patty's glance. "The coffee and croissants were fabulous. Did you make the croissants?"

Patty nodded and grinned. "That's why Nicky pays me the big bucks."

Dominic didn't know where Patty was going with that smart-ass grin, so he said, "Breakfast smells good. Are you ready for us?"

"Sure, boss."

Patty calling him boss wasn't reassuring. Dominic gave her a warning glance as he followed Kate to the table. And whether she acknowledged it or not, she was super polite as they ate.

Patty's French toast was truly decadent, as was a fruit plate that could have been on display in a museum, and the coffee was everything coffee should be: hot, a teeny bit sweet, and strong, with just a trace of austerity to remind you of the reason you drank coffee.

Patty sat at the kitchen table with them and talked about her husband and children. She got up to point out pictures of her family on the kitchen walls—on Dominic's kitchen walls, Kate reflected. And she was actually a little brusque with Dominic at times. She called him Nicky too, like Melanie did. Kate liked that Dominic had people around him who were a part of his life—that he wasn't completely alone.

Dominic worried that Patty was being too friendly and solicitous. But Katherine didn't seem to notice. And when she praised Patty's coffee, asking how she made it, what type of coffee she used, and if she could get some for her grandmother, the ice—if there had been any—had broken, melted, and evaporated into the atmosphere.

Patty couldn't do enough for Katherine. Because, she figured, (1) the very first woman Dominic had brought to this house warranted special treatment and (2) those cuff bracelets Katherine was wearing were really out there for someone like Dominic, who kept his kink private. So Patty actually ran her day's menu past Katherine in the event some of the food didn't appeal.

Kate said, "I eat anything," then blushed so sweetly, Patty didn't wonder that she appealed to Dominic after years of women who wouldn't know how to blush if their lives depended on it.

And when they left after breakfast to go up on the roof to sit in the sun, Patty murmured as Dominic left the kitchen, "She's a keeper, Nicky. You did good."

From the rooftop, the view of the Golden Gate Bridge was postcard worthy, the sun warm as they lay side by side on chaises, the sense of contentment thick enough to cut with a butter knife.

"Happy?" Dominic touched Kate's hand, then slid his finger over the gold bracelet.

She smiled. "Oh, yeah. You?"

"More than you know," he said gently, looking forward to being with her in London. "Sleep if you want. We have until ten."

"And?"

"The attorney comes at ten."

"You sure you want to do this? You don't have to do it for me. I'm not going anywhere unless you want me to."

He kept his voice benign; previous talk of shackling her to his bed hadn't been greeted with approval. "Contracts are routine for me. Humor me, if you don't mind."

"I don't mind. You're the one who's used to exercising his sexual freedom. Exclusivity isn't a problem for me. I don't want anyone else. You know that."

She made it sound so simple, when it had never been simple before.

When he'd never been interested in simplicity when it came to the women in his life. Even Julia had brought with her exotic adventure and thrill-seeking world travel. Now he was happy and content doing nothing, lying here with Katherine, the sun warm on his face, the person who gave meaning to his life beside him.

It was enough.

He didn't need anything more.

And this time he was determined to keep the subversive demons at bay.

While he couldn't change his past or wash away a single bitter memory, he could shape a new destiny, create a new world. Perhaps even learn to understand the meaning of love.

TWENTY-ONE

Dominic's attorney was well dressed in a navy suit that was beautifully cut by a tailor who knew his business, charged what some people made in a year, and sent his clients out in the world with the authority serious money commanded.

Dominic hadn't changed from his sweats and T-shirt. Katherine was equally dressed down, but Chris Robbins smiled politely when Katherine was introduced, pretending he didn't see the cuff bracelets and treating Dominic and Kate with professional deference. Or more likely with the extraprofessional deference awarded to a billionaire client and this woman who'd warranted a change in Dominic's will.

Patty brought in a tray with coffee and cookies, set it on a small table between Katherine and the two men, and left. While Chris extracted several documents from his briefcase, the men discussed the season the Golden State Warriors were having and the point spread from last night's game. They agreed that they needed more rain and that the opera needed more funding, after which Dominic suggested that Chris send the opera whatever he thought appropriate and let Roscoe know the amount.

Chris set a small stack of papers on the table, carefully lined up the edges, and took out a lacquered black pen, quite beautiful, like fine jewelry. He unscrewed the cap and handed the pen to Dominic.

Gee, rich people didn't even have to get up for their own pen, Kate thought, glancing at the desk where several pens resided in a leather canister.

Dominic leaned forward in his chair. "Show us where to sign."

"Would you like to read it?"

"The draft was fine." Dominic turned to Kate. "You should read it though, Katherine." He nodded at the attorney, who slid a copy toward Kate.

"I don't want to."

Dominic gave her a quick look. "I'd advise you read it. Tell her Chris."

Chris smiled politely. "I always suggest a contract be read before signing."

Kate pointed at the papers. "Do you include my e-mail out clause? That's all I need." It meant she could leave, as they'd agreed in Singapore, whenever she wished.

The attorney glanced at Dominic, then ran a quick hand over his thinning hair.

Dominic stared at him for a heartbeat, his expression blank. "Katherine's referring to the revocation clause."

"Yes, of course." Chris swallowed. "The clause is in there."

Kate sat up a little straighter in her chair. "Then show me where to sign."

Dominic gave her a pointed look. "I'm going to make sure your CX Capital contract is reviewed before you sign it. They won't be as amenable as me should you change your mind."

"You're amenable? Really?" She grinned playfully. "Since when?"

"Enough, Katherine," Dominic warned softly, flicking his eyes toward the attorney.

"I expect the nature of our friendship isn't in doubt since Mr. Robbins drafted this contract for you, Dominic," she said as softly.

Dominic sighed. "Then just sign the thing."

"That's what I was going to do before you started giving orders."

Dominic's mouth clamped shut, a twitch appeared high over his cheekbone, and he handed her the pen.

Afterward, Chris Robbins relayed the news to his business partner that not only had Dominic wanted this woman badly enough to sign an exclusivity contract, but that Miss Katherine Hart apparently was not the docile type because she'd argued with Dominic until he'd given up. "Well, not docile except for the handcuffs," he said with a grin and went on to explain the pricey bracelets.

"That's her appeal," Bob Thorp, his partner, said, grinning back in that leering way typical in male discussions of sex. "Docile when it matters, otherwise not docile. Keeps Knight guessing."

"Her only interest was in the revocation clause. She refused to look at the contract. Dominic pressed her and she resisted."

"Did you tell her the revocation clause is worthless?"

"She didn't ask."

"She doesn't know about the codicil to Knight's will either, right? Or do you think she does know and that's why it doesn't matter that the revocation clause is completely ineffectual?"

"No, Dominic was absolutely clear on that. She doesn't know. The codicil was in a separate envelope I was told to put in his desk. I was ushered into his office first."

"So what does this potentially rich woman look like? Something extraordinary, I'd say." Bob adjusted the cuff on his twenty-grand suit. "Maybe she'll be looking for a new friend."

"She's way out of your league, Bobby my boy, so don't get excited. And she's rich only if some meeting Dominic has on Tuesday goes wrong. He's not expecting trouble, he said, but just taking precautions. He didn't give any details beyond that. But Knight Enterprises does business in some dodgy regions of the world. Even with security, there're always risks."

"I still don't know what this extremely clever and apparently too-beautiful-for-me woman looks like." Bob Thorp didn't take his partner's put-down personally. Very few men could challenge Dominic Knight when it came to looks.

"Here." Chris tapped some icons on his phone. "I downloaded the photo from my pen camera. Here."

Bob Thorp laughed. "You and your spy shit," he said, taking the phone. "Oh, baby...she's fine. No makeup, no fancy clothes, and she still blows you away. Leave it to Dominic to find her."

"It's not as though he hasn't been checking out female perfection around the globe both before and after his marriage. His percentages were good he'd find something he liked."

"To the tune of what?"

"Half."

Bob's eyes bulged out like a cartoon character's. "You're fucking kidding me."

"Uh-uh. Half. Signed, sealed, delivered."

"Jesus, she must be good in the sack."

"Don't ever say that to him. The guy's serious about her."

"Yeah, I got that."

TWENTY-TWO

"You have no discretion," Dominic muttered after the door closed on the attorney.

"You of all people complaining. Considering your attorney drafted that contract"—she lifted her brows—"what's the point?" She held out her hands, displaying the cuff bracelets. "Speaking of discretion, you didn't seem to care about these. Because you like this don't you?"

He smiled. "Very much."

"So who's indiscreet now?"

He dipped his head. "Agreed."

She made a check with her finger in the air. "Won that one."

He laughed. "You like to win, don't you?"

"Damn right. You do too. Yin, yang, never a dull moment. That's why—"

"Katherine."

"What?"

"Come here."

She shot a quick glance at the door. "Patty might come in."

"She won't."

"How do you know?" But her voice trembled.

"I know. Now get up and walk over here."

Their eyes met.

"Slowly," he said, his voice serene, his arm resting on

the table, his fingers lightly placed on the contract they had just signed…as though to remind her that her addiction had become legal. To remind her of his incredible power over her.

Dominic's dispassionate voice banished objections and dignity, firm beliefs and any reference to reality. He had only to speak in that soft, lazy tone, look at her with lust in the unfiltered blue of his eyes, expect obedience, and she was instantly wet, her nipples peaked, her sex pulsing in welcome.

Drained of all emotion, save a vast and unconstrained longing.

She stood.

He slowly swung around in his chair, spread his legs, and watched in silence as she walked across the small space separating them. When she came to a stop before him, he looked up from under the dark fringe of his lashes and surveyed her breasts, his gaze fixed and cool. "You're obscenely easy to arouse, Katherine. I've never seen anyone who needs sex as much as you. Your nipples are stiff in seconds." His gaze slowly lifted and a small moment of time unraveled. "Take off your T-shirt. I want to see my tits."

As she pulled off her shirt, he put out his hand.

She dropped the T-shirt in his open palm, and he let it fall to the carpet without taking his eyes off her.

"Touch your nipples for me." His voice sharpened slightly. "Now, Katherine. Do it now."

"Sorry," she whispered, focused on the liquid heat shimmering between her legs, on the flutter of arousal spiking through her body.

"Did you hear what I said?" His voice was rough.

She moved then, prompted by the harshness of his tone. She took her nipples between her thumbs and fingers, gently squeezed.

"Harder."

She tightened her grip, felt the tissue yield, shut her eyes against the spiraling pleasure streaking downward, hot and lush, primitive in its untrammeled beauty. And softly moaned.

"Harder," he ordered quietly.

She increased the pressure, compressing her sensitive flesh, and felt searing desire leap inside her. White-hot lust flared through her body, wildly beating at her brain, and she gasped. With her eyes shut, she whispered, "I need you."

"Are you sure?" he murmured. "Or can anyone fuck you when you're this horny? Do you really care whose dick it is, baby?" He leaned forward, grasping her wrists in a viselike grip. "Do you?" he growled.

His low growl, his savage grip, required a response. Even distracted by a building hysteria she understood. Breathless, fevered, she forced her eyes open, struggling to answer a question she'd hadn't fully heard. Finally she replied in blanket assent. "Whatever you want, Dominic."

Aware of her dilemma, he smiled faintly, his hands fell away, and he leaned back in his chair. "That'll do," he said. He flicked one finger. "Resume."

Incomprehensively, the single word was as potent as the hard thrust of a cock plunging deep inside her. She shuddered as a lurid jolt mauled her senses and her body slavishly opened, eager and willing.

"Jesus, Katherine." His voice was soft as silk, amused. "Do you even know I'm here?"

"How could I not?" Her voice was low and lush, her heated gaze on the only man who made her helpless with longing, who could make her do anything for the pleasure he offered. Then she gripped her nipples, slowly pulled on them until they were stretched taut. "Could you help me?" she said on a caught breath, turning left, then right, offering him an unlimited view. "I can't... reach them with my mouth... but you could."

She took note of his surging erection and, releasing her fingers, slid her hands under her breasts and lifted her pale flesh into high, plump mounds. "Just asking."

Dominic smiled. "Fucking tease." He crooked a finger.

Smiling back, she moved between his legs. "Finally," she said.

"I really am going to have to lock up your pussy. No question," he murmured, gazing up at her from under his half-lowered eyelids.

"Maybe I'll let you."

"No maybe about it. You like to fuck too much. We can't have you out trolling for a one-night stand."

"I promise not to."

He snorted. "Like I believe that."

"Maybe you have to."

"And maybe I don't." He placed his large hands on either side of one breast, curled his fingers, captured her soft flesh, and dipped his head. Just before his mouth touched her nipple, he glanced up and said, "They're working on your chastity belt now."

"You wouldn't!" She tried to jerk back.

His finger tightened. "Of course I would. I can do anything, Katherine." Then his mouth closed on her nipple and he made her forget everything but raw sensation, fevered need, orgasmic frenzy. In seconds she was panting, the throbbing between her legs turbulent, issues of authority and compliance forgotten with her blood on fire and orgasm hovering on the brink.

Then he slid his hands away from her breast, sat back, and quietly said, "Turn around and put your hands behind you."

She stood stunned, insatiable lust beating at her brain.

"Anytime, Katherine. You want to come don't you?"

No, she wanted vengeance, to retaliate by slapping him in the face for his asshole behavior. She didn't want to wait or play games. But vengeance could wait until after she climaxed, she pragmatically decided, so close to orgasm her pulse was pounding in her ears.

She turned.

"We do get along don't we?" he sardonically murmured, drawing the coiled chains from the bracelets. Binding the bracelets together, he placed his hands on her hips and swung her back around. "You can't ever come unless I'm with you. Do you understand?"

She nodded, desire pulsing hot inside her.

"I didn't hear you, Katherine."

"I understand," she whispered, trying to keep from trembling.

"One more thing. I'd like you to apologize for being disagreeable in front of Chris."

His eyes flared wide, hot with temper. "Fuck you."

"Not yet. Apologize first," he said gently.

"No."

"Maybe I can change your mind." Untying her sweats, he slid them down her legs, lifted one foot, then the other, kicked away the puddle of fabric, then slipped a finger inside her.

"That's not fair." But her voice was a wisp of sound.

"I'm not interested in being fair. I'm interested in an apology." He slipped in a second finger, gently stroked her slick flesh. "All you have to do is say you're sorry and I'll let you come."

"I'm not going to."

He slid his other hand over her breast and lazily rubbed her nipple between his finger and thumb, until she was shuddering under his hands, drenching his fingers, panting in a little flurry of need. "You like that? Would you like to come or should I stop? What does winning mean now?"

"I want to come."

"Who can do that for you?"

"You can, Dominic. You can win the next hundred times if you let me come now. Please?"

"Sure, baby. Just making sure you understand who does what to whom in that yin-yang equation."

Her eyes narrowed; even near-orgasmic, her temper was in hot dispute.

He smiled. "Are we clear?"

A long taut silence; he could feel her orgasm begin to ripple up his fingers. He pulled his fingers out, dropped his hand from her breast.

"Should I put your sweats back on, uncuff you?"

She bit her lip, shook her head.

"That's what I thought. I don't need a lengthy apology."

"I'm sorry."

"Thank you, baby." Coming to his feet, he unclasped the bracelets, eased her back onto the chair, knelt, and lifted her legs on his shoulders. Slipping a hand under her bottom, he pulled her close, slid his fingers back inside, gently stroked her G-spot, dipped his head low and tenderly sucked her clit—the pressure of his mouth painstakingly attuned to her swiftly peaking climax. Having gained his objective in clarifying their relative positions, mollified and content, he took particular care to see that Katherine's orgasm was drawn out for long, delirious, soul-stirring moments.

Downstairs in the kitchen, Patty looked up at the frenzied scream, smiled, and went back to her cooking. It was nice that Dominic had someone to play with instead of brooding in his room like he usually did when he was home. Maybe she should make steaks for dinner. If those two kept up their heavy-duty screwing schedule they were going to need some red meat in their diets.

After Kate was once again composed, Dominic changed places with her, lifted her onto his lap, saw to his climax, then another for her, and held her close while they both reached a more tranquil state of mind. Then he said, "Break time? Feel like a swim?"

Kate's head was resting on his shoulder, her arms draped over his shoulders. "I'll watch you."

"You can read a magazine or watch TV. I'll just do a few laps. Now if you're shy, shut your eyes when I carry you downstairs. I have clothes and robes down there."

She sat up, gave him a hard stare. "Don't you dare say Patty's seen you nude before."

Scooping her off his lap, he stood, holding her in his arms. "We met surfing. So that's minimum clothes, but it's clothes. Is that okay with you?" He moved toward the door.

"Have you slept with her?"

"Uh-uh. She and Jack have always been together. They lived in my ratty apartment in Half Moon Bay for a few years, but that's as close as we got to seeing each other nude. Satisfied?" Opening the door, he turned to his right.

"Since I can't send people off to Greenland like you do, I suppose I don't have a choice."

He laughed. "You couldn't get Patty that far north for love or money. She's like you. She's a whole lot of trouble. But she's a damned good cook, so the trade-off's worth it." Another smaller staircase at the end of the corridor led to the lower level. He took the stairs in a fast, smooth descent and entered a lighted room.

Kate nibbled on his earlobe. "Speaking of trouble and trade-offs, Mr. Knight. I know what you're talking about."

He grinned. "At least it's never dull, baby." He set her down in a small locker room with closet-size lockers. "Clothes there." He pointed. "Some of the workout clothes are supposed to fit you. Swimsuits there." He pointed again. "Don't feel you have to wear one if you don't want to. No one uses the pool but me and the water is constantly recirculated and filtered a thousand different ways. I don't like chlorine or chemicals." He lifted his brows. "What are you doing?"

She ran her finger down his arm. "Is this a turn-on for

you too? Look how dark you are." Standing nude under the bright locker-room lights, Dominic's bronzed skin was even more conspicuous. "How dark I'm not. It reminds me of—do you read graphic novels?"

He grinned. "Am I your barbarian fantasy?"

She slid his hand between her legs, looked up, and smiled. "My real-life fantasy."

He pulled her close, slid two fingers inside her slippery heat. "I have this lurid urge to plunder and pillage when I look at your pale fragileness, baby. And it has nothing to do with fantasy. You're so fucking small. It's been tantalizing as hell from the first. Here, look." He half turned her so her back was to him, his fingers still deep inside. "See?" His powerful arm slanted across her body, his hand resting on her mons, his fingers cupping her sex, the two fingers inside her bringing a flush to her cheeks. His skin was shades darker, the black hair on his forearm, the network of veins in low relief faintly visible over his corded muscles in prurient contrast to her creamy skin.

Taking her chin in his other hand, he lifted her face to the mirrored wall. "Look at that." His tall, powerful body dwarfed hers, their skin tones unfiltered dark and light, the divergent images reeking of hunter and hunted, of liberties taken, of urgency and entitlement. "Look how small you are. You're my unspoiled gift, my sweet relief"—he smiled—"my flame-hot riot of need."

Her heart did a little flip because his voice had dropped, as if he were talking to himself. But she knew how little he wished to hear about love so she smiled back, and brushed his arm with her fingertips. "The sensation of being overwhelmed by all this heavy-duty maleness turns me on too."

"It's weird."

"But nice weird. I like that you're stronger than me, bigger...taller, all muscle and mojo."

He circled her with his arms. "I noticed the difference the first time I saw you. I felt"—he blinked, grinned—"probably just lust. I'm not good at distinguishing much else."

She softly exhaled. "You scared me that first day."

"Hey, remember who you're talking to." He bent his head and nuzzled the back of her ear. "You felt something else too."

She turned her head and smiled at him. "I wasn't sure what. Or if I had a chance."

Every woman who stood still long enough had a chance with him in those days. "I'm glad you decided to stay," he said politely, lifting his head. He drew in a small breath. "Sometimes I think of how close we came to never meeting and I start believing in fate. I *never* interview. But Max was busy and he was hot on hiring you so he insisted I fill in; he wanted me to see for myself how good you'd be for the company. And the reason I was late getting there was because I was thinking of blowing you off. Until Max called. Like he knew he had to nudge me."

"And then I said no to you and you freaked."

"I never like no. Although I was pretty sure I wasn't going to get a no when I fucked you."

She turned fully in his arms and looked up. "I might have had something to say about that."

He grinned. "Did you?"

She rapped him on the chin. "Smug bastard."

"Your smug bastard. Get used to it." Although talk of feelings always had a finite time limit for him. Longer now than before, but still not his favorite subject. "Need some help finding clothes?"

"Nah." She was learning to read his restless shifts; although what man liked to analyze his emotions?

He waved toward another doorway. "I'll be out there." And he strode away nude and beautiful as a god.

Kate flipped through a closet of workout clothes, picked out green shorts and a T-shirt, dressed, then settled on a chaise by the pool and watched Dominic do laps in a smooth, easy crawl. She stopped counting laps after a hundred, when he was still going strong, and wandered over to the fly machine. Adjusting the seat and weights, she leisurely worked her pecs. The bracelets were loose enough not to be a problem. It felt good to lift. She'd started when Gramps bought her a Harley for her fourteenth birthday. He'd said, *As soon as you can pick it up when it falls over, you can ride it.* Within a month she could bench press 120 pounds. She kept free weights in her apartment in Boston, but this space was a weight lifter's dream. She leisurely moved down the ranks of machines, testing them out, not killing herself, taking it easy.

Dominic was mentally running through his schedule while he swam. Swimming was his downtime, like meditation, his muscles programmed, his strokes streamlined, automatic, his breathing slow and even. His body moved with mechanical precision, his brain improvised and analyzed.

There was still a lot to do to prepare for Tuesday; he visual-ized landing in Rome and started the countdown again. He preferred not leaving anything to chance. He might take cal-culated risks, but he was never rash.

Kate was slowly working a leg press when Dominic came up a half hour later, wearing a white terry cloth robe. "I'm going to take a quick shower. Do you want to come with me or should I see you upstairs?"

"I'll be up in a while."

Leaning over, he gave her a kiss, then walked away and took the stairs at a run.

Fifteen minutes later, Dominic was showered, dressed in jeans and a faded relic-from-his-past Legalize Pot T-shirt, and was seated at his desk in his office downstairs, talk-ing on the phone. At a knock on the open door, he swung around to find Patty standing there with a surprise visitor. Charlie was smiling at him like he was expecting her. And she'd dressed in female executive mode, as if he cared. Her gray tailored designer suit was couture, her white silk blouse open slightly too much, and she wore enough real jewelry to indicate that she didn't have to work for a living. Which wasn't too far off the mark, because he wasn't sure she actually did much work.

So what the fuck was she doing here? And how soon could he get rid of her?

But he waved Charlie in and pointed at the sofa and then to the phone in his hand. "Uh-uh, Kev, not until next week. No, Wednesday at the earliest." He looked at Patty and brought his free hand to his mouth, mimicking drink-ing from a cup.

Patty nodded and left.

"Roscoe could help you in the meantime if you have any questions. Sure, we'll be back on schedule after Wednesday." He gave Charlie a polite smile. "You got it, Kev." Setting the phone receiver in the cradle, he rose from his chair. Skirting the desk, his bare feet soundless on the carpet, he pulled up a chair from the table in the center of the room and sat.

"Some problem at the NGO?"*God let her say yes because the alternative wasn't anything he wanted to hear.*

Charlie offered him a small bashful smile that might have been effective ten years ago, although even then it would have been a stretch. She wasn't the bashful type. "No, no problem, Dominic. I just wanted to show you the fourth quarter results. They just came in."

Seriously? Since when did he oversee the NGO? He had people who did that. With a silent sigh, Dominic held out his hand. "Sure. I'll take a quick look."

"You can see what we were planning on spending and the actual results. And the new compensation package is a separate document at the end."

Dominic started flipping through the pages, looked up when Patty came in with coffee, said, "None for me," and went back to his reading. He asked a few questions, Charlie inadequately answered them, and he returned to the first few pages to look more closely at the graphs showing the expenditure differences from one quarter to the next.

When Kate walked in, Dominic looked up. "Hi, baby. Come sit." He patted his leg. "You remember Charlie. She brought over the fourth quarter results from Julia's NGO."

"I remember. Hi," Kate said, taking in her dressed-to-the teeth competition. *No way Charlie was here on business.*

Charlie's gaze targeted the cuff bracelets and her hello was frosty. "Working out I see," she said with equal chill.

"Not much." Kate took Dominic's outstretched hand and sat on his lap. "I'm allergic to exercise."

Charlie's eyes narrowed. Dominic's newest slut looked fresh as a daisy in shorts and a T-shirt, without a speck of makeup. Surely those boobs were silicone. No way they were real. The bitch wasn't even wearing a bra. "I have a personal trainer. Actually a celebrity trainer," Charlie added with the kind of hauteur seen only on the stage. "He flies up from LA twice a week."

Fuck it. She was allowed. "Dominic's been helping me out," Kate said, smiling a little shy smile. "It's so sweet of him."

Dominic was tempted to laugh at Katherine's performance art. And he might have, if Charlie weren't breathing fire. "Here, baby," he said quickly, stepping in to defuse the situation. "Take a look at the compensation report from the NGO." He held it out. "You know accounting better than I."

Then Dominic asked Charlie a few more questions with no better results in terms of useful answers, and went back to his reading.

When Kate flipped over a page and her bracelet's diamond clasp caught the light, Charlie's mouth pursed, her eyes narrowed to hot slits, and she quickly debated the danger in speaking her mind. No fool she, her voice was saccharine sweet when she looked at Kate and said, "What lovely bracelets. Such an unusual design. Did you get them here?"

Dominic didn't speak up in the event Katherine preferred her own explanation. The bracelets weren't overtly sexual, the wide gold bands simple enough, and the diamond clasps could have been costume jewelry. Although two of them were perhaps more suggestive than one would have been.

"Dominic found them somewhere." Kate half turned to smile at him. "Did you get them here?"

"My jeweler had them made."

The office suddenly went silent.

Charlie came to her feet in an indignant surge. "Why don't I just leave the report with you, Dominic? It seems I'm interrupting."

"I'll send the report back when I'm finished," Dominic said with his usual air of unflappability.

"Just keep it." Charlie's spine was rigid, each word chafing with affront. "We have a stack at the office."

"Very well." Lifting Kate from his lap, Dominic set her on her feet, moved to the door, and shouted for Patty. "Patty will show you out," he said, turning back and stepping aside to let Charlie flounce past.

A few moments later, when Patty's voice grew faint, Kate glanced at Dominic, who was still standing at the door. "Does Charlie do that often? Bring reports to your home?"

"Never." He walked over to the sofa and dropped into a sprawl. The sofa, like so much of the furniture in the house, was comfortable and well used, the wide-wale corduroy, once a deep forest green, now slightly faded from the sun. "That was pretty fucking transparent."

"You were remarkably polite."

He sighed. "I don't like scenes. And I had no intention of having her stay long. Thanks, by the way, for coming in. I appreciate it."

"I wonder how early in the morning she had to get up to put on all that makeup?"

Dominic smiled. "Meow."

"I don't care. I'd never do what she did. Barge in like that."

"You don't have to, baby. Men come after you. Although I've put up the electric fence in our contract. You're off limits now."

"I'll have to let Charlie know you're out of circulation too."

"Be my guest. It'll save me grief."

"Speaking of grief." Kate tapped the report with her index finger. "I don't know if I should mention something that's none of my business..."

He smiled. "Since when have you been afraid to speak up?"

"This is different. It really is none of my business."

He shoved himself up against the sofa arm. "Forget the buildup. Just tell me."

"I know you pay your employees well, but the compensation packages for Charlie and her assistant are really way above the norm for those positions. I see a lot of pay plans in my business. Those are premium ones. Especially compared to other managers at Julia's NGO. I don't want to make trouble. I'm just saying."

"I don't actually oversee the NGO. Roscoe would know who audits the account." He smiled faintly. "Melanie told me last night I should fire Charlie. I wonder if she knows something I don't know? I thought she was just talking about Charlie's blatant pursuit, but"—he shrugged.

"I'm not saying you can't afford to throw that money away. You can. But personally, I'd wonder how much it pisses off your other managers. Ones that actually know what they're doing." She set the report on the table.

"She couldn't answer a single question could she?"

"Not even half a one."

He grinned. "You want a job?"

"Oh, yeah. I'm just dying to work for you."

"One of these days, baby, I'm going to change your mind."

"You can change my clothes for me if you want," she said with a grin, rising from her chair. "I'm going to take a shower."

"I'll help you."

"You just took a shower."

"Hey, cleanliness is next to godliness."

"How the hell would you know that?"

"I read."

"Not spiritual sermons."

"Should I?"

"It's too late for you."

"That's what I was thinking. But I could wash your hair for you. How about that?"

She lifted her T-shirt up and grinned. "How about

washing something else." Then she dropped her shirt, turned, and ran.

He caught her halfway up the stairs and swept her up into his arms. "You can't get away, baby. Don't even try."

He was very good at washing hair.

Really excellent.

She almost wanted to ask him where he'd learned to be so gentle, but she thought she might not want to know.

TWENTY-THREE

The next few days were perfect. Dominic and Kate played chess with the children several times. Once, they ate lunch at Lucia, taking the armored limo and going in through the back door, although Kate was unaware of the security machinations. And one afternoon—under the same discreet guard—Dominic took Kate to visit Gretchen and then to Tosca Cafe to sample one of his favorite drinks. They were shown into a back room by the owner, Dominic's friend, and they sampled the House Cappuccino, a Prohibition-era brew of chocolate, brandy, and steamed milk. On Melanie's recommendation, Dominic had the de Young Museum stay open late one evening so Kate could see Vermeer's *Girl with a Pearl Earring* in private. As a major donor, his request was granted without hesitation. And after witnessing Kate's ecstatic oohs and aahs as she stood before the small, pristine, almost virginal painting, he was pleased he'd made the effort.

But they mostly stayed in, spending the majority of their time in Dominic's bedroom, coming out on occasion to eat, use the gym, or sit outside on the rooftop deck with its spectacular views of the Golden Gate Bridge. On those fleeting occasions, Patty would summon the staff from next door to quickly clean Dominic's bedroom and bathroom, change sheets and towels, pick up in general, and of course wash the used sex toys,

Kate had timidly inquired who exactly was in charge of that task the first time they'd returned to the room and she'd seen the tidy display all neatly lined up on the bathroom counter.

"Patty's in charge of the house, the cleaning people, the yard men, the billing and deliveries. I don't ask. That stuff all looks clean, right?" Dominic casually remarked. "Patty's more of a stickler for hygiene than anyone. She uses organic everything so we're safe there. You can eat off the floor, she always proudly tells me. So I think the toys are equally wholesome."

A lifted brow. "Wholesome?"

He grinned. "And yet your qualms never last for long, do they, baby?"

"You're shamefully good at corrupting me," she murmured.

"It's not corruption if you're having fun," he drawled lazily. "And I'll always make sure you're having fun." He tipped his head. "So pick out something."

Her question answered with Dominic's habitual disregard for the duties of his staff, Kate followed his suggestion and made a selection. He might not know how the toys came to be arranged and organized so systematically in the bathroom, but he certainly knew how to use them.

The next day, when Kate was discussing a recipe with Patty, he took the opportunity to shut himself in his office and give Justin a call.

"I may hang up abruptly if Katherine walks in," Dominic warned. "Have you found anything?"

"When money's no object it's not a problem."

"Good. Where?"

"Upper Belgrave Street. A nice, two-bedroom flat. Five and a half mil."

"It's settled?"

"Someone in your office here will sign the papers this afternoon. And the account for Amanda has been set up."

"Good. Roscoe said he'd take care of it. You're sure Amanda doesn't mind helping?"

"She's in shopping heaven as we speak."

"Give her a kiss from me. Although tell Amanda if anything needs painting or new carpeting has to be installed, it has to be environmentally responsible, no chemicals, no toxicity. Same with the furniture. All natural finishes, fabrics. Katherine's not a large woman. She can't absorb the same quantities of toxins as someone my size."

"Sounds as though you'd like Katherine wrapped in cotton wool and put in a glass box."

"If only I could," Dominic said drily. "So," he briskly added, "can you have this done by Saturday? We fly in either late Saturday night or Sunday."

There was always only one answer for Dominic Knight. "Sure, no problem," Justin said. "We'll have it ready."

"Thanks," Dominic said. "We'll see you this weekend. By the way, we haven't met. You're just a magnanimous manager from CX Capital helping out a new contractor. You can cover your ass on that, right?"

"Not a problem. I'm a little like you, Nick. I make my own rules."

Dominic laughed. "Glad to hear it. *Ciao*."

Then he made a quick call to Leo.

"I was wondering when I'd hear from you," Leo remarked.

"Life's busy when you're on vacation," Dominic said, the smile in his voice palpable.

"Sounds like it. Everything's going well then?"

"Yes, very. We fly out Saturday though, Sunday at the latest. I'd prefer Saturday. We'll firm up the departure time later. And tell Sese I'm going to need him in London. I'm hoping to talk Katherine into having him serve as her live-in cook. That way there's someone on the inside as well as your crews outside. A little extra security. And Yash better come along too. Just in case."

"I'll tell them. Sese's at his relatives in the Central Valley, Yash is attending some seminar. I'll see that they're back by Friday night."

"How did things go with Tan?"

"Everything went well. They're all gone."

"You're not saying Gora's goon squad flew back to Bucharest?"

"No."

"No repercussions?"

"Only in Bucharest I expect. It should help your negotiations," Leo added.

"Maybe. Gora will run out of guns before he runs out of muscle. But it might make him question his tactics. Tan and his relatives are fine?"

"Everyone's fine."

"I don't suppose—"

"You don't want to know. *I* don't want to know. Tan

sees it as doing you a favor and it's not as though Gora's men had flown in from Bucharest for a vacation."

"Right. Thanks for the update. Gotta go." He set down the phone and smiled at Kate, who was standing in the doorway of his office. "I was talking to Leo. I think we'll leave on Saturday, unless it matters to you. Did you get the recipe you wanted?"

Kate lifted a recipe card she was holding.

"Come here. Show me. Is it something I'd like?"

"As if you care about cooking," Kate said with a smile, moving toward him.

"Hey, I care about what you care about." He swung his chair a half turn and lifted his arms as she approached. "Are you going to cook for me?" He drew her down on his lap.

"Maybe." She gave him a smile. "It's your rice pudding."

"Score." He lightly kissed her cheek. "I'll even help with that. Although," he added, keeping his voice deliberately neutral, "I was thinking you might like Sese to stay with you and cook. You really don't know your way around a kitchen. You like to work long hours, or at least you did in Amsterdam, and Singapore too, according to Johnny Chen. When you're pushing yourself that hard, you need nourishing meals. And Sese will stay out of your way."

"Tempting, but I can't imagine this apartment is very big."

"Let's wait and see." The word *tempting* was a good sign. She wasn't adamantly opposed. And he knew a two-bedroom flat priced at five mil must have some decent-sized rooms.

Their remaining days were nothing but sunshine

and roses, rainbows and bluebirds, unalloyed pleasure—luxurious and momentous. Dominic made sure of that. Whatever Kate wanted, he gave her.

Kate had told herself that first night in Singapore that whatever time she had with Dominic, she wouldn't spoil by thinking about the future. And by and large, she was able to deal with her emotions in a practical way. She was incredibly happy most of the time. Only occasionally, late at night, she'd wake up, terrified, her heart pounding, afraid she'd lost him. But a second later, she'd feel Dominic beside her, or holding her close, and her panic would subside.

For his part, Dominic was feeling a rare tension. He generally had nerves of steel, but with Katherine's safety at issue, with them both in the crosshairs of Gora's relatives, considerably more was at stake. Katherine had already been targeted in Singapore, Gora's men in place before he'd arrived. So he wasn't just gambling with his life, a life he'd viewed as disposable for years. Living held more purpose for him now. Since meeting Katherine, he felt as though he had a future, perhaps even a good one. And he was unprepared to lose either her or that future.

Although on a purely tactical level, Gora was the problem. He was a loose cannon at the best of times, always indebted to his wife's mafiosa family organization, but defiantly independent on the surface. None of which offered a predictable outcome to the meeting on Tuesday.

Money usually worked as leverage, but not always.

There were too many players at the table this time.

And some of them were invisible.

TWENTY-FOUR

Dominic's private plane landed in London Saturday afternoon at five.

Kate had received a text with the address of the sub-let apartment the day before. Justin had offered to meet her there and give her a tour; he was waiting when they reached the flat. Along with Max.

Justin introduced himself to Kate and Dominic and while he showed Kate the flat, Dominic and Max quickly reviewed their plans for Tuesday and arranged to meet at the airport Monday afternoon. Then Max left and Dominic caught up with Justin and Kate in the sleek, stainless-steel kitchen.

"Nice," Dominic said. "I like it."

"It's intimidating for a noncook," Kate said, viewing the handle-less cabinets that soared up to the high ceiling, the large brilliant blue Aga stove, and the even larger refrigerator. The three sinks and sizable wine cooler. "But I'll manage. There's always takeout and pizza."

"Why not let Sese take charge?" Dominic suggested. "You won't even have to come into the kitchen. And with your punishing work schedule I doubt you'll have time." Dominic turned to Justin. "Katherine has a work ethic on steroids. CX Capital is lucky to have her."

"So I've heard," Justin replied with a well-mannered smile. "We're looking forward to her help."

Dominic glanced at Sese, who'd come in behind him. "What do you think, baby? Care to see if Sese can help you out? At least until you get settled in. Your first week or so at work could be hectic."

"I don't know." She hesitated. "Would I be imposing? Sese probably has better things to do."

"Why don't you ask him?" Dominic smiled. "Although keep in mind Sese cooks for a living."

"Divinely as a matter of fact." Kate smiled at the huge mountain of a man standing beside Dominic. Their meals on the plane had been crazy good. "Would you mind helping me out, Sese? It wouldn't be for long. Just until my schedule—I don't know—falls into place."

Sese dipped his head. "No problem."

"Okay." Kate took a small breath. It was her first experience with something so grand as a live-in cook. "I don't have a clue how this works."

"Don't worry about it." A flashing smile. "I've been doing this a while."

"Great." She exhaled. "And I can pay for this," she added, turning to Dominic. "So don't even think about it."

"Perfect. It's settled, then." He glanced at Sese. "Here's your new domain. Starting Monday." Dominic shot a look at Justin. "Is there a cafeteria in the headquarters building or does Sese have to bring in food when Katherine's working late?"

"People generally go out to eat."

Dominic put his arm around Kate and pulled her close. "Sese will see that you have food. Sometimes you forget to eat when you're working. Now, do you have any questions for Justin?"

"How far is the office?"

"My driver will drive you," Dominic said before Justin could answer.

"He doesn't have to."

"Nonsense, that's his job. We'll let him know when to pick you up in the morning and you can call him when you want to be driven home. At least until you get the hang of things," he added smoothly, rather than *You can't go out of the flat without a guard.* "Sese, why don't you get some idea of what Katherine wants you to shop for and I'll see Justin out." Brushing Kate's cheek with a kiss, he moved away and smiled at Justin. "Thanks for coming over."

As the two men walked from the kitchen, Justin drolly said under his breath, "Is she legal?"

Kate wore sneakers, slouch pants, and a long-sleeved T-shirt, her hair unruly as usual, her green gaze luminous; the image of naïf vivid.

"Fuck you," Dominic said, grinning.

"Just asking. She looks fifteen and virtuous."

"Then I'll expect you to protect her from the big bad wolves at CX Capital."

"Jesus, that'll be a full-time job. She's gorgeous. Seriously, how the hell old is she?"

"Twenty-two."

"And she's keeping up with you?"

Dominic gave Justin a hard stare. "That's none of your business or anyone else's. Clear?"

Justin put up his hands. "Sorry."

Dominic smiled. "No problem."

Shortly after, Justin was pouring himself a drink at

home and answering his wife's questions about Dominic's *new friend*. "I think Katherine Hart is more than a piece of ass for him. More than a five-mil flat. Maybe even more than Dominic knows himself. I made the mistake of kidding him about his sex life with her and he bit my head off."

"My, my." Amanda looked up from her chair by the fire, Adam asleep in her arms, and smiled knowingly. "Dominic's protecting her. How lovely, and completely out of character for him." She lifted one brow. "A wedding perhaps?"

"Don't get carried away," Justin cautioned, dropping into a chair opposite his wife. "I'm not sure Dominic's the marrying kind."

"Julia managed."

"Exactly. *Managed* is the word. I think that's why he agreed to marry her. He didn't mind that she arranged his adventures. She didn't manage anything else."

"Just so long as you don't mind me managing your entire life," Amanda purred, blowing Justin a kiss.

"Hey, that's what I signed up for." He grinned. "Do your best."

Which was exactly what Dominic had in mind as well.

With only two nights and a day before he had to leave for Rome, he wanted to make his time with Katherine the very best he could.

Which meant minimum interruptions—no staff, complete privacy.

The moment Sese left, Kate had slipped her arms around Dominic's waist and whispered, "Thank you. I just want to be with you. Just us." She cast a swift glance around the kitchen. "I can probably cook something for you."

Dominic laughed. "You cook like I do—which is inedible. I'll have something brought from my house. It's only a few blocks away. Decide what you want."

"Besides you?"

"You got me, baby. That decision's been made. And you know what? My chef can cook us whatever later. Food isn't high on my list right now. You without clothes is on my list. You without clothes in a bed somewhere—" He looked up. "Where's the bedroom?"

She grinned. "Which one?"

"We have a choice? Maybe both. Maybe I'll chase you all over the flat and fuck you in every room. What do you think of that?"

"You say the nicest things," she purred.

"And you're the reason, baby. You're my happiness and contentment, my reminder that life's beautiful, my everything. Oh, God, baby, don't cry." He gently pulled her close, held her against the warmth of his body. "Everything's going to be good from now on. I promise."

"You're not going to be gone long, are you? Lie if necessary. I miss you already."

He lightly thumbed away the tears on her cheeks. "A few days, that's all," he said softly. "I'll be back before you know it."

She sniffed, swallowed, and tried to smile. "Promise?"

"Yes, promise," he whispered and brought his mouth to hers.

TWENTY-FIVE

Dominic spent the flight to Rome in his office on the plane and when he came out prior to landing, he handed Max a sealed letter addressed to Kate. "If things go wrong," he said, "and I don't make it out of the restaurant. If they use some spy equivalent bullshit that goes on in that part of the world—poison, radioactive isotopes, double cross or triple cross, whatever—make sure Gora doesn't walk out alive. Then give the letter to Katherine."

"Don't worry," Max said. "You're going to be well covered."

Dominic put up his hand. "If I'm dead, I want him dead. Got it?"

"That goes without saying."

Dominic nodded. "Good. I think I'm more use to them alive but God only knows. I thought we'd paid Gora enough to keep the Bucharest factory clean and you saw how that went. Everyone's fucking greedy. As if you don't know that. Now give me the lay of the land on the meeting site."

"The restaurant will be closed. We'll search the premises thoroughly before you go in. Then it's just you and Gora. We have snipers on their snipers. We have men on their foot soldiers and enough arms and ammo at your hotel here to start World War Three. The police won't become involved. Alessandro's taken care of it. We found Gora's jailbait last

night at a convent up in the hills and have her under surveillance. We saw her only once, the walls are high. But she
can't come out without us knowing. And worse comes to
worse, I suppose we could blast our way in. Although the
political scandal might be..." He trailed off and shrugged.
"Well, that's your call. Since Gora doesn't give a shit about
his wife, we have only a couple men on her. She's on vacation in Istanbul. And last, I expect Gora has a price you can
afford."

"If not for Katherine, I'd agree. But he knows how
much she's worth to me. He lost eight men in Singapore.
I'm sure his price has gone up exponentially. And to be
perfectly honest, I can't walk away like I might have in the
past and tell him to do his best or go fuck himself. Not with
Katherine in the picture. It changes everything."

"We can protect her."

"No, we can't," Dominic said. "Not completely. Not
unless we scare the shit out of her—which isn't an option.
And not when she's working in some goddamn office building with thousands of people coming and going."

"So what's the plan?"

"Don't have one other than the usual pile of money that
buys off most anything in the world. I'll wait for Gora to
make his move. I'll make mine. We'll see where it goes."

"At least you've done business with Gora before."

Dominic smiled. "And by that you mean I've paid him
beaucoup extortion money to keep my factory open."

Max shrugged. Both men knew the price of doing business in the lawless regions of the world.

Dominic sighed. "You're right though. Gora's been

dependable. He kept all the small fry scumbags off our backs. And I expect he didn't have much choice when his in-laws put the squeeze on him to steal another twenty million. He likes to live too. Probably even more now with his new little teenage lay." Dominic flicked a finger at the plane door being opened by a flight attendant and smiled. "Ready to rock? Let's go see if we can nail down this deal."

The restaurant was across the street from the Pantheon, the view splendid, the two-thousand-year-old building a thing of beauty, still flawless and sublime. It almost made Dominic turn to Gora and say, "This is really petty shit we're dealing with. Why don't we just put our dicks on the table, see whose is bigger, and be done with it?" But Gora was sitting across from him, dressed by Rome's best tailor, giving him his badass *I'm top dog* look, which didn't portend well.

"So what can I do for you, Gora?" Dominic said, speaking Italian, their common language, settling back in his chair, and thinking he'd dressed down for this party in jeans and a T-shirt. Although the knife blade in the sole of his red sneaker would get him out the door faster than any Savile Row suit. Not to mention, Gora was a lightweight by Balkan standards where no-neck enforcers were standard. His neck wouldn't be hard to crush.

"I need compensation for eight men."

"You shouldn't have sent them. You stole my money. I took it back."

Gora gave him an oily smile and spread his hands palms down on the table. "If it were only me, Dominic, we might be able to come to an agreement. But the organization doesn't like to lose money."

"Then your wife's family should prey on people who don't fight back. They fucked up. What can I say."

"Your girlfriend is in London I see."

He wasn't wasting any time. Just as well. "Yes. For six months."

"That's what I heard."

"I'm not surprised. So let me make myself perfectly clear. I don't want Katherine involved in any of your money problems. So count your fucking blessings. I'll buy my way out instead. How much do you want to make this go away?"

"I don't want money. I need you to marry my girlfriend." Gora quickly put up his hand as Dominic began rising. "Temporarily. She's six months' pregnant and she comes from an old, conservative family who insists she marry well before the child is born."

Dominic sat back down. "And you're afraid of your wife."

"Like you, Dominic, this young woman is important to me," Gora said, ignoring Dominic's comment. "So you see we both face a dilemma."

"You don't come back with the money? How do you explain that to your wife's organization?"

Gora shrugged. "I have enough to cover the shortfall." He smiled. "My business is lucrative too."

"I wish I could help you, Gora," Dominic said, "but I'm not interested in marrying the sixteen-year-old you've been fucking the last three years. Don't look so surprised. Why wouldn't I keep track of you? I'm almost tempted to show the video I have to your wife, but then you'd be dead and who would I deal with then?" A certain level of corruption was inevitable in doing business in the Balkans. That Gora had been useful when Dominic set up his factory in Bucharest was the trade-off.

"I could have you killed instead," Gora said coolly. "How would Miss Katherine Hart feel about that?"

"She did fine before me," Dominic said calmly. "She'll do fine after me. I don't kid myself that I'm indispensable to anyone. That's always a mistake, Gora. To think it matters whether we live or die. The world will survive without either one of us. So don't threaten me. I don't much give a shit. Just like I don't give a shit whether you live or die."

"Let me show you something." Gora pulled out his cell phone, tapped an icon, and handed the phone to Dominic.

The screen held a single photo taken with a night-vision camera. The picture had been taken from a higher sight line—across the street, Dominic noted. Katherine was in her bedroom, seated at the vanity, brushing her hair. Dominic handed it back. "Do I threaten your girlfriend now?"

"If you could get at her."

"I know where she is. She's under surveillance. Your move."

"Take a look." Gora tapped his cell phone again. "This one was taken ten minutes ago, just for you." He reached out and showed the photo to Dominic. Katherine was talking to a colleague in the office. "My cousin is a mail boy at CX Capital." Gora smiled. "It's a brand-new job. Probably temporary, but he likes it. All kinds of pretty girls, he says."

Dominic sat silent for a few moments, then looked at Gora with an empty, dispassionate expression. "Let me tell you a little story, Gora. When I was young my mother sent me to psychiatrists because she thought I wanted to kill her."

"Did you?"

"Why would I tell you what I never told any of the psychiatrists?"

"Is she still alive?"

"This isn't about my mother, Gora. One of the psychiatrists was a pedophile. So I anonymously notified the authorities of his illegal activities like any good citizen would. I told them where his files were. I told them where his photo collection was. I sent them a sample because the stupid shit showed me all that like I'd be interested. You get my drift, Gora? I wasn't quite ten and I'd already learned that you do whatever it takes. Always. Period. So if you harm a hair on Katherine's head, if you even frighten her, if one of your idiots shows himself and frightens her. Okay? Is that clear? I'll take you down, I'll take your wife's family down, I'll do it from the fucking grave. And before you get all blustery on me, your security's not the best. I can get to your little girlfriend. You fucking hurt Katherine and I'll do it. Bianca—right? I'll strangle her with my bare hands. Still want me to marry her?"

Gora gave him a considering look, breathed in and out, choosing his words. "I thought we were going to make a deal."

Dominic said with mild annoyance, "I thought the deal was money. Mine to you. If you need a bridegroom, add the price of some gigolo to stand at the altar with your babe. I just need a fucking number." He tapped his phone in his shirt pocket. "The money will be in your account in five minutes."

Gora hurt people for a living, but he still looked like a skinny accountant in an expensive suit that didn't quite fit him right. And his face had lost some of its badass arrogance now that he was trying to save the deal he needed to please the babe he didn't have sense enough to put on the pill. Although, Dominic thought, after his out-of-control week with Katherine in Hong Kong, he was the last person to talk about sensible birth control. "Look, Gora, I'm as interested in a deal as you are. Only it's gotta be money. And I'm probably going to be sorry I said this, but name your price. Let's get this done."

Gora slowly shook his head. "You know I can promise not to hurt Katherine. My word is good. I'm sure you also know that my Bianca comes from an aristocratic family. So I need you, Dominic, as much as you need me. I play chess too. I know you're protecting your queen." He sighed. "So that said, I need your status, your wealth. Just anyone won't do for her husband. That's why I have men watching your girlfriend. It's the only leverage I have. And I'm not asking you to do this for long. You can have any prenup you want. I don't want your money. After three months, the child is born with a good name; you get a divorce." He smiled faintly. "We know it's a boy. My wife only gave me girls."

Dominic prided himself on his deal making but he was starting to get a bad feeling about this one. Like maybe he was going to get burned. He'd had those feelings before and always walked away. But he couldn't this time. Not with Katherine's life on the line. Not when Gora knew he wouldn't allow her to be hurt. "Jesus, Gora, I expected this to be survivable. Marriage? Christ. Can't you find someone else to take your place as the bridegroom?"

"With the people I know?" Gora shrugged. "Not possible."

Dominic suddenly stood, walked behind the bar, grabbed a bottle of brandy, cracked the seal, poured a slug down his throat, then stood there for a few moments, running all the possibilities through his mind like a Vegas bookie, processing information, calculating tactics and constraints, determining objectives. Gora's people were dumb but they swung a lot of weight. Especially with the factory in Bucharest. Especially in sheer firepower. He *could* maintain a chain reaction of Mexican standoffs: first him, then Gora, then him, threats on top of threats to infinity—all while trying to keep Katherine blissfully unaware and out of danger. But juggling all of these retaliatory balls in the air was going to be a nightmare.

A part of his brain was telling him this might be a good time for a break. He could make a one-stop solution, solve all the myriad problems with a single, unemotional fix. Placate all parties involved and keep Katherine safe. Sometimes taking the weaker side of a deal in chess, taking a tactical loss for a greater strategic gain, was a useful move. A good chess player instinctively knew that.

And he'd always been a numbers guy. Numbers before emotions. That's how he'd made it to where he was. And recently emotion had been reconfiguring his algorithms and fucking with his head.

Maybe he should just put everything on hold. Give

things a chance to calm down. See if he really wanted what he thought he wanted. Focus on the strategic whole rather than the individual parts. Three months wasn't so long.

It was a decision made by a man who had come to view life as explicitly calculable.

Or at least he had until recently.

Dominic turned and walked back. "I have one stipulation," he said, sitting down, putting the bottle on the table and cradling it with his hands. "I'll do my time for you, but Katherine sure as hell won't be. I don't want any misunderstandings. Once the lawyers draw up the papers, Katherine is clear. Completely clear. I'm not leaving London until your hit squad is gone. This is nonnegotiable. You want something. I want something. We're even."

"I'm still eating your twenty million."

"Shut the fuck up, Gora. Quit while you're fucking ahead."

It was agreed. While Dominic drank half the bottle, their lawyers made plans to meet at Dominic's hotel in Rome later that day to draw up the prenup and the preliminary divorce papers. The usual license formalities would be expedited so the marriage could be performed by the end of the week.

Dominic came to his feet. "When I have proof your men are gone, that Katherine is safe, I'll fly back to Rome. *Ciao*, motherfucker."

When Dominic slid into the backseat of his car a few minutes later, he banged on the privacy glass, then held out his hand to Max. "I'll take that letter back."

"Things went well then?"

"Not exactly." As the car pulled away, Dominic folded the letter and slid it into his back pocket. "Give me a minute and I'll tell you. Right now I'm trying to keep from putting my fist through the window."

TWENTY-SIX

Dominic arrived at his house in Eaton Place at eight. Leo and Danny were waiting.

"Tell me again," Dominic said as he walked in. "Reassure me."

"Like I told you on the phone, the apartment across the street's been cleared out," Leo said. "The owner's on vacation in Spain. He doesn't even know Gora's men were there."

"What about the surveillance crews?"

"Gone. As of three hours ago."

"All of them?"

"We followed them to their gates at the airport. Twenty men all told. They left in groups over the course of the last few hours. Some to Bucharest, some to Rome, three to Geneva."

"Gora's brown bagging his twenty mil so his wife doesn't know." Dominic smiled faintly. "Christ, you might almost feel sorry for the little shit if he wasn't so totally fucking up my life."

Danny gave him a commiserating look. "Three months you said?"

"That's what the lawyers wrote down."

"You can't divorce in Italy."

"Christ no. It will take years. I'll divorce in France. The papers are already drawn up and signed. At least I can be grateful that my mother had the good sense to be in Paris when I was born; it gives me dual citizenship. A divorce *par consentement mutuel* is a simple procedure; quick, easy, a rubber stamp by a judge."

"When do you go back to Rome?"

Dominic scowled. "A couple of days."

"Are you going to tell Katherine?"

"I'd rather not. I don't want her living with fear or even the slightest bit of apprehension. And it's not as though this fucking mess can be easily—and truthfully—explained away with the mafia involved." Dominic sighed. "So it's lies, lies, and more lies."

"And the three-month countdown begins," Leo said kindly.

"Yeah. At least there's an end in sight."

Then Dominic texted Sese. *As soon as I get there, you have the night off.*

But a half hour later, when Dominic knocked on Katherine's door, his spirits were low and it showed.

"You're tired," Kate said, taking his hands and pulling him over the threshold as Sese slipped out the back door. "Come sleep. I'll talk to you in the morning."

"I don't want to talk." Kicking the door shut, he pulled free of her hands, swept her up in his arms, and strode to the bedroom. "I just want to fuck." Sex was the constant in his life that overrode all dilemmas and blurred reality—like drugs to a junkie.

"I was trying to be polite." Her smile was close, her breath warm on his cheek with her arms around his neck. "You look really tired. I should tell Sese—"

"He's gone. And I'm never that tired, baby. Not with you."

"How did—"

"Text. I wanted to be alone with you." He was walking fast down the hallway, indifferent to his surroundings; he swiftly strode through the large, high-ceilinged reception room without a glance, swept past the small dining room that Amanda had furnished with an intimate table for two made by Chippendale 250 years ago for a lady who took her morning chocolate in her boudoir with her lover, the carpet beneath it a seventeenth-century Mogul rug faded to a lush rose that may have come from that same lady's boudoir. "Did you have a good day at work?" he asked in a cursory way, as if someone had rapped him on the knuckles and demanded he be polite.

"I didn't wear any clothes," Kate murmured as the sporting prints decorating the hallway to the bedrooms flashed by. "Otherwise things went well."

Dominic's gaze snapped down. "You better be fucking kidding."

"Just checking if you were actually listening to me, Mr. Knight. You seem to be in a rush."

"You got that right," he said brusquely, moving into her bedroom and setting her on her feet. "Take off your robe." He was ripping off his clothes. "Hurry. I missed you."

She knew how he felt. She'd missed him every minute of the day, every second while she was multitasking and actually doing her work. And she'd been waiting for his knock on the door, had almost begun to despair when he arrived.

Dominic was undressed before she'd tossed her robe on a chair and made it to the bed. He picked her off her feet, dropped her on the bed, and fell on top of her with an explosive urgency and a murmured, "Forgive me."

He was frantic at first. She'd never seen him like that. He was always incredibly restrained, as though he could last forever; he *could* last forever. But this time he came almost the instant he entered her, panted "Sorry," and a few moments later proceeded to come again when she climaxed.

"God, you feel...good," he groaned, resting inside her as she gasped for air, his dick still rock hard. "You're going to have to kick me when you can't stand it anymore. I can go all night." His adrenaline was pumped up to the max, from frustration and anger, from lust and horniness, from feelings he couldn't define that burned through his body and brain.

"That works out then cuz I really need you." She ran her hands down his back as though vetting his presence, compelled by her own urgencies, her sense of loss in his absence profound. Dominic had been gone only a night and a day and she'd missed him desperately: the feel of him in her and over her, the pleasure he offered that lit up her world, his warm smile and goodness. And she was filled now with such overwhelming gratitude that he'd returned she was near tears. Shaky. She had her own addictions, and her next hit was in sight. "Oh, hell," she gulped, trying anything to keep from crying, even running through accounting formulas to divert her thoughts. And for a second it worked...until unassailable emotion overwhelmed the flood gates.

"Jesus, baby, don't cry," Dominic whispered, dipping his head and kissing away her tears. "If I did something, I'm sorry."

"I'm...not...crying because...I'm sad," she sobbed, clutching his back with white-knuckled fervor, weeping uncontrollably. "I'm just...happy...you're back."

He clenched his jaw so hard he thought his teeth would crack. Dragging in a breath, he slowly exhaled; then wiping the wetness from Katherine's cheeks with the sheet, he rolled over, sat up, and pulled her onto his lap. "Okay, we both need a quick breather." Reaching over, he picked up the box of tissues from the bedside table, took out a handful, and handed them to her because she was wailing like a baby now.

"Sorry," she hiccupped between sobs, super embarrassed, her nose dripping; she was gasping for breath.

"Everything's good. Cry all you want. I'll get more tissue if you need it." And he held her and handed her tissue and kissed her gently until her tears finally stopped.

"I suppose it's really great to come home to this," Kate said, wiping her eyes for the last time and tossing the tissue. "Every man's dream."

Coming home. He remembered Katherine saying that in San Francisco and it hit him in the gut now just as it had then. "Hey, you're my dream no matter what," he said, overcome by a sudden wave of exhaustion as though his adrenaline had finally given out. He had been kidding himself—his decision in Rome had not been unemotional. He didn't want anything to change. No three-month break, no playing his numbers game.

"Thanks." Her voice was unsteady again; she wanted to believe he meant what he said when she wasn't so sure about anything with Dominic. "Let's talk about nothing until I get myself together."

"You're preaching to the choir, baby." *Nothing* was a helluva lot better than the total mess screwing with his head. "So tell me about your first day at work. Who did you meet? What did you do? Do I have to crack any heads cuz some guys came onto you?"

She giggled.

Which was the point. He had to get through the night. Keep *his* shit together. He asked questions, she answered, and neither did anything irretrievably foolish. She described her first day at work. She told him of the projects assigned to her, the exciting scope of the problems, how she was looking forward to solving them.

"So you like a challenge," he noted lightly. "That must be why we get along. You figure you're going to fix me up someday."

She smiled. "As if I could."

"I like when you try." He shrugged. "Who knows, you might get lucky."

"I'm lucky already," she said, forcing down the tears swelling in her throat. "I have you in my life."

"There you go. Step one. Ten thousand more and you might be halfway to making me human. Remember?" he teased because he could see her struggling to hold back more tears and he'd talk about anything to keep his mind off his looming wedding. "You scolded me once about join-ing the human race. Now, tell me," he said, changing the subject to something even safer, "did you run into Justin today? Or is he on a different floor?"

"I met his wife. She came into the office."

"How is she?"

"Nice. Friendly. A tall, willowy blonde, beautiful of course."

"Why of course?"

"Because Justin makes a very good living so he gets to choose from the classy women. She was pregnant."

"Ah...I was wondering what you meant."

"She invited me to dinner sometime."

"You should go."

"Would you like to come?"

"Sure." *Provided the anticipated explosion over his upcoming marriage was small.*

They settled into easy and meaningless conversation and a few minutes later, Dominic went in search of something to drink. A refuge or remedy; he wasn't sure which. But thanks to Sese, he found a nice supply of Krug Clos d'Ambonnay '96 in the refrigerator and he brought back two bottles.

"With work tomorrow, you'll have to ration your drinking." He grinned. "I, however, do not." Leaning back against the headboard, he pulled Kate under one arm, held a bottle in his other hand, and made a point of asking questions because he wanted to hear her voice. The welcome sound soothed him, kept his bad decisions at bay, and reminded him there was goodness in the world after all, at least when Katherine was near.

He made love to her tenderly after that, like a well-behaved lover, like a man who was memorizing every sensation, every feeling, every touch, every kiss. She purred as he slowly moved in her, he softly growled, her wanting him ratified and endorsed in kind, and no two people were so generous to each other that night. He made love to her with exceptional patience, reading every nuance and subtlety of her arousal, meeting her passionate needs, whether frantic or leisurely, putting all his considerable skills at her disposal. And she gave herself up to him body and soul, responding to his disarming affection, the bounty of his indefatigable dick and as always to his arresting strength and beauty.

He was her temptation and deliverance. He was her life.

He probably should have stopped before he did, but he faced the possibility of three miserable, perhaps lonely, months and he wasn't that unselfish. But he smiled faintly when she said, "I'm going to sleep. You feel good though. You don't have to stop."

"Once more for old times' sake, then," he whispered, pushing into her sleek warmth. And when her eyes opened wide in apprehension, he smiled. "Just an expression, baby. Here's one for now. How about that?"

Afterward, he tucked her in and kissed her good night. "Sleep well, baby. I'm here. I'll wake you at eight thirty." Then he carried in another bottle and watched over her while she slept, feeling comfortless and depressed, pissed that he had no way out of this purgatory.

He silently cursed Gora and Gora's wife's family, which held them both prisoner, reviled the stupidity of a fifty-year-old man who messed with young girls, and wondered when the evil that conspired to fuck with his life would give him a break.

Then he picked up his iPhone, left the bed, strolled into the kitchen, took out another bottle from the fridge, and went in search of a speaker.

The alarm woke Kate. She was alone in bed, but she could hear "Bring It On Home" playing so she didn't panic. Dominic was still here.

She found him lounging in a chair in the living room, nude and beautiful, his eyes shadowed with fatigue, a bottle of Krug in one hand.

He looked up, turned off the music. "Sorry, I forgot to wake you. Did you sleep well?"

She smiled. "I did. You didn't apparently."

He shrugged.

He'd been rehearsing his speech—the one about giving her choices, about him being magnanimous. The one where he told her to go out with others, see more of the world, make sure she knew what she wanted. Enjoy herself. I'll see you in three months when this business deal I'm involved in is over, he'd say, if you still want me.

But she fucked it all up by standing there without a stitch of clothes on, more beautiful than ever, tempting as hell, his eternal Eve. Logic took a hike. Reason flatlined. And if he had had any doubts as to what he wanted before, he was absolutely certain now. When she spoke, her voice was filled with compassion.

"What's wrong?" she asked. She'd not heard Sam Cooke since Hong Kong. "Something's wrong, Dominic. Please tell me."

So he did, or at least he partially did. He had planned to give her his careful speech about the sudden change in his schedule that would take him away from London, how she should think about going out while he was gone, meet other people, make new friends. So much for the best laid plans. "I went to Rome to make a deal," he said instead. "I ran into complications. It's not a white-shoe lawyer or white-hat hacker kind of deal"—he paused, debating how much to say and how to phrase it—"so I'm caught in a bind. I have to temporarily marry someone. In three months I divorce her. That's it."

Kate's legs buckled and she slowly slid to the floor. *Fainting just like in the movies*, she thought. It took her a moment to find her voice and even then it was almost noiseless. "You're kidding."

He didn't immediately answer, struggling to find the right words. Or the words least likely to offend. "This isn't something I'd kid about."

Her normal voice was back, her green gaze turning steamy. "That's a real lame-ass excuse. Can't you think of something believable?"

"Believe me," he said. "It's fucking true." He slid upright, set the bottle on a nearby table, leaned forward, and looked at her, his blue eyes somber. "I'd like to ask you to ignore the whole thing or if you can't, at least wait for me. But it's selfish of me to even consider asking you when this situation is so totally fucked. So I won't."

Why was she surprised? This was Dominic Knight after all. "If you're looking for a way out, just say so," she said, giving herself points for not screaming at him or dissolving into tears.

"Jesus, no. I'm not looking for a way out. I thought we'd spend these six months in London together. Then this god-damn thing happened," he said grimly. "Look, don't move. I'll be right back." Coming to his feet, he quickly strode from the room.

Sad, mad, confused, she wasn't sure she could have moved if the flat was on fire. Her brain was racing, wanting to find a way out, wanting more than anything to find hope in the tumult of her thoughts.

Dominic came back a few moments later, dressed in his jeans. He carried a primrose silk robe and, lifting her to her feet, he quickly slipped it on her, his gaze averted in the event he forgot what was required of him. Then he led her to the sofa, pulled her down onto his lap, and buried his face in her hair.

"This is the only way I know to fix this problem," he said, his voice muffled.

"Who is she?" There wasn't a woman alive who wouldn't have asked.

He raised his head, met her gaze. "I don't know." A half-truth. "I never met her." True.

"Come on—you're marrying someone you've never met? You can do better than that."

He couldn't tell her that without this marriage, her life was in jeopardy. "It's complicated."

"I just can't imagine anything's *that* complicated." She looked at him directly, scrutinizing his face as if the answer lay within. "What's really going on? You must have knocked up someone important. Or are you really just tired of me?"

"Jesus, stop. Did it look like I was tired of you last night?"

"Fucking marathons aren't exactly unusual for you." She sighed. "Are they?"

"You expect me to answer that?" A hint of his temper began to flare.

And the elephant in the room came to life. "You have to admit, it's not unreasonable that I'm questioning this so-called complication. With your history."

He closed his eyes, wishing the three months were over, that he didn't have to have this conversation. "No, it's not unreasonable," he said, slowly opening his eyes.

"Do they want your money?" She needed a reason that made sense, that took away the fear that he didn't want her anymore. "Tell me something I can understand. Because I don't understand this at all."

He blew out a breath. "I really can't talk about it." He hesitated. "That's part of the complication."

"Jesus, Dominic." Her head had begun to spin. "I don't know if I can believe you. It seems to me you could change this if you wanted. Although maybe I'm expecting too much. Maybe you don't want to."

His voice was soft, his eyes gentle. "If I could change this, I would. But I can't. And I understand how hard it is for you to believe me. The whole goddamn thing is unbelievable. But this clusterfuck is mine to deal with, not yours. You're busy with a new job now, you've got your hands full. Maybe it would be best if we took a break for a few months." *It was harder to say than he'd thought. Self-sacrifice had always been for others.*

She felt her world dim, as if someone had abruptly turned off the lights. "Is that what you want?"

"No, it's not what I want," he said, feeling deadly tired. "It's so far from what I fucking want. But I'm trying to be decent. How can I ask you to sit and wait for me? I'd like to more than anything. I'd like everything just to stay the way it is." He held her gaze.

She didn't immediately answer. She turned her head away. Then she looked at him, refusing to let herself be weak enough to cry. "That's asking too much."

"I understand," he said quietly. "It's not fair to you."

She felt something deep inside her give, like a Florida sinkhole that was collapsing under her feet. "Damn it," she whispered, trying to get up. "I'm not going to cry over you. You must do this all the time."

His grip tightened, forcing her to stay. "I don't ever do this." His eyes closed for a second and he took a breath. "I usually say thanks it's been nice. I'm trying to be a good guy for once in my life."

"You become a good guy by leaving me? Is that what you're saying?"

"Jesus, baby. Tell me what you want me to say and I'll say it."

"Tell me you're not getting married."

The silence was oppressive.

"Christ, Dominic. People don't get married because of some murky business deal. If they did, half the people I shut down online would have to get married. They're all crooks. Do you really think I'm that stupid? Jesus, I should have known when you were so super nice last night, when you made me think you actually cared, that I'd get burned in the end. It's fucking Hong Kong all over again."

He gave her a black look. "If only it were that simple. Because when it comes to being burned, I'm being consumed by the flames of hell and you're feeling the heat from blowing out your birthday candles, okay? It's not even close."

"So what I feel doesn't matter? Or not as much as you? Is that right?"

He didn't answer.

"Answer me, damn it."

He stared at her, his jaw tightened. "You wouldn't like my answer."

Fury began to burn through her consciousness. "Fine," she said, the single word whip sharp. "I'm sure you're right. Because you're always right, aren't you? I hope your new wife is fucking docile." She came to her feet, bitchy as hell, and said, "I should thank you for the sex last night. It was great. You were fantastic as usual. And make sure you call off your hired help. I won't be needing them. Now, if you'll excuse me, I have to get ready for work."

He watched Katherine leave.

Jesus, that went well.

If this was love, it sucked.

He got up when he heard the bathroom door shut and finished dressing while Kate was in the shower. The streets were still quiet as he walked the few blocks home. The front door opened before he reached it. His major domo stood at attention beside the pedestal table with the large flower arrangement in the center of the entrance hall.

Dominic nodded good morning to the boy who'd opened the door and spoke politely to the older man who ran his London household. "No calls today, Martin, no visitors either. I don't want to be disturbed. Unless Miss Hart calls."

But she never did.

He hadn't really thought she would.

TWENTY-SEVEN

Kate swore in the shower and swore while she dressed, swore before and after she tried to force herself to eat breakfast, calling Dominic every name in the book. At least it was better than showing up at work red-eyed and splotchy-skinned from sobbing her heart out. She found a cab at the corner and checked her e-mail on her phone as she was driven to work.

She shut her office door the moment she arrived. She normally didn't, but her emotions were shaky as hell and there was no point in having to explain possible tears to more or less strangers. The day passed in a blur. She ate candy bars for sustenance, which was actually the norm prior to meeting Dominic Knight and his host of personal chefs. She'd always consoled herself that Snickers had peanuts, so protein—right? And the sugar high from the candy was a requirement today when her life was so screwed. But her senses automatically responded to a computer keyboard and screen so she was able to function at a tolerable level, her brain navigating the cyber world on autopilot. Although, she wasn't the only one screwed that day. She closed down a hefty list of vulnerabilities, flagging a GTFO before she shut down the hackers' entry points.

At the end of the day, one of the other consultants invited her to join a group going out for drinks. She briefly hedged, thinking, *Go, go! Don't be stupid!* Then she smiled and said, "Maybe next time," because she was already depressed and drinking would only make it worse.

But the minute she reached her flat, she called Meg and whined about no-good men who married other women for no apparent reason and Meg said, "What a fucking liar. I hope you found someone else to sleep with tonight."

Kate laughed. "I'll go out and drag someone in off the street." And she felt a couple degrees better.

"You better fucking mean it," Meg yelled over the phone. "Although maybe someone you know, someone at work, would be less risky," she added in a more thoughtful tone. "Send me a picture of the fun."

Then they talked for a couple hours about badass men, past and present, laughed more than they cried, compared notes on their jobs—Meg's, fabulous and fun, Kate's, fabulous and fun when she wasn't crying, and both ultimately decided that at their age life was still golden—alive with promise and legions of men waiting to be laid.

Before they hung up, Meg asked cautiously, "Are you going to tell Nana?"

"Absolutely not," Kate said. "Especially not about his marriage. I'd get a lecture for not being more careful about the company I keep and all the while she'd be wondering how I could be so gullible. You know Nana—she's anything but gullible."

"Hey, don't beat yourself up. Anyone would be tempted. The man's beyond gorgeous even without the money."

"And unfortunately a grade-A ass. But since Nana already knows the son of a bitch left me once, she won't be surprised he's gone again. So whatever I decide to tell her will be more or less the same old, same old. Speaking of same old, you're still with Luke. That's a record for you."

"I just like him. He's dependable in a serene, unhurried way—easygoing and calming when I'm wired. And he's great in bed and not one bit demanding."

The word *demanding* instantly evoked flame-hot memories that Kate worked furiously to suppress. She wasn't about to recall all the sensational pleasures inspired by a demanding Dominic—making her do things for him, things that—*Stop! Stop!* Sucking in a breath, she said as calmly as she could, "Great in bed is definitely on my wish list."

"I'll be expecting reports on your sex life," Meg commanded with her usual glass-half-full enthusiasm. "Look how much fun you had with what's-his-name. Believe me, he's not the only one with a dick who knows how to use it. Now don't disappoint me. Got it?"

There was only one acceptable answer for Meg. "Got it," Kate said. "I'll let you know."

And she actually meant it. After talking to Meg she was in a much better frame of mind. Meg saw men as functional objects with dicks she could use. Really, it made sense. Why get involved?

While Kate survived the day at CX Capital, Dominic stayed in his library and drank. Max called. He didn't pick up. Max came over. He had Martin turn him away. So Martin brought in a note from Max with his wedding date and time scrawled in large print with a note at the bottom. Danelli villa at Fiesole. Morning coat.

Dominic swore, tore up the note, muttered under his

breath, "Morning coat, my ass," poured himself another drink and finally, late that night, locked the door to the library so he wouldn't go to see Katherine and make what was bad worse.

He came awake on the couch the next morning sputtering and swearing from the water Max was pouring over his head. "I locked the fucking door," Dominic growled.

"Good for you," Max said drily. "Locked doors are child's play. We have to be there tomorrow," he added as Martin waved in house staff to clean up the water.

Dominic groaned, took the towel handed to him, and covered his face.

The next morning, Dominic viscerally understood the term *cruel and unusual punishment*, after undergoing the ordeal of a wedding to someone he didn't know, with guests he didn't know, with a priest who eyed him like he was some pervert. *Not me*, he wanted to say. *I don't do thirteen-year-olds, or sixteen-year-olds for that matter.* But he only answered yes or no as needed, didn't once look at the pregnant young bride, and with a tight smile stood in the blessedly short receiving line after the ceremony.

When the reports had first come in three years ago acquainting him with Gora's newest infatuation, perversion, whatever you wanted to call it, Dominic had wondered what kind of family would allow it.

Now Dominic had his answer: A titled family with heavily mortgaged property and no money. That's who. And when he saw the well-heeled guests, albeit only close family, at the wedding *and* the newly refurbished villa, when he met the parents who sized him up like a prize racehorse, he was reminded of that saying: *No matter how cynical you get, you can't keep up.*

Although he and Gora had already taken precautions to see that no photos would be published and the guests had been warned or threatened into silence, Dominic reminded himself to redouble his efforts in both regards. This Danelli family was out for money and they didn't care whose it was.

He didn't stay for the wedding breakfast, nor did he respond to Bianca's coaxing that was way the hell too friendly. More than most men, he recognized a come-on when he saw it. And once he and Max were in the car and driving away, he mentioned Bianca's overtly seductive approach. "If that little bitch doesn't watch it, Gora will see that she does. Did you notice what she did? She practically crawled up my body, which isn't easy to do when you're six months' pregnant. I thought her parents might say something."

"You're richer than Gora," Max said drolly. "Why would they?"

"That whole scene was surreal. And I don't scare easily."

"You noticed Gora wasn't invited." Max arched a brow. "His money's good enough but he isn't."

"The poor schmuck. He's being played big-time and he's actually looking forward to this child. Tell me not to feel sorry for him."

Max shot Dominic a narrowed glance. "Don't make that mistake. He's a brutal killer."

Dominic nodded. "Never let feelings get in the way. Right?"

"Always a good idea when Gora's involved."

"Gora's problems aside," Dominic said, "we'd better put round-the-clock surveillance on that sex kitten. Bianca's for sale and I don't want to be caught up in some duplicitous scheme that family's concocted. They're like modern-day Borgias."

"We have that covered already. Remember I was the one who did the initial research on the Danellis."

"Well, keep them far away from me."

"That's the plan. Will you be in Paris long?"

"Until this is over."

It was a short drive to the Florence airport. Dominic's plane was ready to taxi the moment they boarded and two hours later, Dominic was in his apartment in Paris. And save for two short business trips in the offing, he planned to stay there. He wanted to be near his French attorney so his divorce papers could be filed as soon as Gora's son was born. Not that he fully trusted any of the other interested parties to notify him. To assure a speedy report, Dominic had come to an agreement with Bianca's doctor: a new Sardinian villa for the doctor in exchange for immediate news of the birth.

Dominic was in Paris for logistical reasons as well. He was far enough away from London so that he couldn't force his way into Katherine's flat—which was a real possibility after a bottle or two. Yet Paris was close enough that he could reach Katherine in under two hours should she call. Not that he didn't wince at his behavior. Christ, he was like a young boy waiting for his first girlfriend to call. He'd never waited for a woman in his life.

So much for unemotional fixes.

He'd tried calling Kate. Usually late at night, usually not fully sober. She never answered.

He'd texted her once and she texted back: don't. The short message was lowercase and ended in a period rather than an exclamation point, but he could feel the ice through the phone. He hadn't done that again.

All of which made the current state of affairs brutal for him.

In desperation, six weeks later, at the beginning of April, he traveled to Minnesota to visit Nana. He'd tried to talk himself out of going. But he had an ache that wouldn't go away, a gut-wrenching sense of loss, a feeling of alone-ness that had never mattered before and now was so deep it was demoralizing.

So he found himself standing outside Nana's door, wait-ing for someone to answer his knock. It was cold in north-ern Minnesota. He should have considered the weather before he left Morocco; he was dressed in jeans, a short-sleeved T-shirt, and sandals. The car he rented at the Duluth airport had been warm so he hadn't noticed until he was standing in the wind on this porch overlooking a lake that was still covered with ice.

The door suddenly opened.

"I'm not giving the money back if that's why you're here," the elderly lady snapped.

Dominic smiled, thought of Kate, and knew where she'd learned to be outspoken. "Obviously you know who I am."

"You hide that private foundation real well. It took me more than twenty hours to sift through all the shadow companies before I found your name on a document." She smiled. "Love the Web. Opens up the whole world, even to people who live in the sticks." She opened the door wider. "Come on in. You must be here for a reason and"—she glanced at his sandaled feet—"you're not dressed for the weather."

"It was warm when I got on the plane."

"What are you, a three-year-old kid?" she said over her shoulder, leading him down a hallway.

"I had a lot on my mind, Mrs. Hart."

"Call me Nana. Everyone does. At least you have an excuse. I suppose what you had on your mind was Katie."

"Call me Dominic and yes, she's been on my mind."

"I have a cousin named Dominic. It's a pretty common name up here. Have a seat." She waved him to a chair in a living room that hadn't changed since the eighties. A hodge-podge of upholstered furniture, nothing matching, framed photos everywhere: mostly Katherine with her trike, bike, motorcycle—his brows went up at that—high school gradu-ation and the prom—he scowled at the good-looking kid standing beside her. There were two recent photos with Katherine smiling on campus, one or two of Nana, one of a man in uniform he assumed was Roy Hart, aka Gramps, and several that must be Katherine's mother, since the resemblance was strong.

"I was wondering if I'd see you," Nana said, sitting down opposite Dominic in a matching Barcalounger. "Thanks, by the way, for the money. I've already told you I'm not giving it back if that's why you're here. With all the cuts in public education, the district needs the money. I didn't mention it to Katie either. There was no reason to tell her. She's not here, if that's why you came, and I'm not telling you where she is."

He knew where she was. That wasn't why he was here. "I was wondering how she's doing."

"How do you think she's doing? A young handsome man like you with bags of money. You can turn any young girl's head. Leave Katie alone. You're out of her league."

"No, I'm not."

"Then you choose to be."

Silence. Then he said, "I'm not so sure about that."

"Too long a pause, my boy. My baby girl needs someone who doesn't have to think about loving her."

Dominic visibly flinched at the word *love*. This wasn't a subject he spoke of in public, or had even considered before Katherine.

"There, you see. You can't do it."

"I'd like to try. I am trying."

"Then tell her."

"She won't talk to me."

"Smart girl," Nana said, her gray perm stirring with her brisk nod. "She was unhappy for quite a while. She's better now, if you really want to know. If you want to help her, you'll leave her alone. She'll get over you. You're not the only good-looking man in the world."

He was pleased to hear Kate was fine; he was displeased to hear she was fine without him. But just talking about her made him happy, so he smiled and said, "She's been doing well in her new business, I hear."

Nana scowled. "Don't try and charm me. I'm an old lady. I've seen it all."

"I'd like to talk about her if you don't mind."

Blunt, honest, a quiet humility in his gaze. "Would you like a drink? You look a little peaked."

"It was a long flight."

"Come downstairs, I'll give you a little pick-me-up. My husband, Roy, made my still years ago when he came back from Nam. He needed something to take his mind off...well, you know what went on over there. He showed me everything I know about making vodka and mine's damn good, if I do say so myself."

"No problems with law enforcement?" Dominic followed her down the stairs to the basement. She was thin and spry at seventy-five, taking the stairs with a little spring in her step.

"I know the sheriff and his father, and grandfather, for that matter, and they know me. I give 'em a few bottles now and then. Everything's copacetic. Sit over there at that table. I'll get us a drink. Blueberry okay with you?"

He almost smiled, remembering his mother's face when he'd brought up Nana's hobby at lunch that day in Hong Kong. "Blueberry would be just fine," he politely replied.

Two drinks later, after Dominic had asked Nana about Roy, about Kate as a child, about small-town living, which was like an alien universe to him; after he'd heard about the new roof on the gym thanks to his gift and the eight teachers they'd been able to hire back with five-year contracts, Nana set her glass down, speared him with her gaze, and said, "You must have set Katie up in business."

"Not personally. Six times removed. I've been able to send a few clients her way, but her success is her own. I have nothing to do with it."

"She liked the flowers you sent when she and her partner, Joanna, set up in business. Purple iris, I heard. Three or four baskets."

It took him a fraction of a second to answer, the room in the Garden House suddenly too vivid in his mind, rocking his world. "I'm glad she liked them."

"She's making lots of money."

"That's the idea."

"Why doesn't she know you've done this for her? It's clear as day."

"You raised her not to be cynical. She's remarkably innocent despite her intellectual accomplishments. It's one of her great charms."

"Hmmph. From an arch cynic."

"I didn't have the advantage of her upbringing. She was fortunate."

"So you're saying money doesn't buy happiness."

"Pretty much."

"And you're wondering if she can fill that void for you."

"I don't know. It's more than that. But she's on my mind a lot. I thought I'd come and see how she was doing, that's all. I should go. I've taken up enough of your time." He came to his feet.

"I won't ask you to promise me you won't pester her because I can see that you will. But she's like her grandpa. You mess with her, she fights back."

He smiled faintly. "I'm aware of that."

"You mess with her and *I'll* make trouble for you. Roy came back from Nam a little bit crazy and some of it rubbed off. Just so you know."

"I have no intention of hurting her."

Nana softly exhaled. "I don't envy you. You don't know exactly what you want."

His smile was sweetly boyish. "I'm trying to figure it out. Or maybe I need to understand how to get it." He pointed at the bottle on the table. "If you ever want to go into business, let me know. Your vodka is first class. I'm always looking for new investments."

She smiled. "You trying to buy your way to my granddaughter?"

He laughed. "I'm not so foolish. Katherine doesn't care about money. I'm assuming she learned that from you."

Nana met his gaze. "Life's about almost everything *but* money. I'm not saying you don't need enough to keep a roof over your head, but after that"—she shrugged—"it's about the people you love. That's what makes life worth living. Sorry about the lecture. I'm an old school teacher. It's in the blood."

"I don't mind. And let me know what more you need for the school. I mean it. My educational foundation is one of my pet projects. Let me give you my cell phone number."

"I already have it."

Dominic's brows shot up.

"Where do you think my baby girl learned to love computers? There's no privacy left in the world. I don't have to tell you that."

Dominic laughed. "In that case, give me a call if you need something."

"Or if I hear something from Katie?"

Kate would have recognized that small startle reflex.

"I'd like that," Dominic said a moment later. "I like to know how she's doing. Thanks for the drink and conversation."

Nana stood on the porch and watched the wealthy young man walk through the snow in his sandals, get into his rental car, and drive away.

She'd never met anyone so alone, she thought.

TWENTY-EIGHT

Their separation wasn't any easier for Kate. Dominic had married another woman. And there was no question in her mind, no matter how she dissected and reviewed their last conversation, that he'd been lying through his teeth. *I have to marry her.* Bullshit. A man like Dominic, who controlled everything as far as the eye could see and beyond? As if he could be coerced into marriage. He didn't want her; he just wanted someone else.

So get over it.

But she must have been reading the wrong *Cosmo* articles. Because getting over someone wasn't supposed to blacken out the sun, shut out the music from the world, bring down the curtain on one's life, or as Gramps would have said, "Make you fire off that last round."

Gramps had always said that like it was a good thing. Like it was time to move on. So she tried.

She dealt with her misery by burying herself in work; she put in long hours, audited source codes and cleaned them up, wrote programming script to stave off cyber attacks, developed new code to keep the site from collapsing under an overload, closed one after another vulnerability on the bank's website. And after Dominic left, she started helping a fellow contractor on weekends in a small office on Bond Street. Together, she and Joanna pounded keyboards and crunched numbers and codes and when Kate was finally ready to collapse, she'd go home and try to sleep. But she wasn't sleeping well, she wasn't eating well, she was trying to distract herself from a cloud of despair that wouldn't lift.

Dominic was in the habit of checking on Katherine's location a dozen times a day, the GPS on her cell phone his personal surveillance, his lifeline to hope, to better times and rosier prospects. When the three months were over, when his divorce was rubber-stamped, he was going to do whatever he had to do to win her back.

There was no question in his mind.

And if she'd ever talked to him, he would have told her that.

He'd also had Max set up security teams to watch Katherine in the event Gora went off the deep end. Each evening, Max reported to Dominic, but his account never varied. "All she does is work. We're running eight-hour surveillance shifts but she isn't. She barely sleeps. CX Capital is getting their money's worth. Her new partner apparently doesn't eat or sleep either."

And so things continued through March and April.

Until a day in early May.

While Kate had become accustomed to not eating or sleeping, her nausea couldn't be so easily ignored. Particularly when she finally paid attention enough to recognize she was sick only in the mornings. After a few moments of panic, she turned to a search on the Web—needing reassurance.

But her search wasn't reassuring.

She still could be wrong, she told herself. Really, how could it possibly be when Yash had given her the shot in Singapore? There must be some reasonable explanation. Recalling a conversation with Justin's wife, Amanda, jogged Kate's memory. Amanda had mentioned her obstetrician's roster of celebrity clients and the doctor's name had sounded movie star-like as well. Bryce Clifton. So Kate called Dr. Clifton's office and made an appointment. Not because she was interested in the celebrity factor, but she expected someone like Amanda would chose a good physician.

Two days later, her nausea not improved, Kate was nervously flipping through a magazine in Dr. Clifton's waiting room, which resembled a cozy country house parlor rather than the chrome and plastic decor normally found in doctors' offices. She was the only person waiting. Apparently, posh doctors didn't stack up patients like they did in the clinic back home.

A nurse came in, summoned Kate in a hushed murmur, and led her to another cozy room painted in warm colors— save for the white-sheeted, stainless-steel examining table. Kate was handed a flower-print hospital gown to put on and directed to a cheerful little dressing room with rose garlanded wallpaper, pink leather chairs, and paintings of pretty landscapes on the walls.

If the goal was to make you relax, it was working.

When Dr. Clifton came in, he introduced himself with well-mannered charm, as if they were meeting over tea, even made similar small talk. Then, he said with a smile, "Let's see what we have here," the nurse helped her lie down, and as he examined her, he spoke softly to the nurse in a kind of medical shorthand.

Then, disposing of his surgical gloves, he helped Kate sit up and said with another smile, "Congratulations, Miss Hart. You're going to have a baby."

"Impossible!" she blurted out.

Dr. Clifton's smile broadened. "You're not the first one I've heard say that."

"But I'm on the contraception shot." Kate schooled her voice to a more polite tone. "How is it possible?"

"The shot isn't infallible, my dear. Were you not told?"

"But I was told the percentages were extremely small. Obviously," she said, trying to remain calm, when her pulse was racing, "not small enough. Have you any idea how far along I am?" she said, frantically trying to count back.

"You're approximately twelve weeks, Miss Hart. When was your last period?"

She told him that since the shot she'd hardly had a period. And he did some calculations. "You're due in early November—I'd say the tenth."

Kate went pale. A bona fide date made it terrifyingly real.

The doctor patted her shoulder. "Would you like to lie down for a few minutes? Many patients need a moment or so to absorb the news. Or would you like me to call some-one to come and see you home?"

"No!"

"Well, then," he said tactfully, because he'd seen other young women like Miss Hart who were concerned with their privacy, "the nurse could show you to a quiet room where you could rest."

Kate shook her head, sat up straighter. "Thank you, but that's not necessary. It's just a shock—when you think you're protected." And stark and clear, the words *Don't use that. Okay?* rang through her mind. It had been her decision that first night they were together in Singapore.

So she couldn't blame Dominic for not using a condom, although she'd love to, since he'd broken her heart—twice. *She* was to blame though. No one else. Which just went to show how much havoc a tall, dark, shockingly handsome man could cause when a woman wanted him.

Soon after her return to work, Kate realized she couldn't possibly maintain the pretense of professionalism when her life was in complete free fall. So she begged off sick, telling her fellow consultant and weekend accounting partner, Joanna, "It's just a migraine. I'll be fine tomorrow."

An unfortunate lie, since Joanna actually had migraines, which meant that Kate had to endure a recitation of a long list of remedies that were only marginally effective, and she had to try to discuss her symptoms with some personal awareness. She mostly punted by nodding at appropriate moments and repeatedly saying, "That's it—exactly."

After making her escape, overcome with nausea, she quickly ordered a pot of tea in the café downstairs, found a quiet corner seat by the window, and immediately drank down half a cup. Tea actually helped her queasiness she'd discovered.

Then sitting quietly, nursing her tea, she felt her stomach settle, and resorting to the slow countdown she'd learned from Gramps, she tried to relax. There were times he'd waited for days in enemy territory for a target to come into his sights, he'd said, and when he could barely move for days on end, he needed to say calm. Jesus, she missed him. Her eyes filled with tears. She missed Nana too and she smiled, thinking of what Nana would say when she told her she was going to be a great-grandmother. She'd probably say, *Beat that news, Jan Vogel,* because Jan was always bemoaning the fact that she didn't have grandchildren. And in a hidden away spot that had resisted all her best attempts to scour her life of Dominic's presence, she wondered for a fleeting moment what Dominic would say.

Nothing probably. He was good at not answering.

Then she saw a young mother pushing a pram and she was instantly transfixed. She watched until they moved out of sight and then began to notice other prams and strollers with babies in the passing pedestrian tide—and toddlers, and girls and boys on their way home from school. She'd catch her breath from time to time, as though suddenly the sight of babies and young children left her breathless and spellbound. As if she were aware for the first time of the miracle of birth.

But a small panic also underlay her astonished wonder.

And a faint unsettling doubt washed over her in irresolute waves.

Jesus, what was she going to do with a baby?

That same afternoon, Dominic was surprised to get a call from Max well before their regularly scheduled time.

"I just wanted to let you know, Katherine went to Harley Street," Max said.

"Yes, I already know." *GPS in action: map, street, address, name.*

"She went to see a doctor."

"Yes, I know. To get her contraception shot. It's been three months."

"She didn't get her shot."

Dominic shifted slightly in his desk chair and glanced at the clock in his Paris office as if on some subconscious level the time was significant. "You know that?"

"You wanted me to be thorough."

"And? Cut the drama. If you have something to say, say it."

"She's pregnant."

Dominic sat up like a shot. "Impossible."

"Apparently, that's what Katherine told the doctor."

Dominic swore softly. "A fucking three percent chance? And the casino still wins? Jesus."

"I didn't know the odds, but the nurse mentioned it. I chatted her up. Nice older woman, two children, a new grandchild—"

"Christ," Dominic muttered. "You're sure?"

"Positive."

"Fuck." He slumped in his chair, shut his eyes.

"Katherine might decide she doesn't want it."

Dominic's eyes snapped open and a collection of raw memory raced through his brain, images of Katherine fifty different ways. "I'm not sure that's a solution," he said, a brooding note in his voice.

"It might be for her."

"We'll see about that," Dominic curtly replied. "Have

a car waiting at Heathrow. I should be there in an hour, twenty." Dominic was already punching numbers on his desk phone.

"Katherine's still at work. You probably shouldn't embarrass her there."

"I'll see the doctor first. George, file a flight plan for London. I'll be at the plane in fifteen minutes." Dominic slammed down the desk phone, came to his feet, and spoke into his cell. "Thanks, Max. Gotta go."

TWENTY-NINE

The traffic from Heathrow had been an utter nightmare, so three hours later, Dominic was in Dr. Bryce Clifton's personal office, his shoes leaving prints in the plush carpet as he crossed the large room. The paneled office was elegantly appointed, the eighteenth-century fireplace still in working order, a real Canaletto on the wall, antique furniture artfully placed to best show its lines. The doctor clearly made a very good living. Dominic almost asked, *Is Amanda Parducci your patient?* but he didn't want to involve her. Katherine wouldn't have found this man otherwise though. Clifton wasn't the kind of doctor who advertised.

"Please, sit," the doctor smoothly offered. Dominic's name had granted him immediate access.

"Thank you." Dominic chose the larger of two Sheraton armchairs placed before an impressive desk and sat.

Dr. Clifton took note of Dominic's double-breasted, navy with white chalk stripes vicuna suit. "Anderson and Sheppard?"

Dominic flicked a quick glance downward. "The lapels always give it away, don't they?" He'd worn the fifty-thousand-dollar suit for a reason. The world's rarest and most expensive fabric was an indulgence for only the very wealthy. It was official notice of his status.

"Yes, indeed. A signature feature." The doctor showed

his perfect teeth in a polished smile; his hair implants were equally impeccable. "Now, how may I help you?"

Dominic returned the doctor's smile. "You recently saw a Miss Katherine Hart. I'd like to know the particulars of her visit."

"That's impossible, of course. Patient confidentiality, you understand." The doctor's smile was still in place. He folded his hands on his immaculate desktop. "The law is quite clear, Mr. Knight."

Dominic's brows lowered marginally and his smile was only slightly less pleasant. "Spare me the lecture, Doctor. I know all that. But the matter is of some importance to me," he noted gently, rather than hit the smug bastard.

"Then you should take it up with Miss Hart," the doctor said irritably, unfamiliar with being countermanded.

"I intend to. But she's back at work and she doesn't like to be disturbed." Dominic's voice was exquisitely restrained. "I couldn't help but notice your Canaletto," he added, glancing at the beautifully framed and lighted painting. "*The Horse Guards*—isn't it?"

"Yes." The doctor immediately preened. "It was done when Canaletto was in England."

"He has a way with light, doesn't he? Atmospheric. You can almost feel the sun. I've seen another rendition, but not so fine a one as yours. Have you had it long?"

"It's been in my wife's family for generations," the doctor said proudly.

And yet it was in his office—greedy fuck. Although that might make things easier. Dominic took his phone from his suit coat pocket, quickly brought up a few screens, and leaning forward turned the phone to the doctor. "Have you seen this Canaletto? *The Doge's Palace*. It's equally good."

"I have." The avaricious light in the doctor's eyes was bright as a beacon. "The Hamilton Gallery has had it for sale since March."

"Why don't I buy it?" Dominic said smoothly. "What's your address here?" He knew the address. He just wanted a commitment from the doctor.

Ten seconds.

Fifteen.

Dominic leaned back, tapped the screen a few times. "There. I can always use another Canaletto if you don't want it." He looked up and smiled at the doctor. Then he stared at the screen for a second more before he chuckled. "Douglas said he'd open his reserve whiskey for me. I've bought a few things from him over the years. Where should I tell him to send it?"

Dr. Clifton struggled with his conscience for only a few seconds more. Then he gave Dominic his address.

Dominic keyed in the doctor's address, turned off his phone, and slipped it back in his pocket. "They'll deliver it tomorrow at two. I hope you enjoy it. Now then." He needed confirmation, not secondhand information.

"You understand my responsibility to my patients," Dr. Clifton said, looking Dominic in the eye like any good horse trader who never gives anything away.

Dominic smiled. "Of course."

"So I can neither confirm nor deny that Miss Hart is twelve weeks' pregnant. Nor can I confirm or deny that she is in excellent health."

Dominic sat quietly for a moment, absorbing the quick shot of happiness. Then he came to his feet. "Thank you, Dr. Clifton." He dipped his head. "It was a pleasure to meet you."

Dominic left the office, a million thoughts tumbling through his brain, a continuous flicker of a smile twisting his mouth as he got in his car and was driven to Eaton Place. According to the doctor, Katherine was three months' pregnant. Which meant he *should* have used a condom the night she'd had the shot. He smiled faintly. As if any man alive could have refused her huge, pleading eyes when she'd said softly, "Just don't. Please?"

But fond memories aside, he had a problem on his hands.

Because he was still in hock to Gora for two more weeks or slightly more, depending on the birth of Gora's son.

An inflexible interval. On the other hand, he expected it would take at least that much time for any woman to plan her wedding. So he had only to say, *Let's get married in three weeks* and no further explanation was required. Although the timing was the least of his problems. Getting Katherine to talk to him was the dilemma. He hadn't had much luck in the last ten weeks.

Hours later, when Max called to tell him that Katherine was home, Dominic was still unsure about how to approach her.

With no real plan yet, his emotions all over the map, and his entire world in flux, Dominic found himself standing on Katherine's doorstep, the sun a faint golden glow behind him, the horizon streaked with the brilliant magenta of sunset.

He knocked on the door and saw a curtain twitch on one of the street windows.

He knocked again, louder this time, using the brass knocker.

"Go away!"

Katherine's voice was sharp, clear, hostile. And on the other side of the door now, not near the window. "I'm not going away," he said, raising his voice just enough to make his point, but not enough to draw attention. "Open the door."

"No!"

She heard a key turn in the lock, wondered if she could hold the door shut, but even before the thought was fully formed, Dominic had shoved the door open and was standing on her threshold. Looking breathtakingly handsome, casually dressed in a blue blazer and jeans, every hair neatly in place, tall and dark and treacherously beautiful. *Oh God…do not respond to all that irresistible maleness.* "Where did you get that key?" she snapped instead.

He ignored her question and gave her an almost invisible raking glance, taking in her loose-fitting T-shirt and sweats. "How have you been?"

"Fine. Perfectly fine. You?" She held out her hand for the key.

"Shitty. Really shitty." He put the key in her hand because he could have more made. "May I come in?"

"No."

"We should talk."

"There's nothing to talk about."

He glanced up and down the street, still lively with people out enjoying the May evening. "We can talk about your having my child out here on the steps or we can talk about it where the tabloids won't be taking pictures."

"How do you know about that?"

He ignored her glare. "Contacts."

"Meaning?" she said, her voice even more pissy.

"Max told me."

"How did *he* know?"

"You'd have to ask him."

"Are you still stalking me?" she hissed, the term spitting bullets appropriate to the occasion.

"Not personally, no," he said, immune to imaginary bullets and glares and hisses and anything else that stood in the way of his mission. "Now, may I come in?"

She didn't move.

"Did Nana tell you I visited her a few weeks ago? She might enjoy the tabloid pictures. Or CX Capital. The gossip rags always have the smuttiest headlines."

She almost stopped breathing. "You went to see Nana?"

"She didn't tell you? We had a nice visit." He dipped his head. "I'm not going away until we talk about this. So we can do it on the street or in private. Your call."

She stepped back.

"I appreciate your giving me some of your time," he said softly, following her in and shutting the door.

She faced him, her jaw firm, her eyes cold. "Say what you want to say, then get out. Go back to your wife."

He took a small breath, intent on avoiding the fight she

wanted. "My wife is a technicality," he said carefully. "I'll be divorced in two weeks."

"Well, then go back to her for two weeks. Have you had your baby yet?"

He looked startled. "Baby?"

"Yes, the one you didn't tell me about, the one you just confirmed with that revealing little twitch," she said snidely. "You're not always completely expressionless after all." *She'd always suspected it would be the only reason someone could force Dominic into a shotgun marriage.*

"It's not my child."

"That's what they all say."

"I'm not saying that about you."

"Maybe you should. We didn't spend that much time together. What—a grand total of three weeks? Although that's probably a record for you. One-night stands. That's more your style, isn't it?"

Jesus, he didn't like scenes. He'd done a lot of keeping his mouth shut and waiting in his life. And this wasn't an argument he wanted to have. "I don't have a style, Katherine," he said quietly. "What I'd like to talk to you about is our child. As a matter of fact, it pleases me that you're having our baby."

She raised her hand to shut him up. "Fuck you, Dominic. You can stop that bullshit right now. I'm not interested in anything you have to say. I'm not interested in whether you're pleased or not." Her voice was taut with indignation. "You walked out on me twice. That's twice too many," she snapped, the fury in her eyes a hostile glow. "So this is my baby, not yours. Mine. Do you understand? You have nothing to do with it." Her voice was rising. "So I really don't want to hear a goddamn word from you! Now or ever!" She was screaming now. "Get your ass out of here!"

Feeling a wave of relief that she wanted the baby, he said, very softly, "Calm down for a minute. Let's—"

"Don't tell me to calm down, you son of a bitch!" she shrieked. "I'm not calming down! I may never calm down! If you think you can walk back in like nothing happened and pick up where you left off, you're crazy!" Her fists were clenched at her sides, her face was flushed. "Now get the fuck out!"

For a fleeting second Dominic considered picking her up, taking her to bed, and screwing her until neither of them could move. That usually worked with her. But she was really pissing him off; it probably wouldn't be wise. She wasn't the only one with a quick temper. Dragging in a breath of restraint, he forced himself to speak in a conciliatory tone. "Could we please talk about this like adults, Katherine? This baby involves me even if you don't want it to. I'm the father. I can prove it with a paternity test if necessary. Although I'd prefer coming to some reasonable agreement."

"About what, Dominic? About you fucking whomever you want—what the hell—marrying anyone you want, and I get to sit at home having your baby? Tell you what," she snarled. "How about you knock up someone else and go talk to them. I'm not in the talking mood. So fuck off or I'll call the bloody police!"

He leaned in close, his gaze blue flame, his jaw clenched so tight he could feel it in his shoulders. "This discussion isn't over," he said in a low, grating rasp. "Not on your fucking life. You'll be hearing from me." Then he spun around, pulled the door open, and stormed out.

He didn't even hear the door slam behind him as he strode down the steps, angrier than he could ever remember being.

Even angrier than he'd been in high school when he'd beat the shit out of a whole lot of bruisers and bullies.

Although Dominic and Kate could have contested peak anger levels.

Kate was so close to blowing a fuse, she actually flopped into a sprawl on the sofa, started some deep breathing, and turned on the TV in an effort to distract herself. Mother. Fucker. Did he have a gigantic set of balls or what? Just knock on the door, ask to come in, and proceed to take over as father to her child like he had any fucking right when he was married to someone else. Jesus!

She flicked to the Weather Channel that was always capable of zoning her out and sure enough, by the time the weatherman was droning on about the weather patterns over Africa she was breathing normally again. She really did have to be more considerate of her health now, turn over a new leaf in terms of her lifestyle. Learn to relax. She'd have to eat three meals a day too—like seriously—no messing around. The mental prompt brought her to her feet and she walked into the kitchen. Opening the refrigerator door, she stared at her semiempty fridge. Except for the champagne she hadn't drunk because it reminded her too much of Dominic, the entire contents of her fridge consisted of a bag of nearly three-month-old apples, some shriveled lemons, and lettuce so gross she'd need disposable gloves to touch it. Christ, everything was gross. She shut the door, ordered a pizza, and went online to see if she could find a grocery store that delivered.

She was eating for two and she didn't want an unhealthy child because she was too stupid or lazy to put good food in her mouth. She let out a sigh of relief when she found a grocery delivery service; she ordered everything she liked and set up a delivery time for tomorrow after work.

But when she arrived home the next day, her refrigerator was already stocked with wholesome food, and dozens of prepared dishes like those Patty had packed in San Francisco, with the same kind of directions for cooking or heating or not heating. She could have killed Dominic for breaking and entering. But she smiled a little too. He was thinking of the baby. Damn him. Then everything went crazy in her head like it always did when Dominic was super nice and super kind and caring.

But she got herself under control a few seconds later when she thought of his wife.

Faithless prick.

His agenda, his entire life, was always purely selfish; damn the rules and norms and common courtesies. If he wanted something he took it. Not this time though, not with her. A faithless prick wasn't good father material. No more than Dominic had been good Prince Charming material.

But his numerous shortcomings didn't mean she wasn't going to eat all that really great food stacked in her fridge. She had to think of the baby, not just her own bitter, woman-scorned resentments.

A few blocks away, Dominic had talked himself into a more reasonable frame of mind, shortly after he'd returned home and put his plan B into operation. Smother her with kindness, show her he could be whatever she wanted him to be, take care of her and the baby. No way he was giving up after he'd been waiting three months to have her in his life again. Although now, with a baby in the picture, they were past any kind of casual arrangement. They'd have to marry—quickly. Which meant he was going to have to grovel big-time.

But, hey, whatever it took.

He half smiled. A woman who didn't want him, though. That was new. Different.

He'd have to rethink his game plan.

Very late that night when Kate was almost asleep— sedated as she was from a wonderful dinner and two servings of rice pudding—Dominic texted her. *Did you enjoy the food? My chef was asking. And if you have any menu requests, just let me know. I had rice pudding for dinner. How about you? Sleep well, baby.*

She didn't answer, but she didn't text *Don't* either.

Dominic noticed, but waited another hour just in case.

Then he smiled and poured out the rest of the whiskey he'd been drinking.

He had to stop overimbibing. He was going to be a father. And he refused to be a fucking asshole like his father. So temperance and sobriety were on the docket. No more bottle or two every night, no more hotheaded anger, no more temper tantrums.

And since he had only two weeks to change Katherine's

mind about taking him back, doing it completely sober would set a better tone. He wanted her to be happy with him again, maybe even a little in love again, because she really should be a willing participant when he married her the second his divorce was final.

Because their wedding was inked in on his calendar whether she was willing or not.

THIRTY

Dominic's campaign to win back Kate's affections was of Napoleonic proportions, but then he had both the resources and intensity of a revolutionary general. He had two weeks to secure his objective and failure wasn't even a consideration.

Max had men monitoring the doctor's activities in Rome, the attorney in Paris was on call, and a judge was ready to sign the divorce decree. Gora was in Rome as well, awaiting the birth of his son. All the outside actors were under scrutiny and on pause, biding events.

Dominic had talked to Melanie last night and asked a favor of her. That morning, he'd just finished speaking to a wedding planner Liv recommended, stipulating at the onset that their discussion was to be kept strictly private. He'd received a haughty glance, as if he'd accosted the elderly woman, and barely concealing her affront, she'd said, "Everything we do, Mr. Knight, is done in complete confidentiality. Our clients demand it."

"Perfect," Dominic had said, not sure he dared smile when she had her nose in the air like that. But he chanced it anyway and added as insurance, "I may not have mentioned it, but I'm more than willing to pay a premium for your advice when our time frame is so limited." That brought a smile to her face and confirmed the age-old principle: money talks.

His wedding plans *en train*—all final decisions Katherine's of course—he waited for his next appointment. The matter with the jeweler was quickly settled. The man was to assemble an assortment of his best diamond rings and have them ready to show to Katherine. "I apologize for the short notice," Dominic said. "I hope it's not a problem."

For the price Dominic was paying, problems were non-existent. And the jeweler expressed that sentiment with affable warmth. After the man was shown out, Dominic had his car brought around and set off on an unprecedented errand.

Meanwhile Kate was lying in bed eating chocolate cake because dessert after a completely nutritional breakfast of scrambled eggs, bacon, and fruit was certainly allowed, even under her new health regime. And she'd skipped coffee and had only chocolate milk this morning. So whether it was her sizable intake of chocolate that gave rise to her euphoria or the fact that Dominic's staff had cleaned her entire flat yesterday, she was sleeping on freshly ironed sheets, had showered in her bathroom that now contained stacks of washed towels instead of piles of dirty ones, or simply the fact that being taken care of was...well, really sweet and she wasn't as angry with Dominic as she had been.

Stupid, she knew. The man was Svengali after all.

Still...and it nearly killed her to think it—she missed him.

A short time later, Dominic was standing outside a shop on Marylebone High Street waiting for the shopgirl to get her key to work in the door. He'd depended on Liv for all his recommendations, including this very small store selling children's clothes. He was about to impatiently say, *Good Lord, let me do that*, when the girl finally managed to turn the key in the lock. She was completely flustered by the presence of the stunningly beautiful man who'd been waiting for her when she arrived. If only she'd worn a nicer dress, she was wistfully thinking, spent more time on her hair, put on more dramatic makeup.

Although once inside the shop, it was Dominic's turn to be befuddled. He'd never set foot in a children's clothing store. His gifts for Melanie's children had always been toys. So he stood just inside the door, surveying the minimal space and the glass case in the middle of the room filled with tiny, colorful, handmade shoes. He wondered what it was that he needed and wanted and how to ask for those things without revealing his identity. The tabloids would have a field day with this photo.

He came awake from his daze at the sound of a throat being cleared and a timid, "May I help you, sir?"

"I need baby clothes," he said gruffly. "If you could show me some," he added more graciously, "I'd appreciate it."

What a lovely deep voice. "Do you have anything special in mind?" she asked, hoping he'd smile and say *You.*

"No, no—ah—I'm not sure."

There was a small silence.

"Is it for a boy or a girl?" the young lady asked, because clearly the gorgeous rock star in her shop didn't have a clue what he wanted. Dressed in jeans and a black leather jacket so supple it looked like silk, with his dark, ruffled hair curling softly over his jacket collar and his long-fingered hands flexing slightly, he was seriously doable.

"The baby's—not—" He took a small breath.

"Not born yet?"

He nodded.

"Something for a newborn then."

Dominic blew out the breath he hadn't realized he'd been holding. "Exactly. That's what I need. No blue or pink. Something neutral."

"White is always nice," the pretty blonde said, knowing she'd be posting this on Facebook as soon as he left the shop. "This way, sir." Lord, she wished she dared take his picture, because her friends would all be green with jealousy that she'd breathed the same air as him.

Dominic followed her to a rack on the wall where tiny little garments hung on tiny little hangers. As she took them out one by one and held them up, he said yes or no, mostly yes, or asked a question that made it plain he knew next to nothing about newborns. He bought everything she had that wasn't blue or pink, gave her a company credit card that didn't help her at all in terms of his identity or even in terms of the company name. She'd never heard of Green Infinity Industries. As for his signature, no one could possibly decipher it.

"I need everything boxed and wrapped—ribbons and that sort of thing. Not individually, a few larger boxes perhaps. Someone will pick them up this afternoon. Thank you very much," he said with smile. "You've been a great help."

A really dazzling smile, she thought with a sigh, watching him from behind the counter until he slid into the backseat of the swank black car.

Dominic briefly considered buying maternity clothes but wasn't quite up to entering that arena, feeling slightly intimidated for the first time in his life. Not that he wouldn't do it, if that's what Katherine wanted. He was in full accommodation mode.

Which reminded him. Flowers. Was that too trite? Too clichéd? Maybe something small, delicate, sweetly scented. What was that fragrance that reminded him of Katherine? Did she wear perfume? Jesus, why hadn't he paid attention?

In the end, the young woman in the flower shop near his home suggested lily of the valley with tiny white roses, the small bouquet tied with a white silk ribbon. He carried it to Katherine's flat, let himself in, chatted with his staff, who were there cleaning and doing dishes and laundry, placed the simple crystal vase on her bedside table, set a small sealed envelope beside it, and, stepping back, smiled.

Fuck, it felt good just to be here again.

Strange how happiness could be so simple.

When Katherine walked into the flat after work, she wasn't surprised to see the pile of packages on the foyer table and the chair, two larger ones on the floor. Beautifully wrapped packages with white and yellow bows. Or she wasn't very surprised. What she had to admit was that it pleased her, and that was slightly more difficult. She almost immediately called herself to task; Dominic just wanted something he couldn't have. She was a challenge for him.

But when she walked into her bedroom to change into something comfortable, she saw the small bouquet on the bedside table and felt her stomach do a little flip-flop. Had he been here? As she approached the bed, she saw the note and, picking it up, sat on the bed. Peeling the seal open, she pulled out the small card and read the two lines.

> I'll try to be a good father.
> I'll try really hard.
>
> > All my Love,
> > Dominic

Tears slid down her cheeks. She thought of his bleak, unhappy childhood during which neither parent cared and her heart ached for him, for this promise for his child, for the poignant sadness in that hope. And all her resentments melted away when they shouldn't. When she should know better. When the thousand issues that still confronted them couldn't be exorcised by hope alone. Falling back on the bed, she shut her eyes and let her mind go blank.

Everything was too complicated, the situation a total mess, any solution still fraught with difficulty.

She was too tired to deal with it now.

Then as if on cue Kate's phone rang. The one on the bedside table. The number no one ever called.

Stretching for the phone, thinking it must be a mistake, Kate's hello was tentative.

"Is this a bad time for you? Were you sleeping? This is Melanie."

Kate shoved herself into a sitting position against the headboard. "No, I just came home from work. I was just resting for a minute."

"How are you?"

"Fine," Kate said cautiously.

"Don't hang up on me now, but Dominic asked me to call you. He said you might hang up."

"I'm too tired to make that decision."

Melanie laughed. "Good. Then all you have to do is listen. Dominic told me about your good news. He's thrilled, and I never thought I'd see him happy about having a baby. But he's worried that you won't forgive him...for everything that's happened. So he asked me for help...and he never does that, not even when...well you know about all that when he was a kid. He'd come home from those ghastly sessions and I'd say, 'Do you want me to hold you?' and he'd always say no. Then he'd turn on the TV and watch cartoons. So I'd sit and watch cartoons with him. I think he liked that but he never asked. So you see, when Dominic is willing to ask me for help, he's—well—desperate. So if you could see it in your heart to talk to him, I'd be pleased and I know he'd be over the moon."

Kate's heart had started racing as Melanie talked, but she said carefully, "I can't picture Dominic over the moon about anything."

"Believe me." Melanie's voice was subdued. "Dominic's"— she took a breath—"I've never heard him like this before—at a loss. Alarmed enough to turn to me."

"You know he's married," Kate said, a betraying little quiver in her voice.

"I also know it's only temporary," Melanie said quickly. "Dominic didn't give me the details, but Matt knows and he told me Dominic had no choice."

"Are you sure?" Kate wished she hadn't sounded so wretchedly hopeful.

"I'm positive. Absolutely positive. Matt wouldn't lie to me. And the child isn't Dominic's. Matt was emphatic."

"Wow," Kate breathed softly, wondering how crazy she was to feel like an overgrown child who had all her birthday and Christmas wishes come true at once.

"I expect Dominic hasn't mentioned that he deals with some very strange and occasionally dangerous individuals. I've been aware of it for a long time. Apparently this situation was more untenable than usual. You might ask Dominic about it, although I'm not sure he'll tell you. Matt's that way. He doesn't like me to worry. He runs into problems from time to time. When large sums of money are involved, some men resort to unsavory practices."

"Jeez, even there?"

"You'd be surprised. But, truthfully, I don't really want to know." Melanie laughed softly. "There are times when I don't mind being taken care of."

"I know what you mean. Dominic's been in full nurturing mode."

"Well, good. You can use all the nurturing you can get right now. Are you having morning sickness?"

Kate sighed. "Unfortunately."

"I might be able to help."

The women talked for another few minutes, Melanie told Kate to call her with any questions about her pregnancy or anything else, and ended by saying, "Don't be too hard on Dominic. He loves you. He actually said it. I almost fainted."

THIRTY-ONE

Kate heard the knock on the door.

But Dominic didn't let himself in as he might have; he waited for her to answer.

And when she opened the door, she saw the boyish smile she only rarely saw, the one she suspected all the high school surfer girls had seen: his eyes creased with pleasure, the lazy curve of his mouth pure temptation.

"Hi." He looked at her differently now, always searching for new clues in the mystery that was unfolding, although only the most subtle changes had occurred in her body— well hidden tonight in a pair of Mrs. Hawthorne's kitten print cotton pajamas that he'd bought for Katherine in Hong Kong.

"Hi," Kate said, breathless at the sight of him, like the first time she'd seen him in Palo Alto. He looked incredibly young, wearing jeans and a faded blue T-shirt with a peace sign. She was half in love with him again despite everything and she knew it.

"May I come in?" He dipped his head, his hair fell forward, he pushed it back behind his ears with his thumbs. "How are you feeling?" His glance drifted to her stomach.

"Good." She held out her hand, because she wanted to more than anything. "I always feel good at night." His large hand closed around hers with the gentleness that always surprised her in such a large man, and she felt a small familiar warmth stir her senses.

"Thanks for inviting me in." His blue gaze was clear, open, his voice nakedly grateful as he stepped into the foyer and shut the door.

"Thanks for all those." Kate gestured at the pile of wrapped packages.

"You should open them." He smiled. "It was quite a shopping trip for me."

"I will later."

He didn't know if the word *later* was good or bad. Whether it meant later when he was here or later after he was gone. "I want to apologize for anything and everything, for all I did and didn't do," he said quietly. "For the things I said that hurt you."

She was briefly silenced by the haunted look in his eyes. "I said my share of hurtful things too. Come on," she said, tugging on his hand and moving down the hallway. "Talk to me."

He'd never been so happy to hear those words. In the past if a woman said she wanted to talk, he'd always headed for the door. "Thanks," he said again, really meaning it.

Kate gave him a sideways glance as they moved down the hallway. "You might change your mind about that. I'm going to ask you a lot of questions."

"That's okay."

"Really?" Her surprise showed.

"Look, baby, I'm just so happy you're letting me in, I don't care what you do. I've been in hell the last few months. Like the last time you were gone. So read me the riot act, I don't care. I'm just going to say yes to everything you want."

She stopped, looked up at him, her brows slightly drawn. "You're freaking me out a little."

He smiled. "Too polite?"

"Just a little bit."

A hint of amusement flickered in his eyes. "Maybe I'll piss you off later when I tell you about our wedding plans."

"Oh, yeah," she said, her nostrils flaring. "That'll do it. Maybe I don't want to marry you."

"I'd really like you to, but just a second." He dropped her hand, walked back to the packages, and pulled out a small shopping bag tied with a large white bow and a yellow-ribboned package. Coming back, he took her hand again, smiled with tantalizing languor, and said softly, "Where would you like to talk?"

"Don't look at me like that." She frowned. "This is a serious discussion."

"The reception room then?" He was on his very best behavior.

"I call it a living room."

"Perfect," he said with a diplomatic smile. "Do I get to touch you or is this a separate chairs situation?"

"Separate chairs." It was too easy to fall under his spell, to respond to that soft voice and warm smile, when she was teetering on the edge already. "You have a lot of explaining to do," she said quickly, as if her treacherous senses needed a reminder of her vast suffering the last months.

"Ask anything. Really." *Except for Gora. Openness had its limits.*

But once they were seated across from each other, Dominic leaned forward, his gaze direct and animated. "Tell me about the baby first. I promise I'll answer your questions afterward." He held out his hand, twitched his fingers, and smiled. "I'm a bundle of nerves and excitement."

Seeing him like that with a smile lighting up his face stirred up a cloud of butterflies in her stomach. But loving him wasn't enough. She couldn't forget that; every woman he'd ever smiled at wanted him. "I can't tell you anything because I don't know anything," she said evenly, but her heart rate was rising despite her silent lecture. "This is going to be a steep learning curve for me."

"Let me help you. Let me do whatever you need done." He forced himself to stay seated when he wanted to get up, lift her up into his arms, and hold her for a decade or longer. "You shouldn't have to do anything but sleep and eat and stay healthy. I'll do the rest."

"Please, Dominic." She swallowed hard. "Slow down. We have to back up a little first."

He took a small breath. "Okay."

"Melanie called," she began, watching him take that small breath, seeing the almost invisible flinch.

"I know."

"She told me that Matt knows why you got married."

"He does." These would have to be minimum answers.

"But you can't tell me." She clasped her hands in her lap and went very still. "Or you don't want to."

"No, it's just that I'd rather you didn't know." This was the scariest conversation of his life. He couldn't lose her again. "Mainly," he said, picking his words with great care, "I don't want you frightened."

"Maybe I'm not that easily frightened."

He set his hands on his knees and studied them for a moment before he looked up. "I think you would be. Please, it's almost over. I know how clichéd this sounds but please trust me on this."

"Melanie said you sometimes deal with unsavory characters, that Matt does too. Is that what this is about?"

He nodded. "In your business, you see corruption too. Criminals, thieves, cons, large and small. Matt and I deal with corruption at a personal level, not once or twice removed, and not from behind a computer screen. Since you can't help me on this, you'd only worry unnecessarily." He leaned back, stretched out his legs, and stared at his sandaled feet for a moment. "Now that you're pregnant," he said quietly, "I want to protect you even more. In two more weeks this all goes away. Talk to Melanie. She'll tell you to leave this kind of bullshit to Matt and me."

"Two weeks? For sure?" She didn't want to feel such relief or want him with such helpless longing. But then her insurgent psyche spoke up. *He wants to protect you, you idiot. How can that be bad?* She felt better, like chivalry might still exist, like maybe Dominic had some Prince Charming in him after all. "After two weeks, then things go back to normal?"

His gaze was teasing. "As normal as they are between

you and me." He smiled. "You're a real handful, baby, and I mean it in the nicest way."

"Then maybe you should think twice. Maybe you should find someone more amenable. I'm sure the line of willing candidates is long. You don't have to marry me just because I'm having your baby."

As if, he thought. "That sounds like I'd better get down on my knees."

It was her turn to smile. "Tempting."

"Hey. I'm not talking about sex, Katherine. I'm serious about this marriage." And coming out of his chair, he picked up the small shopping bag and package, closed the distance between them, sank slowly to one knee, and put the bag in her lap. "Open it," he said. "Please?" he quickly added, because he's spoken a shade too bluntly and her mouth had started to purse. "Sorry. Really. Give me a break. I've never done this before."

She blew out a breath. "Me either."

For a few moments only the sound of ribbons sliding and paper crinkling broke the silence.

Kate looked inside the bag and went motionless.

Why did he suddenly feel as though he were standing in front of a firing squad? "Take your pick, baby," he said, velvet soft, as if too loud a sound would startle her from her trance. "Or take them all. I didn't know what you'd like."

She still didn't move.

Christ, he could hear the bolts sliding back on the rifles. "Don't break my heart, baby," he whispered.

The look in his eyes almost made her cry. This was a

man who never asked anyone for anything, who had faced every adversity alone.

She put her hand in the bag, saw his shoulders relax, saw him slowly smile, and knew what loving someone meant. It meant taking away a young boy's hurt, laughing at a strong man's smile, closing your eyes when he touched you because you were melting inside. She smiled faintly. Or having him line up little boxes on your pajama-clad legs as you take them out and hand them to him. But even loving him with all her heart, she couldn't stop herself from saying, "So much, Dominic."

"Not really," he replied casually. "I left most of them at home."

"Oh God, Dominic."

"Come on, baby. If I have to learn to be more open with you, you have to learn to deal with my money. It's yours too. Okay?" He stared at her, gave her a small smile. "Okay?"

She took a breath, swallowed hard. "Okay."

"See, it's not so easy to change is it?" he murmured, beginning to open the ring boxes. "But we're going to do it. Come on, baby"—he touched her bottom lip gently—"we can do anything, you and I."

She nodded, slid her fingers over his hand. "It must be the baby," she whispered. "I feel like crying every second."

"Cry all you want. I'll buy a tissue company. You'll never run out."

She laughed.

"Hey, I mean it. Melanie cried all through her pregnancies. But pick out a ring first, then I'll show you my love letter, then you can cry."

She looked at him in surprise. "You wrote a love letter?"

"Yup." Then he opened each box, slid the rings on her fingers—one through ten, all enormous diamonds.

She looked at the glistening display, bit back her comment about the outrageous expense, and pointed. "This one."

His eyes glinted with pleasure. "I was hoping you'd say that. It's my favorite too."

The diamond solitaire was a forty-carat, D-flawless, emerald-cut stone that had just come on the market. A rare jewel the likes of which appear in the cutting rooms perhaps once every ten years.

Sliding off the other rings, Dominic casually dropped them on a nearby table, then turned back. Taking her hand in his, he said with ceremonial formality and a more typical breathtaking smile, "Would you do me the honor of marrying me, Miss Hart?"

For a second Kate was overcome by the immensity of the question and the smaller fear that she loved him too much. That he was too easy to love not just by her, but by every woman.

Months past questioning his feelings, Dominic put his hand to his ear and grinned.

A big breath, an answering smile. "Yes," Kate said.

Leaning forward, Dominic touched his forehead to hers and whispered, "Thank you."

"My pleasure," she said as softly.

"The pleasure is all mine, baby." He cupped her face lightly, then sat back on his heels, picked up the small package, and put it on her lap. "Just look. See what you think."

He watched her unwrapping the package with an uncharacteristic restlessness. "You can tear the paper," he said and proceeded to do just that. Tossing the wrapping aside, he nodded at the small box.

"This?" she said teasingly.

He lifted his brows ever so faintly. "Are you looking for a spanking?"

"Maybe."

"And maybe I'll give you one if you open that."

"How can a girl refuse?"

"No shit."

She punched him.

"I was referring only to you, of course."

"Damn right you'd better be." But she was smiling too, until a second later, when she lifted the lid on the box and her eyes filled with tears. The tiniest little onesie lay inside, white and precious and achingly beautiful. She lifted it up and sniffled, "How did you think of this?"

"How could I not? That's all I think about. You, me, a baby, unimaginable happiness." Reaching out, he brushed the tears from her cheeks. "I'm glad you like it. I bought everything they had that wasn't blue or pink. I'll bring in the rest of them later."

"You must have made some shop clerk's day."

"Maybe. So long as I make your day, that's all I care about." Sliding his hands under her legs, he picked her up with ease and sat back down on the chair with her in his lap. "There are some cute little shoes made in France too—one pair is high tops in bright green leather. They're for either boys or girls," he added just in case. "I have no preference."

"I thought every man wanted a boy."

"It doesn't matter to me. I only want to make you happy."

"Is that why you wrote your love letter?" Her voice was buoyant, her gaze sunshine bright. "I've never had a love letter before."

"Then we're the perfect pair because I've never written one before." He reached back, pulled a folded envelope from his jean pocket, and handed it to her. "Don't judge me too harshly." He smiled a slow, lovely smile. "It's an amateur effort."

She opened the envelope, pulled out the single page, and unfolded it; Dominic's script was bold and vigorous as ever, like the man himself.

He watched her read what he'd written on the plane and given to Max when he wasn't sure he'd survive his meeting with Gora. He'd always been fatalistic, indifferent to his future. That was the first time he'd cared whether he lived or died.

Dear Katherine,

By some great act of fortune, you've been brought into my life and I find myself in the unlikely position of caring deeply about another human being. For the first time. For the very first time. And I am overcome with fear.

If I don't return, I want you to know that I love you with all my heart, my soul such as it is, and my once purposeless spirit—that now has purpose. I only knew hopelessness before I met you and now

I know hope. You've given me my life. And for that
and a thousand other nameless wonders, I love you.

With you always in my thoughts,

Dominic

She looked up with tears in her eyes. "You really didn't
know if you were coming back?"

He shrugged. "An issue with one of those unsavory
characters. But the gravity of the situation made me realize that you were the only person in the whole world who
mattered to me." A faint smile warmed his eyes. "And now
junior or juniorette is added to my list. It helps if there're
two"—he ran his hand over her flat belly, then glanced up
at her and smiled—"when it comes to dealing with a baby.
We'll be happy—all of us. My word on it."

She looked at him, thinking that maybe miracles did
come true, that if you wanted something badly enough
some benevolent spirit conferred it on you. "I've only ever
wanted you—from the very first."

He smiled, remembering her letter in Hong Kong. "With
reservations."

She smiled back. "*Despite* reservations."

"You've had me from the first, baby," he said tenderly.
"In some deep, strange, new place I didn't even know
existed. And you have me now"—his smile was soft with
love—"and forever and a million years after that."

"Don't ever leave me again," she whispered.

"I won't. Not ever." He dipped his head and held her
gaze. "May I kiss you now? I'm asking because I don't want
to frighten you. I've been too long in the wilderness."

"I may frighten you back." She suddenly went still, afraid she was coming undone.

He shook his head. "Never, baby. Won't happen." Then he very gently took her face in his hands, lowered his head, and just before his lips met hers, whispered, "We'll get it right this time. I promise."

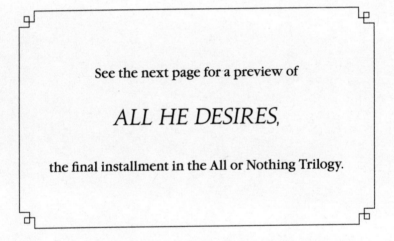

See the next page for a preview of

ALL HE DESIRES,

the final installment in the All or Nothing Trilogy.

ONE

Dominic's blue gaze was warm with pleasure as he freed the top button on Kate's pajama top. "I feel like a kid at Christmas who gets to open his special present."

"Then if you'll undress for me"—Kate's voice was lazy with content—"we'll both get a special present."

His grin was wickedly sexy. "That'll take two seconds."

"Maybe you'd like to reword that," she said, instantly testy, the blur of women in his past, the sex photos, tabloid and otherwise, not easily forgotten.

He looked up into a pouty face and stormy eyes and his fingers stilled. "How about I take my time undressing? This is all about what you want." *Because he had what he wanted.* "Just let us know the schedule."

Mollified or embarrassed or both, Kate softly sighed. "Lord, I'm even more jealous than before. I'm going to blame my crazy baby hormones because I don't want to think of myself as some jealous bitch." She smiled faintly. "Tell me you don't mind or I'll burst into tears again."

He laughed. "Whatever you do is fine, baby." Then his voice went soft. "If there were nine circles of hell, I was in the tenth without you, okay? Nothing you can do will even begin to replicate that fucking misery. So jealousy, tears, whatever—hit me with it, I don't care."

Her smile was sunny again. "Really. I have carte blanche?"

"Damn right. You're nurturing this baby for us. You're allowed anything. You want something, let me know. I'll find it for you. You need a shoulder to cry on, I'm here. You have a craving for something, it's yours." Framing her face in his palms, he dipped his head. "Because I'm good at getting what I want," he whispered.

"And you want me."

"You have no idea, baby."

"Even if I'm fat?"

He grinned. "Depends how fat, I suppose."

She punched him.

His gaze was lit with amusement. "Okay, so we'll take all the scales out of our houses."

"Your houses."

"Hey." He looked at her, his mouth pursed.

"Our houses—in three weeks," she added with a grin.

"I'll have to spank you softly now, but don't think I won't if you get too mouthy, Katherine. We're not going to argue about money. What's mine is yours. End of discussion."

She wiggled her hips.

"Are you trying to change the subject?" But his dick got the message loud and clear and swelled noticeably.

"I am," she purred. "I hate talking about money. And for your information, pregnancy makes me even more sexy."

He stared at her. "It does?"

"No doubt in my mind."

He exhaled softly and ran through a few quick trial questions, because even with Max's surveillance, there was the possibility someone had been missed. Then, drawing in a breath, he said carefully, "I'll ask this only once and I apologize in advance because I have no right to ask when we weren't together, but did you—"

"Only my vibrator—or yours actually," she interjected because he was trying so hard to be polite.

He blew out a breath. "Sorry. It shouldn't matter but it does."

"Tell me about it," she muttered, shoving him away as jealousy instantly soured her mood again.

He wouldn't have had to move; he was more than a hundred pounds heavier than her. But considering their very recent detente, he did. Smoothly rolling away, he rested beside her in a lounging pose, his head propped on his hand. "Come on, baby, it's almost over," he said softly. "And the minute my divorce is stamped by that judge in France, we're getting married. You should tell Nana."

"Don't change the subject. I should whip your ass," she said, although after Dominic's sweet earnestness, her tone was less grumpy.

Encouraged, he smiled. "If that changes the subject, be my guest."

She grinned. "Really?"

"Fucking A. I don't want to talk about this or even think about it." He'd agreed to a temporary marriage to ensure Katherine's safety—although she was unaware of her danger. He wanted to keep it that way. "But seriously," he added, "you should give Nana a head's up. I'll send a plane for her, but still, she might like some warning."

"I can't call her and tell her that you're married, I'm pregnant, and if all goes well, you'll soon be divorced *and* should that happen, then we'll get married. Not only does that sound like some scam, but I'd like to see your divorce papers before I call her. Nana will have her shotgun loaded and pointed at you when she gets off the plane unless everything's settled. You met her. So that can't be a surprise."

"She didn't seem unreasonable," he said. "We got along."

"Jesus, did you charm her too?"

He grinned. "You mean I actually charmed you?"

"To the extent that we'll soon be parents," she noted sardonically, running her hand over the slight rise of her belly.

"Lucky me," he murmured, placing his hand on her stomach. "I mean it, Katherine. You don't know how pleased I am that you're having my baby." Leaning over, he took a chance, kissed her cheek, and gave himself a mental high five when she didn't balk. "But if you prefer, call Nana when everything's resolved."

"Jeez, Dominic, you make it sound as if you forgot your umbrella and as soon as someone's brings it to you, life's back on track."

"The degree of difficulty doesn't concern me, so long as we get out lives back." A muscle twitched along his jaw, a sudden chill invaded his eyes. "And I promise you, we will."

"You sound like you did with those bankers in Singapore. Can you stop? It's scary."

He ran his hand over his eyes in a literal gesture of nullification. "Sorry," he said, smoothly, the cold belligerence extinguished from his gaze. "And now if you can wait a few minutes before you whip my ass," he added, cupping her small belly in his large palm, "I'd like to say hi to our baby." Bending low, he murmured, "I'm your daddy. We're going to have fun, you and me and Mommy. You're going to be the center of our world, did you know that? And if you want a pony you can have one," he added playfully, then looked up and rolled back. "They can hear, right?"

"I think so. I'm completely ignorant. I almost had a pony but Gramps balked at cleaning the stall. Did you have one?"

"Uh-uh. I never wanted one, but maybe the baby will take after you. Did you hear that?" He brushed his palm over Kate's belly. "Your mommy wanted a pony." He glanced at Kate. "I think we'd better get some baby books. Neither of us knows what we're doing. In fact, let me call Melanie. She can overnight some to us." He pulled his phone from his jeans pocket.

"Now?"

"It's early afternoon in San Francisco. If she buys them today, we'll have them tomorrow. We can't shop for them or the paparazzi might see us. If some of my staff buy them, we're no better off. So Melanie's safe." He grinned, punched in a name on his directory. "Instant gratification. I want to learn about babies. Not that I didn't help Melanie with her first two, but when it's not really your job, you just do what you're told. This is *our* baby. I want to know *everything*. Hi, Mel. We need some baby books. All you can find. Send them overnight. No shit, I'm excited. Why wouldn't I be? Yeah, yeah, cute. How about it's better, okay? Like a hundred times better. Don't give me any more grief. Just send them. No, you can't talk to Katherine now because I'm talking to her. Yeah, actually talking. Good-bye." He punched End and tossed his phone on the bedside table.

"What's a hundred times better?"

"Nothing. Mel was being clever, that's all."

"Tell me."

"It's raunchy."

"Now I really want to know."

He made a face. "It was a long time ago."

"Jesus, Dominic. Do you ever want a piece of ass again?"

"Watch it, baby. That's not negotiable."

"Maybe I have something to say about it."

"Not as much as me," he said in a soft growl.

She sighed. "I couldn't anyway. This pregnancy makes me soooo horny. But I *could* be too tired for sex. I *am* tired a lot."

"Oh Jesus...okay. But don't get pissed. It's just surfer slang. When you're surfing in waves that should kill you and you're in the jaws of a wind tunnel that should destroy you and you know you can't control it, you just let goooo. You lay into the warp and ride it clean through a cannon blast of green spit. And when you come out the other side alive, we call that kind of ride the next best thing to a three-way. That's all." Or that's all he was going to tell her. She'd freak at the real three-way stuff.

"That's not so raunchy. It's cute."

"Glad to hear it." *Really glad. He was off the hook.* "So." He pointed at her pajama buttons. "May I?"

"It's always a yes, damn you. Sometimes I wish I had more control."

He smiled, looked up from sliding a second button free. "I like that you don't."

"Still. It's always too easy for you. It always has been, I expect. I hate to be one of the crowd."

It stopped him for a flashing moment, the thought that he'd do any of this for anyone but her. Risk his life, offer an open-ended bribe of millions to Gora, marry some horny little bitch who was looking to augment her family's bank account. "You're one of a kind, baby, not one of a crowd," he said gently, back to his unbuttoning. "I've never asked anyone to marry me before. I've never considered having a baby with anyone before. I've never been in love like this before. Would you like that in writing? On a billboard somewhere. I could do a press release. In all modesty," he said with a small smile, sliding the last button free, "it would be a worldwide news flash."

"I want it in skywriting," she said, deadpan, before she grinned. "And thank you. For someone who always had more confidence than I needed, this baby is screwing with my head. It's really strange."

"It doesn't matter. I like you strange or any way at all. Ummm.... this I like a lot," he murmured, having brushed aside her pajama top. "They're bigger." He looked up. "When did that happen?"

"Are you sure? I haven't noticed."

"I'm sure, baby. You've been working too hard if you haven't noticed these." He slid his hand under the curve of one large breast and gently lifted. "We're going to have to fly Mrs. Hawthorne over to see that you have some bras that fit."

"No."

"Later then." He sat up and cupped her other breast.

"No, not later either." They'd had this fight before.

"Then you're going to have to wear some bulky sweaters because these aren't for public display." He moved his fingers and very gently squeezed her swollen nipples. "These are for me."

"I'm guessing the baby gets first dibs on my boobs. Oh, God, that feels good."

He looked up, smiled. "Then I'll settle for seconds. Apparently, parental self-sacrifice starts early."

"Even earlier than that." She raised her brows. "My breasts are incredibly sensitive now and I'm practically in heat twenty-four/seven. So I'm going to need some of your personal attention—like constantly."

"Jesus," he breathed. "My dick heard that. Are you sure it's okay?"

"Don't you dare even think that," she hissed.

"My mistake. Although we should talk to a doctor just to make sure."

She glared at him.

"Tomorrow. Not now. A female doctor. I didn't like Clifton."

"You're not undressed yet," she said, ignoring his comments, only half-listening, her attention focused on her impatient desire, on the steady throbbing between her legs, particularly on Dominic's opened jeans and his obvious erection beneath his blue-and-white-striped boxers. "I'd like the two-second undressing if you don't mind."

"Would it matter if I did mind?" he said with a grin, ripping off his T-shirt.

"I *am* going to whip your ass if you don't hurry." Then

she drew in a shaky breath, her eyes filled with tears, and she whispered, "I've really missed you."

He was undressed in under two seconds. So grateful for the love radiating from her eyes, he would have given her the world wrapped up in a bow and delivered by pixies if she'd asked.

But the one thing he knew she needed he delivered. Quickly settling between her legs, he smoothly entered her, drove in more gently than usual despite her protestations that everything was fine.

Her *fine* and his were still in contention.

"Dominic! Please!" she cried, hotheaded and hot-blooded, hurriedly wrapping her legs around his hips, her arms around his back, dragging him closer.

He carefully moved deeper, ignoring, or rather disregarding, her nails sinking into his back. It wasn't possible to actually ignore them.

"I'm going to cry if you don't let me come!"

So he compromised, not because female tears disconcerted him, but because he wanted to please her. And in lieu of added depth, he flexed his stiff, thick dick upward and rubbed it back and forth over her pulsing G-spot. "We're seeing a doctor tomorrow," he said, rough and low. "Say yes or I'll stop."

"Yes, yes, yes...oh yes," she sighed, her nails sliding off of his back. "Do that again."

"This?" His pain level blessedly reduced, he obliged her with his well-trained dick and steel-hard thigh muscles, pressing gently against her G-spot and clit, once, twice, several more times, before moving slightly in and out, side to side, then back to her favorite entertainment site while she panted and gasped in wonder and delight, softly moaning in rising hysteria.

And he did what women around the world loved him for—over and above his money. He fucked like an artist: with natural talent, an almost indecent technical competence, and the well-honed gift of accurately gauging female arousal.

Like just about *now*, he decided, sliding his long, slender fingers over the curve of Kate's hips, under her soft, round ass and lifting her so his rigid erection pressed hard into her throbbing cushiony mound of tightly concentrated bliss.

"Oh God, oh God, oh God..."

He watched with a faint smile and a well-behaved, disciplined dick as nearly breathless now, she careened at volatile, breakneck speed over the orgasmic edge and climaxed with only the tiniest of screams.

Which served as musical background to his own satisfying climax.

"Don't move," he whispered, a few minutes later, unwrapping her legs and setting her feet on the bed. "We need some towels."

"I can't move," she breathed, her eyes still shut. "I may never move again."

Her sweet naïveté always pleased him. Sex was so fresh and new to her. Every climax unalloyed delight. "So I don't have to worry about you escaping while I'm gone?" he said, rolling off the bed.

"You don't have to worry about me ever escaping. That should frighten the hell out of you."

She still hadn't opened her eyes, her voice syrupy with content.

"On the contrary, baby," he said, over his shoulder as he strode away. "It saves me the trouble of dragging you back. Because you're mine, as in permanently, until the end of time."

The sound of his voice died away as he walked into the bathroom.

Instantly feeling deprived, as though bereft of love and pleasure, as if the light of the world had dimmed, she suddenly opened her eyes, sat up, and cried, "Dominic!"

He appeared in the bathroom doorway, holding a stack of white towels. "I'm here, baby." He didn't take exception to the panic in her voice because he knew too well that feeling of loss. "I'll always be here. In fact, I'd like to tie you to my wrist if you'd let me," he added, walking into the bedroom. "We have to talk about that."

Falling back on the bed, she felt her heart rate begin to slow. "Everything's suddenly so intense, super emotional, bordering on hysteria. I'm jumpy and misty-eyed over everything and nothing at all."

"It's just the baby. We'll talk to a doctor tomorrow, get some basics on prenatal moods, read those books from Mel, and just be happy about all these new changes you're going through. I don't care how jumpy you get so long as you stay within eyesight. You're not the only one flipping out." Tossing all but one of the towels at the foot of the bed, he sat beside Kate, used the towel for her, then him, dropped it on the floor, lay down beside her, and pulled her into his arms.

"You really spoil me," she murmured, snuggling closer. "I could get up and wash. I shouldn't be so lazy."

"I like to spoil you. Don't worry about it." This from a man who wasn't in the habit of spoiling women, other than with his talented dick. From a man who had a staff at all his homes so he didn't have to bother with mundane practicalities.

"Are you tired? I'm a little tired." Her voice was already sliding into sleep.

He glanced at the clock. *Christ, it wasn't even nine.* "I'm good, baby, but we should think about going home. You're going to need more and more sleep. And if we wait too long, it won't be safe for you to travel."

Immediately roused at the mention of abandoning her work obligations, Kate came marginally awake. "I can't go home. I still have three months on my contract with CX Capital." She sighed. "And Joanna expects me to do my share with our clients."

Dominic was careful to keep his voice neutral. "Do you want the baby born over here?"

"I don't know. I haven't given it any thought."

Maybe someone should. "I can get you out of your contract," he offered. "I can also find Joanna a replacement for you."

"Could we talk about this later?" Her eyes were drifting shut again. "I'm too tired to think."

"Sure, baby. Go to sleep." It looked as though he was going to have plenty of time to work in the evenings. Which wouldn't be all that bad since he was planning on spending as much time as possible with Katherine—once he talked her into going home. Because any contract could be broken; CX Capital could find another forensic accountant somewhere in the world. Maybe not as good as Katherine, but that wasn't his problem. As for Joanna, he could pay her enough so she could hire whomever or how many others she wished to replace Katherine. Again, not an equivalent in terms of ability, but fuck if he cared.

Dominic was in love for the first time in his life, but that didn't mean he was undergoing a personality change. He still expected to control his world and the people in it. As for Katherine, he was willing to compromise. To what extent depended entirely on her.

Once she was fully asleep, he left the bed, pulled on his jeans, picked up his phone from the bedside table, and walked into the reception room. Dropping into a chair, he punched in a name and waited while his cell rang and rang and rang.

"Am I interrupting something?" Dominic said when Justin finally picked up.

"We're at the symphony. I walked out into the corridor."

"I won't keep you then. I'll talk fast."

"Take your time," Justin said. "It's some benefit. They're droning on about the foundation's financial goals."

"How hard will it be to break Katherine's contract?"

"Not hard. Why?"

"We're having a baby. For your ears only. I'm caught up in some complicated problems right now, so none of this is public information."

Justin knew better than to ask. If it was complicated for Nick, it was quasi legal. "Are congratulations in order?" he asked, like any man would knowing Dominic's track record.

"Yes, very much in order. I'm marrying Katherine. And I'd like to take her home before it's too dangerous for her to travel. She, on the other hand, is telling me she can't break her contract. I'm hoping to change her mind. If and when that happens, could you take care of things for me at CX Capital?"

"Not a problem. Bill will be sorry to see her go, but he'll live. By the way, I'll be expecting a wedding invitation. I never thought I'd see the day," Justin noted drolly. "No offense."

"None taken. I wouldn't have placed any bets on me remarrying either. The actual wedding plans are up to Katherine, though. If she decides to invite more than family, I'll send a plane for you and Mandy. Speaking of Mandy," Dominic said pleasantly, "you must be a new daddy by now. How're Mandy and your daughter?"

This Nick who asked about babies and children still threw him for a loop. After the briefest of pauses, Justin said, "The baby was born three weeks ago, and mother and daughter are doing fine as they say. Also, the nurse and nanny are super. Mandy's actually getting enough sleep to enjoy a night out."

"Then you'd better get back to her. What did you name the baby?"

"Don't ask. It's a family name."

"Yours or Mandy's?"

"Her grandmother's name. Beatrice."

"That's not so bad."

"I guess. The baby's cute as hell, though so that'll help even with a name like Beatrice."

"So you're saying she looks like her mom," Dominic said sportively.

"Thank God, yes. And seriously, I'm happy for you and Katherine. Kids are great."

"I'm beginning to understand that. It's pretty fucking exciting."

Justin stood in the corridor of Royal Albert Hall after the call ended and let the stunning news settle in his brain. Not only was the man he'd thought least likely to marry about to marry, but Dominic Knight was, in his own words, *pretty fucking excited* about having a child. He wouldn't have bet a penny on either eventuality ever occurring. Dominic's relatively brief marriage aside, he'd always been the poster boy for serious kink and vice.

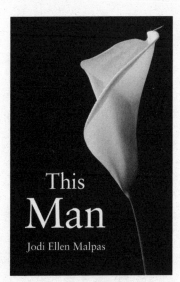
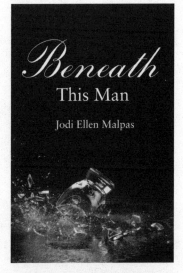
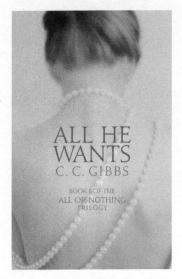
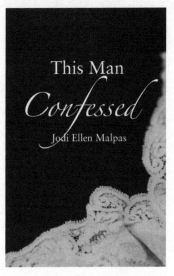

ABOUT THE AUTHOR

C.C. Gibbs is the pen name of *New York Times* bestselling author Susan Johnson. She lives in the Midwest, at times in Northern California, is married with three children and considers the life of a writer the best of all possible worlds. Bringing characters to life allows her imagination full reign, while the creative process offers fascinating glimpses into the machinery of the mind. And last but not least, researching anything, but particularly a book like ALL HE NEEDS—thank you Google—is great fun!

Learn more at:

www.SusanJohnsonAuthor.com

Twitter, @CCGibbs

Facebook.com/CCGibbsAuthor